Rue considered her options. "Run."

Primrose looked her up and down doubtfully. Rue's pink dress was stylishly tight in the bodice and had a hem replete with such complexities of jet beadwork as to make it impossible to take a full stride without harm.

Rue disregarded her own fashionable restrictions and Prim's delicate gesture indicating that her own gown was even tighter, the bodice more elaborate and the skirt more fitted.

"No, no, not *that* kind of running. Do you think you could get Uncle Rabiffano to come over? I feel it unwise to leave the safety of the potted plants."

Prim narrowed her eyes. "That is a horrid idea. You'll ruin your dress. It's new. And it's a Worth."

Prim tisked in annoyance but drifted off with alacrity, making first for Rue's discarded shawl and then for the boyishly hand-some werewolf. Moments later she returned with both in tow.

Without asking for permission—most of the time she would be flatly denied and it was better to acquire permission after the fact she had learned—Rue touched the side of her uncle's face with her bare hand.

Naked flesh to naked flesh had interesting consequences with Rue and werewolves. She wouldn't say she relished the results, but she had grown accustomed to them.

It was painful, her bones breaking and re-forming into new shapes. Her wavy brown hair flowed and crept over her body, turning to fur. Smell dominated her senses rather than sight. But unlike most werewolves, Rue kept her wits about her the entire time, never going moon mad or lusting for human flesh.

Simply put, Rue stole the werewolf's abilities but not his failings, leaving her victim mortal until sunrise, distance, or a preternatural separated them. In this case, her victim was her unfortunate Uncle Rabiffano.

By Gail Carriger

The Parasol Protectorate
Soulless
Changeless
Blameless
Heartless
Timeless

The Custard Protocol
Prudence
Imprudence

The Parasol Protectorate Manga
Soulless: The Manga, Vol. 1
Soulless: The Manga, Vol. 2

Finishing School
Etiquette & Espionage
Curtsies & Conspiracies
Waistcoats & Weaponry
Manners & Mutiny

GAIL CARRIGER

www.orbitbooks.net

Copyright © 2015 by Tofa Borregaard
Excerpt from *Soulless* copyright © 2009 by Tofa Borregaard
Excerpt from *The Unfortunate Decisions of Dahlia Moss* copyright © 2015 by Max Wirestone

Cover design by Lauren Panepinto, Type design by Chad Roberts
Cover photography by Shirley Green
Cover Illustration by Don Sipley/Michael Roberts
Cover copyright © 2016 by Hachette Book Group, Inc.

Orbit
Hachette Book Group
1290 Avenue of the Americas
New York, NY 10104
www.orbitbooks.net

Printed in the United States of America

RRD-C

Originally published in hardcover in Great Britain and in the U.S. by Orbit in March 2015
First U.S. trade paperback edition: February 2016

10 9 8 7 6 5 4 3 2 1

Orbit is an imprint of Hachette Book Group.
The Orbit name and logo are trademarks of Little, Brown Book Group Limited.

The Hachette Speakers Bureau provides a wide range of authors for speaking events. To find out more, go to www.hachettespeakersbureau.com or call (866) 376-6591.

The publisher is not responsible for websites (or their content) that are not owned by the publisher.

Library of Congress Control Number: 2014956789 (hardcover)
ISBN: 978-0-316-21225-0 (trade paperback)

CHAPTER
ONE

The Sacred Snuff Box

Lady Prudence Alessandra Maccon Akeldama was enjoying her evening exceedingly. The evening, unfortunately, did not feel the same about Lady Prudence. She inspired, at even the best balls, a sensation of immanent dread. It was one of the reasons she was always at the top of all invitation lists. Dread had such an agreeable effect on society's upper crust.

"Private balls are so much more diverting than public ones," Rue, unaware of the dread, chirruped in delight to her dearest friend, the Honourable Miss Primrose Tunstell.

Rue was busy drifting around the room with Primrose trailing obligingly after her, the smell of expensive rose perfume following them both.

"You are too easily amused, Rue. Do try for a tone of disinterested refinement." Prim had spent her whole life trailing behind Rue and was unfussed by this role. She had started when they were both in nappies and had never bothered to alter a pattern of some twenty-odd years. Admittedly, these days they both smelled a good deal better.

Prim made elegant eyes at a young officer near the punch. She was wearing an exquisite dress of iridescent ivory taffeta with rust-coloured velvet flowers about the bodice to which the officer gave due appreciation.

Rue only grinned at Primrose's rebuke – a very unrefined grin.

They made a damnably appealing pair, as one smitten admirer put it, in his cups or he would have known better than to put it to Rue herself. "Both of you smallish, roundish, and sweetly whole-some, like perfectly exquisite dinner rolls."

"Thank you for my part," was Rue's acerbic reply to the poor sot, "but if I must be a baked good, at least make me a hot cross bun."

Rue possessed precisely the kind of personality to make her own amusement out of intimacy, especially when a gathering proved limited in scope. This was another reason she was so often invited to private balls. The widely held theory was that Lady Akeldama would become the party were the party to be lifeless, invaded by undead, or otherwise sub-par.

This particular ball did not need her help. Their hosts had installed a marvellous floating chandelier that looked like hundreds of tiny well-lit dirigibles wafting about the room. The attendees were charmed, mostly by the expense. In addition, the punch flowed freely out of a multi-dispensing ambulatory fountain, a string quartet tinkled robustly in one corner, and the conversation frothed with wit. Rue floated through it all on a puffy cloud of ulterior motives.

Rue might have attended, even without motives. The Fen-churches were *always* worth a look-in – being very wealthy, very inbred, and very conscientious of both, thus the most appalling sorts of people. Rue was never one to prefer one entertainment when she could have several. If she might amuse herself and infiltrate in pursuit of snuff boxes at the same time, all the better.

"Where did he say it was kept?" Prim leaned in, her focus on their task now that the young officer had gone off to dance with some other lady.

"Oh, Prim, must you always forget the details halfway through the first waltz?" Rue rebuked her friend without rancour, more out of habit than aggravation.

"So says the lady who hasn't waltzed with Mr Rabiffano." Prim turned to face the floor and twinkled at her former dance partner. The impeccably dressed gentleman in question raised his glass of champagne at her from across the room. "Aside from which, Mr Rabiffano is so very proud and melancholy. It is an appealing combination with that pretty face and vast millinery expertise. He always smiles as though it pains him to do so. It's quite... intoxicating."

"Oh, really, Prim, I know he looks no more than twenty but he's a werewolf and twice your age."

"Like fine brandy, most of the best men are," was Prim's cheeky answer.

"He's also one of my uncles."

"*All* the most eligible men in London seem to be related to you in some way or other."

"We must get you out of London then, mustn't we? Now, can we get on? I suspect the snuff box is in the card room."

Prim's expression indicated that she failed to see how anything could be more important than the general availability of men in London, but she replied gamely, "And how are we, young ladies of respectable standing, to make our way into the *gentlemen's* card room?"

Rue grinned. "You watch and be prepared to cover my retreat."

However, before Rue could get off on to the snuff box, a mild voice said, "What are you about, little niece?" The recently discussed Mr Rabiffano had made his way through the crowd and come up behind them at a speed only achieved by supernatural creatures.

Rue would hate to choose among her Paw's pack but if pressed,

Paw's Beta, Uncle Rabiffano, was her favourite. He was more older brother than uncle, his connection to his humanity still strong, and his sense of humour often tickled by Rue's stubbornness.

"Wait and see," replied Rue pertly.

Prim said, as if she couldn't help herself, "You aren't in attendance solely to watch Rue, are you, Mr Rabiffano? Could it be that you are here because of me as well?"

Sandalio de Rabiffano, second in command of the London Pack and proprietor of the most fashionable hat shop in *all* of England, smiled softly at Prim's blatant flirting. "It would be a privilege, of course, Miss Tunstell, but I believe that gentleman there...?" He nodded in the direction of an Egyptian fellow who lurked uncomfortably in a corner.

"Poor Gahiji. Two decades fraternising with the British, and he still can't manage." Prim tutted at the vampire's evident misery. "I don't know why Queen Mums sends him. Poor dear – he does so hate society."

Rue began tapping her foot. Prim wouldn't notice but Uncle Rabiffano would most certainly hear.

Rabiffano turned towards her, grateful for the interruption. "Very well, if you persist in meddling, go meddle."

"As if I needed pack sanction."

"Convinced of that, are you?" Rabiffano tilted his head eloquently.

Sometimes it was awfully challenging to be the daughter of an Alpha werewolf.

Deciding she'd better act before Uncle Rabiffano changed his mind on her father's behalf, Rue glided away, a purposeful waft of pale pink and black lace. She hadn't Prim's elegance, but she could make a good impression if she tried. Her hair was piled high atop her head and was crowned by a wreath of pink roses – Uncle Rabiffano's work from earlier that evening. He always made her feel pretty and ... tall. Well, taller.

She paused at the refreshment table, collecting four glasses of bubbly and concocting a plan.

At the card room door, Rue reached for a measure of her dear mother's personality, sweeping it about herself like a satin capelet. Personalities, like supernatural shapes, came easily to Rue. It was a skill Dama had cultivated. "Were you anyone else's daughter," he once said, "I should encourage you to tread the boards, *Puggle dearest*. As it stands, we'll have to make shift in less public venues."

Thus when Rue nodded at the footman to open the card room door it was with the austere expression of a bossy matron three times her age.

"But, miss, you can't!" The man trembled in his knee britches.

"The door, my good man," insisted Rue, her voice a little deeper and more commanding.

The footman was not one to resist so firm an order, even if it came from an unattached young lady. He opened the door.

Rue was met by a cloud of cigar smoke and the raucous laughter of men without women. The door closed behind her. She looked about the interior, narrowing in on the many snuff boxes scattered around the room. The chamber, decorated without fuss in brown leather, sage, and gold, seemed to house a great many snuff boxes.

"Lady Prudence, what are you doing in here?"

Rue was not, as many of her age and station might have been, overset by the presence of a great number of men. She had been raised by a great number of men — some of them the type to confine themselves to card rooms at private balls, some of them the type to be in the thick of the dancing, plying eyelashes and gossip in measures to match the ladies. The men of the card room were, in Rue's experience, much easier to handle. She dropped her mother's personality — no help from that here — and reached for someone different. She went for Aunt Ivy mixed with Aunt

Evelyn. Slightly silly, but perceptive, flirtatious, unthreatening. Her posture shifted, tail-bone relaxing back and down into the hips, giving her walk more sway, shoulders back, jutting the cleavage forward, eyelids slightly lowered. She gave the collective gentlemen before her an engaging good-humoured grin.

"Oh dear, I do beg your pardon. You mean this isn't the ladies' embroidery circle?"

"As you see, quite not."

"Oh, how foolish of me." Rue compared each visible snuff box against the sketch she'd been shown, and dismissed each in turn. She wiggled further into the room as though drawn by pure love of masculinity, eyelashes fluttering.

Then Lord Fenchurch, unsure of how to cope with a young lady lodged in sacred man-space, desperately removed a snuff box from his waistcoat pocket and took a pinch.

There was her target. She swanned over to the lord in question, champagne sloshing. She tripped slightly and giggled at her own clumsiness, careful not to spill a drop, ending with all four glasses in front of Lord Fenchurch.

"For our gracious host – I do apologise for disturbing your game."

Lord Fenchurch set the snuff box down and picked up one of the glasses of champagne with a smile. "How thoughtful, Lady Prudence."

Rue leaned in towards him conspiratorially. "Now, don't tell my father I was in here, will you? He might take it amiss. Never know who he'd blame."

Lord Fenchurch looked alarmed.

Rue lurched forward as if under the influence of too much bubbly herself, and snaked the snuff box off the table and into a hidden pocket of her fluffy pink ball gown. All her ball gowns had hidden pockets no matter how fluffy – or how pink, for that matter.

As Rue made her way out of the room, she heard Lord Fenchurch say, worried, to his card partner, "Which father do you think she means?"

The other gentleman, an elderly sort who knew his way around London politics, answered with, "Bad either way, old man."

With which the door behind her closed and Rue was back in the cheer of the ballroom and its frolicking occupants – snuff box successfully poached. She dropped the silly persona as if shedding shape, although with considerably less pain and cost to her apparel. Across the room she met Prim's gaze and signalled autocratically.

Primrose bobbed a curtsey to Uncle Rabiffano and made her way over. "Rue dear, your wreath has slipped to a decidedly jaunty angle. Trouble must be afoot."

Rue stood patiently while her friend made the necessary adjustments. "I like trouble. What were you and Uncle Rabiffano getting chummy about?" Rue was casual with Prim on the subject; she really didn't want to encourage her friend. It wasn't that Rue didn't adore Uncle Rabiffano – she loved all her werewolf uncles, each in his own special way. But she'd never seen Uncle Rabiffano walk out with a lady. Prim, Rue felt, wasn't yet ready for that kind of rejection.

"We were discussing my venerated Queen Mums, if you can believe it."

Rue couldn't believe it. "Goodness, Uncle Rabiffano usually doesn't have much time for Aunt Ivy. Although he never turns down an invitation to visit her with a select offering of his latest hat designs. He thinks she's terribly frivolous. As if a man who spends that much time in front of the looking glass of an evening fussing with his hair should have anything to say on the subject of frivolity."

"Be fair, Rue my dear. Mr Rabiffano has very fine hair and my mother *is* frivolous. I take it you got the item?"

"Of course."

The two ladies drifted behind a cluster of potted palms near the conservatory door. Rue reached into her pocket and pulled out the lozenge-shaped snuff box. It was about the size to hold a pair of spectacles, lacquered in black with an inlay of mother-of-pearl flowers on the lid.

"A tad fuddy-duddy, wouldn't you think, for your Dama's taste?" Prim said. She would think in terms of fashion.

Rue ran her thumb over the inlay. "I'm not entirely convinced he wants the box."

"No?"

"I believe it's the contents that interest him."

"He can't possibly enjoy snuff."

"He'll tell us why he wants it when we get back."

Prim was sceptical. "That vampire never reveals anything if he can possibly help it."

"Ah, but I won't give the box to him until he does."

"You're lucky he loves you."

Rue smiled. "Yes, yes I am." She caught sight of Lord Fenchurch emerging from the card room. He did not look pleased with life, unexpected in a gentlemen whose ball was so well attended.

Lord Fenchurch was not a large man but he looked intimidating, like a ferocious tea-cup poodle. Small dogs, Rue knew from personal experience, could do a great deal of damage when not mollified. Pacification unfortunately was not her strong point. She had learnt many things from her irregular set of parental models, but calming troubled seas with diplomacy was not one of them.

"What do we do now, O wise compatriot?" asked Prim.

Rue considered her options. "Run."

Primrose looked her up and down doubtfully. Rue's pink dress was stylishly tight in the bodice and had a hem replete with such complexities of jet beadwork as to make it impossible to take a full stride without harm.

Rue disregarded her own fashionable restrictions and Prim's delicate gesture indicating that her own gown was even tighter, the bodice more elaborate and the skirt more fitted.

"No, no, not *that* kind of running. Do you think you could get Uncle Rabiffano to come over? I feel it unwise to leave the safety of the potted plants."

Prim narrowed her eyes. "That is a horrid idea. You'll ruin your dress. It's new. And it's a Worth."

"I thought you liked Mr Rabiffano? And *all* my dresses are Worth. Dama would hardly condone anything less." Rue deliberately misinterpreted her friend's objection, at the same time handing Prim the snuff box, her gloves, and her reticule. "Oh, and fetch my wrap, please? It's over on that chair."

Prim tisked in annoyance but drifted off with alacrity, making first for Rue's discarded shawl and then for the boyishly handsome werewolf. Moments later she returned with both in tow.

Without asking for permission – most of the time she would be flatly denied and it was better to acquire permission after the fact she had learned – Rue touched the side of her uncle's face with her bare hand.

Naked flesh to naked flesh had interesting consequences with Rue and werewolves. She wouldn't say she relished the results, but she had grown accustomed to them.

It was painful, her bones breaking and re-forming into new shapes. Her wavy brown hair flowed and crept over her body, turning to fur. Smell dominated her senses rather than sight. But unlike most werewolves, Rue kept her wits about her the entire time, never going moon mad or lusting for human flesh.

Simply put, Rue stole the werewolf's abilities but not his failings, leaving her victim mortal until sunrise, distance, or a preternatural separated them. In this case, her victim was her unfortunate Uncle Rabiffano.

Everyone called it stealing, but Rue's wolf form was her own:

smallish and brindled black, chestnut, and gold. No matter who she stole from, her eyes remained the same tawny yellow inherited from her father. Sadly, the consequences to one's wardrobe were always the same. Her dress ripped as she dropped to all fours, beads scattering. The rose coronet remained in place, looped over one ear, as did her bloomers, although her tail tore open the back seam.

Uncle Rabiffano was mildly disgruntled to find himself mortal. "Really, young lady, I thought you'd grown out of surprise shape theft. This is most inconvenient." He checked the fall of his cravat and smoothed down the front of his peacock-blue waistcoat, as though mortality might somehow rumple clothing.

Rue cocked her head at him, hating the disappointment in his voice. Uncle Rabiffano smelled of wet felt and Bond Street's best pomade. It was the same kind of hair wax that Dama used. She would have apologised but all she could do was bow her head in supplication and give a little whine. His boots smelled of blacking.

"You look ridiculous in bloomers." Prim came to Uncle Rabiffano's assistance.

The gentleman gave Rue a critical examination. "I am rather loathe to admit it, niece, and if you tell any one of your parents I will deny it utterly, but if you are going to go around changing shape willy-nilly, you really must reject female underpinnings, and not only the stays. They simply aren't conducive to shape-shifting."

Prim gasped. "Really, Mr Rabiffano! We are at a ball, a private one notwithstanding. Please do not say such shocking things out loud."

Uncle Rabiffano bowed, colouring slightly. "Forgive me, Miss Tunstell, the stress of finding oneself suddenly human. Too much time with the pack recently, such brash men. I rather forgot myself and the company. I hope you understand."

Prim allowed him the gaffe with a small nod, but some measure of her romantic interest was now tainted. *That will teach her to think of Uncle Rabiffano as anything but a savage beast,* thought Rue with some relief. *I should have told her of his expertise in feminine underthings years ago.* Uncle Rabiffano's interest in female fashions, under or over, was purely academic, but Prim didn't need to know that.

He's probably right. I should give up underpinnings. Only that puts me horribly close to becoming a common strumpet.

Speaking of fashion. Rue shook her back paws out of the dancing slippers and nudged them at Prim with her nose. *Leather softened with mutton suet, resin, castor oil, and lanolin,* her nose told her.

Prim scooped them up, adding them to the bundle she'd formed out of Rue's wrap. "Any jewellery?"

Rue snorted at her. She'd stopped wearing jewellery several years back – it complicated matters. People accommodated wolves on the streets of London but they got strangely upset upon encountering a wolf dripping in diamonds. Dama found this deeply distressing on Rue's behalf. "But, Puggle, darling, you are wealthy, you simply must wear *something* that sparkles!" A compromise had been reached with the occasional tiara or wreath of silk flowers. Rue contemplated shaking the roses off her head, but Uncle Rabiffano might take offence and she'd already insulted him once this evening.

She barked at Prim.

Prim made a polite curtsey. "Good evening, Mr Rabiffano. A most enjoyable dance, but Rue and I simply must be off."

"I'm telling your parents about this," threatened Uncle Rabiffano without rancour.

Rue growled at him.

He waggled a finger at her. "Oh now, little one, don't think you can threaten me. We both know you aren't supposed to change without asking, and in public, *and* without a cloak. They are all going to be angry with you."

Rue sneezed.

Uncle Rabiffano stuck his nose in the air in pretend affront and drifted away. As she watched her beloved uncle twirl gaily about with a giggling young lady in a buttercup-yellow dress — he looked so carefree and cheerful — she did wonder, and not for the first time, why Uncle Rabiffano didn't *want* to be a werewolf. The idea was pure fancy, of course. Most of the rules of polite society existed to keep vampires and werewolves from changing anyone without an extended period of introduction, intimacy, training, and preparation. And her Paw would never metamorphose anyone against his will. And yet...

Prim climbed onto Rue's back. Prim's scent was mostly rose oil with a hint of soap-nuts and poppy seeds about the hair.

Given that Rue had the same mass in wolf form as she did in human, Primrose riding her was an awkward undertaking. Prim had to drape the train of her ball gown over Rue's tail to keep it from trailing on the floor. She also had to hook up her feet to keep them from dangling, which she did by leaning forward so that she was sprawled atop Rue with her head on the silk roses.

She accomplished this with more grace than might be expected given that Prim *always* wore complete underpinnings. She had been doing it her whole life. Rue could be either a vampire or a werewolf, as long as there was a supernatural nearby to steal from, but when given the option, werewolf was more fun. They'd started very young and never given up on the rides.

Prim wrapped her hands about Rue's neck and whispered, "Ready."

Rue burst forth from the potted palms, conscious of what an absurd picture they made — Prim draped over her, ivory gown spiked up over Rue's tail, flying like a banner. Rue's hind legs were still clothed in her fuchsia silk bloomers, and the wreath draped jauntily over one pointed ear.

She charged through the throng, revelling in her supernatural strength. As people scattered before her she smelled each and every perfume, profiterole, and privy visit. *Yes, peons, flee before me!* she commanded mentally in an overly melodramatic dictatorial voice.

"Ruddy werewolves," she heard one elderly gentleman grumble. "Why is London so lousy with them these days?"

"All the best parties have one," she heard another respond.

"The Maccons have a lot to answer for," complained a matron of advanced years.

Perhaps under the opinion that Prim was being kidnapped, a footman sprang valiantly forward. Mrs Fenchurch liked her footmen brawny and this one grabbed for Rue's tail, but when she stopped, turned, and growled at him, baring all her large and sharp teeth, he thought better of it and backed away. Rue put on a burst of speed and they were out the front door and onto the busy street below.

London whisked by as Rue ran. She moved by scent, arrowing towards the familiar taverns and dustbins, street wares and bakers' stalls of her home neighbourhood. The fishy underbelly of the ever-present Thames – in potency or retreat – formed a map for her nose. She enjoyed the nimbleness with which she could dodge in and around hansoms and hackneys, steam tricycles and quadricycles, and the occasional articulated coach.

Of course it didn't last – several streets away from the party, her tether to Uncle Rabiffano reached its limit and snapped.

Rue transformed spontaneously back into a normal young lady – or as normal as is possible with a metanatural. She and Prim ended their run on their posteriors at the side of the road. Prim quickly stood, undid her bundle, and threw the rose shawl about Rue's naked form.

"Spiffing! What a whiz. Now, hail a hack, would you, please, Prim?" Rue tucked the shawl about her as neatly as possible and reseated the wreath about her head. It was all hopeless – her hair was loose, her feet bare – but with no other options, Rue found it best to make an effort to ensure one's appearance seemed intentional.

Prim handed over the dancing slippers.

Rue put them on, trying not to feel the aeration of her nether region. Not so long ago, split bloomers had been all the rage – she couldn't imagine why. She tucked a lock of hair behind her ear, knowing she looked like a light skirt. Only with no skirt.

Fortunately for them, the hackney cab driver had seen far stranger things around London in his day. "Ladies." He tipped his hat. He was clearly taking his cues from Prim's impeccable gown rather than Rue's ridiculous lack of one. He also seemed taken with Prim's winning smile and long lashes.

"Oh, how kind of you to stop, good sir," Prim simpered.

As if it weren't his job, thought Rue, but let her friend work her magic. Taking her cue from the simpering to act the part of an invalid.

Primrose recited Dama's address. "Quickly, if you please – we are in some distress."

The driver was concerned. "Is the young lady well?"

Rue stumbled helpfully, pretending faintness as she climbed into the cab. She didn't have anyone to imitate in this matter; everyone she knew was in excellent health. Thus the act might be a tad overdramatic, but the driver looked adequately troubled on her behalf.

"Oh, sir!" Prim widened her eyes, pulling his attention back. She wobbled her lower lip. "Tragical accident."

"I'll get you there as quickly as possible, miss." Suddenly converted into a white knight, the driver whipped his horse to a trot.

Rue's adopted father was a rove vampire of considerable style and vast means. He operated outside hive sanctions and fashionable restrictions – always claiming that the latter was the reason he left. He controlled a gossip network of dozens of fashionable young dandies, several exotic trade concerns, the political position of potentate advisor to Her Majesty Queen Victoria and, perhaps most importantly, had been *the* dominant influence on male evening dress in London since the death of Beau Brummell half a century earlier.

He received the two young ladies in his drawing room with both arms extended and his new favourite toy, a large multiphase appearance reparation kit, strapped to one arm. "My darlings, my darling girls. My *Puggle*! My little rosehip! How lovely. How *very lovely* to see you both." Dama always behaved as if he hadn't seen an acquaintance in years. "Time between visits," he usually said, "is *irrelevant* to vampires. We are old and often forgotten – people know we will always be there, thus we vampires *very much* like to be remembered." He wielded verbal italics as if they were capable of actual bodily harm. Not as unlikely as one might think since, with him, word emphasis sometimes did cause incalculable pain.

Primrose ran into the vampire's arms with alacrity, hugging him in an excess of emotion for a young lady of quality. She was rather too fond of the rove for her hive-bound mother's comfort, and thus did not get to visit him as frequently as she liked.

Rue, although equally pleased to see him, was confined to clutching his gloved hands and exchanging air kisses in the French manner, a technique they had adopted to prevent her skin from touching his inadvertently. Tonight, caution was required in spades as she wore nothing more protective over her ruined bloomers than a Chinese silk dressing-gown she'd grabbed on her way in.

Dama would comment on her improper state of dress. "Puggle, lovest, *must* you appear in such a very *Grecian* manner?" He winced as if ruminating on an overabundance of chitons with which he had once had personal affiliation. Which he might have. Rumour had it that Dama was very old indeed. Rue never asked; it was considered beyond the pale to ask a vampire his age – literally. But she paid attention to the precise way he executed certain vowels when speaking. If anyone consulted her – which no one ever had – she would have said Greek in origin.

"I'm wearing a very respectable dressing gown," she protested. Dama's drones kept a full selection on hand in the front parlour for when Little Miss returned in *a state* as they called it. The drones always chose beautiful, highly decorated, full coverage dressing-gowns. They were terribly concerned with Lady Prudence's dignity and reputation. More so than she, much to their distress.

"Yes, dear, but this is my drawing room, *not* a Turkish bathing house."

"Your drawing room, Dama dearest, has seen far worse."

"Too true, too true. There might be something in the idea, come to think on it. Bath houses ought to come back into fashion soon, everything is about steam this century already. I should invest. Here, put this in your hair at least." He popped open his appearance kit and ejected a ribbon and two long emerald hair pins.

Rue took them with an arched eyebrow. "Silver-tipped? You expecting trouble from the neighbours?"

"One can never be too careful with werewolves around." The vampire gestured for the two ladies to sit, pausing to remove his gloves and hat. Rue only then registered that he had been about to go out.

Prim took possession of the end of a gold and cream brocade chaise next to an aged calico cat, trying not to disturb the
decrepit creature. The cat opened one bleary eye and croaked at
her politely. Prim scratched the animal's head in response.

Dama watched in approval. "You look very *nice* this evening,
Primrose, my petal! I take it your mother did *not* have a hand in
choosing that particular dress?"

Prim flushed at the compliment. "Certainly not! Fortunately
for me, her attention is otherwise occupied with hive matters and
my wardrobe is mostly my own to command. Although she still
doesn't trust me with hats."

Rue bounced over to sit next to Dama, pulling out the snuff box.

The vampire leaned away from it, peering through a monocle
he didn't require, as though intellectually intrigued. "Was it *difficult*, my sugarplum?"

"Not at all. I wasn't able to be quite as subtle as I hoped, so had
to borrow wolf off Uncle Rabiffano to escape."

"Oh, poor boy." The briefest of pauses and then Dama flittered
his fingers in the air. "Given your birth parents, my pudding,
I suspect *subtlety* will forever be beyond your ken. Perhaps we
should work on that?"

Rue wasn't offended. *Why be subtle when a good dose of the supernatural worked perfectly in most situations?* "You're probably right."

"You know, Rue, someday you will be in a pickle with no vampire or werewolf nearby and then what will you do?" Prim was
ever the voice of reason.

Rue considered. "Act like you, of course, dear Dama."

The vampire was not to be flattered out of his parental concern. "And if that doesn't work?"

"Probably hurl a heavy object."

Prim muttered to the cat, "Lacking *subtlety* is not the only
familial similarity."

"What was that?" Rue looked at her sharply.

"Nothing at all." Prim widened her eyes and continued petting the feline.

Rue said, in an effort to shift matters, "Dama, I do wish you'd give me something more challenging to do."

"All in good time, my sweet." The vampire reached for the snuff box but Rue held it away from him protectively in her bare hand, a hand he wouldn't dare touch.

"What's *this*, Puggle?" Dama tossed his blond locks and pouted. Given that he had what one admirer had once described as the face of Ganymede on earth, the pout looked very well on him. Which he knew, of course.

"Nope." Rue could resist the pout. "First tell me why it's so important."

The lower lip wobbled.

Primrose hid a smile at the vampire's theatrics, so very like her own earlier that evening.

Rue waggled the little box temptingly back and forth out of the vampire's reach.

They all knew he could not take the box away from her, even with supernatural speed. The moment he touched her skin, Rue would have his vampire abilities *and* still be in possession of the snuff box. The vampires called her soul-stealer, the werewolves called her flayer, the scientists metanatural, and there hadn't been one like her for thousands of years. She'd spent her childhood spoiled and studied in turn, combating three overbearing parents. It made for interesting results. Results like the fact that even the most powerful rove in the whole of the British Empire could not extract one snuff box from her if she didn't want him to.

"*Troublesome infant*," grumbled Dama, and stopped the simulated pouting.

"Well?"

"It's not the snuff box, nor the snuff, my little *limpet*."

"Oh?"

Dama crossed his arms. "Did you examine it closely?"

"Of course."

The vampire arched one perfect blond eyebrow – exactly the correct shade, slightly darker than his hair. Artificially darkened, of course, but then his hair was artificially lightened every evening. Dama left nothing to chance, least of all his own appearance.

Rue stood and went to retrieve a pair of high-powered glassicals from a nearby sideboard. She popped them on, the single magnification lens emphasising her left eye to such an extent as to seem grotesque. Even though, if asked, Rue would have said her eyes were her best feature.

She checked the snuff box over carefully, running her hands along the sides. Soon she spotted the secondary catch inside the box, buried in snuff. It was tiny and hidden beneath the lid's silver hinge.

"Careful!" warned Dama, too late.

Rue pressed the catch. The top of the inside of the box flipped open to reveal a hidden chamber underneath. Of course, this sprayed snuff everywhere, covering Rue's head and chest in a fine coating of peppery-smelling brown powder. The glassicals protected her eyes and Rue was so taken with her discovery that she didn't bother to brush the snuff from her hair and décolletage.

Prim stood – the cat murmured an objection – and marched over, partly to examine the discovery, partly to repair the damage to Rue's appearance.

"What is it? More snuff?" she asked, applying her handkerchief with vigour.

Inside the bottom compartment of the box was more vegetative matter.

Rue shook her head, snuff puffed out of her hair. "No, the leaf is too big. A new breed of pipe tobacco?" She was already sticking her nose down to sniff. She couldn't get through the scent of snuff, however. She wasn't in wolf form, so she hadn't the nose to distinguish nuances.

The vampire tut-tutted and used a silk scarf to clean his adopted daughter's face. "No, darling, no, not tobacco."

Rue crowed out the only other possibility. "Tea!"

Dama nodded. "Indeed. A new kind, *Puggle*. They tell me it grows better, faster, and in a wider range of climates than the Chinese varieties. Can you imagine the possibilities in India if this turns out to be a viable beverage?"

Rue frowned. "You'd be stomping all over Bloody John's territory. No wonder you wanted this to be secretive." The East India Company was referred to as Bloody John as it was mostly backed by vampire hives. If Dama wanted a controlling interest in a tea farm overseas, he was going up against other vampires. Vampires whose interest − as potentate − he was supposed to protect. A delicate matter indeed.

Dama twinkled at her. "I'm going to check this leaf against the British palate. If it's drinkable, I'm investing in eight thousand plants and you, *my darling Puggle-girl*, are going to India to meet said plants, ascertain the location and acquisition of land, hire supervisors, and commence distribution."

Primrose was pleased. "India? Lovely! Weren't you just saying we should get out of London, Rue?" She looked to her friend for approbation.

No one, not even Dama, questioned the fact that Primrose would go with Rue. Prim always went with Rue. Besides, Rue couldn't very well travel as an unmarried young lady alone.

"Dama. What a delightful scheme. But − and I don't mean to throw a spanner − what do I know about tea-growing? I'll need native contacts familiar with the territory and climate." But Rue was already considering her options, and Dama only nodded. "And, more importantly, who are you going to test the tea on?"

"Your *mother*, of course, Puggle," replied the vampire. "Can you think of a better option?"

"Unfortunately, no." Rue grimaced, snapped the secret compartment shut and closed the snuff box. She went to hand it over to Dama but then held on to it.

"India, did you say, Dama?"

"*India*, my darling heart. I have specialist tea contacts in that area ready to meet with you and facilitate this endeavour."

"Of course you do." But Rue was smiling.

"Doesn't everyone have specialist tea contacts?" Dama smiled back.

"Mother and Paw approve your plan?"

"Ah, yes, well, I haven't exactly *talked* to your blood parents on the subject yet."

"Oh dear," said Prim. She adored Dama and his drones, and could cope very well with vampires, having been raised in a hive, but she was rather terrified of Rue's blood parents. The formidable Lord and Lady Maccon were both prone to yelling loudly and bashing the noggins of those whose opinions did not mesh with theirs. Even though they had grown up best friends, Primrose had rarely been exposed to them. Rue had rarely been exposed to them, for that matter.

Primrose was frowning. "How will we *get* to India?"

Dama brightened. He had been waiting for this question. "Aha! Now that, my posy, is an answer I believe Puggle here will *very* much enjoy."

Rue, intrigued, gave him what he wanted – the snuff box.

Dama took it carefully so as not to disturb the contents or to touch her hand. He slid it inside his waistcoat pocket. The waistcoat was made of gold lace over fine teal silk with jet buttons, and looked to be so tight a pocket would not accommodate a gooseberry, let alone a snuff box. Nevertheless, it disappeared within, as if by magic.

The vampire was about to tell them more when his head jerked up. He bared his fangs, showing the full length. His nostrils flared as if he scented something in the air.

Rue was instantly on guard. "What?"

Dama held up one unnaturally pale hand to quiet her. His perfect face, too beautiful, narrowed and became hunter-like. "Intruder."

The door knocker reverberated sharp and loud.

They all jumped to stand.

A rustle and a clatter emanated from the hallway and a drone's pleasant voice said, "What ho?" to whomever was on the other side of the door. There was a soft murmur of exchanged pleasantries. Then the drone said loudly, trained to be at a level that his vampire master could hear from the drawing room, "No, you may not come in. Not invited. But I'll fetch her for you, if you insist."

A moment later a tentative knock came at the drawing room door. "My lord?"

"Yes, Winkle?"

Winkle trotted in. Winkle was one of Dama's current favourites. He was a devilishly exotic-looking chap, with features that hinted at Far Eastern or possibly Pan Pacific ancestry. His hair was as glossy and as black as jet mourning jewellery, his dark eyes tilted becomingly and his face was completely free of any topiary. He smiled easily and often with the merest hint of dimples. He also spoke several languages and played the clarinet beautifully. Good traits to look for in any man, Dama informed her, as it led to a very strong tongue. Rue had made a mental note of the advice and tried not to wonder as to the particulars.

"Wimbledon hive vampire at the door, my lord, sent to fetch Miss Tunstell."

Prim stamped her little foot in annoyance. "Queen Mums. Bother her."

Winkle grinned. "You know she doesn't approve when you

visit this house. She'd rather you chose the den next door and kept up the pretence of only associating with werewolves."

"I wish it *were* only a matter of vampire politics," grumbled Primrose. "Excuse me, my lord, but you must know, Queen Mums simply doesn't approve of you. I think it's your fashion choices."

Dama did not look offended. "My dear, I cannot think of a better reason to dislike a person! I must say, for my part, I strenuously object to her hats. Positively everywhere these days, massive hats, massive hair. It's so regrettably *poofy.*"

Prim looked frustrated with them both. "Oh really, *vampires!*"

Winkle was relatively new to Dama's household and had not yet determined the intricacies of the relationship between Lord and Lady Maccon, their daughter, Lord Akeldama, Baroness Tunstell, and her daughter. As far as he could gather, politics dictated that Lady Prudence be adopted by a rove vampire to keep her safe from the hive vampires' fear of metanaturals, hence Lord Akeldama's bringing her up rather than her blood parents. Lady Maccon and Baroness Tunstell had been friends since childhood, as incomprehensible as such a relationship might seem, hence Miss Primrose's companionship of Lady Prudence. But why some of them didn't get along, and others avoided all contact, remained a mystery. So he said tentatively, "Your mother prefers her child visit werewolves over a rove?"

Prim shrugged. "Odd vampire to have any children at all, you might say."

What Winkle didn't know was that Ivy Tunstell's metamorphosis to vampire queen had been unplanned, unexpected, unprecedented, and highly unlikely. The entirety of London had yet to recover from the decades-old shock. The fashion for overly decorated hats was only the latest marker of Baroness Tunstell's sudden – by vampire standards – presence in supernatural high society. The fact that as a newly made queen she'd arrived with a complete hive of four male vampires – all of them quite old, quite rich, and quite powerful – and six foreign drones was beyond the limits of acceptability. The fact that all were *Egyptian* was beneath contempt. The consequences of such horrendous behaviour was as expected – Queen Victoria gave Mrs Tunstell a baronetcy. What else could the aristocracy do with such a travesty in its midst but absorb it entirely? The baroness had been declared *an original* and integrated into the ton. Her family's connection to trade and her actor husband were quietly forgotten, the skin colour of her hive members was blatantly ignored, and she was invited to dine at all the best houses. Not that she could leave her hive as a tethered queen, but invitations were sent. Her ridiculous hats were accepted by ladies of standing and ill repute with equal alacrity. Even the Parisian designers were producing the occasional platter-shaped monstrosity replete with entire scenes of crocheted sheepdog herding. Within a year of contact with the Wimbledon Egyptians, as the hive was sometimes called, the more daring London dandies had taken to coloured shirts, sashes about the waist, and the odd gold bracelet or two. Dama had needed to be very firm *indeed* with his more modish drones. Mr Rabiffano, as the world's only fashionable werewolf, had remained amused and aloof from it all.

Baroness Tunstell, though a vampire queen, never lost her suspicion of other vampires. Her close friendship with Rue's soulless mother and werewolf Paw left her pro-werewolf in a way that had not been seen in a vampire for centuries. Thus Baroness Tunstell was considered by the supernatural set to be quite modern. Countess Nadasdy, queen of the nearby Woolsey Hive had been heard to call her, on more than one occasion, both fast *and* forward. In vampires, that was almost a sign of respect.

But for Primrose, who'd gone up against the Baroness of Wimbledon's overprotective nature since she was born, and for Rue, who'd often been included in the smothering, Aunt Ivy was a *problem*. Being a vampire queen in control of a twitchy transplanted hive full of foreigners only exacerbated a temperament ill-suited to either command or parenting. It was just *like* Aunt Ivy to send one of her vampires after her daughter when there was no sign of danger. And even more *like* her not to acknowledge what a tremendous social faux pas this was.

Primrose was mortified. "Oh, Lord Akeldama, I do apologise! How horribly rude. I am abjectly sorry."

The blond vampire relaxed, but only slightly. A hive-bound vampire simply did not visit the house of a rove without sending a card first! Such matters of etiquette existed for very good reasons.

Rue was annoyed on Dama's behalf and amused by her friend's discomfort. Prim was usually so poised. "Really, Prim, doesn't your mother ever learn?"

Prim hurried to gather up her wrap and reticule. "Sadly, no. I apologise again, Lord Akeldama. Please excuse me. Rue, I'll call tomorrow. Just after sunset?" She bobbed a curtsey and blew them both a quick kiss before hurrying to intercept her mother's vampire before he actually caused *an incident* by trying to enter Dama's home, without invitation.

Rue watched her friend depart. "Why must we be cursed with such troublesome parents?"

"My dear Puggle," objected her Dama in mock injury, "what could you possibly be implying?"

Rue shifted next to him and carefully rested her head on his well-padded shoulder. "Oh, not you, of course, Dama. Never you."

"That's my girl."

CHAPTER
TWO

For Queen and Custard

Rue watched her mother's face for signs of distress. The aristocratic features remained inscrutable except for a slight flare of the nostrils. Rue touched her own nose, checking for signs of expansion. It was a characteristic mannerism adopted whenever she was in Mother's company. She'd developed it as a child, worried that her nose might suddenly, out of envy, begin to grow into a similar beak. It hadn't yet but it still *might*.

Rue's mother wrinkled said protuberance and swished the tea carefully about her mouth as though she were a French wine expert in imminent danger of expectorating. Except, of course, that Mother never expectorated. Apart from the indecorous idea of an aristocrat spitting, she would abhor *the waste* of tea.

Rue had never entirely forgiven her mother for naming her Prudence. Despite a shared and inexplicable love for treacle tart, their relationship was contentious at best and combative the rest of the time.

Rue's mother was a veritable battle-axe, boasting a shape not unlike that of a tragic soprano in a Germanic opera, only with less inclination to throw herself off bridges. In fact, she was not overly demonstrative about anything, least of all bridges. Not that Rue felt she suffered from the lack. As muhjah to Queen Victoria herself, Mother had an empire to manage which should take precedent over such inconsequential distractions as fashion, household management, and child-rearing. All three of which she left in the capable hands of Dama. With good reason, for if asked, Rue had no doubt that Mother would have stated, in tones of mild disgust, that the vampire was not only better at such mundanities, but actually appeared to enjoy them.

Her mother took another sip of the tea and then rendered judgement. "Aggressive malt overtones, lots of smoke, a little like licking the inside of a fireplace."

Rue added, "In the best possible way, I'm sure she means to say, Dama."

Dama, perched on the edge of his seat like some brightly coloured bird, nodded. "Like Lapsang?"

"Yes. Lapsang, but brighter, more acidic tones. Good for blends, I'd hazard a guess. And Lapsang does very well these days, I am given to understand." Rue's mother put the tea-cup down as firmly as if it were a dog she had just instructed to *stay*.

Rue added, "Oh yes, it's served in only the very best drawing rooms."

Dama positively gleamed in excitement. "Ah, my dearest, darling, Alexia *bonbon*, I *knew* you would have all my answers for me." He might even have bounced slightly.

Rue's mother determined that settled the subject, and turned to her daughter. "And what have you been up to this evening, infant?"

Rue bridled at the tone of her mother's voice. She wished she could act like someone else around Mother – pretend to be Uncle Rabiffano, for example. But it was useless to even try: her mother always brought out the worst in Rue. Which is to say, Rue's actual personality proved impossible to repress and all acting ability deserted her. When Lady Maccon used *that tone of voice* Rue was irreversibly thirteen again. "I was at the Fenchurches' ball with

Primrose, as I informed you I would be. Would you believe the Stilton on the cheese plate was misplaced? And they had the latest floating dirigible lighting arrangement from Quimble's – a ridiculous expense. And Mrs Fenchurch was positively vulgar – she must have worn an entire breastplate of diamonds."

Dama obligingly switched his delight from tea to gossip. "Were they paste? I'd wager they were paste. His business concerns have taken a tragic downturn recently, did you hear? Very weak indeed."

Unlike Dama, Rue's mother was not to be misdirected. "Ah, then you weren't running through London in your bloomers? Oh good. I did hear this wild rumour about a werewolf in bloomers. And I thought to myself, here now, none of my dear husband's pack are *that* experimental."

Dama looked intrigued. "Are you quite certain?"

Rue snickered, imagining the fuzzy uncles in bloomers. She could see, perhaps, on a lark, some of Dama's drones bouncing about in lacy pantaloons, but not a werewolf. They were much more dignified.

"You must be mistaken, Mother." She stopped smiling and tried to be prim, crossing her hands delicately in her lap in a modest manner.

Mother tapped her parasol, an impossibly ugly accessory she dragged with her everywhere day or night, dinner party or ball. "Yes, I suppose I must. You couldn't possibly have had anything to do with, perhaps, the acquisition of this unusual tea?"

Rue looked affronted. "I've no idea to what you are referring, Mother."

Accustomed to her daughter's stubbornness, Lady Maccon turned to the vampire. Her famous Italian glare pierced Dama. "What are you two hiding?"

Dama looked equally innocent. "Us? Nothing, gooseberry pearl. *Nothing* at all."

Lady Maccon leaned forward and grabbed Dama's hand. At the contact, the vampire turned mortal. Her power wasn't like Rue's – she didn't take on the vampire's abilities, and the effect wouldn't last once she let go, but she did turn him human. It was this skill that made her soulless, and made most vampires loathe her upon the very realisation of her preternatural state. Of course, once her personality asserted itself, vampires tended to loathe Rue's mother for her *own* sake.

"Lord Akeldama, I will not have you involving my daughter in some seedy tea extraction mission!"

Dama sat back, affronted. "My darling *girl*."

Rue leapt to his defence. "When has Dama ever done anything even remotely seedy?"

"Of course, infant, permit me to rephrase. I will not allow you to involve my daughter in some *stylish* tea extraction mission, either."

"Could we say 'stylish tea infusion mission'?" Dama suggested meekly.

Rue was not going to let her mother coerce her Dama. She mounted a secondary defence. "Pish-tosh, Mother. May I kindly remind you that I am all grown up and perfectly capable of making my own tea-related decisions."

"Like rampaging around London in your bloomers?"

"I wasn't in human form, no one knew it was me. At least, not until the tether to Uncle Rabiffano snapped."

"So it *was* you? Oh dear me, the scandal! You'll have to retire to the countryside until it blows over at the very least. How will we keep this out of the popular press?"

Rue felt like stamping her foot, but didn't on principle. "Of course it was me. And I will certainly not go to the countryside."

"I hope you learnt something from this," said her mother, looking a little hopeless.

"Frankly, all I learnt is that I must give up bloomers. Perhaps a short silk underskirt would work better? It's the tail, you see, it rips the seams."

"And what on earth has happened to your *stays*, young lady?"

"Pshaw, Mother. I gave up wearing corsetry years ago. Far too inconvenient. And so old-fashioned."

"Oh mercy me, how did I not know this? What kind of child have I raised?"

"I got permission!" Rue whined.

Her mother whirled on Dama. "This is what comes of *your* overindulgence! My daughter prancing around in split bloomers!"

Dama only smiled, his fangs politely tucked away. "My dear *sugarplum*, be reasonable. I would never allow my daughter to go without proper foundation. It wasn't me who gave her said permission."

Rue's mother threw her head back and yelled at the top of her lungs, "Conall! Get your furry posterior in here post haste!"

Rue giggled. "Paw's got great hearing but he's at the Bureau tonight. Even he can't hear you all the way across London."

Her mother's face was all thunderclouds. "Give up stays, indeed! With your figure? To think, you've been *dancing* without support. Lordy, lordy. The uncontrollable wobble of it all! And now bloomers as well?" She turned to Dama as a new possible ally rather than enemy in the matter of her daughter. "My dear lord, how are we to remedy the catastrophe that is my progeny?"

Rue would have none of it. "Mother, it's done. Besides, why should I obey the bounds of polite dress?"

"Because, infant, you are a *proper gentlewoman*. The daughter of two lords and a lady. You have *standards* to maintain." Her mother was moved to impassioned gesticulation for emphasis. It was the Italian ancestry that did it.

Rue rolled her eyes.

Her mother turned again to Dama. "What are we to do with her?"

"Ah, good, Alexia my *gherkin*, I'm *delighted* you brought that question up. I do believe that what our Puggle requires is an *occupation*."

Rue's mother sputtered.

Dama was ready. "Now, now, my dear, cast your mind back some quarter century or so. I do believe you once got into a great deal of trouble yourself, all because you hadn't an *occupation*. Now, you are settled into your duties, I have my potentate responsibilities, your husband has BUR, even Rabiffano has his hat shop. Puggle needs the same, don't you, *darling*?"

Rue would hardly have put it like that, but since she was keen on the idea of travelling, she nodded, and watched her mother for an adverse reaction.

Whatever incident Dama alluded to seemed to do the necessary because her mother's imminent boil-over subsided. She twisted her parasol about in her grasp and actually gave the matter serious thought.

She caught Rue's eye. "I suppose, were you an ordinary child, you'd be married by now. And since you've been vampire-raised, people have mostly stopped trying to kill you. I worry, that's all. What will become of you?"

Rue was touched. "Aw, you actually love me."

Alexia Maccon scooped her child in closer to her on the couch with one arm and kissed her temple. "Of course I do, infant."

Rue hid a smile. Sometimes it was too easy. "So, this ball I was at . . ." *Before you get hold of tomorrow's gossip rags.*

"Very well, tell me all. What's the situation with the tea? What did you do to poor Uncle Rabiffano? And why were you gallivanting about London in your bloomers?"

Of course, poor old Mother became quite agitated all over again at the idea of her precious daughter travelling to India. Although, as Rue pointed out, it was most certainly the countryside. Dama reminded Lady Maccon of her own misspent youth which, much to Rue's surprise, appeared to include plagues in Scotland, a mad dash across Europe, and one ill-advised trip to Egypt. "At least with Puggle here, we can see her well prepared, properly outfitted, and decently dressed."

"Really, Mother, I had no idea you were so reckless. You seem so very staid."

"I'll have you know, infant, I was a madcap adventurer of epic proportions. Not that you should take that as permission, mind you."

"So you agree I should go to India?"

"What did I *just* say?"

Rue crossed her arms and glowered, looking rather too much like her Paw for anyone's comfort level. "I can take care of myself. Did you forget the little fact that I can steal supernatural abilities?" Nothing irritated Rue more than overprotectiveness. Except possibly flat champagne.

"Infant, there are times when there are no vampires or werewolves around. Not to mention daylight hours rendering you powerless. Also, I am not the *only* preternatural in existence and able to thwart you."

"I have other skills," Rue grumbled.

Her mother looked her up and down as if she were a military captain evaluating Rue for a mission. Then she turned back to Dama. Some silent signal passed between her parents. Dama had trained Rue in mysterious ways and Lady Maccon knew of Rue's theatrical abilities, even if she rarely witnessed them first-hand, and preferred not to think about the ramifications.

"Oh, very well," Mother capitulated, "but take this. You'll need it. Very hot in India, I understand." She handed over her parasol, an ugly if well-meaning gesture.

It was a good thing to have Mother's approbation, for even
Dama hadn't the persuasive powers to convince the Alpha of
the London Pack that his daughter traipsing around the empire
was a good idea. Lord Maccon might be firmly wrapped around
Rue's little finger, but when her safety was at stake he could be
militant. It would take Mother's cajoling to bring him on board.
Rue had never inquired too closely into her mother's skills in this
arena. Suffice to say that, on those occasions when Lord and Lady
Maccon argued most virulently, a *pattern* inevitably emerged.
They disappeared to their private quarters in disagreement and
re-appeared in accord, generally to Mother's way of thinking.
Rue's mother was fond of saying, "I am always right. Sometimes,
it simply takes him a little time, flat on his back, to realise this."

"India, infant, is going to take me most of our daytime repose,"
was her mother's assessment before they took to their beds before
dawn.

"Oh, Mother!" It was nice to know her parents still enjoyed
physical expressions of affection even at their advanced age, but
also very much *not* nice to know.

The matter was thus settled, as far as Rue was concerned. She
retired before her Paw returned home with the certain knowledge
that plans would continue the next evening.

Rue came down after sunset in a dove-grey visiting dress trimmed
with black velvet and white beadwork to find Dama and his
drones preparing for a trip. The vampire, unlike his hive-bound
fellows, often went out on the town, taking in the latest play or
opera, occasionally calling upon his mortal acquaintances. Every
such jaunt was an event, for everyone and everything in con-
junction with the expedition must be aesthetically coordinated.

Tonight, Rue's appearance in the grey dress occasioned a line-up, two drones on either side, as they were to make up a party of six in the landau.

Winkle was instructed to go upstairs and change immediately as his yellow waistcoat did not go with Rue's muted colour palette. The drone returned in a sage vest, carrying Rue's hat. Queen Ivy's millinery influence dictated this accessory be a massive affair richly decorated in what looked like the flattened corpses of three seagulls. Rue thought it rather detracted from the beauty of her dress but Uncle Rabiffano insisted it was the *very latest thing*, and Uncle Rabiffano was *never* wrong about hats.

"Was Mother successful, do you think?" Rue asked Dama as he helped her into the coach. The horses sported grey tassels at their bits and the coachman a grey silk top hat.

"You are in some doubt? My Puggle of little faith."

Rue smiled. "Of course. Silly me. It's Mother. She always gets her way."

"Mmm," said Dama. "Except, of course, when you do." He made room for his four drones to join them.

They made a very fetching picture, and Rue was delighted with the entire outing. She savoured the envious looks of the other ladies parading through Hyde Park. Rue was accompanied by five of the best-looking men in all of London, and was still young enough to enjoy the envy and not mind that it had little justifiable cause. For young women of burgeoning romantic hopes, these men could provide only decoration and conversation rather than amorous solace or entanglement. They were, as far as any *lady* was concerned, like the fake fruit on Baroness Tunstell's favourite hat – entertaining, pretty, and apparently delicious but not actually useful in the event of starvation or even an attack of the nibbles. Rue, secure in this knowledge, was free to enjoy their company without expectations. Which she did, to the mutual entertainment of all.

Dama directed the driver through Hyde Park and out onto the Edgware Road towards Regent's Park. Far less popular and less populated by the supernatural set, Regent's Park was quiet at night. They drove along one side before turning in towards a dense plot of trees near Boating Lake. There, in the centre of a petite forest, sat an abandoned cricket pitch now occupied by a small but cheerful family of squirrels and Dama's latest acquisition.

"Oh, Dama! She's so beautiful." Rue was embarrassed to find herself actually clutching both hands to her breast like the heroine of a romantic novel, for there in the middle of the pitch was moored the most amazing airship she had ever seen.

Rue was particularly fond of floating. She'd spent many a summer's day up in Dama's personal aircraft, *Dandelion Fluff Upon a Spoon*. He himself never used it of course, but kept it on the roof because it was the kind of possession that a man of means kept on his roof. Dama always made the appearance of doing what was proper and modern. He would never want to be thought old-fashioned – that was for other vampires. When Rue turned sixteen, the drones taught her to fly old *Fluff*. Since then, Rue had never missed the opportunity to bundle Prim up in hair muffs and goggles, pack a suitable picnic, and take to the skies. Prim grew to enjoy it more than she would admit and had invested in a wardrobe to complement.

"I don't want to be thought an outdoorsy sort of female," she initially objected.

"Don't be silly, Prim – everyone is taking to the skies these days. It's not only the country set. It's not like we're riding horseback or something passé like that."

"But, Rue, I'm all too often seen on wolfback. If I take to floating as well, people will say I'm – oh, I don't know – *athletic*."

"They will say no such thing. The height of your heels alone belies any suggestion of brawniness."

That hadn't helped – the mere mention of "brawn" nearly gave Prim hysterics. Through dint of cajoling and application of a very handsome drone to assist with lessons, Primrose eventually allowed herself aboard.

But this dirigible was utterly unlike such a poky little craft as old *Fluff.*

"Dama, she's perfectly topping."

"She is rather, isn't she? I commissioned her several years ago, before some of the technology was even ready. Now she has all the very latest of everything, from navigation to habitation to mechanics to munitions. She's lighter, better, faster and more deadly than *anything,* even Her Majesty's floatforce. And, my darlingest of puggles, she is *yours* to command."

Rue was moved to italics by the gesture. *"Mine?"*

"Indeed. I think you two will get along swimmingly. Or should I say *floatingly?"*

The coach pulled up next to the beautiful ship and the drones jumped out.

Winkle helped Rue to step down and she approached the dirigible reverently.

It wasn't as big as one of Her Majesty's mail ships but it was large. Rue suspected the gondola alone of being about the size of Dama's town house, if the house were tipped on its side and made into the shape of a streamlined boat.

Dama said, "We took our cues from the basket homes of the balloon nomads of the Sahara and sourced an extremely light bendable wood from China for the hull." The wood in question was a lovely golden colour. Rue stood on tiptoe to run her hand along one beam reverently.

The ship bobbed, straining against its mooring ropes, eager to take to the skies.

"May I go inside?" Rue pleaded, her golden eyes big and shining – almost a match to the exotic wood.

"Of course you may, my *petal*. Although you will permit one of my drones to accompany you and excuse me the pleasure?"

"Oh but, Dama, she's moored very low, can't you...?"

"Best not to risk it, my love. Ropes can snap and then we'd suddenly be beyond the limits of my tether. I am an *old* vampire, little Puggle, and I did not get so old by being reckless."

Rue nodded and in lieu of Dama, grabbed Winkle's arm. They made their way up the creaking gangplank and onto the main deck of the ship. The open squeak decks, below the massive balloons, seemed protected enough from the helium above to not cause undue voice modification. Although Rue suspected that, in the case of a leak, the poop deck, which was raised the highest, might be a danger zone – that would make for a funny sort of command.

The navigation centre on the poop deck was made to look like an old-fashioned ship's helm, but it was the design aesthetic rather than any indication of dated engineering. The balloon could be inflated and deflated by means of either helium or hot air, or both, depending on local resources. A paddle propeller below aft did most of the steering and propulsion with a single mainsail off the stern for use in high-floating in the aether currents. When down, the mast looked like the tail of an inquisitive cat.

Rue was only disgruntled by one thing.

"Pigeons!" She dropped a surprised Winkle's arm and charged across the deck, waving at the roosting birds like a mad woman with her parasol. Rue had an abhorrence of pigeons. Some childhood encounter involving a stolen sausage roll was to blame. The birds squawked and flapped off. Rue in turn flapped at a nearby deckhand. "Keep them away, would you, please? Repulsive creatures."

"Yes, miss," said the deckhand, eyes wide at this erratic behaviour.

"I don't like pigeons," Rue felt compelled to explain. "And I think you're probably supposed to call me *captain*."

"Who *does* like pigeons, captain?" wondered the deckhand philosophically.

Belowdecks in the forecastle were crew quarters, and in the stern, officer quarters. Rue wholeheartedly approved of the lavish captain's chambers, featuring a wardrobe with sufficient room for most of her shoes. There was a nice-looking mess and a galley which included the latest in refrigeration boxes and every possible pot and pan, even crumpet rings. Rue supported this excess – she was awfully fond of crumpets. A beautifully decorated stateroom sat across from a smoking room, down from a sickbay-meets-laboratory and a few guest berths.

The lowest deck was made up of a hold at the fore, with ample room for supplies and other necessities, and a massive chamber aft. This proved to be engineering, containing coal bunkers, boilers, and the very latest in steam engines charmingly designed to look like a bank of cheerful chubby teakettles.

Rue was not a particularly handy person. Her nature had never led her into much interest in how things worked. She felt the important thing with machines was that they *did* work and when they did, she appreciated it. When something broke, she identified the closest possible expert and asked them – nicely of course and with remuneration – to fix it. Thus much of what passed for mechanics, gadgets, instruments, and devices on the ship was beyond her ken. But she liked the teakettles.

"I'll need to hire a chief engineer and navigator first," she said, concerned with the care of the technology around her.

Winkle nodded, mouth slightly open. "I can see that you would."

The ship already boasted a skeleton crew: a smattering of deckhands and decklings scampered above while firemen, greasers, and sooties manned the one active boiler kettle. This motley collective stood to attention at the appearance of a lady among them. Caps were doffed, awkward murmurs were made, and Rue felt guilty at having imposed herself upon them.

"Pleased to meet you all," she said after the senior greaser had performed some bumbling introductions. "I am Lady Prudence Akeldama and I will be your captain."

The revelation that their skipper was a female aristocrat seemed not to bother any of the young men one whit. Either someone had already warned them or they had been selected for their forward-thinking. Rue scrutinised her nascent crew more closely. Only then did she realise that the senior greaser and at least half the firemen and sooties were in fact *female*. She wondered where Dama had found such workers but was secretly delighted. Rue was not, to the best of her knowledge, a lover of women, but she did have a number of lady friends and enjoyed having females around. This might be because she'd been raised, mainly, by two tribes of men, one scruffy and werewolf, the other tidy and dandified. It'd be nice to go traipsing around the globe with a fair representation of the fairer sex. She could institute a proper teatime without grumbles.

She grinned at them all, dressing herself with a bit of her Paw's leadership style mixed with a touch of Dama's technique for making announcements to the drones. "Ladies and gentlemen, it will be, I am sure, an honour to serve as your leader, and to become better acquainted with you all. We are going to have some grand adventures, you and I. Probably not dignified, knowing me, but grand."

The assembled company perked up. Their fears over the evident youth and inexperience of their captain, Rue hoped, were now mollified by the indication of her egalitarian nature and good-humoured approach to life. A few of the sooties smiled back, their smudged faces brightening in anticipation.

After a moment's thought, Rue added, "Very good. Carry on."

As one, the little crew dispersed and went back about their business, steps lighter for having met the Young Lady Captain.

Rue turned to the senior greaser, knowing the importance

of getting this woman to trust her. The greaser was a strapping female in her early thirties, her frame long and lean and well-muscled. She had reddish-brown hair cut short and a voice almost low enough for a man. Rue trusted Dama to have found her the very best, but this woman also looked unkempt, gruff, and gloomy. Not to her vampire father's ordinary taste at all.

"How do you do?" Rue said, sticking out her hand in the American fashion.

"Miss," answered the woman, not shaking it.

Rue was tolerably certain the greaser should have said captain. Still, it was better to be nice, even in the face of insubordination. She retracted her hand. "Might I know your name, senior greaser?"

"Phinkerlington, miss. Aggie Phinkerlington." She spat it out as if it should mean something significant.

"Very pleased to meet you, Greaser Phinkerlington." Rue moved her assessment from gloomy to outright sullen and bad-tempered.

"Miss?"

"I trust you will keep her up until I can fix the officers in place?"

"Am I not doin' so already, miss?"

"Of course you are. Thank you for you proficiency." Rue was a little taken aback by the bluntness; it bordered on incivility.

The woman jerked her head. *Was that a nod?*

With an internal sigh, Rue said, "Dismissed."

Aggie Phinkerlington sauntered off, leaving Rue perturbed. Not that she hadn't met a number of people who hated her on sight. Her metanatural state had made her the target of preju-diced antipathy on more than one occasion. Still, it was outside of enough to be disliked for no apparent reason whatsoever. She'd simply have to win Miss Phinkerlington over. She wondered if pretending to be more like Primrose would help.

Winkle, all forgotten standing next to her, said, "She might be a bit of a problem, that one."

"We shall see," replied Rue. "I'm beginning to suspect problems are about to become my business. Now, where shall we——?"

She was cut off as one of the teakettle boilers nearby shrieked loudly and then exploded in a great flash of heat and steam.

Rue reacted on instinct, flattening herself to the floor of the soot-covered chamber. Winkle was right there with her. He had excellent reflexes for a fop.

"What the devil?" Rue turned her head, trying to see through the smoke. All she could make out was Winkle's dark eyes, wide in shock. His top hat tumbled off and rolled towards a pile of kindling.

There were shouts and Greaser Phinkerlington began yelling. The smoke and steam cleared slowly to reveal sooties running everywhere.

The floor of the chamber began to lean as the ship lurched to one side.

"Keep her steady, keep her up!" hollered Phinkerlington. "Puff, Spoo, Kip – man the redundancy boiler, get her stabilised fast. Wute, Ribbin, Jikes – find out what's wrong with boiler primary. Firemen? Where are my firemen?"

The chaos resolved itself into a controlled scurry under Phinkerlington's orders.

Rue stood, dusting herself off – glad she'd chosen to wear grey. She offered a hand to Winkle, who looked a bit shaken by the experience. He stood and retrieved his hat, examining both it and the state of his knees with a distressed expression.

To take his mind off the problem of attire, Rue commented, "She's very good at her job."

"Unfortunately, she isn't as good at personality," replied the drone.

"Dama has his priorities. Personality can be improved upon – efficiency is a natural talent."

Winkle chuckled. "Very wise indeed."

As they watched, the activity became a well-coordinated hum, the floor levelled out, and soon everything was more or less back to normal.

Aggie Phinkerlington gave Rue a look that suggested she would never forgive the young captain for having witnessed this shameful debacle.

Rue grinned hopefully at her.

The senior greaser spat out of the corner of her mouth and went back to work.

"Charming," said Rue.

"Don't you worry about Aggie, captain," said a small voice. One of the young sooties, barely twelve if she was a day, stood next to her, cap in hand. "She's a crotchety old thing, but she's fair."

Rue smiled softly down. "Thank you . . . ?"

"Spoo, captain. She shortens all our names, better to shout quickly-like."

"Thank you, Miss Spoo."

"Just Spoo'll do."

"Spoo," came the yell from Greaser Phinkerlington. "Stop your dawdling!"

Spoo popped her cap back on and scampered off.

Rue left the ship reluctantly, already planning which gadgets, tea, weapons, china, and shoes she would be packing for India. She'd have to see if Uncle Rabiffano could take the air sickness long enough to give her tips on decoration and furnishings. She emerged to find Dama sitting on the footboard of his coach, chatting amicably with his drones. He looked up as Rue came trotting over, wafting Winkle in her wake.

"Dama, she's glorious."

"*Delighted* you approve, Puggle. But what happened to your face and your *lovely* achromatic dress?"

"Problem with one of the boilers."

"We thought we heard a shriek and a bang."

"And you trusted me to sort it and didn't send a drone to investigate? Dama, how lovely of you."

"My dearest Puggle, my whole life with you has been a series of explosive events. Why should this be any different?"

"I shall take that as a compliment," said Rue happily. "This one was not my fault – I feel compelled to defend my honour. And anyway, it's nothing that can't be fixed, said the horrible Phinkerlington creature."

"Ah, you met Aggie, did you, Puggle my pet? Not to worry, she grows on you."

"Like mould?"

"And like mould she can be very useful."

"And tasty on cheese?" Rue was thinking of teatime.

"I wouldn't go *that* far, my little petunia blossom." Dama hopped lightly down and came to stand next to Rue, looking back over to the ship. "She still needs a few light touches by way of adornment."

Rue was proprietorially offended on the ship's behalf. "She's perfect."

"Now, my little *Puggle-muffin*, no insult intended. I merely wished to point out that her balloon needs to be oiled and painted. You'll have to select the colour palette. Make me proud, *please*, darling dewdrop? Also you need to name her."

Rue was nothing if not decisive. "Can I have it painted red with black spots, like a great big ladybug?"

Dama let out an uncharacteristic bark of uncontrolled laughter. "I should have guessed. And the name?"

Rue considered and then, after taking into account the pale golden nature of the amazing Chinese wood and the generally warm spirit of the craft said, "*The Spotted Custard.*"

Dama suppressed a slight snort. "Are you certain, my brilliant child?"

Rue's chin went up. "She'll be spotted and custard is my favourite food."

Dama didn't question her further. "One of the drones will see her registered." He reached into his emerald-green waistcoat pocket and pulled out a list. "Now, you require additional crew. I've already selected deckhands and three stewards, but you'll need more domestic staff and, of course, officers. Here's my list of recommendations." He handed the bit of paper to her, almost nervously.

Rue would never have thought Dama capable of apprehension. Then she looked down the list. It was not very long and one name instantly jumped out at her. "Oh, bosh! Percy? Must I?"

"Now, Puggle, he's the best man for the job of navigator in all of London. Who's not already committed to queen, country, or contract. Do be *reasonable*. He's smart and capable and used to being bossed around by a woman."

"But he's a pollock. And he whines. And he's easily distracted."

"He knows all about the history of *every* country in the British Empire. He can find out about almost anything else."

Rue capitulated with a grumbled, "Prim won't like it."

"He speaks six languages," weaselled her adopted father.

"And ignores instructions in all of them!"

Dama pursed his lips and then faced the lion's wrath. "You haven't finished the list."

Rue perused further. Then she encountered the name Dama was really nervous about. "Absolutely not."

"Now, now, Puggle, *darling*—"

"Dama! No."

"Just think about it, my dear. He is absolutely perfect for chief engineer."

"She'll never let him go."

"Which *she?*"

"Either *she.*"

"I think you'll find he's got a mind of his own these days."

"Oh, you think so, do you? That's a manifold problem. I don't like men who won't listen to my mind over theirs."

"He designed most of the boilers and steam engine controls on *The Spotted Custard.*"

Rue shook the piece of paper at Dama in violent exasperation. "Of *course* he did. I should have known from the kettles."

"And he might have mentioned recently to Winkle how eager he is to leave London for a while."

"Got some poor young tradesman's daughter pregnant, did he?"

Dama was truly appalled at such crassness. "Prudence Alessandra Maccon Akeldama, that is *enough.*"

Rue admitted she might have gone a little far. "I suppose you did just give me charge of the best ship ever made. I could think about it."

"Perhaps even meet him?"

Rue sighed. "I do love you, Dama, but sometimes you can be the most vexing of all my parents."

Dama accepted victory and shifted to look fondly over at his cadre of drones. "Come along, darlings, we must take the Puggle to the train station. She must visit Woolsey Hive."

The drones were re-enacting the balcony scene from *Romeo and Juliet* over the edge of the middle squeak deck of the ship. Winkle was back on board, draped in a tablecloth for hair and gesticulating dramatically at his doomed lover below.

Rue could not resist one last complaint. "He's so very *difficult.*"

"The best ones are, my darling." Dama's eyes were misty with memory.

Woolsey Castle was situated some two hours outside London in particularly lush countryside. The rolling unspoiled beauty of it gave most vampires the screaming willies, for vampires vastly preferred city life. The Woolsey Hive had settled in a swarm of desperation, and was as ill-suited to the green as a family of goats would be to sitting in the House of Lords. Since their move, the Express Whistler, intended to steam straight through to Barking, would stop at an unmarked and unnamed station by special request. No one but the conductor knew the location and everyone was afraid to ask. From that station – the Countess's Crouch as some called it – there was a tiny automated tram that puffed up the long low hill to Woolsey proper. The tram only ran if the vampires approved the visitor, and there were still check-points to clear, manned by large, muscled drones with more cravat than cranial capacity.

The most aggravating aspect of the Woolsey Hive was not its location, rustic though it might be to a young lady of Rue's urban sensibilities. Nor was it Woolsey Castle's appearance, that of a hodgepodge manor house with too many flying buttresses and too little symmetry. No, the most irritating thing about Woolsey Hive was its queen, Countess Nadasdy.

Countess Nadasdy was always *extremely* nice to Rue. Most vampires were, outwardly. Woolsey Hive made a *particular* effort – an unpleasantly *particular* effort. Lady Prudence Akeldama was *always* invited to all hive events. Never had a single gold-embossed invitation passed Rue by since she first came into society at seventeen. The countess made it a *point* to leave her inner sanctum, the back parlour, and walk out to meet Rue in the hallway any time Rue visited, a courtesy she did not extend to muhjah or dewan. She *never* failed to compliment Rue on some part of her attire, seeming genuinely interested in what the young people were wearing these days. She intended Rue to be aware of her approval of Rue's unflaggingly stylish choices. As if Rue would dare go calling less than perfectly turned out with Dama for a father and Rabiffano for an uncle.

None of this made up for the fact that the entire hive would quite happily see Rue fried like an apple fritter and take turns dipping her into the brandy sauce. Quite frankly, it was not comfortable paying a call on an aristocrat who wanted one dead, particularly not when that aristocrat is a very old vampire of means and social skill. It became, in a word, incommodious.

"My dear Cousin Prudence." The countess advanced, both gloved hands out in the greeting vampires extended to family members. Vampires took the concept of adoption seriously. In the hive mind, Rue was solely and entirely Dama's daughter. The Maccons had relinquished their lawful right to her, and as such their parental control. The fact that they remained next door was a source of aggravation but not contention. As long as Rue was legally the child of a vampire, she was one of theirs. And by George they would treat her as such.

The countess grasped Rue, carefully, by the upper arms. Her hands were well shielded from Rue's skin by several layers of cloth. The vampire kissed the air a good six inches away from Rue's cheek. "Welcome. To what do we owe the honour of you gracing us with your delightful presence?"

She was laying it on rather thick, but Rue was Dama's daughter and, if nothing else, she could entertain and rebut flattery in all its forms.

"My dear Cousin Nadasdy, how stunning you look this evening. Is that a new gown? How very modern."

Rue was not exaggerating. The outfit was lovely – a bloodred velvet reception gown with rose-printed cream silk sleeves, divided overskirt, and scalloped hem, all trimmed in the barest hint of Chantilly lace. The countess wore her honey-coloured hair piled in a profusion of curls atop her head with red roses nested throughout. She was a mite round for such an elegant gown but she carried it off by dint of regal bearing and the certain fear always bestowed upon those in her company that she was far more interested in nibbling one's neck than anything else. Even fashion.

"Do come in, Cousin Prudence. You are always invited. But such an unexpected call. And *without* a chaperone. We did not receive your card. Did it go astray?"

"No, no, forgive my horrid bumbling. I must presume upon our familial relationship to call unannounced. I did not have time to send 'round as this is a matter most urgent. Since we are practically family, I thought this once I could leave off my customary escort."

"Well, then, my dear cousin, do not stand on ceremony. Come right through, do." The countess was sickeningly obliging, gesturing Rue magnanimously into the hall. The entranceway of Woolsey Castle was decorated in shades of wine and cream, beautifully complementing the countess's dress, a fact that may or may not have been accidental. A stunning crystal chandelier in the shape of a dirigible dangled from the gilt ceiling and the very latest in mechanised hem cleaners rested near the door. Valuable works of art decorated the walls, set off by what could only be original Greek statuary. The Woolsey Hive took stately elegance seriously. There wasn't a whole lot they could do about the exterior appearance of Woolsey Castle but they took great pains that the interior be beyond sumptuous. There were drones and vampires lurking nearby, any number of whom glared at Rue out of hard, unkind, glittering eyes.

"No insult intended, dear cousin," replied Rue, anxious to get out of the cloying atmosphere of the hive quickly. "But it is actually your ward I wish to see."

The countess was taken aback at such a request. "Quesnel? But I thought you two loathed each other."

"Now, now, cousin, *loathe* is such a strong word. We have been known to clash on a few occasions."

The countess raised one perfectly arched eyebrow. "Indeed? I believe you once stole poor Ambrose's vampire abilities merely so you could dunk Quesnel into the duck pond."

Rue blushed. Admittedly, Quesnel's behaviour had been very bad indeed, but she had escalated matters more than she should. "That was a long time ago."

The queen looked misty-eyed. "Was it? Ah, time passes so oddly for you mortals."

"She was eight," said a mild tenor voice, tinged with a slight French accent. "I was down from university. I remember it well."

Rue whirled to face Quesnel.

The man advanced towards her.

Quesnel Lefoux was one of the few males Rue had ever met whom she could not manage. He was unlike the large gruff werewolves of her father's pack, easily swayed by feminine wiles. Nor was he like the effete elegant courtiers of Akeldama's domicile influenced by whispered gossip and cheeky innuendo. Quesnel Lefoux was a different breed entirely, which accounted for a great deal of Rue's difficulty with the man. He would not be categorised. He was of medium build and medium height. He moved like a dancer but had the manners of an academic and an inflated opinion of his own repartee. He smiled easily and was inclined to wit rather than wisdom despite his being one of the most brilliant mechanics of the modern age. He was a terrible flirt, which everyone blamed on his being French. To cap the offence, Rue's acting abilities always failed her around him. As a result, he was prone to either making her head spin with banter, or overwhelming her with the desire to dump tea on his head, sometimes both at the same time.

"Lady Prudence, to what do I owe this unalloyed pleasure?" Quesnel took her hand and bent to kiss her wrist, lips whisper-soft and actually daring to touch skin. He was entirely human and had nothing to fear from Rue in that regard. Except that she badly wanted to box his ears for the impertinence.

Instead Rue simply withdrew her hand as soon as was polite. She resisted the urge to rub at the spot his lips had touched. "I was looking for you, Mr Lefoux. If you could spare me a moment?"

Quesnel exchanged a pointed look with the vampire queen.

Countess Nadasdy shrugged – the barest hint of a movement so as not to upset the drape of her gown. There was a dangerously covetous look in her blue eyes. However, she made no objection to the proposed private assignation.

Quesnel tilted his head. "Very well, mon petit chou, come into my lair. Or would you prefer a walk around the grounds?"

Rue decided it was best to keep matters in the open. "The grounds. I could use the fresh air."

Quesnel offered her his arm, which Rue took, almost scared of his warmth.

He led her through the hall and out the back into the beautifully tended grounds. Before leaving the house, he casually paused to unstrap and toss aside a whole mess of gadgetry. It was a mark of how unsettled the man made her that Rue hadn't noticed it until that moment.

"What's that?" she asked.

He dismissed the advanced assemblage. "Tools mostly. I find it useful to have everything on me when I'm working. But they get in the way the rest of the time, when one has lovely visitors to attend."

Woolsey had once been home to Rue's father's pack. In fact, she had been born there, but had never lived in the place herself. It still bore a few signs of wolf occupation. The occasional scratch mark, silver chains in a hall cupboard, and extensive dungeons underground. Over the last two decades, the countess had done her best to improve Woolsey, with only modest success. The castle itself was a patchwork of buildings, for it had been added to by a variety of owners with wide-ranging tastes, including several Alpha werewolves. It proved that even with a millennium of knowledge not every house could be made beautiful.

The grounds were a different matter. The vampires had hired a veritable army of attractive gardeners. The countess, confined inside, could only appreciate them at night – both grounds and gardeners – from the windows of her abode. But she did both, frequently. Much had been done to make the view from above, as well as the walk within, a delight to the eye. There were gazebos and fountains, ponds and dells, bird baths and statues, not to mention an elaborate maze of creamy gravel with contrasting topiary and a cluster of silver birches at the centre.

Under the three-quarter moon, Quesnel led Rue along a winding black-stone path, passed well-tended shrubs, beautiful herbaceous borders, rows of fruit trees, and the occasional Grecian temple. They talked of mutual acquaintances, asking after each other's families until they arrived at a picturesque pond with water-lilies and weeping willows all around.

Rue looked at it thoughtfully. "Is that *the* pond?"

"Why, yes, it is. Such a high-spirited young thing." Quesnel rubbed his posterior as though still remembering landing on it.

"Who? Me or you?" Rue wondered.

"Both, I suppose."

Rue was willing to let bygones be bygones if he was. "Mere childhood kerfuffles."

"Speak for yourself. I was fully grown and should have known not to tease a spoiled metanatural. I should have also known the rest." He led her to a marble bench.

They sat.

"What rest? That I'd be strong enough to dump you in a pond at eight years of age?"

"That you'd eventually grow up beautiful with a very long memory."

He really was a horrible flirt. "But still spoiled? Is that an apology? Accepted."

He raised golden eyebrows at her. "And?"

"Oh, no, I'm not apologising for dunking you. For all I know, it might need to happen again."

Quesnel laughed. "Touché. Ah, so, what did you need to see me about, mon petit chou?"

"I've been given an airship."

"I know. I built her. Or at least part of her. Fantastic, isn't she? I do excellent work. Particularly with kettles."

Rue swallowed down any snide remarks at this blatant arrogance. "Dama thinks you're the best candidate for chief engineer. At least on short notice. We're going to India. What do you say?"

Quesnel did not answer, only gave her a strange look.

Rue babbled, "It'd only be this once. I should think we could easily find a replacement for you after. I could . . ." She trailed off, uncomfortable.

Finally, Quesnel said, "That's the most oddly phrased invitation I've ever received. Sweet, of course, but odd."

Rue immediately stood. "Well, if you don't want to accept that's perfectly understandable. I only said I'd ask. I know you're awfully busy and that the countess and your mother like to have you at their disposal."

"Now, now, pretty lady, don't be impulsive." Quesnel grabbed Rue's hand to keep her from walking off and pulled her back to sit next to him. "Did I say no?"

"It'd be much easier if you did."

"Now, chérie, when have either of us ever taken the easy route?"

"Good point. So you're willing?"

He smiled at her, his eyes crinkling up at the corners. Rue knew from past experience they were a disturbing violet colour, but under the moonlight they were silver. He said, "Of course I'm willing."

Rue said, "Oh bother," before she could stop herself.

"See, I knew you wanted me there."

Rue gave him an exasperated look. "Couldn't you say you had other commitments?"

"When I could torture you for weeks on end in a confined space?"

Rue sighed. "I suppose I can somewhat see the appeal."

At which, Quesnel Lefoux slid closer and put one arm about her, leaning her back in exaggerated mockery of a Shakespearean lover. "Several weeks aboard ship and you will be unable to resist me."

Rue batted at him. "Stop it, you ridiculous man."

Quesnel dived in to administer a loud buzz of a sloppy kiss on Rue's cheek.

"Mr Lefoux!"

He snickered at his own theatrics and let her go. "Who else has signed on?"

Rue extracted a handkerchief and made a point of wiping off her cheek. "We've got a skeleton crew right now. I'll recruit Primrose and a few others. I'm going to call upon a possible navigator this very evening."

"Primrose Tunstell? Topping." On those few occasions when they had met socially, Quesnel always seemed to enjoy Prim's company. Rue wondered if she detected genuine interest in her friend or if he was simply being Quesnel about it. He did so enjoy the company of women; the ship wasn't all that big. Either one could prove awkward. Primrose was also a terrible flirt but she had a propensity to actually fall in love, which Quesnel avoided. Besides, if Quesnel felt the urge to be rakish he ought to be rakish with *her*. Rue was better equipped to withstand his overtures.

"Why India?" Quesnel asked.

"Ostensibly, tea."

"Ostensibly?"

"Well, Dama is sending me."

"And you think he has an ulterior motive?"

"When doesn't he? Fond as I am of Dama, he is still a vampire. Not to mention the potentate. Mainly, I think he's giving me something to do. So I don't get into any real trouble here. Cause a scandal in London that even all my parents can't extract me from."

Quesnel, horrible creature, did not make the appropriate noises about how unlikely that should be. "Good point, mon petit chou. Anything else I should know?"

"There's a very disagreeable redhead under you as senior greaser."

"Aggie Phinkerlington?"

"You know her already, do you?"

"Of course I do. We're grand old chums. Protégée of my mother's."

"Of course you're friendly. And naturally, she knows your mother. Isn't that simply spiffing?"

"Ah, chérie, I shouldn't fret. You'll manage to keep us all in line somehow."

He was a dozen years older than her, but Rue wasn't going to let that impinge on her authority. "And don't you forget it. I'm your captain on this trip and..." She paused, searching for an appropriate threat. "I'm certain they have duck ponds in India."

Quesnel grinned. "Speaking of which." In a terribly fast movement for a mortal, he stood, scooping Rue up into his arms. He was strong for a mere inventor – probably from moving all those steam engine kettles around.

Rue protested, wiggling.

Quesnel stilled and looked deeply into her eyes. His glittered with guile.

Rue's stomach sank. Was he going to try to kiss her? She was both terrified and curious. Rue had allowed herself to be kissed before, of course she had, she wasn't that old-fashioned. But not by Quesnel.

He bent down, face more serious than she'd ever seen it, looking actually handsome instead of boyishly cocky.

She opened her mouth to protest but found she hadn't any words.

He leaned in closer.

And then she was hurtling through the air to land with a tremendous splash on her posterior in the duck pond.

Rue emerged sputtering but feeling in more control than she had since she first entered Countess Nadasdy's abode. "Mr Lefoux, this dress is a *Worth*." Her lovely grey gown had been through quite a lot that evening, what with the boiler explosion earlier and now this.

"Had to be done, mon petit chou. If you're to be my captain shortly, I can't spend weeks cooped up on an airship with you, constantly faced with the mad temptation to dump you overboard. You must see the necessity of getting such things out of the way now?"

Oddly, Rue did. "I understand your reasoning." She waded out of the pond with as much dignity as possible, trailing lily-pads. Uncle Rabiffano's lovely hairdo sagged and the seagull hat was a non-starter. It floated away, looking as if something monstrous had drowned.

Quesnel stepped up to help her out of the pond. Rue took his hand warily. But he acted the perfect gentlemen, just as if he hadn't tumbled her in.

"I suppose I'll have to leave Percy until tomorrow now, unless I'm lucky enough to dry out on the way back to town."

"Percy?" Quesnel let go of her hand.

Rue almost slipped back into the pond. She recovered her balance and glared at him. He remembered his manners, embarrassed. However, when he tried to assist her in dumping water out of her boots, she issued him a sharp, "Shoo!"

Quesnel did not try again but he did not let the matter of Percy drop. "Professor Percival Tunstell? Are you in earnest? Please tell me you aren't in earnest?"

"What, you thought you were the only impossible man I'd have to deal with? Much as I hate to admit it, Dama is as right about Percy as he was about you. He's my best option. You two will have to get along. Without dunking each other in ponds, I hope. He's unlikely to be as understanding as I."

"But he's so very annoying."

Rue cocked her head. "Funny, that's pretty much exactly what I said about you."

Quesnel was so centred on the fact that he might be trapped on a dirigible for weeks on end with Professor Tunstell that he didn't bat an eyelash at this insult. "I don't know what anyone sees in that man."

"I did hear a rumour that he inadvertently stole something from you last season. I hardly gave it credence at the time but I take it the rumour's true? Care to elaborate?"

Quesnel bit his lip. "How on earth did you hear such a thing?"

"You forget about my father's pack. Terrible gossips, werewolves. Worse than Dama's drones."

"Are they really?"

Rue nodded gravely. "Yes, less circumspect and louder about

it. Plus the drones are actually more interested in politics and fashion than the liaisons of others. If he didn't steal your waist-coat, hat, or social standing, they don't give a fig. The werewolves, on the other hand, like to be tangled in relationships. And if they don't know the details, they'll make them up."

"I see." Quesnel, raised in a respectable sort of hive, clearly didn't *see* at all. "But if Pompous Percy's coming I don't know if I..."

"Oh no, you can't back out now. I have your word. And you dumped me in a pond. Fair dues, Quesnel."

"You called me Quesnel. How nice. Now, how about calling me *sweetheart*? Wouldn't that be even nicer?"

He was incorrigible. Sensing the imminent return of her customary urge to poke Quesnel Lefoux in the eye, Rue decided to make good her escape. She gave the man an insultingly brief curtsy before lifting her damp skirts high and saying, "I bid you good evening, *Chief Engineer Lefoux*. We leave in three days, with the aether current. Do tender my regards to your mother and beg my leave of the countess? I should be getting on."

Quesnel bowed, taking the hint for once. "Lady Prudence. I look forward to our next meeting."

Rue sniffed. "So do I, as long as it's a good deal less soggy."

CHAPTER

THREE

Rue's Problem with Redheads

Professor Percival Tunstell moved out of his mother's hive in Wimbledon and accepted a post as Oxford don the moment he came into his majority. After being summarily dismissed from Oxford for his radical theories on the transcendental sprout-shaped nature of the aetherosphere, he rented a decrepit bedsit behind the British Museum, off Russell Square. "The better to facilitate my studies," he explained to his aggrieved mother.

Nor would he tolerate vampire guards. Primrose, his dearly beloved and barely countenanced twin, might secretly enjoy the status conferred by a persistent supernatural escort, but Percy spent the lion's share of his days cooped up in his library researching the breeding habits of sand fleas. He did not require a vampire nanny. Nor, for that matter, did the fleas. After the third of his mother's minions returned to the Wimbledon Hive with slashes from a wooden letter opener, Baroness Tunstell stopped sending them. Percival Tunstell was nothing if not a great fan of learning. If that education involved sharp pointy sticks, he applied himself just as diligently as to other forms of research and with far more uncomfortable results to those around him. In the end, Queen Ivy gave up mothering her son, and Percy stopped poking her vampires with letter openers.

Rue knocked loudly on the door to his apartments.

Nothing.

She knocked again.

She waited.

She knocked a third time.

Eventually, Percival Tunstell himself answered. The gentleman was wearing a smoking jacket and tweed trousers and carrying a heavy Latin tome. He glanced up at Rue, his skin pale as any vampire's, spectacles perched at the tip of his nose. Percy, it must be acknowledged, was quite good-looking for a bluestocking ginger fellow, but terribly peaky about it.

"Oh. It's you."

"Where's your footman?"

"Dismissed him, kept interrupting my reading."

"With something sensible like food, I suspect. May I come in?"

"At least you don't have my ghastly sister with you."

Rue took that as permission to enter.

Percy resumed reading his book, walking slowly down the hallway away from her.

Rue followed. "You'll be happy to know she's doing well."

"Who is?"

"Your sister."

"Oh, is she? How unfortunate. It would do her some good to be in ill health for once."

"Percy, how can you be so tiresome?"

"Rue, I'm terribly busy at the moment. What do you want?"

"Why, what are you busy doing?"

"Agricultural research. I think it might be good for the great British jam industry to move from quinces to crab-apples for pectin production."

"Oh, indeed? Is there a jam industry of any note?"

Percy continued on as if he hadn't heard. "But the relative ratios of storage to fruit gelatine are proving difficult to calculate.

Plus if crab-apple trees require more water, then things may tip back in the quince's favour. Do you know?"

"Do I know what?"

"If they need more water."

"No, I don't. You might ask a farmer."

"Don't be ridiculous. There must be a book on the subject."

Rue decided this conversation could go on for hours. "Percy, your country needs you."

"I highly doubt that."

"Very well then – I need you."

"Don't tell fibs, Rue, it doesn't suit."

Rue took the book away from Percy and said, "I'm flying an airship to India and I require you to be my ship's researcher, librarian, and navigator."

"You're sotted. Have you been drinking? I think you've been drinking." Percy looked mildly concerned. "Do you need to sit? Should I ring for tea? I believe that I still employ a valet." He made room for her on an armchair by removing the enormous pile of scientific pamphlets occupying it.

"Percy, I am entirely sober and in earnest. What I've said is all true. Don't you think you would enjoy leaving London for a while?"

"No, I do not."

"You could bring your books along," she wheedled, wondering if *The Spotted Custard* could take the extra weight.

"My books are quite fine where they are, thank you very much."

"It would get you entirely away from your mother."

Percy's eyes sparked slightly. "But not my sister, I assume. Since you two have been joined at the hip since we were knee-high to a biscuit."

"Prim will stay out of your way, I promise. The ship will be swarming with handsome young men to distract her."

Percy snorted.

Rue tried a new tactic. "Wouldn't you enjoy seeing some of the exotic lands you've studied?"

"Not particularly. All evidence seems to suggest that they are dirty, hot, messy places riddled with disease and chilli peppers. I loathe chilli peppers."

"But what about all the bits that haven't been written about? Subjects untapped, discoveries waiting to be made. Percy, you could become the world's expert on the..." Rue flailed, grappling, and then said triumphantly, "Sacred napping practices of the Punjabi wild cabbage."

"Do cabbages have napping practices?"

"They might. And how would you know if you didn't join me?"

Percy considered. "You make a valid point. Some of my research books on the subject of India are quite dated and inexcusably superficial in their treatment of native culinary practices. After all, how can one avoid chilli peppers if one doesn't adequately track their movements and migration patterns?"

"Chillies have migration patterns?"

"Don't interrupt. Where was I? Oh yes. Of course, I read Hindustani and Punjabi and if I could get my hands on some primary sources I shouldn't be disappointed. But couldn't you and Primrose pick those up for me and bring them back?"

"No." It was Rue's turn to be difficult. "We most definitely could not."

Percy looked at her. "No, I suppose you would have no earthly idea what a true academic requires on the matter of chilli peppers."

"As you say."

Percy paused. "Very well, I shall come," he capitulated suddenly and with great decisiveness. "Where is that valet with the tea?"

"You never rang for him."

"I didn't? Oh well. When do we leave? It should only take me a month or so to pack."

"The evening after tomorrow."

"What?"

"I shall send Dama's carriage for you. *The Spotted Custard* is moored in Regent's Park. His driver will know the way. I'll have him call tomorrow afternoon in case you'd like to take some books over early and settle them in. And you'll need to research aether current navigation and aerial maps of India."

"I will? That sounds rather jolly. *Spotted Custard*, eh? New kind of pudding, is it? Delish. Can I finish with the quinces first?"

"No, the quinces will wait."

"I understand that's one of the advantages."

"What?"

Percy explained, animated. "Quinces store very well, better than crab-apples. In cellars, and cupboards, and wardrobes, and hatboxes, and what have you."

"Oh, do they? Very interesting, Percy dear. Perhaps I'll have Cook order some for the journey. But you'll still have to change study subjects for the time being. India, I'm afraid, must take precedence."

"Hard taskmistress," Percy grumbled.

"I'm sure you'll become accustomed to it. You may bring the quince books along. You might have time to read as we float."

Percy didn't answer. He was at one of his shelves, combing through scrolls, rolled-up maps, and current charts.

Rue rang for the valet.

A harried young personage appeared. Rue gave him a funny look. Had Percy elevated the boot-black boy in lieu of any other household staff?

"Pack your master's portmanteau for a float to India, a month or more's journey. Please don't forget his daily necessities. You know how he gets when he's researching. And try to keep him from bringing too many books. I'll be sending around a carriage tomorrow around teatime. Please ensure the first load is aboard and that he goes with it to see to his quarters. You'll also be joining us since someone has to look after him. I hope that's agreeable. I will, of course subsidise your remuneration. We leave the evening after next, currents permitting."

The young man was not at all discombobulated. In fact, he looked thrilled. Well, life with Percy was probably extremely dull. "And Footnote, miss?"

"Footnote?"

"Himself's cat."

Upon hearing his name, said cat stood up from behind a pile of books and swayed over, emitting a chirrup of inquiry.

"Whatever possessed Percy to acquire a cat? He can't even take care of himself."

The boy suppressed a chuckle. "The cat acquired us, I'm afraid, miss."

"The best ones always do." Rue chucked Footnote under the chin. He emitted a mighty purr of approval. Rue was lost. "Oh, bring him along. Every ship should have a cat. Perhaps he can help with the pigeon problem."

"Very good, miss."

Footnote flopped over onto his back, presenting his chin for further scratching. He was an attractive animal, mostly black with white markings, as though smartly dressed for the theatre. Better dressed than Percy ever was, that's certain. Rue left off cat-worshipping reluctantly.

The valet made his farewell bow.

"Oh," Rue added before he shut the door, "bring Percy up some tea, please."

"And nibbly bits," mumbled Percy, digging through scrolls, maps flying, not looking up.

"And nibbly bits," added Rue. Footnote trotted after the valet, possibly intrigued by the mention of nibbly bits.

"Yes, Lady Prudence."

"Oh dear, have we met before?"

"No, my lady, but I've heard of you. And I guessed that you couldn't be the Honourable Primrose Tunstell."

"No? We do look alike."

"Yes, my lady, but himself's not yelling at you."

"A good point you make there...?" Rue trailed off, questioningly.

"Virgil, my lady."

"Ah, I see why Percy hired you. He always has had great affection for the ancient scribes."

"My lady?"

"The tea, please, Virgil."

Virgil made her a second bit of a bow and scampered off. Footnote biffed along after him, tail up with the tip tilted like a small, furry flag.

Rue turned her attention back to Percy, "Nice young man, Percy. No idea what he's doing with you."

"Good name," muttered Percy.

Rue sighed and made her way through the chaos of books and out into the hall. "I shall see you soon."

Percy came to the study door and waved a dismissive map at her. "Unfortunately."

Rue knew Percy well enough to realise that this was the best she was going to get out of him so she let herself out with as much dignity as possible. She did trip over a small stack of *Beeton's Englishwoman's Domestic Magazine and Fashion Tips* next to the automated hat cleaner in the hallway. Since he was entirely the opposite of *fashionable* Rue was mystified by their presence. One never knew why with Percy.

Thereafter, Rue spent the majority of her waking hours on *The Spotted Custard* supervising the hiring of the last of the deckhands and staff, meeting her crew, redecorating her chambers, and ensuring they had adequate stores for the journey. Scientists had recently shown that sunflowers were a great natural disinfectant of the poisonous humours in the upper atmosphere. Just to be on the safe side, Rue had twelve potted sunflowers brought in for the decks, fresh-cut placed in all the rooms, and dried clustered everywhere else. She even stocked seeds for regrowing or consumption, whichever seemed best. Sufficient puff pastry was also of paramount importance, although perhaps not so public a health concern. Lady Prudence Akeldama had quite the sweet tooth and it was impossible for her to imagine a journey of a week, let alone a month, without an adequate supply of custard and puff pastry.

This frazzled the cook. "It's the milk we'll run out of first, captain. It does tend to spoil."

Rue considered the matter seriously. "I shall coordinate stopovers for milk restocking. We would have to regardless, for the sake of the tea. I require milk in my tea every day, several times a day."

The cook wrung his hands together. "Yes, captain."

"And cheese – Miss Tunstell loves cheese."

"Of course, captain."

"Prepare a list of perishable necessities not adequately covered by our admirable refrigeration facilities – one should be timed weekly and the other once a fortnight. Let me see what are our most limiting supplies and what I would have to endure if we are only able to make bi-monthly stopovers."

"Yes, captain, but the fuel?"

"Is not your concern. Although I understand some of the empire's outpost aether-stations carry both coal and milk."

The cook gave a little bow. "Aye aye, captain," and he ran off to tend to his lists.

A massive crash above distracted Rue from her galley coordination. "Great ghosts, what's that?" Her exclamation was met with shrugs from the kitchen staff.

Rue marched topside. The loading gangplank was down and the main deck was crawling with confused crew. An entire flock of hats had landed and were nesting near the quarter deck. A massive overturned trunk and hatboxes rolling everywhere appeared to be behind the millinery invasion.

Primrose had arrived.

Or at least Primrose's accessories had arrived.

Rue looked over the railing. The lady in question was standing in an open-topped carriage gesticulating wildly with two parasols as a stream of footmen unloaded an entire other carriage full of baggage.

Rue waved. "Cooey!"

Prim looked up. "Oh, Rue, you wouldn't believe the bother."

"Why all the hats?"

Prim gave her an exasperated look, easy to see even at a distance and under the shade of a wide bonnet trimmed with silk butterflies. "It's the only way she would let me come."

"Who?"

"Gracious me, Rue. Need you ask? Mother, of course."

"Of course. Was she terribly difficult to persuade?"

"Terribly. And she only gave me permission when I promised to bring a hat for every possible crisis, land or air, rain or shine, England or India, sweet or savoury. It was a nightmare. I was at Château de Poupes for *over four hours* last night. Four hours!"

"How is Uncle Rabiffano? Still upset about me stealing his form?"

"Not at all. Much better now actually, as I spent a vast amount of Queen Mum's money at his establishment. As you can probably tell by all the hats he foisted on me. Mother should never have

opened that unlimited purchasing account. Your Uncle Rabiffano takes terrible advantage."

"Shall we stop yelling? Come aboard. I'll give you tea.
You can tell me all about your shopping woes. We've got this
marvellous kettle tube thing, mounts above the reserve in
engineering and runs directly to the galley. Allows for hot
water at any time in a veritable instant, as long as the boilers are
running."

"I'm sure that's quite a spiffing notion but can it wait? After
I've supervised the unpacking, I really must make some calls. I'm
surprised you don't have to."

"In that case I'll come to you." Rue made her way down the
gangplank, almost knocked off it by two footmen carrying
between them another massive trunk. "More hats?" Rue asked,
not too surprised.

"Parasols, miss," grunted one.

"Oh, dear," said Rue.

She attained the ground safely and went to hand Prim down
from the carriage, there being no gentlemen around to perform
the obligation, and the footmen all occupied with baggage. Prim
looked to tumble out soon, she was waving her parasols so vigor-
ously, as if guiding a floatillah of airships into land.

"Goodness, Prim, you'll do yourself an injury. Come down
from there."

Prim came down, fanning herself with one hand and prodding
at a clumsy footman with her parasol with the other. "Careful
with that, Fitzwilliam!"

"You know we are only going for two months at the very most?
This is not the Taking of the Fortress of the Fashionless."

Prim sighed. "It was much easier not to argue with Queen
Mums on the subject. Besides, the more I packed, the less I'd
have to go back for. Speaking of which, do you think I could stay

aboard tonight before we leave? Best not to give her the opportunity to change her mind."

"I'm surprised she let you come at all."

Prim nodded. "You and me both. I think it helps that she
doesn't know Percy's joined up. Both her precious eggs in one
floating basket—? There will be histrionics the entire time we
are away. London is going to be in for it when she finds out."

"Aunt Ivy doesn't know I've got both of you?" Rue looked
uncomfortable. Prim might see her mother as mainly an annoying busybody, but Aunt Ivy was still a vampire hive queen with
all the power and authority that that incurred. She could make
life very difficult when she was unhappy, which London had reason to know – personally.

"He hasn't told her. You know Percy. Could be intentional or it
might have legitimately slipped his addlepated mind."

"Oh, yes, speaking of your horrible brother, Dama's carriage is
arriving. I sent it 'round to retrieve him."

"Really?"

"To be fair, I sent it to retrieve his books. Percy was bound to
follow."

"Safe assumption."

The carriage in question – a gilt horse-drawn affair, like something from a nursery rhyme, complete with trailing blue rib-
bons and enamel panels depicting beautiful romantic tableaux
of goose girls and Greek heroes – pulled up next to them. Percy,
an incongruous occupant for even the most ordinary of carriages,
unfolded from within, rumpled and harried. He still wore his
favourite smoking jacket, although he had substituted cream
linen trousers for the tweed with the result that he looked rather
like a cricket player cross-bred with a librarian. He'd forgotten a
hat and his red hair was sticking up wildly in all directions in a
fair imitation of a werewolf after full-moon night.

His little valet followed. Virgil's eyes were wide and mouth slightly open as he caught sight of the dirigible and the chaos of luggage surrounding it.

The Spotted Custard now boasted a completely finished exterior. Her balloon had indeed been painted bright red with black spots and coated in the necessary lacquers and oils to make her weather-resistant. She shone in the late afternoon light like some large, fat, round seedpod. The trim of the gondola section was picked out in shiny black, a stark contrast to the pale blond wood. Railings and other details shone darkly beautiful in the late afternoon sun. Dama had insisted that black was the perfect choice, being a colour that matched anything. "Now, when you lean *picturesquely* against the railings, my Puggle, your dress will never clash."

"Very well reasoned, Dama," had been Rue's straight-faced response.

Percy looked about with utter indifference.

"Well, Percy," said his sister, drawing his attention to her presence. "What do you think?"

"Why name the craft after a comestible and then decorate it like a Coccinellidae?"

Rue knew better than to attempt reasoning with Professor Percival Tunstell. "Because I like it that way."

Percy wrinkled his nose at her and then, distracted, leapt forward. "Do be careful – those documents are hundreds of years old!"

Rue summoned Percy's valet with a subtle gesture. "Virgil, be a dear and steer him up that gangplank and down below into the library, would you, please? Spoo here will show you the way."

Spoo obligingly appeared at Rue's elbow and nodded at the young valet. "Oi up, me duck?" she said, or something equally unintelligible.

Virgil looked askance at the soot-covered girl, near his own age but remarkably scruffy and laddish by comparison. "Good afternoon," he said, remembering his manners. Then he looked up at

Rue, panicked. "Himself won't like it if this one goes anywhere near those there scrolls."

Rue grinned. "Ah, good. Spoo, follow those trunks, pretend to be helpful and try to touch them but don't actually do so."

"If you say so, captain." Spoo, irrepressibly good-natured, trotted off to do exactly as she had been instructed.

Percy instantly panicked and ran after the girl as she rendered – what Percy was certain was – smudgy doom upon his trunks and satchels of books. Everything else was forgotten as he followed the sootie's stubby form in gangly worry. Virgil brought up the rear carrying a wicker picnic basket that was yowling in protest, and a good quality hatbox. At least Percy would have one top hat on board. And his cat.

"Good. That's him safely ensconced," said Rue.

"You're not worried he'll escape?" Prim watched her brother with affectionate exasperation.

"I've given instructions for the footmen and porters to wall him in with his own books. By the time he reads his way out, we should be ready for float off."

"You'll leave a feeding hole?"

"I'm not a monster." Rue looked up in time to see yet another conveyance barrelling towards their not-so-secret location. "Speaking of monsters."

This contraption was no horse-drawn carriage but a steam-powered locomotive of a most unusual design. It was insect-like in appearance, constructed rather like a pill bug, although it was not intentionally decorated as such – like *The Spotted Custard* – but only appearing bug-like out of necessity. It was more utilitarian than beautiful, its exterior comprised of darkened metal panels shelling into one another like scales. It belched steam from below this carapace, and smoke from two stiff antennae.

The steam roly-poly subsided to a stop and a hatch at its top popped open. Quesnel Lefoux's boyish head poked out.

"Good afternoon, ladies." He tipped his hat. He, of course, was impeccably well turned out.

"Mr Lefoux, how do you do?" Prim gave the inventor a warm smile.

Rue nodded, her own smile slightly forced.

"Like that, is it?" Primrose looked at Rue sideways and then suddenly caught sight of something aboard ship that needed her attention. "Oh dear, my skirt tapes appear to be in some danger. The sooties are turning them into slingshots. If you would excuse me." With which she opened one of her parasols, a frothy white affair with small green embroidered leaves, and bustled up the gangplank. She was wearing a sage travelling dress with cream lace sleeves and collar decorated with more embroidered leaves. Prim had such an enviably effortless style. She used the second, closed parasol, with equal effortlessness to prod her way through the masses.

Quesnel came over. "And where has the charming Miss Tunstell gone? Was it something I said?"

"Perhaps the cut of your jib offends," suggested Rue.

"I assure you my jib is very well cut indeed." Before Rue could sputter he changed the conversation. "I can't say I approve of what you've done with the place. Why the spots?"

"I like spots."

"She's rather over-decorated for a dirigible."

"So she should be. You stick to your jibs and leave the dirigible to me."

"A man, mon petit chou, has only one jib." Rue did sputter at that. "Now, what did you decide to call her?"

"*The Spotted Custard.*"

Quesnel couldn't suppress his snort of derision. "Goodness, that sounds like a disease of the unmentionables."

"You and your jib should know," Rue shot back without thinking.

"Jealous of my experience, mon petit chou? You've only to ask and I'd be happy to teach you all the rigging."

Rue tried not to be shocked or intrigued – after all, she had rather asked for it. She was actually tempted to open negotiations on that very subject right then and there. She'd wager he *could* teach her a great deal, and she was quite curious. Instead she stuck her nose in the air. But it was a retreat and they both knew it.

Quesnel didn't press the advantage, instead assessing propellers, belay lines, sail, and smoke stack. "*N'importe quoi*. Who cares about the name as long as she floats smoothly?"

Rue arched her brows at him. "Well, that would be your responsibility now, wouldn't it, Mr Chief Engineer?"

"A responsibility at which I have no doubt I shall excel." He became distracted by Prim gesticulating wildly at a deckhand. "Why is the Honourable Primrose Tunstell accompanying us? What purpose could she possibly serve? Is it a safe journey for a woman of her delicacy?" Quesnel seemed genuinely concerned.

Rue sniffed – he didn't give a toot for *her* delicacy. "Don't worry about Prim. All will become clear."

They watched as Primrose flirted and parasolled her way through rank and file on the main deck, in a matter of moments organising the entire crew into a streamlined baggage transportation troop. Rue would have had to act like Paw and issue orders. Primrose simply manipulated everyone into doing what she wanted. It was impressive.

"*That* is the Honourable Primrose Tunstell's *purpose*, as you so delicately put it," said Rue.

As Quesnel's own bags were already being unloaded and whisked up the gangplank under Prim's expert guidance, the engineer could only say, "Remarkable. I stand corrected."

"I believe you might want to become accustomed to the sensation."

Quesnel turned twinkling violet eyes on her. "This is going to be such fun."

Rue laughed. "Yes, yes, it is." She spent a moment appreciating those eyes before Quesnel's attention was once more caught by something on the ship.

A redhead appeared on the main deck, and it wasn't Percy.

"Goodness," said Rue. "What's she doing outside the boiler room? She never leaves the inner sanctum."

Aggie Phinkerlington waved a hand at Quesnel and yelled, "Thought those were your bits I saw loading in."

Quesnel shouted back, "What would you know of my bits, you beastly woman?"

"More than I ever wanted to, you repulsive boffin. Come on up, see what they've done with all your original bits. I think you'll like it."

"I'd better – you know how seriously I take my bits." Quesnel turned to Rue and doffed his hat. "Until later, chérie." He began to stride towards the gangplank.

"Chief Lefoux?"

He paused gratifyingly quickly. "Yes, captain?"

"Staff meeting in the stateroom in one hour. I expect to see you there. Don't let Greaser Phinkerlington and those bits distract you for too long."

Quesnel gave a half-smile and another tip of his hat. "Of course not, captain."

Primrose put her tea-cup down without a clatter, her big brown eyes delighted. "You didn't lie about the tea, Rue. It is quite

excellent. This is going to be a far more civilised journey than I
initially thought."

Rue huffed. "Goodness, I hope not. Life can be too civilised,
don't you think?"

Prim was genuinely shocked by such a statement from her
Lady Captain – as the crew had taken to calling Rue.

Quesnel said by way of explanation, as though he were on far
more intimate terms with Rue than her closest friend of twenty-
odd years, "Now, Miss Tunstell, you know our girl here, raised by
werewolves. Gives one a healthy scepticism of polite society. Not
to mention a charmingly forthright nature."

Percy grunted, either in agreement or disapproval – it was
impossible to tell which. He was nibbling a biscuit and reading a book. At the table! However, Rue was pleased to see that
the book addressed the complex subject of aetheric currents – so
at least it was relevant to their trip. Of course, it seemed to be
a treatise on the currents above the Mongolian Steppes but one
couldn't quibble.

In addition to Quesnel, Percy, and Primrose, a few of the staff
were also present – the head steward, the purser, and the cook all
stood uncomfortably at the back of the room, despite having been
invited to join the aristocracy at table.

Rue turned to them first in order to alleviate any discomfort.
After a brief hesitation, she settled on imitating her mother at
her most docile. It was a challenging personality to wear – a
modulated aggressive temperament mixed with eager interest. It
required the eyes be widened slightly, the nose elevated but not
too much, and a touch of a smile about the corners of the mouth.
It bordered on arrogance, so Rue had to take great care with her
wording. "If you're certain you won't take tea, shall we get on to
business right away? I've called you here to introduce you to the
Honourable Primrose Tunstell – she will have charge of the daily

staff. She is, in effect, my clerk meets butler meets housekeeper meets batman."

"My goodness," muttered Percy. "How the mighty have fallen."

"Do be quiet, Percy," snapped his sister.

Rue continued, "I assure you Miss Tunstell will execute her duties efficiently and thoughtfully. She will settle all shipboard disputes that do not require official judgement. In these matters she speaks for me. Is that understood? My concern must be the floating of the ship and the safety of those on board, not to mention making our destination in good time. I do not wish to be bothered with trifles." Rue hoped she didn't sound too autocratic, but Paw always said that authority must be established from the beginning. Rue was afraid her concern over puff pastry and sunflowers might have initally come off as too domestic for a real captain. Nevertheless, she couldn't help but add, "Except those trifles of the pudding variety."

The three heads of staff nodded enthusiastically.

"Very well. Dismissed. Feel free to take your own tea in the mess. We shall remain here for the next half-hour."

The staff hurried away, relieved.

Rue waited until they had gone and then dropped her act. "Was it wrong of me to invite them to sit?"

Prim said, "Give them time to get to know you, Rue. Staff is not accustomed, as you are, to thinking of everyone as pack."

Rue nodded. "I take your point. If I am to be Alpha here, I must maintain some official distance?"

Prim sipped her tea. "Something like that."

Rue turned to Quesnel. "Report on engineering, Chief Lefoux?"

"Looking good. Boilers are steaming, coal bunkers are full, water tanks are topped, sooties working hard. It's a good crew and a well-stocked situation."

"Your estimate of first-needed refuelling?"

"We should be fine for a week at least. More if we catch the right aether currents and can use the mainsail rather than the propeller."

"Good. Cook's stores estimate matches that – let's try to keep it that way, shall we? Speaking of currents, Professor Tunstell, have you charted our course?"

Percy pulled out a rolled map and plopped it down on the table. He attempted to unroll it several times but it kept snapping shut. Rue signalled to the others and they all grabbed the edges on his fourth try, holding it open for him. Without a thank-you, Percy bent over the image now displayed.

It was a peculiar-looking thing, a rough sketch of England, Europe, and the Mediterranean overlaid with arrowed swirls and lines. "We're making for the Maltese Tower," said Percy, pointing. "If we can catch the Gibraltar Loop south and then the Mediterranean Shifter west, we could make it there in two days. That's our ideal course. If we miss the transfer puff, we can take the European Flow here and shoot for the Constantinople Tower instead. It's further away but we should make it in three days, four at most. It's the current-hops we have to worry about."

Quesnel interrupted, giving the navigator a critical look. "How's your hop technique?"

Percy arched an eyebrow. "Perfect, of course. In theory. The ship had better handle smoothly."

Quesnel could play that game. "Smoother than butter, as long as your probe points are accurate."

"Of course they're accurate! Are you accusing me of not researching the aetherosphere properly?"

"I'm accusing you of inexperience."

"Oh, and you've floated a ship of this size and design regularly over long distances, have you?"

Rue banged her free hand down on the map-covered table top. "Gentlemen. Enough. None of us has done this before and all of

us are likely to make mistakes. Including me. Well, except Primrose, of course. She's perfect."

Prim blushed. "Aw, Rue – too kind."

Rue soldiered on. "The important thing is to act within the
best of our knowledge and with confidence in front of the crew.
We must look like we have done this before. And do try to get
along in public." She stood to emphasise her point. She hadn't
her mother's figure but she wasn't a delicate creature either. Rue
knew how to get a gentlemen's attention, and she wasn't averse
to using that skill in her capacity as captain. She drew a deep
breath. Both Percy and Quesnel sat up straighter in their chairs
and stopped glaring at each other to glare at her instead.

Rue continued, "We need only get along for this one mission.
If everything goes smoothly, we should be home in less than a
month. Then we can all go our separate ways. Agreed?"

They all looked at one another.

Primrose said quickly, "Agreed."

Quesnel crossed his arms over his grey waistcoat and leaned
back. "Agreed."

They all turned to look at Percy. "Very well," the redhead said
reluctantly. Then he added, "I suggest we catch the morning current. The Gibraltar Loop should be over London at about nine."

Rue and Prim looked at him, askance. Neither of them had
ever been up before eight in the morning, except on those few
occasions when they were viewing that untenable hour from
the other side. Being raised by vampires and werewolves made
one quite nocturnal.

"Not possible. Dama has a bon voyage party planned for after
sunset. I think perhaps two hours or so after that is a superior
departure time."

"And I must make the rounds this afternoon, leave my card,"
added Primrose.

"Why?" Percy asked, genuinely confused.

"Oh really, Percy. One cannot simply leave town without *telling* people. It's not done."

Percy shook his head at the ridiculous politeness of it all and consulted his maps and timetables. "That's not ideal, but we could catch a lesser current and hook up with the loop over the mainland here." He stopped talking and began calculating, completely ignoring them all.

Primrose put down her tea-cup. "Well, Rue, if there's nothing else—?"

"Of course. Very well. Dismissed."

Quesnel left with alacrity, doffing his hat and winking at Prim. Percy didn't look up.

Rue decided to leave him to it. She walked Primrose down the gangplank and saw her back into her carriage. There was something off about her friend's attire. An under-used part of Rue's brain, the part that belonged to Dama's drones, was bothered by her friend's outfit. But since Primrose never made mistakes in fashion, Rue ignored her inner drones and returned to ensuring all was shipshape.

Rue was at dinner in the stateroom at around midnight when Primrose returned to the ship. Footnote had found his way over from the library and graced her lap with a purr. This was most likely due to the delicious smells coming from her plate, but Rue was disposed to be honoured by his presence. She had thought to return home to Dama's that night but with so much to do, and a cat in her lap, it seemed easier to stay aboard and test out the facilities in a dry run. Kill two pigeons with one stone, as it were.

"Oh, Prim," she said, looking up from her manifest, "I forgot

you'd be back. Would you like some supper? S
She trailed off. "What on earth is the matter?"

Prim's face was a picture of distress.

"Rue, it's awful! My reputation...in tatt
recover from the scandal." She paced about in a
lock of her hair might actually have fallen out of place.

"My dear, what's wrong?" Rue bribed Footnote to the floor
with a bit of chicken skin. Then she stood to console her friend
with an arm about the waist.

Prim trembled in agitation. "I hardly dare speak of it."

Rue lowered her voice. "Prim, were you caught *in flagrante?*"
Rue could hardly suppose this to be true – Primrose was a horrible flirt but she wasn't a hardened flirt. As far as Rue knew, Prim
had never even entertained a gentleman in private. In this, Prim
was the more circumspect of the two of them.

Prim resumed pacing, gesticulating, and talking – likely to
knock some carefully placed decorative item over in her agitation.
"I was making my calls, presenting parting compliments *pour dire
adieu*, the rounds and such, as you do."

"You didn't use the wrong size card, did you?"

"The very idea! I am not absent of all sense of decorum. *Of
course*, I used the larger format. But you see, oh, it's just too bad..."

"Primrose Tunstell, what has happened?"

"I made near a dozen calls and it wasn't until I got to the duchess's that I realised. Oh, Rue, I can hard bear think – the shame
of it all."

"What *is* it?" Now Rue was getting annoyed. Primrose was
drawing things out for dramatic suspense.

"I wore the wrong outfit."

"Is that all?" Rue realised that was what her inner drones had
been upset about that afternoon. Primrose had been wearing a
travelling dress, not a visiting dress.

Queen Mums will *never* forgive me. A travelling outfit for evening calls? Should she hear of this, should it get back to her, I'll never live it down. And of course I returned home to the hive and her drones saw. I wondered what they were tittering about. Then I got to my room and looked in the glass and right there, on my head, a *sun hat*. At night! And a *travelling gown*. Oh, the shame of it. I went back down immediately and begged them not to tell. But they can't hold their tongues, not for more than one night."

"This is a serious business." Rue schooled her expression into one of deep concern. It hardly mattered that she thought it ridiculous – Primrose was in distress and such perturbation must be honoured.

"Queen Mums practically invented the idea of specialty hats. And to pair one with an inappropriate dress? I might as well have worn my bicycling outfit to her dinner party."

"Practically?" interjected Rue. "She *did* invent the idea."

"Oh, Rue, what are we to do?"

"Issue a statement of apology to the popular press?"

"Please don't be facetious at a time like this. No, there is only one thing for it – we must leave London at once."

"What, early? Before the party?"

"Yes – early. Just as Percy suggested. The better current is tomorrow morning anyway. As if I could show my face at a party when word of this gets out."

"But Dama would never forgive me."

"Dama would forgive you anything."

"Good point. Except possibly wearing a sun hat for evening calls."

Primrose was too distressed for the joke. "Oh, goodness, what if he finds out too? Rue, we must leave! Immediately!"

"Agreed. The hat requires it. Do be more careful from here on out though, please. I wouldn't want my ship to get a reputation."

Primrose nodded earnestly. "Not a hat will be left unturned. This I vow."

Rue took a last bite of supper. "Well then, we will have to finish preparations tonight. Luckily most of us are still on board. Percy's trapped in the library. Quesnel elected to stay overnight as well. I'll make sure the rest of the crew is here, if you'll check on the staff and the supplies?"

"Of course."

Rue stood and addressed the cat. "Let's find out what time that optimal morning current was. Coming, Footnote? I need to talk to your master. Prim, you'd better come too, help mollify the beast."

Footnote burped at her and led the way to the library. The two ladies followed.

Percy was not pleased to have the plans changed again so soon. "But I did all the calculations for the more complicated night departure. Now you want to go back to the first float scheme?"

"Yes. We decided you were right all along," said Rue, swiftly forestalling further objections.

Percy sputtered to a halt. "Oh. Well, yes, naturally. Of course I was right."

"So what time is that superior current you found for us?" Rue pressed.

Primrose wore a look of distaste at Rue buttering her brother up but held her tongue since it was her fault.

Percy scattered his notes every which way, looking for the earlier schedule. "Eight minutes past nine in the morning."

Prim couldn't help it: she groaned. "Such an inhuman hour."

"Such an unfashionable hour," corrected Rue. "All too human — that's the point. It's after sunrise. No supernatural parents to see us off. No drones."

Rue couldn't help a little thrill at the idea of sneaking away. She adored all three of her parents but they were awfully prone to drama. Paw would cry – she knew he would. Lord Maccon might be the biggest, baddest Alpha werewolf in all England but he was a big old softy where his daughter was concerned. Mother would order her around. Dama would fuss over her clothing selection. Better to escape in secrecy. Thank goodness for Prim's unexpected fashion faux pas – it was going to make Rue's life so much easier.

They left Percy to formulate the new float plan.

FOUR

A Floating Custard

The Spotted Custard left London on her maiden voyage with much less fanfare than one might expect from the departure of two of London society's darlings.

Thinking they were to leave that evening, Rue's parents, the Wimbledon Hive, and the Woolsey Hive had agreed for once to coordinate *the* outdoor event of the supernatural season. They planned a moonlit masquerade in Regent's Park with invitations accepted by many of the best kinds of people. Provisions included unlimited champagne and sanguine fluid, treacle tart and blood sausage. The event would have played host to the season's most extravagant dresses and fantastic hats. The next day's papers referred to its cancellation as a *scandalous upset*; several young debutantes went into serious emotional declines. The precipitous departure of the guests of honour did not, many felt, warrant the event's demise. Lady Prudence and the Honourable Primrose Tunstell were, in hushed whispers, thought to as have behaved in a very shabby manner indeed. Why should they spoil everyone else's fun?

Rue and Prim knew none of this.

Rue's thoughts were of her hapless Dama, who would be frightfully disappointed. He did so enjoy a fuss, and if it couldn't be over him, his Puggle was the next best thing. He'd have had his outfit planned and all the drones furnished to match. Then again, he might have predicted Rue's sneaking away early.

Only Quesnel's mother came to witness their departure, arriving in the steam roly-poly. How she'd found out was anyone's guess. Drone Lefoux merely hugged her son goodbye and stood quietly to the side while he made ready for float-off. She was statue-like – a bony older woman with short cropped hair and a preference for gentlemen's garb that the age of American novelists had ensured was no longer as shocking as it once had been. Quesnel checked the rigging, conferred with the ground crew, and re-boarded with a final wave. As the mooring ropes were pulled up, his mother removed her hat and held it to her breast in the attitude of a mourner.

Rue, Prim, and Percy assembled on deck. Percy took the helm behind and above the others, his face drawn in concentration. Primrose had supervised the installation of a large parasol over his poop deck navigation area, a pretty red one to match the balloon, which rather clashed with Percy's hair but would keep him from acquiring additional freckles during the journey. Prim was overly worried about her brother's freckles. Quesnel, of course, disappeared below to supervise engineering.

They floated up smoothly, if rather more round and cheerful than elegant. Once clear of the trees, the propeller whirled to life, driving them forwards, preparing to push them into the correct current once they broke into the aetherosphere. Then, quite unexpectedly, the chimney off the stern belched out two great burps of smoke along with a tremendous flatulent noise.

Rue could feel herself blushing, for this was not the dignified float-off she had imagined. Some pigeons, all unnoticed until that moment, squawked and left their roosting spots on *The Spotted Custard*. Rue gave them a dirty look.

Percy let out a bark of laughter.

"Is that normal?" Prim wondered.

"It's fine, only somewhat lacking in gravitas," Rue assured her hopefully. She looked up. "And you're never going to let Quesnel forget it, are you, Percy?"

"Certainly not." The redhead grinned at her.

"It is going to do that every time we lift off?" wondered Prim.

"Very probably. Design flaw, I'm afraid," said Percy, grinning even more broadly.

"Ah well, these things will happen." Rue looked over the railing. The trees of Regent's Park began to blur together, then the buildings around it became visible, then they too lost detail, and finally London herself was spread out below in one big dirty blob. The pigeons accompanied them up a short way. Rue shouted at them about the brief nature of their future existence and they lost interest, gliding lazily back down in search of statuary.

Thus unchaperoned, *The Spotted Custard* farted again and floated sedately upward.

Rue did not see, hidden under the trees on one side of the clearing, a tall couple. The woman wore no gloves and held the man's massive hand in one of hers – fingers interlaced, skin touching skin. Lord Maccon had once been a strong enough werewolf to stand under direct sun, but he was getting weaker, and his wife's touch was now vital during daylight.

He still looked as big and as strong as he had when Rue was a child, but he slept each night touching Lady Maccon, mortal, shaved each morning, and had aged ten years to Rue's twenty as a result. His dark brown hair was salted with grey but it was worth it. His wife's touch was the only medicine that staved off the Alpha's curse of age-born madness. As far as Conall Maccon was concerned, ageing slowly was a worthwhile price to pay.

Alexia leaned her dark head on her husband's shoulder and said, "Good enough now, my love? She's safely away and on her own."

"Indeed," Conall grudgingly agreed, nestling his chin into his wife's curls. Alexia had forgotten to wear her hat. "But safe?" He whispered the query into that glossy hair, still as thick and dark as when they had first met. He'd sat one evening upon a hedgehog and never forgotten – the hair, the magnificent figure, or the hedgehog.

Alexia squeezed his hand. "She'll survive and thrive in India. It will be good for her to be away from all of this. All of us."

"Yes, but will India survive her?" the werewolf wondered legitimately.

Alexia chose to tackle his underlying concern and not his sarcasm. "She has resources and friends. That's the best one can ask for in life. And I gave her a parasol."

"Oh, indeed, was it *the* parasol?"

"No, simply *a* parasol. She's not ready for *the* parasol . . . yet. I'm taking this journey as a test of worthiness."

"You think she will be ready when she returns?" Conall drew back to look down into her face.

Alexia's brown eyes were thoughtful. "I think this will temper her. Travel is very broadening for the mind, don't you find? Our daughter is a sharp edge but of the kind that could grow dull, stuck here in London."

"I hate it when you are reasonable, wife."

"I know, but you really ought to be accustomed to it by now."

"Never. It's one of your many charms." He bent and kissed her deeply, a safe thing to do, hidden from prying eyes by trees and an early hour.

Alexia blushed like a schoolgirl under her tan skin but leaned eagerly into his kiss. "Ridiculous man." She pulled away. "Now. Don't you think it's time we considered your retirement?"

Conall glowered. His amber eyes, so like his daughter's, went hard. "Are you saying we should send a summons?"

"To Scotland?" His wife was thoughtful. "Perhaps."

"India. Kingair is billeted in India at the moment."

Alexia turned all nose, like a hound scenting a fox. "You knew that when you let her go, didn't you? Of course you did."

"Why else would I have permitted it?"

Alexia was relieved but unwilling to praise his fatherly interference. She returned to the subject at hand. "Do you think Biffy is ready?"

"Oh, he's ready. It's only, I'm not certain that I'm ready to let go."

Alexia cupped her husband's cheek with her free hand. "You let go of our daughter today, next to that . . ." she trailed off.

"A pack is no small thing, my love. Even balanced against a daughter. And I still have a little time left, I think."

Alexia had confidence in her adored, if frustrating, husband. "Then you must use it to reconcile yourself to our future."

"I hate it when you're right."

Alexia grinned. "Almost as much as when I'm reasonable?"

He growled at her. "Possibly more."

The moment they hit the aetherosphere, Rue fell instantly and entirely in love with her new ship. They crossed into the blurry nothingness of aether, losing sight of both the world below and the sky above. It was a great scientific mystery that the aetherosphere was invisible, except when one was inside it. And inside was a treacherous space to be. However, Rue's ship took to the currents with such grace it was almost as though they were still floating in normal air.

Percy was equally charmed. "This is what she was made for. Goodness, feel her go." His self-importance gave way before a misspent youth tagging after Rue and Prim as the girls took *Dandelion Fluff Upon a Spoon* out for yet another illegal jaunt. Percy might be a bluestocking but he did love to float. It was one of the reasons he took Rue's job offer.

The *Custard* slid smoothly through the aether where any other ship would have shuddered and jolted. Percy examined the Mandenall Pudding Probe's dial. It was set for the Gibraltar Loop but the first hop into a current was always the hardest. The moment they entered the aetherosphere they began drifting with the local idles southward.

"Take us up, please," said Rue.

Percy pressed down hard on the puffer button to put a little more rise into the balloon, and they glided up and began drifting east.

"And again, please," ordered his captain. Rue was enjoying command. Especially over Percy. "This time, bring her nose around to the south."

Percy puffed the *Custard* up once more and engaged the propeller to maximum. It farted loudly and they started a slow spin. At that moment, the Mandenall emitted a squirt of viscous milky liquid, not unlike rice pudding. This was how it had earned it its name. This was also the only sign they would get that they were directly below the correct current.

"There she is – the Gibraltar Loop," crowed Rue. "Hop it, Professor Tunstell, on my mark. And . . . mark."

Percy engaged the puffer once more and the ship rose up, hooked into the current, and began drifting.

Rue grinned in pleasure. "That's our lift – let's button it down."

Percy went into a flurry of dialling things to the correct places and cutting all steam power to the propeller.

Rue called out to the deckhands to raise the mainsail and the *Custard* came about beautifully, hauling fully to sit entirely within the Gibraltar Loop.

They all held their breath, hoping that they had settled into the correct side of the Loop – the one that went towards Gibraltar rather than away from it. The probe could tell them the right current but not whether it was heading in the right direction.

Percy checked his compass.

"Steady on course, captain – floating the Gibraltar south-bound," he crowed.

"Next hop?" Rue wasn't about to let him glory in his accomplishments for too long.

Percy instantly sobered. As dangerous as the first hop could be, it was hopping between charted currents that took real skill. He took out his pocket watch and snapped it open. "Four hours, twenty-six minutes."

Rue smiled. "Excellent. More than enough time for tea. Carry on, navigator."

"Captain," said Percy slightly sarcastically, but it was good enough for Rue.

The boiler room was a busy hum of activity: sooties scampered to and fro guiding the coal feeders, firemen manned the kettles, and greasers oversaw the smooth coordination of it all. It wasn't a big crew but they managed to look substantial by being everywhere at once. Quesnel stood to one side, watching in confident superiority. Aggie Phinkerlington slouched next to him, occasionally barking out an order. The two had worked out a system that

involved Quesnel calmly and softly pointing out some flaw and
Aggie yelling at someone about it.

"How's she floating, chief engineer?" Rue asked.

Quesnel acted as if he hadn't noticed her until she spoke.
Although there was no doubt he had been aware of her presence
the moment she entered the room. "Perfectly, captain. As if I
should design anything less than sublimely efficient."

Rue decided to play along and not prod him in the ribs with a
tong. "Compliments from ship's navigator – the *Custard* hopped
the aether beautifully. We are right on course."

"Compliments from old Percy? Stoats might float."

"Mr Lefoux." Rue pretended shock. "Language."

Aggie said, "Our captain's a real lady, boffin. Respect her as
such." The look on her face suggested this was meant to be an
insult.

Rue only bobbed a regal curtsey, acting like Primrose at
her most haughty. "Thank you kindly for the support, Greaser
Phinkerlington." She continued to Quesnel, "However, I was
wondering about the noise."

"What noise?" Quesnel was all innocence.

"You know, the noise the propeller makes when she cranks up,
out of the smoke-stack."

"No, I don't know. Can you make it for me?"

"No, I most certainly cannot! It was slightly, well . . ." Rue lowered her voice. "Flatulent. Percy suggested it was the result of a
design flaw."

"Oh, he did, did he?" Rue couldn't tell if Quesnel was pretending to be offended or genuinely upset.

"Is it going to make that sound every time we crank up?"

Aggie snorted out a laugh. "Troubles your delicate sensibilities,
does it, Lady Captain?"

Rue openly acknowledged this fact – she didn't think it a
character flaw. "Well, yes, it does rather. Not to mention Miss

Tunstell, whose sensibilities are far more delicate than mine. And there are appearances to consider."

"Pox to appearances," said Aggie rather aptly.

"Now, now, Greaser Phinkerlington," remonstrated Rue. "Some of us have to think of every possible angle. What if we need to be stealthy or sneak away from a situation?"

"In a ship painted like a ladybug?"

Rue was beginning to suspect Aggie of disliking her decorative choices.

"Paint," said Rue quite primly, "can be covered over. Farts cannot."

Aggie bristled. "Don't you argue semantics with me, you prissy—"

Quesnel, trying hard not to laugh, interrupted what looked to be quite the argument. "Very well, captain, I'll look into correcting the noise, or at least stoppering it over when we're in grave need."

Rue nodded. "That's all I ask. Now if you'll excuse me." She glared at Aggie. *Prissy. I'll give you prissy.* She pretended to be Mother at her most autocratic – stuck her nose in the air, put her shoulders back, and narrowed her eyes at the horrible female. This seemed to give Aggie some kind of minor apoplectic fit.

"So soon, mon petit chou?" said Quesnel, swooping in to grab Rue's hand, bending over it gallantly.

"Gladly," said Aggie at the same time.

Rue returned above deck feeling she had mainly lost that particular conversational battle. But disposed to be pleased that she had at least got what she wanted out of Quesnel.

The second hop didn't go quite as smoothly as the first. For one thing, it took Percy by surprise. Fortunately, he'd stuck the

Mandenall Pudding Probe up and set it to register correctly, but
it squirted out the current cross-point a good quarter-hour before
he'd calculated it should. Since the crew was relaxing over suste-
nance at the time, this was rather an upset to everyone.

They were taking tea on the main deck. Primrose had requisi-
tioned deck chairs and small side tables, and Cook had provided
them with a large pot of a most excellent Darjeeling blend and
some buttery little crumpets with clotted cream and jam.

Prim was playing hostess, outfitted in a black velvet travelling
suit with purple swirl detailing – not unlike one of Percy's aether
current maps – and a large purple hat lavishly decorated with silk
roses.

Rue had opted to only pack and wear her most military-
inspired gowns – she felt this better suited her role as captain.
She wore a travelling dress of navy blue with black cord stripes,
the jacket featuring prominent gold buttons and a crossover
front. It was almost plain and would have given Dama heart
palpitations with its severity. Her hat was an oval of navy straw
with an up-tilted front and a very large feather spilling over one
side which looked pleasingly piratical. The ensemble suited her
beautifully, emphasising by contrast her womanly figure and
mercurial expressions.

Percy was slurping his tea while reading a book on the micro-
fauna of the aetherosphere and the threat inherent in such creatures to the vital humours of chronic aetheric travellers. Percy
was a bit of a hypochondriac. His outfit of tweed and mismatched
jacket combined with floating goggles and tool strappings was
hardly worth mentioning. Although he had stuck a sunflower in
his button hole for medicinal purposes.

Quesnel, slightly smudged but presentable, chatted amiably
with Primrose. He wore a day suit of steel grey with a green
waistcoat, which perfectly corresponded to both his occupation
and standing. He refused, it must be admitted, to wear his top

hat while in engineering, although he had religiously donned it whenever above deck.

Even with Percy and Quesnel at odds, the teatime conversation was civil. Prim was adept at inane chatter and applied it with such dexterity that even her brother had to bow to her consummate skill. With Rue gamely holding up her end of the gossip, the gentlemen didn't stand a chance.

Until the probe squirted.

Virgil, who was manning the helm in his master's stead, gave a squawk of surprise not unlike that of the pigeons earlier. The sticky stuff plopped onto his shoe. Having been told to alert Percy should anything out of the ordinary occur, the valet sent up a wail of distress. Everyone but Prim jumped up, scattering crumpets, and dashed to the poop deck to ascertain the nature of the catastrophe.

"What? What is it?" Rue demanded.

Virgil pointed an accusatory finger at the probe and then his shoe. "That thing *excreted* at me."

Percy paled beneath his freckles. "Already? But it's far too soon. We shouldn't be hitting the Mediterranean Shifter for another fifteen minutes."

Quesnel said, "Your calculations must be off."

"My calculations are *never* off!"

Quesnel was already running for the stairs, removing his hat at the same time. "Well, explain that to me later, O wise one – right now we've a hop to make with limited preparation and less time. Lord save us all."

Rue tried to look debonair and calm. She thought about Uncle Rabiffano, and allowed herself the hint of a dandy's slouch. She thought that she might – at least – be fooling the decklings.

Percy continued protesting at Quesnel's vanished form. "The current must have moved from its last charted location – there's no way I could have predicted—"

Rue interrupted him. "Never mind that now, Percy. Virgil, stop squealing and use a handkerchief to clean your shoe. There's a good lad. Percy, grab the helm and prepare for a hop."

Percy's eyes widened. "But I'm *not* prepared."

Rue gave a rather ferocious grin. "No time – we're making this hop now. It'll be a good test of the *Custard*'s mettle."

Percy stared at her. She did look a mite crazed.

"Now, Percival!"

Percy sprang into action. He yanked at levers and cranked dials, getting the ship out of flotsam status.

Rue ordered the mainsail pulled in. It took the decklings longer than she liked. She'd have to run some drills on them to improve speed.

"Propeller at the ready?" she barked.

Percy grabbed and cranked over the appropriate bar. "Ready, captain."

The Spotted Custard farted.

Rue chose to ascribe it to nerves. "Steady, girl," she said to the ship, then to Percy, "Which nodule registered? Are we dropping or lifting to catch the Shifter?"

Percy examined the probe. "Lifting, captain."

Rue picked up the speaking tube that connected her to engineering and pressed the button that would sound a bell there.

"Yes?" Quesnel's voice was almost snappish.

"Prepare for a puff, chief engineer."

"I don't know about this. We're pushing her."

"She was made to be pushed or Dama wouldn't have given her to me."

"As you say, mon petit chou." She heard Quesnel turn away from the tube and murmur into the hubbub, "It's a lift, Aggie – have them stoke all boilers hot."

There came the sound of Aggie yelling.

Quesnel returned to Rue. "Ready, chérie."

"Here we go!" Rue hung up the speaker tube and turned to face Percy.

"Do it, Professor Tunstell. Now, please."

Percy pressed the puffer button to give the balloon its boost.

They bobbed out of the Gibraltar Loop into the loose uncharted swirls of the Charybdis currents. *The Spotted Custard*'s balloon caved in at several points as the dirigible was buffeted in various directions at once. The gondola section shook. Prim, still seated in a chair on the main deck, gave a little squeak of alarm and dived to secure the tea things.

"Find that current, professor," Rue ordered, her heart in her throat.

"Almost there, captain, a little higher," reassured Percy, looking utterly terrified.

He pressed the puffer button again.

They rose, but the balloon began to collapse inward on the leeward side. The gondola lurched to starboard as the balloon caught one current, while the lower part of the ship caught another. The two halves were being torn apart. If they weren't quick, the gondola could separate from the balloon entirely and they would spiral down to certain death far below.

"Not enough power," yelled Percy.

Rue battled the tilt of the deck, reaching for the speaking tube, holding her hat to her head out of instinct. She lifted the tube to her mouth, pressing the alert.

"What now?" came Quesnel's voice, oddly calm under the circumstances, only that extra French to his accent indicating stress.

"More heat to the boilers, please, Quesnel," said Rue, forgetting to use formal address in her fear.

"Since you ask so nicely, mon petit chou," was Quesnel's pleasant reply.

Rue nodded at Percy. "Again."

Percy gave *The Spotted Custard* another puff.

The ship rose up in a quick bob, hooked in and then...

Everything levelled out, the balloon returned to its chubby ladybug state, the gondola hung straight down as if it had never tilted. Everything went calm as a loon floating serenely on placid waters.

Rue set the tube down with a whoosh of breath overset by a terrible temptation to give in to wobbly knees and collapse to the deck. But as captain she had no time for such silliness. She turned to Percy. "Everything as ordered, Professor Tunstell?"

Percy blinked at her. "Erm. Yes, captain. A completely seamless hop, as I predicted."

"Indeed, seamless." Rue arched an eyebrow at this outrageous statement. She turned to Virgil who was lurking to one side with a group of panting decklings. They'd only just managed to lower the mainsail in time for the hop.

"Deckhands, decklings, everyone still solid? Virgil?"

"Floating pretty, Lady Captain," said Virgil with a grin. He'd recovered his aplomb with the remarkable speed of the very young. The other decklings only seemed able to nod, awed by what had just occurred.

Rue picked the speaker tube back up.

"What now, chérie?" came Quesnel's voice, now devoid of accent.

"How's everything in engineering?"

"Bit of a bumpy ride but we weathered it well and good. Couple of welts and bruises, the odd small burn, nothing requiring Matron. Got us a coal spill to clean up if you could spare any hands from up top?"

It was certainly a good thing no one needed a surgeon, as they didn't have one on board. Rue pointed at the decklings. "You six, report to engineering. Back up here post haste, mind you. We'll need that sail up again shortly. You two to the crow's nest – I want eyes on that current. You two stay on deck at alert."

They sprang to do her bidding. Virgil wandered over.

"Six coming down to you now, Mr Lefoux," said Rue into the speaker.

"Ta, mon petit chou." This time Quesnel hung up on her.

Rue replaced the tube and went to attend to her last concern.

"It's a good thing you started out bossy before you were given command," Primrose said from where she sat, slightly swallowed by a partly collapsed deck-chair.

"Are you well, Prim?"

"One tea-cup down. But it was empty, thank goodness, so nothing spilled. And the pot's still warm. Would you like a refresher?"

Rue, feeling all-conquering and victorious, waved a casual hand about her head in what she felt was a field marshal manner. "Just pour it, darling, just pour it."

When she returned to her seat, however, it was to learn that all the crumpets had overturned to land buttered-side down on the deck. "Why must that always be the case?"

"Laws of the unnatural humours," sympathised Prim before sending Virgil to Cook for some more. "And lemon curd please this time, not raspberry jam. Lemon is so much better with crumpets, don't you feel?"

"Indubitably," replied Rue, sipping her tea.

They made the Maltese Tower in just under three days. Percy bragged that this was almost – although not quite – a record. "Next time we could do it in two and a half if we kicked in the propeller more frequently."

"I'm not pushing my sooties and tapping the fuel reserves

so you can have a record on the slates with the Royal Society," replied Quesnel.

They were enjoying a nice supper in the mess hall. Or at least it could have been nice. Cook had managed macaroni soup, roast pork ribs, cabbage, and Napier pudding. Unfortunately, Percy and Quesnel's constant squabbling could upset even Rue's iron stomach.

Rue put down her knife and fork to glare at them. "Don't you two ever stop?"

"Everyone needs some form of entertainment, mon petit chou," replied Quesnel with a charming smile.

Percy returned to his book, a treatise on the health benefits of sea-bathing versus aetheric emersion. They had unsuccessfully tried to stop him from reading at table. In the end, Rue had insisted he wear a pinafore if he continued to try to eat *and* read, but if he had already finished his meal, she no longer objected. He seemed perfectly able to participate in the conversation, even when he was to all appearances entirely absorbed by the written word.

When Quesnel would have said something more to aggravate the navigator, Rue shook her head at him. "Leave the poor thing be. For goodness' sake, what exactly did he steal from you to make you so annoyed with him all the time?" she wondered, knowing the question was both intrusive and daring.

Primrose put a hand to her mouth in shock. "Rue, should we discuss such things at the table?"

"We should if it continues to impinge upon everyone's enjoyment of social discourse."

"Fair enough." Quesnel hit her with twinkling violet eyes. "So discuss."

Rue tried to arrange herself to look sympathetic. "Was it a woman?"

Quesnel inhaled his cabbage and began to cough.

Rue slapped him on the back, hard, and Prim passed him wine.

When he had swallowed two full glasses and wiped his eyes, Rue said, "Well, was it?"

"Not to put too fine a point on it, yes." Quesnel actually blushed, something he did rather well given his fair skin.

Rue, who had her mother's swarthy complexion, had always considered it rather a blessing that she didn't blush easily. It made her, she fancied, seem cool and untouchable. But if she could do it as prettily as Quesnel, she might try in the future.

Primrose jumped to her brother's defence. "To be fair, Percy is like that."

Quesnel looked at her. "Like what? A poacher?"

Percy pretended to remain above the whole conversation, although he was obviously listening closely.

"No. He's deadly attractive to the ladies. Always has been, since Rue and I were little."

At that, Percy rolled his eyes and Quesnel looked offended.

Rue tried to swallow a smile. "I don't think you're helping matters, Prim."

Prim amended her statement. "Not that you aren't handsome yourself, Mr Lefoux."

"Thank you," said Quesnel immodestly, giving her a seductive glower.

Rue kicked him under the table. He didn't even flinch.

Prim continued, "Not that I could possibly understand the appeal, but females are always flirting shamelessly with Percy. He's quite the ladykiller, aren't you, brother dear? I understand our dad was a bit of a dasher as well in his day."

Percy looked at his sister. "Tiddles, I don't know what you think you're doing but it isn't helping."

"Not that he *tries* to be a ladykiller. Of course. He simply can't stop himself."

Percy grumbled at his book. "Oh no, it's my dashing good looks."

The funny thing was, of course, Primrose was perfectly correct. At any given ball, Percy inevitably found himself surrounded by young ladies angling for a dance. After suffering what amounted to two sisters, Percy was a marvellous dancer and all the society mothers knew it. They also knew that he had powerful relations without being a risky supernatural proposition himself. Untitled, yes, but rich was almost as good, and he ranked high with the sunset crowd by association. One could overlook his parents' theatrical background and his own curious case of bluestocking fever in favour of such amenities as money, connections, and appearance. As for the young ladies, there was something about his academic snobbery that drew them in like butterflies to a flower – a gawky, uncomfortable flower. They even liked the aloofness. One could never expect to be flattered by Professor Tunstell. Exposure to Percy at a ball, Miss Prospigot had announced recently, hands clasped to her lips, "was positively *soul quivering*".

Primrose continued, "He's always getting himself accidentally engaged. That's why he withdrew from polite society, isn't it, Percy? Tired of breaking all those hearts."

Quesnel sat back, watching the interchange with eyebrows arching so high they almost ate into his hairline. "Very noble of him."

Rue felt compelled to add, "Sad to say, Mr Lefoux, but she's perfectly correct. I can't explain it either."

"So you haven't fallen victim to the professor's unavoidable allure?"

Rue baulked. "I should say not. He's practically family. Why, I find you far more appealing than old Percy here."

Prim said, "Hear hear."

Quesnel looked suddenly pleased with life.

Percy slammed his book closed. "Really, girls! I hardly know the medicine from the ailment."

Quesnel said, "It's a strange back-handed compliment, ladies, but I'll take it."

Rue sighed, realising that this was all her fault and that she had opened up a topic of far greater intimacy than she should have, being the captain. "I do apologise, gentlemen. And of course, Mr Lefoux, if Professor Tunstell poached your lady-love, whether by accident or design, it is bad form, to say the very least. Professor, did you . . . poach, as it were?"

Percy snorted. "This conversation is ridiculous. Why should I care for the leavings of a mechanically-minded Frenchman?"

Quesnel stood at that, face flushed. "I say, that's too far."

Rue sighed. "Gentlemen, forgive me – this is getting us nowhere. I had hoped to clear the air so things could be more pleasant. That seems unlikely at the moment. Shall we adjourn?"

Percy was already up and away, extra helping of Napier pudding in one hand, book in the other.

Quesnel turned to look at Rue as if he felt he owed her an explanation. "It's the principle of the thing, chérie. Ungentlemanly behaviour. You know my heart belongs only to you. The sunshine of my life, the moon on my horizon, the—"

"Yes, of course, dear. The pearl of your necklace, the rose of your garden." Rue rolled her eyes and tried not to be actually flattered.

"Oh, yes, those are good too."

Rue sighed. "Scoot off, Quesnel, do."

"You are all sweetness and light, mon petit chou."

Rue did not rise to the bait. Nor was she going to ask him to stop calling her *mon petit chou*. He knew it galled her but as long as he confined it to the semi-privacy of the stateroom, she would ignore it.

"Shoo to you too."

Quesnel strode out and Rue sat back down with a sigh.

"More tea?" Prim's eyes were dancing.

"Thank you. Prim, was that a foolish thing to discuss?"

Primrose remained silent.

"It can't only be some silly painted lady, can it? Aren't you dying to know why they hate each other so?"

"Certainly not." Prim's tone indicated she probably already knew and that it had something to do with the twin connection. Often it was difficult to remember that Percy and Primrose were related, let alone twins, but a lifetime of experience had given Rue a sense of when she was intruding on their sibling bond. She was about to attempt a new line of conversation when the most amazing sound emanated throughout the ship. It was a new noise entirely and it seemed dangerous.

Rue and Prim leapt to their feet and made for the poop deck as quickly as their skirts would allow.

CHAPTER

FIVE

The Maltese Tower

The sound, which was a like a gargle meets a warble, only extremely loud, turned out to be *The Spotted Custard*'s version of a proximity alarm. It had been activated by a deckling in the crow's nest. The young lad swung himself down to report that the Maltese Tower beacon was dead ahead in the murk of the aetherosphere. His glassicals – the far-focus set handed out to any who manned the nest – amplified his watery eyes into huge blue orbs under the gaslight of the deck lanterns.

"Very good, young sir," was Rue's reply. "Now back up with you, please, and let us know when we reach docking drop-down juncture."

"Aye aye, Lady Captain." The boy gave a floppy salute before pulling himself back up via a series of rope ladders ending with one long swinging run up the side of the balloon.

"Ah, to be young and agile again," said Primrose.

"We were never that young," replied Rue.

"More to the point, we were never that agile," said Prim with a soft smile.

Rue huffed her agreement and turned to Percy, who had put away his book and resumed the helm the moment the alarm sounded. At least he had a sense of responsibility. "Prepare to drop out of aetherosphere as soon as we reach docking juncture point."

"Yes, captain," replied Percy, face a little drawn. "I had assumed."

Rue spared a moment to worry that this job might be too much for even his arrogance. "Percy, have you ever docked a ship of this size?"

"Not exactly," replied Percy.

"And what *exactly* does 'not exactly' mean?"

"I've read about it."

"Oh dear. Should I call Mr Lefoux up to take over from you?"

"Absolutely not. I'll do perfectly well." Percy's face went from fearful to fiercely determined.

Pleased with herself for manipulating him properly, Rue said, "I'm sure you will."

The crow's nest hollered down, docking juncture spotted. Rue squinted into the swirling miasmic grey, not unlike London during the Great Pea Souper of 1887. Just ahead she thought she could make out . . . a lamp-post.

Or what looked like a lamp-post, except that it was only the top half of one and Rue knew that it only seemed small because they were still far away. In actual fact, the beacon was very large indeed. It was birdcage in shape and lit from within by a miasmic orange gas.

Rue ordered, "Deck hands pull in the mainsail, navigator prepare to drop out of aetherosphere on my mark." She went to the speaking tube and bonged the boiler room.

"Yes?" barked a female voice.

"Greaser Phinkerlington?"

"You were expecting an opera girl?"

"Please prepare to engage the propeller."

"We're always prepared for that." In an aside Rue was probably meant to hear, Aggie added, "Imbecile."

Rue gritted her teeth and tried to think of sticky sweet buns. "Very good. Thank you for your efficiency."

Before Aggie could add anything more snide, Rue replaced the tube.

"I could grow to hate that woman," she said to Primrose.

Prim patted her back condescendingly. "You handled it well – bad language never won fair maiden."

"Prim, dear, I don't think that's how the saying goes. Nor do I think Phinkerlington would like being called a fair maiden."

Prim grinned. "Precisely my point."

The decklings scrambled to bring in the sail. Rue watched, plotting how to run speed drills. Also, they'd benefit from one among them being put in charge of the others for the sake of efficiency – there seemed to be a lot of squabbling. One of the deckhands was supposed to have them under orders, but he seemed at a loss coping with an overabundance of youthful exuberance. An internal hierarchy might work to everyone's advantage.

By the time the mainsail was down, they were almost upon the beacon.

"Professor Tunstell, three, two, one, mark," Rue said, trying not to sound panicked.

The Spotted Custard sank as Percy activated the anti-puffer. Rue's stomach went up into her throat. It was rather like bobbing on a large wave. They slid through the Charybdis currents easily this time, but unfortunately hit a strong current below that dragged the airship westward away from the beacon.

"Again, professor," ordered Rue.

Down they bobbed a second time. And a third. And a fourth in quick succession. This was followed by a buffeting spin through another set of fiercer Charybdis currents. Then they were blessedly

out. The aether mists cleared and they were floating down through
a star-filled sky. Rue wondered, not for the first time, what the
aetherosphere looked like from above. And what, in fact, the layer
above the aetherosphere was made of – was it even breathable? She
was not alone in this curiosity – aether scientists discussed the out-
ersphere as if it were a desirable undiscovered country, and were
always concocting new ways to go higher. So far, however, no one
had managed to break through.

Percy cranked up the propeller, and *The Spotted Custard* farted
excitedly. Slowly, they swung around to face their original direction of travel, and before them, under the silvered moon, was the
upper docking section of the Maltese Tower, the beacon rising
above into the aetherosphere.

Rue scurried to the front rail of the forecastle, looking out over
the bowsprit at the Sixth Pinnacle of the Modern Age.

The Maltese Tower, one of the Eight Wonders of the British
Empire, was as impressive as one might hope. It looked like nothing so much as an immense piece of elaborate cooking equip-
ment – a massive circular oven pot with peepholes and windows
and multiple spatulas sticking up and out, only facing the wrong
way with their handles in. These spatulas made up the docking
ports, a few already boasted dirigibles, ornithopers, and other airships, fresh into port, mooring ropes out. Some were under main-
tenance, while others were taking on helium, water, or coal. The
tiny forms of dock workers scampered along the spatulas like
ants along cake servers. The dock of the Maltese Tower resembled
a shipyard, only miles up in the air. Not, of course, that Lady
Prudence should have any idea what a shipyard looked like.

Rue wasn't impressed because what made the Maltese Tower
one of the Eight Wonders of the British Empire wasn't its beacon,
nor its docking port, but its bottom half.

For when one looked down, it was as if the Maltese Tower kept
going for ever, braced and supported by scaffolding so colossal

it required most of the island of Malta as its base. This part also looked like an endless stack of kitchen utensils. It was held up not by its own structure, but by hot-air balloons staged all along in a random pattern, balloons that were moved by the winds so that the whole tower swayed one way and then the other under the influence of various breezes. Like some underwater sea worm meets jumble sale.

It must be terribly troublesome in a storm, thought Rue.

The Maltese Tower seemed to have been built with any available material: fabric and net, wood and steel, a massive bicycle here, bits of boat there, very small houses, the occasional train carriage. Rue knew people lived and worked up and down the tower, an entire culture sustained by aetheric travel, but she was hard-pressed to think it wondrous.

Prim came to stand next to her. "Gracious me! It is hideous, isn't it?"

"Oh, I don't know." Rue was disposed to be optimistic. "If one squints, it might be called attractively biological. See those parts, dangling. They are like seed pods."

"Presumably they're actually habitations and workshops."

Rue ignored her friend's lack of romantic vision. "The balloons and air tanks there are like leaves stretching upward."

"I don't follow."

"No, you never do." Rue was resigned. Primrose was a creature of practical elegance and the Maltese Tower was neither.

They watched as enormous dumbwaiters, carrying coal, moved sedately up one side of the tower on thick cables. There were long tubes winding around and sucking up water from the Mediterranean, filtering and siphoning, destined for the great ships that docked far above but tapped all the way along by workers and inhabitants. Rue remembered reading somewhere that the Maltese Tower had a dedicated side business in the salt trade.

Percy guided *The Spotted Custard* forward gingerly, heading for a port on the nearside. The *Custard* seemed to be going rather fast.

"I should prefer it, professor, if we didn't actually *crash* into the Maltese Tower," said Rue.

"Yes, captain, I guessed as much."

The Spotted Custard sped up as she caught a breeze.

"Percy!" said Rue, voice rising.

"Everything is in order, captain."

Rue lifted the speaking tube. "Cut the boilers, please."

"Anything for you, mon petit chou," Quesnel's warm voice acknowledged the command. Rue was decidedly relieved it wasn't Aggie.

She added, "Once we're docked, please come up for a discussion on the matter of shore leave."

"It would be my pleasure," replied Quesnel.

Rue replaced the tube with the feeling that her engineering staff was doomed to be a problem, one way or another.

Percy toggled the switch that reversed the propeller to the sound of triple flatulence. *The Spotted Custard* stuttered, jerking to a slower speed, almost sedate. They glided in and nosed up next to one of the spatulas, subsiding into stillness with one final tremendous *ptttttt* noise.

"Not the most dignified of arrivals," commented Primrose.

Percy snipped at his sister: "I thought the point was not to crash."

"You did very well, Percy, on that front. And I would appreciate it if you were consistent in this matter," praised Rue.

Percy looked at her sideways to see if she were humouring him and then subsided onto a nearby deck-chair in a funk.

Quesnel appeared above deck mere moments later. The ubiquitous smudges gave him a rakish look which Rue wished didn't suit him quite so much. It was horribly annoying of him to look dashing. She ignored his smudgy adorableness. He cocked his head at her engagingly.

With Prim and Percy already close at hand, Rue called the meeting to order. "Let everyone under you know, please, that we will be departing from the tower in exactly one hour. Staff and crew are allowed to explore, but they'd better be back in time. Of course, security measures must be taken to protect the *Custard*, so half the personnel for each station must remain behind. I don't care how you make the decision of who's allowed leave but you had better make it fast. Also, one of our command chain should remain behind."

Not unexpectedly Percy said, "I'll stay."

"Of course you will," said Quesnel, "but that hardly improves security." He didn't await Percy's rebuttal, instead lifting the speaking tube to engineering. "Aggie? Draw lots for shore leave. Three-quarters of an hour only, so pick a few with pocket watches. What? No, I don't care if you use it as a reward. Why, has Spoo been acting up *again*? Well, if you don't like the chit, reassign her, for goodness' sake. I'm sure they could use the help on deck. Yes, yes, very good. Of course you have to stay – who else will make certain we take on the right amount of coal and water? Yes, well, that's the way it is." He put the tube down. "Sometimes, that woman!"

Rue looked at him in genuine surprise. "Only sometimes?"

Prim bustled off to consult the head steward and cook to deter-mine who might be allowed off-ship and what supplies they required. She returned shortly, having somehow found the time to change into a walking suit of black taffeta with a pattern of embroidered rings in gold and burgundy. She wore a matching black hat perched forward on her head, decorated in gold braid and tufts of burgundy feathers and carried a black parasol.

"Very nice," Rue said enviously.

"Thank you." Primrose twirled for full effect. "Queen Mums chose this one as my shore-leave-expedition-and-visiting-over-curry outfit. She has odd notions about Indian foodstuffs, my Mums. I think she was traumatised during her own travels."

Rue nodded. "Should I change?" Primrose was always wise in the matters of attire.

Primrose gave her a critical once-over. "No, I don't think it necessary."

Rue puffed under the praise. She couldn't help it – Prim was just so elegant, it was nice to garner approval from her. "Shall we, then?"

The ladies linked arms and, without further ado, left the ship. Percy took that as permission to retreat to his library, leaving Virgil at the helm. Quesnel, after a moment, strode after Rue and Prim. Rue peeked over her shoulder to see him making hasty repairs to his smudges with a large white handkerchief. She mourned the loss, and then reprimanded herself for it.

The two young ladies made their way along the long spatula handle towards the centre of the docking port. The whole tower was illuminated via a variety of artificial sources, from gas chandeliers and tubes of glowing orange fog to massive brightly coloured paper lanterns. Since they were clearly women of some standing, the dockworkers parted before them by rote. A few snide remarks were muttered as they passed, but Rue and Prim stuck their noses in the air and pretended not to hear. Quesnel followed a few steps behind, eyes wary. The workers were mainly intent upon *The Spotted Custard*, dragging pipes, carts of fuel, and other necessities towards it.

Rue frowned, watching as the supply lines targeted her ship. *The Spotted Custard* didn't require all that much. "I haven't signed off on any of this. Where's the tower steward?"

Only then did she register the fact that a group of her own staff and crew – including sooties, greasers, firemen, deckhands, deck-

lings, stewards, and scullery maids – trailed in their wake like
school children out for a jaunt in the park. It was an odd spectacle
and made Prim and Rue, at the head of the procession, feel suddenly conspicuous.

Rue became aware of a new kind of bustling. The workers
parted before her to reveal an officious elderly gentlemen wearing
full evening attire and a red sash across his breast like a military
general. He held a leather ledger and a long double-ended stylus.
He was using both, rather indiscriminately and not as designed,
on any dockworkers who did not get out of his way quickly. "Bad
minion!" he shouted at one boy, snapping the lad's ear with the
stylus.

Behind him stomped two men in uniform guiding between
them a steam-powered tea trolley loaded with devices, boxes,
aetherographic transmitting slates, and other necessities of
bureaucracy. Rue thought it a grave misuse of a perfectly nice tea
trolley.

The man with the sash stopped, snapped his heels together,
and stood to attention, blocking their path. He looked Rue and
Prim up and down and then turned to Quesnel, dismissing the
ladies as mere fripperies.

"Your ship, sir?" he asked without introduction. "Travelling
gypsy barge? Circus troupe? I don't have anything in the annals
expected for today under *entertainment* or *ladybug*."

Quesnel gave him a funny look. "Her ship, *sir*," he said, tilting
his head at Rue, emphasising the sir as a marker of the lack of
proper conversational approach.

The little man's eyebrows went up but he turned to Prim and
Rue. They were quite the pair, parasols closed and masquerading
as walking sticks, hats tilted forward although there was no need
for shade, arms linked, expressions disapproving. Rue carried her
mother's parasol, which was too ugly to match any of her outfits,
but was more sturdy than any of her fashionable ones. This one,

felt Rue, could really cause damage to a noggin if applied with enough enthusiasm. Somehow this made her feel more secure about life in general.

The ladies regarded the man with eyes of steely disinterest. Well, to be fair, Prim's eyes were more a melted cocoa of mock reproach, and Rue's were the twinkling tawny of barely contained amusement. But it was hard to see this fact through the hats. Rue spared a moment to wonder if Aunt Ivy's insistence on hats wasn't a precaution against sub-par acting abilities.

Rue adjusted hers to a steeper angle, the better to hide her twinkle.

The officious man cleared his throat as though expecting them to speak first.

They continued looking at him in silence.

Rue up-tilted her nose in the air, and drew her shoulders back, using physicality to grow more aristocratic. Prim didn't need any help – such things came naturally to her.

Finally, the man bowed. "Senior Tower Jerquer, Gresham Stukely at your service."

"Mr Stukely," said Rue and Prim in chorus, curtseying.

"Your, erm, ship, ladies, it's not in my registry. That's illegal docking, add to that non-notification, add to that unauthorised personnel, add to that after-hours fees, add to that—"

"Oh dear me," said Rue to Prim. "Daddy promised, didn't he, that she would be on everyone's books? How terribly upsetting. He *promised*!" Rue spun her ugly parasol against the metal walkway in agitation. She channelled the most snobbish of Dama's drones in her voice – enunciating all her vowels as though hampered by particularly large teeth.

Prim instantly fell into the game. "Yes, he most certainly did. Silly Daddy. Oh *sister*, what are we to do?" Her voice wobbled in distress.

Rue admired this greatly – Prim was very good at being distraught. Rue's forte was bluster, a native ability inherited from her blood parents, so she went with that. "Did he give us paperwork to that effect? I simply cannot remember. You know I'm terrible with anything of the notation inclination." She turned to the official, batting her eyelashes, and reached for the part of her that could talk like Dama at his most supercilious. "Just a little world tour, you understand? Of course you do. You have a very understanding brow. Daddy thinks we need *culture*. Of course, we had to come here first. The Maltese Tower is the *last word* on culture. Poor Daddy couldn't come, sadly bedridden. It's the aetheric particles – they caused him to come over all flopsy. But he did say it was *settled*. I'm sure he did say that. Or was that Mr Barclay? You know Mr Barclay, don't you, Mr Stukely? Oh, you must – *everyone* who is anyone knows Mr Barclay the *banker*?" When all else failed – overwhelm with inanities.

Prim widened her big brown eyes in distress. "Oh, sister, this is terrible, so terrible! What are we to do? Oh, no, are we going to be detained, or questioned, or searched, or...?" She trailed off, looking as though she might cry. "I feel faint. Where's my *sal volatile*? We won't be locked away, will we? I don't think I could stand it, not a small bare room. No trim at all."

Rue put an arm about Prim in a sisterly manner, hushing and comforting her. "I'm certain this nice gentlemen will help us, won't you, kind Mr Stukely? My sister, you understand, is delicate. *Très, très* easily overcome by nerves. Poor dear sister."

The jerquer was himself overcome with remorse and the need to be a hero to such obviously innocent and, more importantly, wealthy young women. "Oh, now, ladies, normally an unregistered craft, well, we would have to at least question—"

Primrose began to sob. One fat tear dripped down her perfect rosy cheek. Rue suppressed the urge to clap.

Quesnel watched this entire exhibition with a well-hidden grin. He was not, Rue noticed, employing his hat, but had merely sunk his chin down into the high points of his collar and cravat in the manner of an undertaker.

Mr Stukely twitched at Prim's whimpers. "Perhaps, just this once, a small fine? It is a very nice craft, very colourful, obviously not unlawful with such carefree decorations." He glanced over at *The Spotted Custard*, deluded by the bright black-on-red spots into disregarding its smooth deadly lines.

Rue compressed her lips. This was, of course, part of her intent with the *Custard*'s decoration. If Dama had taught her nothing else, it was that the outrageous was often one's best disguise. *It is a very great thing, my Puggle, not to be taken seriously*, he had once said. If two young ladies of high society showed up on one's tower claiming a pleasure tour, it was more believable if their dirigible looked like an enormous, friendly beetle.

Rue latched on to the little man's last words. "Remuneration for your troubles, did you say, my dear Mr Stukely? How kind you are. How very kind. How much did you say? Not that a lady should talk such details but, as you see, we are currently without our abigail."

The little man cleared his throat, flushing red, and then, so he would not have to mention the number out loud, scribbled it down with the stylus on a corner of his ledger and showed it to Rue. Rue took note of the amount, as well as the details and rosters of the other ships in dock, helpfully listed on that very ledger. There were no familiar names.

Without flinching, she reached into her reticule and extracted the sum in question, handing over the coins. Pittance indeed – she did not even need a banknote. Which was a good thing, as it would not have been drawn on Barclay's.

The jerquer carefully counted, noting that the sum was well over the requested amount, over by enough for it not to be a mistake. He pocketed the excess with alacrity and instantly became their good friend. "Ah, thank you very much, ladies. And a very good afternoon to you, Miss . . . ?" He trailed off.

Without pausing Rue said, "Miss Hisselpenny."

Prim, who was sniffling after her pretend bought of crying, turned a snort of surprise into a new sob.

Rue thumped her on the back. "There now, *sister*, buck up. It's all dandy and daisies now. This nice gentlemen will take care of everything. Won't you, very kind sir?"

The nice gentlemen in question was looking dazed. "And what ship name should I put on the registry?"

"*Dandelion Fluff Upon a Spoon*," replied Rue.

"Very good, Miss Hisselpenny."

"Will there be anything else, my good sir?"

"No, ladies. Thank you for your cooperation. Your steward?"

"Is aboard and will handle all the necessities. My purser will pay you any additional monies for supplies and stores. Is that the right way of it?"

"Yes, indeed, Miss Hisselpenny."

"Thank you again, kind sir." Rue delicately passed the man another handful of coinage. She also flashed him a brilliant smile.

Mr Stukely, bowled over by both the gratuity and the smile, doffed his hat, and the two ladies continued on their way without further impediment. Although their deft interactions with the official seemed to have made them more of a spectacle rather than less.

Quesnel tilted his hat at the man sympathetically and followed after them. He caught up as they attained the door to the central area of the port. "Why the façade?"

Rue looked at him, surprised. "Did you miss the part where this was a covert mission? One should try to keep one's identity a secret."

"Especially when one is the world's only metanatural, daughter of some very famous aristocrats?" Quesnel nodded at this precaution.

"Don't discount Prim either – she's got some infamous parents herself."

"But the names you chose!" Quesnel looked as if he really would laugh.

Primrose said, affronted, "Hisselpenny is my mother's maiden name, and *Dandelion Fluff Upon a Spoon* is Lord Akeldama's pleasure dirigible. They are perfectly respectable names."

Rue explained, "If one must lie, make it memorable. Hisselpenny is a name which, if called out in a crowd we would both respond to, and that ship name is easy for us to remember and exactly the moniker two frivolous ladies of fashion would give to their craft."

With which Rue determined she owed Quesnel no further explanation, and pushed open the door into the docking centre.

"Oh, my goodness me!" she squeaked.

It looked rather like the Reading Room of the British Museum, only a great deal larger and without any books in it. Instead there were stalls selling wares around the edge, like at a street fair with various interesting-looking sculptures, booths, and gatherings in the middle. The place was humming with humanity, some fashionable, many questionable. Somehow the centre harnessed part of the orange light of the beacon far above, and it spilled down into the interior in umber shafts.

Quesnel said, "Only you didn't tell your crew, my beautiful witless wonder."

Rue turned back to her chief engineer. "What was that?"

"About your plan to change the names of everything. You didn't tell your crew, yet you gave them permission to leave the ship," explained Quesnel carefully. "Aren't you worried they'll spoil the act?"

"Oh dear, good point. I do hope they don't go blabbing." Rue frowned, calculating the time. They had only three quarters of an hour left. How much harm could the crew do?

Quesnel nodded to the gaggle of staff still behind them. "I think most of them witnessed your antics."

Rue wasn't certain "antics" was a dignified way to describe a lady but before she could reprimand her chief engineer, Spoo stepped forward. "Yes, Chief Sir and Lady Captain. That was a pretty nice show you put on there."

"Why, thank you, Spoo," replied Rue.

"You're all right, Lady Captain, but this one was a real corker." Spoo gestured with her thumb at Primrose.

Prim smiled down at the small person in a queenly manner, causing the young sootie to blush. "Such accolades. I was born to carry on a theatrical legacy, but sadly fate had other plans for my family."

"Fate or Egypt?" wondered Rue.

"There's a difference?" Prim looked wistful. Egypt was where her mother had turned vampire. The girls knew few particulars, but they understand that everything had changed for everyone after Egypt, 1876.

Spoo said, not following, "I'll make sure everyone knows who and what we are and what names we belong to while 'round the tower."

"That is very much appreciated, Spoo," replied Rue.

Spoo, after a quick hushed conversation with a few of the other sooties, scampered back to *The Spotted Custard* to waylay anyone else who might disembark or have cause for conversion with dockhands.

Rue and Prim exchanged a look. They were unused to having to widen the scale of their schemes. Adjustments must be made for this new course their lives had taken.

"We'll plan better next time," Rue assured her friend.

"Yes, I think we ought," Prim agreed but was already distracted by their surroundings. "What a very odd sort of place this is."

Quesnel moved forward to pat her arm reassuringly.

Primrose took it eagerly.

Rue felt a tiny pang but brushed it off as girlish silliness.

Someone dragged a noisy nanny goat past them. Across the way, two men with turbans argued in an exotic language about a clay figurine of a pregnant snake or possibly a cow without legs. One of them had a monkey sitting on his shoulder. Off to one side was a row of massive cages inside which paced tigers, hyenas, and other toothy carnivores. The Maltese Tower clearly did a brisk trade in exotic animals. A stall nearby displayed racks of valves and rows of sprockets in tempting stacked pyramids, as a fishmonger might lay out his wares.

Quesnel's eyes lit up and he drifted in that direction.

Primrose, on the other hand, had spotted a promising-looking jewellery vendor and began to walk the other way.

Before they could get far, Rue grabbed each by the arm.

Quesnel looked down at her gloved hand on his sleeve. "What now, chérie?"

"How about exploring together? Get the lay of the land? I've never been to a docking tower before, have you?"

Quesnel's shook his head.

"But...sparkles," said Prim forlornly.

"We can shop after a bit of a wander and a nice nosh, what do you say?" Rue's eyes were shining hopefully.

Primrose said, suspiciously, "Tea?"

"Tea in a proper tea-shop. There must be one somewhere. All the best towers have tea-shops. Fortnum & Mason has three."

Nothing else could possibly draw Primrose away from rubies. "Oh, very well."

Quesnel was disposed to be agreeable. "The opportunity to spend more time in your glorious company, how could I resist?"

"How could you, indeed?"

Quesnel gave Rue big violet puppy eyes – back and forth between her and the stall of gadgets.

Rue relented. "Very well, you may acquire gadgets on the ship's account. A few, mind you. I'm not made of money. And nothing too greasy."

Quesnel brightened.

Primrose looked pathetically at her.

"No, dear." Rue was firm. "I don't think I could convince even Dama that we needed jewellery on the ship's account. Spend your own money."

They shifted so Quesnel was in the middle, as was proper and, arms linked, the three strolled the perimeter.

Rue enjoyed herself immensely. The tower was fascinating. It was so unlike her experience in London, with the exception of the theatre district. Even so, one rarely saw day labourers in the West End during fashionable hours. Yet here was surely every possible example of human life. Not to mention a wide range of objects and animals. They saw so many small dogs carried about the person that Primrose said, "Do you think I should return to the ship for Footnote? I could wrap him around my neck. Everyone who is anyone seems to be wearing a pet."

"What footnote?" wondered Quesnel.

"Not what, who. My brother's cat."

Rue said, "While it does seem the thing to do, and I know you like to follow the very latest styles, you would look somewhat less fashionable with scratches all over your face."

Primrose nodded. "Quite right, of course. I notice no one is using a cat – probably too difficult."

"One for cat-kind," said Rue. "Best not used as accessories."

Quesnel, only just following their rapid-fire banter, asked,

"Wait. Miss Tunstell, your brother brought a *cat* on board my ship?"

"My ship," corrected Rue without rancour.

"I beg your pardon, but why?"

Primrose said, "Why not?"

Rue added, "All the best ships have cats."

Quesnel decided not to press the point.

They continued their perambulations. When they encountered a group of clearly inebriated greaser types, Quesnel insisted the ladies hold tight to their reticules to protect the contents, and their parasols to protect their personages. Quesnel himself – not of a particularly threatening stature – afforded them only the protection of having an escort with both arms occupied. One of the rougher elements made their ineffectual appearance clear by shouldering in close and issuing the trio a lewd remark.

Rue, accustomed as she was to werewolf behaviour, was less upset than she ought to be by rough talk. Certainly, Dama would have reprimanded her for not taking greater offence. But then Rue had never quite grown into as much of a lady as her vampire father had hoped.

Primrose, on the other hand, was shocked and experienced such distress at the application of the phrase "a fine mouthful of muffin, there, ho ho" to her good self as to make it necessary to ascertain the location of the nearest restorative teahouse *immediately*.

"It is not, certainly not, that I am unaware of the compliment," said Prim, panting from modest heart palpitations. "But perhaps the young man might have used a more delicate turn of phrase. *Mouthful of muffin*, I say!"

Rue patted her on the arm. "You did very well, dear."

"I thought it verging on poetical." Quesnel's violet eyes were sparkling.

"Oh indeed, you chomp of cheese pie?" shot back Rue, hoping to distract Prim.

"Yes, O slurp of sweet syrup."

Prim attempted a giggle but it was clear she was still overset from the encounter.

Quesnel's brow furrowed in real concern as he realised that her trauma was genuine. He paused his banter. "Perhaps, ladies, this is not an ideal environment. Should we return to the ship?"

"Certainly not!" objected Rue. "Prim and I can take a little rough talk, can't we, Prim?"

Prim sighed. "Ask me that after we've found tea."

And then there it was – a beacon of light within the mists of mixed society, a diamond in the mud, a teahouse in the rough. A quaintly old-fashioned little shoppe complete with pink and white scroll paint, flowers in the window, lace curtains, and silver bells at the door. Outside stood a number of differently sized gilt cages and a polite little sign suggesting if patrons did not deposit their animals there, said animals would also be supplied with tea. And one never knew how tea would affect a goat.

Quesnel steered them towards it and they attained the tinkling entrance with no further distress to ear or wellbeing.

"What an exhilarating place the Maltese Tower is," said Rue, nodding to the hostess and taking the proffered chair with ease.

Primrose folded into hers with evident relief. "Perhaps a tad uncivilised?"

Rue agreed but added, "I like it."

Quesnel disposed of their hats and returned to sit. "Mon petit chou, you are a strange creature. Lovely, of course, but strange. Are you feeling better, Miss Tunstell?"

Prim was still pale. Rue knew from experience that this was nothing a nice pot of Assam couldn't put right, plus a bit of gooseberry charlotte and maybe some candied orange peel.

Quesnel's solicitousness was touching, if rather more than strictly necessary. Still, Rue was disposed to think kindly upon anyone who liked Primrose. She was accustomed to losing male attention to her friend, and couldn't really fault anyone for it. Much as Percy was deadly attractive to the ladies, his sister had a similar effect on the gentlemen. Rue gave a little mental sigh. No one would ever describe her as deadly attractive. She brightened a bit. Perhaps she could aspire to just deadly?

A girl in a pink and white striped pinafore arrived to take their order, and in a very short time they had a pot of tea, an orange with sugar on it for Rue, a gooseberry charlotte for Prim, and a welsh rarebit for Quesnel. Quesnel admitted shamefully that he did not very much like sweets. Dangerous character flaw, that.

Despite the revelation of this appalling shortcoming, it was a delightfully refined repast. Prim's colour returned and Quesnel resumed distributing his attention equally. They might even have been said to be having a good time . . . until the lioness attacked.

CHAPTER
SIX

A Lioness in a Teahouse

Of course, it was startling. It's simply not the thing one expects of a teahouse, even when travelling abroad, even miles up in an airship docking tower. *Especially* not miles up in an airship docking tower. But there was most assuredly a lioness among them. She came in through the front door, setting the bells tinkling like any ordinary patron, and then setting everyone screaming. Rue thought this a little much; after all, if a lioness wanted tea, why not give it to her? The animal in question was a sleek, beautiful creature, all golden fur and rippling muscles, but apparently intent on wreaking carnage and not on ordering tea. Whatever else was going on in that furry head, the cat clearly did not appreciate teahouses.

Do cats, Rue wondered, *as a rule object to teahouses? If so, then there is something very much to be said in favour of dogs.*

"But there is a *sign*!" objected Primrose in semi-shock. "A *sign* indicating pets aren't permitted. Really, some people."

While Primrose protested the indelicacy of it all, Rue resorted to some of Dama's less official training. She shoved their table over and grabbed Prim by the arm, pulling her down to take refuge behind it. Not that the lioness was firing projectiles, but Rue thought that at least if they were out of sight they might enjoy a modicum of safety.

Everyone else ran for the door or the kitchen.

Quesnel, with disturbing calm, stripped off his jacket and rolled up one shirtsleeve to expose an emission device strapped to his wrist. It looked like it might shoot long bullets or possibly darts.

He crouched down behind the table. It was a tight fit for three, two of them in walking gowns, for it was after all only a tea table. Quesnel peeked around one side, wrist up, and aimed.

"No clear shot," he said, turning to the ladies. "That beast is fast."

People were yelling, furniture crashed, teapots shattered. The lioness was intent on maximum ruckus, overturning all the tables while servers stumbled out of her way, cakes flew through the air and the bells on the door reverberated as patrons pressed together seeking exit. There was panic everywhere but . . .

Rue straightened up to look over the edge of their makeshift barricade.

"What are you doing? Stay down!"

Rue batted Quesnel's restraining hand away. "She's not hurting anyone."

"What?"

"The lioness, she's not actually doing anything to people. It's only objects. Right now, she is savaging a sweets tray."

Prim remonstrated: "Rue, she has upset many perfectly decent pots of tea. I call that a serious offence, if nothing else."

One huge paw appeared on the edge of their table-top, then another, and then a smooth sandy-coloured head peaked over and looked at them. The cat's whiskers twitched, giving her an aura of accusation. Rue had a horrible moment of swallowing down laughter – it was as if they were playing a game of hide and seek.

She met the cat's gaze. Oddly enough, the animal had brown eyes. Rue didn't think cats could have brown eyes. But then, who was she to question anyone else's eye colour? Given hers were an odd sort of yellow.

Quesnel raised his wrist and took aim.

"Wait, stop." Rue put a hand on his arm above where the weapon was strapped and pushed down. Quesnel resisted. He was remarkably strong. Rue took a moment to be impressed – he didn't *look* physically fit.

Rue and the cat stared at one another.

The lioness blinked.

Rue blinked back. "I don't think she intends to hurt us. I don't think she means to hurt anyone."

The cat tilted her head back and forth, gaze sliding between the three of them. She looked at Primrose for a long moment and then, in an amazingly fluid movement, she leapt over the table, grabbed Rue's hideous parasol up in her mouth, turned, and charged out of the tea-shop by way of one of the front windows. Which were not open, mind you. The resulting crash resulted in several more screams. Pandemonium reigned outside in the assembly area as the cat skidded through the crowds there, parasol firmly clutched in her teeth.

Rue was not amused. "Come back here, you mangy beast! That's *my mother's* parasol." Rue hiked up her skirts, regardless of showing ankle to the entire tower, and gave case.

Quesnel and Prim, still crouched behind the table, barely registered her impetuous action. Both tried to rise at once and got caught up in the tea things and each other so that by the time they reached the broken window of the tea-shop, both lioness and Rue had vanished into the milieu of the Maltese Tower.

Rue chased the parasol and the cat through the crowd. The assembled personnel seemed mainly annoyed by the disturbance. A few were quite upset by a rampaging lioness with an ugly accessory in her jaws – but their concern seemed more to do with the risk to the parasol rather than the presence of the lioness. Rue also garnered dirty looks. After all, since she was chasing after the beast, they assumed it was her lioness off-lead. The cat relaxed into an easy loping pace, fast enough so that Rue could not catch her but slow enough for her black tail tip to be ever beyond Rue's reach, like an extremely frustrating fishing lure. Rue wished one of her father's pack were nearby – if she could steal wolf form for a while she could certainly catch the blasted creature. Not that any werewolf could withstand being up so high and so close to the aetherosphere.

The lioness dodged between two food booths – one which dealt in fish and chips, the other smelling of curry. Behind the stands was a shanty town of dockworkers' hovels made of old scrap metal and stretched fabric. Laundry dangled between and above the makeshift structures. Rue charged through, blissfully unaware of the impracticality of a lady of means running with skirts hiked up – and no bloomers – into what amounted to a sky-high slum.

The cat flicked inside one of the not-quite-buildings and Rue paused, suddenly aware of her surroundings. There were only a few people visible but she had the distinct impression of many eyes upon her. This was someone's home she was about to enter, without invitation. Dama's face appeared before her, finger shaking madly. Vampires were very taken with proper invitations. Then again, there was a lioness inside with her parasol! If anyone could think of a better excuse for barging in uninvited, she'd like to hear it.

So Rue barged.

There was no door, only a weight of bright material hanging long and heavy in the entranceway. Rue parted it and cleared her throat. "Um, pardon me, is anyone home?"

No answer.

"Yoo-hoo. May I come in, please? It seems your lioness has possession of my accessory."

When still no one answered, Rue pushed through the fabric.

It was dim inside after the brightness of the station with all its gas lighting and colourful activity. It took Rue's all-too-human eyes a moment to adjust. She simply stood still and waited.

The room was tiny, pleasantly furnished with a mismatch of crates draped in bright swathes of cloth and pretty cushions of varying shapes and sizes – so many pillows, in fact, that they fell about, littering the carpeted floor. Glass baubles, strings of shells, golden fringe, and large tassels dangled from hooks and protuberances. It reminded Rue of a fortune-teller's caravan or possibly a peddler's covered wagon. Not that she'd had occasion to see many, but she could imagine what they might look like.

It was empty. No cat. No parasol.

Then out of the shadows and through a curtain of wooden beads walked the most unbelievably beautiful woman Rue had ever seen.

Rue's perspective on beauty was not confined to those of British high society, although she could certainly see Prim's loveliness, a classic English rose with milky complexion and dark chestnut curls. She could also see the Nordic beauty in her troublesome Uncle Channing for all his objectionable arrogance and uncertain temper, a chilly combination of ice and ivory. But she could also see beauty in the Fisk Jubilee Singers, all ebony and lace and sweet melodies, and in the copper-coloured drones Aunt Ivy had inherited with her Egyptian vampire hive.

This woman's skin was a dark tea colour, her eyes huge and almond-shaped. Her cheekbones were high enough to etch glass and her neck was long and impossibly graceful. Her nose might be a tad assertive by British standards, straight and dominant, and her lips, though full and well-shaped, were set firm.

Rue's breath actually whooshed out of her.

Finally she breathed in and coughed. All she could think to say was, "Are you on the stage? You should be."

The women looked nonplussed and then, in a subtle shift of posture, she changed, becoming less showy and more dangerous about her beauty. Rue watched this, flabbergasted. How had she done it? Here was an acting skill Rue did not possess. Primrose, for most of their adult life, had used her appearance as if it were some delectable dessert. For the first time Rue realised that beauty might also be applied with power, like a particularly stinky but highly desirable cheese. Rue knew that she herself could never pass for anything more than *cute*. *What does that make me in the after-dinner beauty metaphor?* she wondered. *The digestif? A sweet, alcoholic afterthought with possible vicious consequences.*

By that time the shock had worn off, and Rue could feel every hackle she had inherited from her werewolf father rise. If she had been in wolf form, her tail and ears would be down and her canines exposed. As it was, she smoothed out her skirts, straightened her spine, and prepared to do battle with every tool from her other father's repertoire. Unless she had missed her guess, the best approach was to be very polite and outwardly ridiculous. She reached for her vampire father's personality and donned it as if it were some sparkly diamond make.

"How do you do?" she said. "Amazing!" She waved a hand about, taking in the colourful surroundings. "Charming fabric and cushions and things you have here." Perhaps not her best opening sally, but true.

The woman was taken aback, but she clearly spoke English and knew some etiquette, for her response was a musically accented, "How do you do, Lady Prudence?"

"Ah, you know my name – we are already acquainted?" Rue was certain she would have remembered.

"No, but I have been eager to meet you since I learnt of your existence."

Rue winced. Was this stunning female one of *those* fanatics? The ones crazy to encounter a real live metanatural? How disappointing. Rue tried to change the subject. "Was that *your* lioness I met recently?"

"In a manner of speaking."

Rue followed this line of thought, familiar as she was with Footnote and Dama's Madam Pudgemuffin. "Ah yes, cats – difficult to speak of in terms of ownership as a rule. I'm afraid she rather, um, borrowed something from me."

"Indeed?" The woman glided forward slightly. She wore a long robe of white silk. "Is this the object in question?" She produced Rue's parasol from some fold of her attire. It looked, if possible, more ugly by contrast to such impossible loveliness.

The flowing swathes of fabric seemed to be all the strange woman wore. They wrapped up once about her head like the veil of a mourner, around her body, and then draped back over her shoulder in a cascade. Her dark hair was long and loose and aggressively straight, and she wore no jewellery or cosmetics of any kind. Rue suspected this woman of being bare-footed as well – her steps were absolutely silent. Rue sniffed but could detect no prominent smell – perhaps a hint of amber but nothing more. She wished, once again, for wolf form.

The woman handed the parasol to Rue. It seemed none the worse for fangs and a bit of cat slobber.

"Thank you very much, Miss...?" Rue trailed off, hoping for an indication of identity.

"You may call me Sekhmet."

Without doubt that was not the woman's real name.

"Very well, then. Thank you, Miss Sekhmet."

Rue turned to leave, oddly frightened to present her back. If they were not hundreds of storeys up in the air, she would have said that this woman was supernatural. But no vampire queen would go unprotected or live in a slum, quite apart from the fact that a vampire tethered to the Maltese Tower would be known throughout the empire. And no werewolf Rue had ever heard of could withstand heights. Wolves could handle travel by sea but not by air.

Rue was almost at the door when that smooth voice lilted at her: "A moment more of your time, if you would be so kind, skin-stalker?" Her English really was good.

This encounter had rapidly taken a turn from extremely odd to entirely surreal. Rue turned back and the woman approached. Rue realised that she had been wrong. She did wear jewellery – a single chain about her neck from which dangled two small charms – one looked like a sword and the other a shield.

"Trust me, Miss Sekhmet, you have my attention." *As I am certain you are accustomed.*

A tiny smile tilted the lady's full lips. "I am one of those who respects what you are and does not fear it. There are few – very few, I am sad to say – like me left to fight for your rights, skin-stalker. None of them is in India. I would not go there, if I were you."

Rue frowned. "How did you know I was going to India?"

No answer.

"Well, while I appreciate the warning, you must understand that I can't change my plans on the whim of some stranger in robes."

"Plans? Then you are being sent to India on purpose? So you know? And your parents – they know too?" A pause. "This is not good."

No, thought Rue, *this isn't good. Obviously this Sekhmet represents a counter-tea interest, after the new plants. And foolishly I've revealed too much.* Rue plucked at her parasol, brushing away cat saliva. *Yech.* She stumbled on, awkwardly, intent upon giving away nothing further. "Nice as you seem, Miss Sekhmet, and grateful as I am for the return of my . . ."

She trailed off. She was speaking to an empty room. The beautiful woman had vanished. Rue poked about, searching the small space, three rooms all similarly covered in colourful cloth and pillows, and no evidence of the woman, the lioness, or even a regular occupant.

Rue made her way back through the station. The tea-shop was closed and men in black uniforms with a white cross insignia were picking their way through the wreckage. Not wishing to attract unwelcome official attention, Rue decided it was best not to present herself.

Quesnel and Primrose were nowhere to be found. Rue was not particularly concerned. Nor did she feel abandoned. If Quesnel was a gentlemen, which Rue suspected he was – deep down, duck ponds notwithstanding – he would take pains to see Prim back to *The Spotted Custard* safely before returning with reinforcements to find Rue. A smart man would bring Aggie Phinkerlington – that woman could scare the willies out of anyone. Even a lioness.

Disorientated, Rue set out to walk around the circle, figuring she'd eventually recognise something. The station was no less crowded, but Rue felt less of a spectacle alone and accompanied only by her parasol. Still, she was well aware of the danger of being without a chaperone in a strange station. She cocked an ear. No one was even speaking English! Shockingly, the common language seemed to be some form of Italian.

As a result, Rue was on her guard when a whisper of a presence sidled up next to her.

She was profoundly relieved to find it was only a smallish, thinnish female. She was uncomfortably close, touching Rue and keeping pace. The woman was shrouded in cloth, including her head. Unlike Miss Sekhmet, her robes were colourful. Rue might have thought she was merely pressed close by the crowd except that she said, quite distinctly, "Puggle?"

At first Rue thought she misheard – it was such an out-of-place word to come from that figure in this location. Like seeing a kingfisher with a diploma.

"Are you...Puggle?" The woman's accent was strong but not so strong that Rue could misinterpret.

The only thing visible, her dark eyes, were intent and serious.

Only Dama called Rue Puggle. She got excited, realising what this meant. "Oh, is this...? Oh my goodness! Are you trying to have a clandestine encounter with me? Espionage and codes and such?" She almost clapped her hands. "Oh, please tell me you have a secret message?"

"Ah, I see you are much as family lore described."

Rue was taken aback. "Have we met before?"

"Not so much as either of *us* might remember. My name is Anitra."

"Oh, ah, I see," said Rue, not seeing at all. Clearly the name should mean something, but it didn't. Although it was very pretty.

At Rue's obvious confusion Anitra added, "My people," she paused, soft and delicate, "float."

Rue shook her head.

"Ah well, we do like to be forgotten." Anitra shrugged under the swathes of fabric. "I have something for you from Goldenrod."

This confused Rue further. "Pardon?" *Was Goldenrod one of the fated specialist tea contacts?*

"You left precipitously – he was not best pleased." Anitra tutted in disgust and then reached into the folds of her robes and produced a slim literary volume. "I am to give you this, should he need to communicate with you."

It was an innocuous book, cheaply made with a pink canvas

cover, without a doubt some ill-informed travel guide from a London publisher. It was so utterly unexpected and out of character that Rue took it automatically, stopping right there in the tower street to glance it over.

Rue opened it to the title page and read out, her voice rising with incredulity, "*Sand and Shadows on a Sapphire Sea: My Adventures Abroad* by Honeysuckle Isinglass? A young lady's travel journal. But these are two a penny in the bookshops back home. Why on earth would I need . . . ?"

But for the second time in as many minutes, Rue found herself abandoned by a female in the middle of conversation. "Goodness, hasn't anyone any manners on this station?" she asked the disinterested crowd.

Then, looking up, she noticed to her relief that she had found her way to *The Spotted Custard.* Or at least found her way back to the doorway leading to its dock. Her ship bobbed softly outside the glass some distance away. She did not consider the fact that as they walked together, Anitra had been guiding her back.

Clutching her rescued parasol in one hand and *Sand and Shadows on a Sapphire Sea* in the other, Rue headed home. She felt that she had had enough cryptic encounters with mysterious females to last a lifetime. After all, that was *three* in less than a half-hour — if one counted the lioness.

As it turned out, Rue was the last aboard. The deckhands were already pulling in the mooring ropes as she trotted down the spatula handle towards *The Spotted Custard.* Prim and Percy were on the poop deck in deep discussion.

As Rue made her way up the gangplank, Spoo saw her and gave a wave.

"Lady Captain, where you been?" the scamp wanted to know.

"Nowhere special."

"Had us worried, you did." Spoo was sporting a spectacular black eye. Rue didn't feel they were on intimate enough terms to ask why.

"Apologies, Spoo." As Rue put her foot on the main deck a large blond bullet hit her from the side and twirled her around so that her back was pressed flush against the railing.

Quesnel grabbed her by the shoulders and actually began to shake her. "Don't *do* that!"

"Mr Lefoux, unhand me!" objected Rue, whacking at him with *Sand and Shadows on a Sapphire Sea* and greatly tempted to use the parasol. *Such impudence.*

The gentleman in question seemed to have temporarily lost hold of his senses.

He pulled her in and wrapped his arms about her in a rather nice hug which Rue tried to imagine was like that of one of her many uncles but which was neither scruffy nor fruity-smelling, and gave her heart a little boost in a way the uncles never had. For one breathless moment she thought he might actually kiss her, right there at the end of the gangplank in full view of her crew, with blatant disregard for all propriety. He drew back and looked at her lips, his violet eyes very focused, but then he merely hugged her again. His hands pressed hard against her back. She fancied she could feel the roughness through the many layers of her dress. They must be rough, all that handling of sprockets and spigots and such.

Eventually, Rue managed to extract herself. "Mr Lefoux!" she said severely, because she ought.

"How could you?" said the engineer, looking more harried than it suited his customary persona of urbane intellectual meets boyishly charming flirt.

"How could I *what*?" Rue replied, attempting to make reparations to her hair, which had survived a mad dash across the Maltese Tower but not the enthusiastic regard of her chief engineer.

"Just disappear like that, running off after a raging lioness? I thought we had lost you. I thought you'd end up disembowelled in the nearest warehouse. I was just about to mount a rescue. Spoo was going to come, weren't you, Spoo?"

"Of course I was," said Spoo, looking forthright.

"Well, as you can see, you thought wrong. I found the parasol but not the cat." It was pretty close to the truth of the matter.

Quesnel took a deep breath, rediscovering his devil-may-care self. "Of course you did, mon petit chou, so silly of me to doubt you." He backed away. Rue wondered which was really the act — his previous concern or his standard behaviour.

"Exactly. Now, is everyone else back on board?" Rue looked over at Prim, who was smiling at Rue's discomfort and Quesnel's display of concern, and Percy, who was frowning down at his book.

Percy ignored her question but Prim glanced at a roster. She had scripted it neatly, like a party invitation, on pale yellow paper.

"Looks like," said she, running one glove-covered finger down the list and whispering out a count. "Yes, everyone back except you. Shall we get on?"

"By all means," replied Rue, skirting around Quesnel at a wary distance. The Frenchman ran his hands through his hair distractedly. He then realised he'd knocked off his hat when he'd grabbed Rue and went looking for it. By the time it had been recovered, Spoo having chased it down the gangplank, he was calmness itself, and Rue had made her way up to navigation.

"Professor Tunstell?"

Percy put down his book and took up position without looking at her, the sourpuss.

Rue turned back to Quesnel. "Chief engineer?"

Rue fancied she sensed a certain reluctance to go below, which was ridiculous, of course. Quesnel was simply an emotional Frenchman who had thought her dead and reacted as he would a missing sister.

He gave her a cheery smile. "Delighted you retrieved your parasol, captain."

Rue looked down at the item in question. "Oh, yes, me too. Gift from my mother. Hideous, of course, but it has sentimental value."

"Of course it does." Quesnel looked at the parasol as though it hid some secret and then he disappeared below.

Rue turned to her topside crew, giving Percy the nod. "Prepare for float-off, Professor Tunstell."

She then put down her parasol and lifted the speaking tube.

Aggie Phinkerlington said, "Yes?" sharply from the other end.

"Mr Lefoux will be with you shortly. Prepare for float-off."

"You shouldn't scare him like that, miss," remonstrated the mechanic.

"I beg your pardon!" Rue was genuinely shocked at a reprimand from an underling.

The greaser did not seem to care that Rue took offence at the intrusive comment, compounding insult with instruction: "Next time, don't be so impetuous."

Rue hung up the speaking tube without reply, afraid she might say something unforgivable.

"Well, I say!" said Rue to no one in particular.

Percy looked up from twiddling his knobs and levers. "Gave you a talking to, did she?"

"Are you going to lecture me as well?"

Percy, blast him, took that as permission. "You're captain of a ship now, Rue. You can't go tearing off willy-nilly like you did when I was in short pants."

"Wonderful. You *are* going to have at me."

Percy rolled his eyes. "Next time, think about your actions

before you take them, all right? You don't have werewolf or vampire skin to fall back on. Up here in the skies, you're as mortal as the rest of us."

Rue bristled. Was he implying that she used her metanatural abilities as a crutch to get out of sticky situations?

Percy went back to preparing for float-off, so Rue turned to her last and best ally, Primrose.

Prim was looking inscrutably placid.

Rue knew that expression all too well. "Really, you too?"

Prim arched one eyebrow.

"Oh, bother," said Rue. "We'll talk about this later, after the hops. I do have an excuse."

"Darling," said Prim. "You *always* have an excuse."

Rue ignored this. "Percy, what's our course looking like?"

Percy grimaced. "I hate to do it, but our best option is the Tripoli Twister. The Damascus Draw is smoother and more reliable but that'll add an extra day to the journey, possibly two."

Rue grinned. After being roundly scolded for taking unnecessary risks, she was obstreperous enough to stay with the theme. "Twister it is. Get the Pudding Probe up and calibrated."

Percy's face was blank. "I guessed you'd say that. The Mandenall is already set. Shall we proceed?"

Without further ado *The Spotted Custard* cast off, wound up her propeller, farted gently, and eased her way out of the Maltese Tower docking port. She glided sedately up into the aetherosphere, a fat satisfied ladybug.

Little differentiated this series of hops from those previously except that they were a great deal more bumpy. The *Custard* handled the intervening Charybdis currents with aplomb, as did Percy, who was now almost comfortable with the procedure. The first two hops went as specified by charts and calculations, but the Tripoli Twister was one of the highest, and one of the hardest to stay the course. They'd need to reef the mainsail for the rough breezes. The decklings were scrambling about, belaying ropes and tying items down as if *The Spotted Custard* were facing a storm. They were all more seasoned floaters than Rue and her officers. A few of them had even run the Twister before. For all of them, the Tripoli Twister was considered a worthy challenge, one that would yield bragging rights once they returned to London. Very few ships dared the Twister for any distance and the *Custard* was about to try for the full course.

Percy eased them up several more puffs – there must have been a dozen in total. Then the Mandenall Pudding Probe spat and they knew that directly above them swept the Tripoli herself.

Rue shouted to the deckhands, "Everything secure?"

"Aye aye, captain."

"Decklings?" Rue asked.

"All buttoned down, Lady Captain, ready on your mark," answered a familiar chipper voice.

"Spoo? What are you doing abovedecks?"

"Transferred position, captain. Bit of a snafu down below. You don't mind, do you? I've worked topside before."

"Certainly not."

Spoo seemed to have become unofficial leader of the decklings in a very short space of time. Some kind of coup? Rue supposed she would have to make it official if the girl proved capable. For now she was glad to have someone whose name she knew to yell.

"Wait for it," Rue instructed the girl and turned to her next concern. "Primrose?"

Her friend was solemn-faced, seated primly off to one side of the navigation area, parasol raised against the grey nothingness of aetherosphere, hat pinned firmly down. Rue trusted her to have warned the steward, cook, and purser so that the inside staff was prepared.

Prim tilted her chin in acknowledgment.

To free her hands, Rue tossed Prim *Sand and Shadows on a Sapphire Sea* for safekeeping.

Prim caught it easily.

Rue picked up the speaker tube. "Boiler room, are you ready?"

"We have never been more so," came Quesnel's reply.

Rue said to Percy, still holding the tube so Quesnel could overhear, "Make the hop, Professor Tunstell, on my mark. Three, two, one, and . . . mark."

Percy pressed the puffer. *The Spotted Custard* jerked up, caught the current, and began to shudder uncontrollably. It was as if the whole gondola section of the ship was shivering from cold.

"Percy, what the devil?" It felt like they were nested inside the current – why was this one so different from the others?

"Almost in, captain." Percy reached down and twisted something. The ship rose up an infinitesimal amount. The propeller whirred madly. The ship began to tilt sideways as though being pushed from the side. The main deck angled more than was comfortable. Anything not fastened down began to slide. Including Primrose, who looked resigned to the indignity.

Percy grabbed the tiller and wrenched it upright. "Come on, sweetness," he growled, straining against invisible aether forces.

Rue dashed over and reached for the other side of the tiller, pushing at it with all her might to assist his pulling. She was tougher than she looked – Dama's drones liked to arm-wrestle on occasion to keep themselves in shape for competitive whist. Together they managed to push the ship upright and facing the correct direction: due east.

The Spotted Custard stopped shuddering and settled into a bobbing motion.

Percy gave Rue a relieved nod.

Rue stepped back, shaking out arms trembling from effort. Then she bounced a little at their success. "Victory is ours, current!"

She remembered her duty as captain. "Decklings, mainsail up if you would."

Spoo began to point and shout. The decklings hopped to it with no discussion – the sootie already had them better trained than whoever had previously been in charge. Rue began to suspect that Spoo's black eye had something to do with her jump to head deckling.

The sail was raised in no time and Rue definitely approved of Spoo in her new position. As soon as it hooked the breeze, the *Custard* stopped shaking and smoothed out.

Rue relaxed but only for a moment, for her ship began to spin. *The Spotted Custard* was still floating upright with the current, east – the aetheric particles told them that much – but the sail had caused her to start rotating like a sedate top, slowly, clockwise, round and round. It was disconcerting.

Rue leapt to help Percy with the helm but her navigator shook his head.

Rue was incredulous. "This is it?"

"They don't call it the Tripoli *Twister* for nothing."

The sensation, while not unpleasant, did make Rue slightly dizzy. "And how long are we in this waltz?"

"Three days, I'm afraid. Best not to look out into the grey, they say."

Rue could believe it – the sensation was perturbing, to say the least.

"Very good. I shall head below. If you're well up here? I believe your sister would like her chance to lecture me now."

Percy's eyes twinkled. "Aye aye, captain. Although I think it's jolly unfair I must miss the spectacle."

"You have the deck, Professor Navigator, sir." Rue made her way over to Primrose who seemed recovered from her deckchair slide. "Things are tip-top up top – to the stateroom for a scolding?"

But Prim no longer looked like she wanted to lecture Rue – instead, she was wiggling the little pink book as though it were some strange new species of musical instrument worthy of further examination in order to make it toot.

"That can wait. First, Rue my darling, my sweet, my precious..."

"You sound like Quesnel – what has your bloomers in a twist?"

"Language," said her friend without rancour.

"I await your pleasure." Rue's voice was laden with sarcasm.

"What are you doing with my mother's book?"

Rue felt a tingle of shock. Instinctively, she looked around to see if Prim had been overheard. Apparently not, so she hissed: "Aunt Ivy wrote a *book*? Wait, wait. Aunt Ivy can write?"

CHAPTER
SEVEN

Honeysuckle Isinglass's Secrets Revealed

I believe I can quite confidently claim that Aunt Ivy has never written anything more strenuous than a note to the butcher in her entire life." Rue was circling the meeting table, her main sensation being near-paralytic confusion. Although, obviously not *exactly* paralytic as she was quite definitely circling.

Primrose sat placidly, hands crossed in her lap, eyes crinkled in amusement. "Terrible dark family secret. I hardly dare spill..." She allowed herself to trail off, heightening the suspense.

"Aunt Ivy is really Honeysuckle Isinglass?" Rue gave up confusion in favour of the thrill of discovery.

"Well, to be perfectly correct, Honeysuckle Isinglass is really my mother, the Baroness of Wimbledon. The hive thought it was beneath a vampire queen to publish a travel memoir, so she had to take a pen name. You know how vampires are – the respectability of the supernatural mystique, the gravitas of the blood, the nobility of the fang, all that rot. Pity, really – the book might have done better if people knew who penned it."

"Oh, was it received poorly?" Rue tried not to grin.

"Very badly indeed. Why on earth did you buy it, Rue? It's about Egypt, not India, you do realise?"

"Primrose Tunstell, do not change the subject. Explain Honeysuckle Isinglass."

Prim elucidated further. "Queen Mums wrote it a few years after her metamorphosis. It's supposed to be based on notes she took while visiting Alexandria, you know, with the acting troupe and your parents back in 1876. When we were still in nappies."

"Aunt Ivy takes notes?"

Prim ignored this and continued. "It is an alarming piece of literature. Percy is particularly embarrassed by its existence."

"I suppose Aunt Ivy is ridiculously proud of it?"

"Ridiculously. Of course, no one else ever mentions it if they can possibly help it, and Queen Mums rarely manages to bring it up in casual conversation. Not that she doesn't try."

"But, honestly – Honeysuckle Isinglass?"

"I believe that was *your* mother's invention."

"My mother will have her little bouts of fun."

"The two of them must have been holy terrors in their day." Primrose puffed out her cheeks at the idea.

"If that book is any indication, they were certainly *something* – probably unholy." Rue paused to consider. Aunt Ivy was so silly and mother so powerful, they must have been such an odd paring. She snorted. "Honeysuckle Isinglass *indeed*."

Rue picked up the slim travel memoir in question and paged through it. *"The amber sun sinks slowly into the tourmaline sea, a blooming peony of beauty surmounting the waving undulations of the silken sapphire depths. All unobserved, our heroine wanders along the wave-licked shores, a young lady with a soul overfilled with sentiment for the pulchritude of the bejewelled landscape radiating before her, her feet attired in Mademoiselle Membrainoux's finest kid slippers. The* slush slush slush *of the sparkling iridescent waves marries to the breathless beating of her engorged heart—"* Rue had to stop. "Crikey, Prim!"

Prim was giggling into her hand. "I know. It's *so* bad."

Why, wondered Rue, *has a supposed acquaintance named Anitra*

given me a badly written slim travel memoir authored by a vampire?
And does it have anything to do with my parasol being stolen by a lion-
ess? And who's Goldenrod? Rue snapped the book shut and turned
it about in her hands, shaking out the pages, hoping for a hidden
message, a dried flower, something. But there was nothing there,
not even a suspicious stain.

"I should read it for clues but, Prim, I don't think I could
bear it."

Prim said, "I do understand. And they are unfortunately ubiquitous. I mean, Queen Mums insisted they print simply thousands of them. They were so resoundingly disparaged by the
critics, they were somewhat taken to heart by those who eschewed
the intellectual set. Now all the very worst libraries have one. I
can't believe you haven't encountered it before."

"Neither can I. I can only speculate that my mother pre-
vented copies from entering my sphere for fear of linguistic
contamination."

"Why *did* you buy it?" Prim pressed.

"I didn't – it was given to me by an old friend."

Prim stopped giggling and looked up. "You have *other* old
friends?"

"Apparently. This one was so old I don't remember her. Gave
me her first name only – Anitra."

"How terribly indelicate."

"You're telling me. Then she handed me that book."

"Even more indelicate," agreed Primrose. "Was that the reason
you were late back to the ship? What happened to the lioness?"

"Well, that resulted in a different mysterious female. Name of
Miss Sekhmet. I followed the cat into a shack, and then a beautiful woman swathed in silk came out, knew who I was, gave me
back my parasol, and warned me to stay out of India. Then, when
I was walking back to the ship, this Anitra person accosted me in

public, also swathed in fabric, said that Goldenrod sent her with that book. And that was it."

"Pull the other one."

"If I were going to fib, wouldn't I come up with a better story?"

Prim considered this and made a show of straightening the bodice of her travelling suit, carefully checking all the buttons. "I suppose so. But what does it *mean?*"

Rue shrugged. "I've absolutely no clue but I think we had better put this slim travel memoir in a safe place."

"My brother's library?"

"Good idea. We might have a hard time finding it again but then so would anyone else. He's up top right now – shall we risk it?"

They made their way out of the stateroom but not before Prim had put a hand on Rue's arm.

Oh dear, thought Rue, *here it comes.*

"You thought you were going to get out of it," said Prim. Rue's expression was wary.

"Very well, if you must. Go on."

"Rue, and I mean this most kindly, but perhaps in future you should act with a little bit more *prudence.*"

"Oh, ha ha, thank you very much. Is that all?"

"And I shall be writing a letter to your mother to post as soon as we land in India on the subject of your choices thus far."

"You are a very hard-hearted female."

Prim made a kissy face at her and that was that. No further scolding was needed – twenty years of friendship has its benefits.

The two ladies made their way to Percy's quarters, one half of which was also the ship's library. The suite had started out as one of the largest but now looked as if it were the smallest. The arched chamber was a warren of books with stacks and shelves and piles everywhere. The beams supporting the deck above were the only component of the *Custard* still visible. Somewhere there must be walls but it was difficult to spot any. There was no doubt in either of their minds that Percy had some manner of organisation system in place, but they couldn't figure it out.

"Yoo-hoo?" called Rue into the stacks in case there was someone else infiltrating.

Footnote appeared, stretched at them in his version of a bow and sniffed their shoes. They stood still, allowing him to do so until, gatekeeper-like, he magnanimously began leading them through the books, tail high.

"Lady Captain?" Virgil appeared, wearing an apron and carrying one of Percy's boots, obviously in the middle of blacking them.

Footnote sniffed his feet and then flopped over on top of them.

"Ah, Virgil, you wouldn't clock a tick about Professor Tunstell's filing system, would you?" asked Rue.

"Not exactly, captain. Of course, you could always ask one of the ladders."

"Pardon?" said Rue.

Virgil put down the boot. Footnote transferred his affection to this interesting new smell. Virgil approached a ladder which hung from a long top rail that snaked about the perimeter of the room. Clearly the ladder was designed to slide for easier access to the highest shelves. Rue had thought it quite ordinary, except for being metal instead of wood, but Virgil seemed to know otherwise. On one side, down near the first rung, was a dial, and the ladder had a cranking mechanism with a pin reader at the railing above. The railing was perforated at multiple points with patterns of holes so that when the operator set the dial, the ladder would roll along until its pins dropped into the matched holes, stopping the ladder abruptly at a prescribed point.

Rue said, all innocence, "The professor lent me this slim travel memoir and I wanted to return it. To the, erm, the section with travel journals."

Virgil bent down and clicked the dial over to the number seven. Rue made a mental note. The boy jumped onto the ladder and flattened himself against it, clutching with both hands. He then pressed a button on one side and in a puff of steam, the ladder whooshed off more rapidly than Rue thought possible. With an audible click, it stopped some distance away behind the stacks.

"This way, Lady Captain," sang out Virgil's disembodied voice.

Rue and Prim wended through the shelves and piles of books. The ladder was near the only porthole left unblocked in the room. Virgil jumped off.

"Of what type is the travel book, Lady Captain?" he asked.

"Bad?" said Rue cautiously.

The boy grinned. "No, I meant what part of the world, flowery retelling or solid factual detail?"

"Oh. Egypt."

Primrose added, "And flowery. Definitely flowery."

Virgil led them around the back of two chairs, both covered in rolls of maps, metal scrolls for aetherographic transmitters, and current charts. He pulled one of the chairs away and pointed down to a shelf near the floor stacked with small, cheaply made, slim travel memoirs. There were an awful lot of them. Fortunately, none of the others was pink. Percy, great collector of the written word though he may be, evidently did not already own a copy of his mother's infamous work. Rue tucked the volume in among its fellows in as innocuous a location as possible.

She straightened. "Thank you very much for your help, Virgil."

Prim asked, "Does my brother have anything in a less flowery vein on travelling in India, do you know?"

"Over here." Virgil pointed up at a higher part of the same

shelf. The books there had been disturbed and stuffed with bits of notepaper marking pertinent sections. Percy had obviously been following instructions to read up on their destination.

Prim stood on tip-toe to read the spines. She selected *The Complete Indian Housekeeper and Cook* by Flora Annie Steel and Grace Gardiner.

"Thank you kindly, young man. I believe this will do nicely."

They made their farewells to Virgil and Footnote, both young males pleased to have been of assistance but eager to get on with their regular tasks – in Virgil's case, as boot-black, and in Footnote's, interfering with the boot-black.

"What is that about?" Rue pointed to *The Complete Indian Housekeeper and Cook* clutched in Prim's hands as they exited.

"Best to give Virgil something more to report to my brother than us returning a book. If we *took* something from his collection, Percy will focus on that and forget the one we added."

"Very nice tactic." Rue respected Prim's manipulative talents.

"Besides, this looks like an interesting read."

At which statement Rue, who preferred adventure novels, was properly horrified.

Three days later, they left off their slow spinning, to the great relief of all. It had become disorientating, even in the grey nothingness of the aetherosphere. Prim had stopped taking tea on deck, claiming the stateroom was more restorative. Rue made a vow to eschew the waltz at future balls – it may be old-fashioned of her, but she had a newfound respect for the quadrille.

Percy de-puffed them expertly into a more relaxed and standard current, the Central Hyderabad Waft, which would take them on to India and down towards Bombay. From the maps, Rue knew that they must be above the Baghdad Environs at the moment, but the aetherosphere provided no evidence to this fact. Much as she loved to float, Rue was finding that she preferred the slower method inside the actual air, where one could see the landscape below.

It would take another three days to reach Bombay but Rue insisted they continue without pause. This might tax their stores and leave them low on fuel, but there was no convenient tower near the Hyderabad Waft. They'd have to go to ground for a restock, and dipping down would severely waste hours.

Everyone was prosaic about this decision except Primrose, who panicked over the prospect of running low on milk. She instructed Cook to take all non-dairy essentials, including Rue's favourite custards, off the menu until further notice – all milk being required for tea – and even considered extracting the Swiss condensed reserves out of storage.

"I don't think we need go that far," was Rue's response to the idea.

"Extreme measures," hinted Prim darkly.

Despite her friend's doom talk, they made it to Bombay with little fuss and no shortage of milk. They de-puffed out of the aetherosphere to find India spread below them like a great red and brown apple fritter nestled in a pool of blue sauce. There were sprinkles of green jungle, which, if one continued the comparison, meant the fritter was mouldy.

Rue had no idea if Bombay was typical of the colonies, but it was not typical of any city she'd ever visited before. Which she guessed meant the onus was on her to change what she considered city-like. It was lyrically beautiful, a place of colour and spice. Aunt Ivy would have waxed most verbose at the sight. Possibly even written another slim travel memoir.

Rue, while impressed, was frightened of flowery language even when faced with such an amazing sight as Bombay.

"Oh, my," was the sum total of her commentary, as Percy

guided them slowly through the atmosphere, ever downward towards the mass of buildings, dirigibles, roads, rails, and humanity that made up the First Great Port of the Great British Empire.

Later, Rue added to her eloquence with, "Gracious me."

Bombay was, ostensibly, a peninsula, but it looked from above more like an island, surrounded on almost all sides by water. Percy was directing them towards the southern-most tip where a parade ground gave way to an old cemetery and the Colaba Battery. A muddy beach along the western edge had been misappropriated for airship use and was dotted with dirigibles, ornithopters, and balloons, plus associated loading docks and mooring points. The airships were tied down using long lines fixed to bollards set into the ramparts of the parade ground. In cases of very high tide, the airships were given lee to rise up above the water. It was impossible to board at such times, but given the crowded city, this made for a sensible use of an otherwise unreliable beach.

Fortunately, it was low tide as *The Spotted Custard* floated in to ground.

The ship caused no little fuss upon arrival. Bombay and her resident regiments were accustomed to airships in many shapes and sizes but *The Spotted Custard* was a cut above the rest, and rather shiny. Officers liked flash, particularly red flash, and they were suitably impressed by a large ladybug bobbing into port. A few of the off-duty foot even wandered over to see who might disembark from such an impressive ship.

Also, as Rue was to shortly discover, the native population appreciated transport disguised as animals.

"Let's give them a show as we disembark, shall we?" suggested Rue to Prim's evident delight.

Primrose was fond of the military – rather too much for Aunt Ivy's comfort; Rue a little less so, as she grew up with werewolves who were always attached to some regiment or another.

"Shall we change?" suggested Rue.

Prim was grinning.

Rue turned to her crew, busy battening down the *Custard* for docking. The mainsail was in, the mooring ropes out, and the propeller wound down.

"You all right from here on without me, Navigator Tunstell?"

Percy nodded without bothering to reply.

Rue wondered if she should ask him if he wanted to come along but, knowing Percy, calculated that this was a waste of breath.

The two ladies linked arms and headed across the poop deck to the ladder down to their quarters.

Since the idea was to impress, they chose two of their best walking dresses – after consultation to ensure the outfits would display well together. Primrose selected a lemon-yellow organza with black velvet trim in petal-like layers over the skirt and black flower appliqué on the bodice. It had a wide black velvet belt to emphasise the slenderness of her waist. The sleeves were the latest in leg-of-mutton cut with wide black ribbon cuffs. And, of course, it boasted a matching black hat decorated with yellow bows and a huge ostrich plume out the back.

Rue went with a burnt umber Indian silk Worth. Dama was dear friends with Jean-Philippe and had a standing order in for Rue – new gowns every season. Dama referred to the older Worth's demise earlier that year as the Great Tragedy, and had consoled Jean-Philippe with copious flowers, bolts of silk, and letters of condolence. Jean-Philippe had responded with, among other things, this very dress. It was simpler than Prim's gown, with a slashed bodice and overskirt. Out from the skirt peeked crêpe of a slightly darker umber, and from the bodice a Madras muslin of cream with brown flowers. The edges of the gown were bordered in more of the crêpe, with collar and cuffs of brown velvet. A patten of cream appliqué over the bodice echoed that of the black on Prim's lemon gown. Rue's sleeves were narrow and cut high with a lace trim. Her hat was a great deal more modest – of flat Italian straw with one brown velvet bow and three umber silk roses. Together they looked rather like excited mobile tiger lilies.

Both ladies carried parasols against the Indian sun – Rue rejected her mother's as too ugly and borrowed a brown lace one from Prim. Prim had, of course, a matching lemon-yellow number with black edging. They looked, as Spoo whispered behind their backs, a *treat*, and might have strolled through Hyde Park at the height of the season with not a single nasty remark from any patroness of high society, not even the anti-supernatural set.

It was wickedly hot. By the time they crossed the deck and strolled down the gangplank, Rue thought she might be melting. She blessed her own irreverent nature and shape-shifting inclination which allowed her to forego stays and undergarments. To wear anything more than outward modesty required, even for the sake of decency, was patently ridiculous. Poor Prim looked likely to faint after only a few minutes' walk. She did not sweat of course, not the Honourable Primrose Tunstell, but there was a certain sheen to her face that delicacy might term a *damp aura*.

Rue expected Bombay to play host to the bustle of an exotic marketplace as her mother had described Alexandria. But the place was remarkably still. They were in the imperial section of the peninsula and not the city itself, but she could see the tops of buildings outside the ramparts and even there Bombay seemed... well...dead.

Prim said, "Perhaps respectable folk stay in during the hottest part of the day."

A few boys in white shifts, brown limbs exposed, scampered by, tossing a large fruit back and forth. Here and there a stray dog wandered, but that was all.

"Either that or there's a plague," replied Rue, making light and then regretting it at Prim's panicked expression.

They walked along the beach or – properly – mudflats, and then up onto the promenade around the edge of the barracks. This brought them closer to the city proper, looming beyond the walls of what Prim said were the Cotton Godowns and the Victoria Bunder. Beyond the walls were rows of massive trees forming a demarcation between representatives of Her Majesty Abroad and *everyone else*.

The city was pleasingly unfamiliar in shape and smell. The rooftops were all red or covered in coloured tiles. They boasted tall spires or the occasional onion-shaped protrusion. It had its fair share of empire builders too – sky trains, massive rotary carriers, and evidence of other steam transport was everywhere, from rails to divots to cycle hooks. Unlike London, all these machines were decorated. The local sky rail, likely used for transporting goods from warehouses to shipyards up and down the peninsula, loomed high above the buildings. It too was at rest in the heat of the day, hanging from its one massive cable. It featured all the expected components – steam vents, smoke stacks, guidance arms – but it had been made to look like a large elephant. The elephant had huge ears made of brightly coloured animal skins and chains of fresh flowers and paper lanterns garlanded about its neck. Rue marvelled at how close this sky rail came to breaking the Clandestine Information Act, entering the realm of Forbidden Machines. The elephant component must be purely decorative and have no independent protocols, doing nothing more risky than running up and down its cables like any other delivery steamer – only prettier. Otherwise, surely it would have been destroyed.

Rue grinned. England had brought steam to India, but the locals were clearly insistent that steam be attractive. She liked it very much. It was irrepressibly cheerful, a word Rue doubted anyone had ever used to describe a sky train before.

Primrose, the aestheticist, clearly felt the same, for she revived out of her wilted state long enough to remark in wonder, pointing down near the water with her parasol. "Would you look at that? I think it's a garment washer, but it looks like a monkey. Charming, quite charming."

Rue pointed at the sky rail.

Prim gasped. "How lovely!"

A voice behind them said, "You admire our Ganesha, ladies?"

Rue and Prim turned to find themselves face to face with an officer in uniform and two customs officials. The officer looked youthfully good-natured but the customs men were sweating profusely and seemed unhappy at being forced to move around.

Rue and Prim curtseyed prettily.

Rue said, "My dear sirs, we do apologise for calling you out in such heat. Had we not been in need of a restock we should have waited to land until a more respectable hour."

"No need to apologise," replied the officer. "It happens regrettably often. The currents carry at their whims – science wills it so. If you ladies would step over to the shade just there? We can dispense with the paperwork as soon as may be."

The two native gentlemen merely murmured, "Madam Sahib," and allowed the officer to lead the social interchange.

A small table and few spindly chairs were arranged under the shelter of some glorious flowering tree. Rue and Prim stepped.

Rue contemplated enacting one of her schemes. Miss Sekhmet had warned of danger. Should she reveal her true name? She looked to Prim for assistance in determining tactics.

Primrose was busy fluttering her eyelashes at the officer. She was equally identifiable. The name Tunstell had quite the reputation due to the baroness's hats. Everyone knew that the Wimbledon Queen had had two children pre-metamorphosis because it had been quite the scandal at the time. Thus they couldn't register the ship under Primrose or Percy's names either. They might use Quesnel, but Rue wasn't entirely certain that if she registered *The Spotted Custard* under his name, the Frenchman wouldn't gleefully abscond with it.

Fortunately or unfortunately, the decision seemed to have been taken entirely out of Rue's hands.

The officer gestured for the ladies to sit and introduced himself: "How do you do? I'm Lieutenant Broadwattle. On behalf of Brigadier Featherstonehaugh, I am charged with welcoming you to Bombay." He looked back and forth between them before hazarding a guess. "You are Lady Prudence Akeldama? And you are the Honourable Primrose Tunstell?"

Rue swallowed a smile. "Other way around, but not to worry – it happens all the time."

Prim simpered at the young man. "Fortunately, we are such dear friends we do not mind being mistaken for one another."

"On some occasions we even encourage it," added Rue.

"Ah, well, two such delicate ladies must, perforce, accompany one another."

Rue was not one to be distracted by flattery, even by a dasher in uniform. "You were alerted to our imminent arrival?"

"You are earlier than expected, but we did have an inkling. The brigadier expressed his particular interest once the pack informed him of your connections. You're aware that Bombay's regiment is honoured by a werewolf special forces attachment?"

Rue brightened – *shapes to steal*. "Oh, how nice. Anyone I know?"

"The Kingair Pack?"

Rue winced. "Ah. I see."

Prim looked at her sharply. "What?"

"Fringe relations. They advised Brigadier Featherstonehaugh of my coming?"

The officer nodded, smiling nervously at her reaction.

"Now I know why Paw didn't fight harder to keep me home," said Rue. "Werewolves. Interfering busybodies, the lot of them."

"Rue, language," remonstrated Primrose, fidgeting awkwardly in embarrassment.

Like a true gentleman, Lieutenant Broadwattle moved the conversation on. "Unfortunately, pressing business makes the brigadier unable to welcome you himself. Nevertheless I am charged with informing you as to his profound honour at being graced by a visit from the daughters of such collectively esteemed vampires, Tunstell *and* Akeldama." Rue could read the truth behind that statement – they were an inconvenience. The officer continued, "I suggest, however, that you keep your ancestry private. We have tried desperately to civilise this country but vampires, I'm afraid, are not at all liked in India. Natives categorise them as Rakshasas, a folkloric daemon. We are told that the cultural practices of vampires are less sanguine in this part of the world. Although I have not had the pleasure myself."

The two customs officials winced noticeably at the word *Rakshasas* and made small hand gestures to ward off evil. They were both Indian, heads wrapped in cloth, with dark eyes and impressively full beards.

The young officer moved swiftly on. "Werewolves, on the other hand, are most welcome. Many animals are considered, at least partly, sacred in India. Although they have no native packs – wrong climate – the werewolf curse is thought a blessing . . . with sufficient full-moon controls, of course."

"How novel," said Rue.

"Not to mention forward-thinking," added Primrose, smiling warmly at the two native men. She was trying to show that she had no hard feelings for their vilification of her relations.

One could not blame a people for disliking vampires. Vampires were like Brussels sprouts – not for everyone and impossible to improve upon with sauce. There were even those in London who disapproved of Dama, and he was very saucy indeed.

The young officer managed a weak smile. "If we could get on to the minutia, ladies? Because of your connections, we have tried to make this as simple as possible. Of course, in casual conversation when you are home, perhaps a favourable mention in polite company on the efficient nature of my regiment?"

"I assure you, thus far, we will have nothing but glowing things to say about the Bombay company."

Lieutenant Broadwattle smiled radiantly, his slightly homely face made handsome by good cheer. "Here are your papers of registration for the airship. *Spotted Custard*, as I understand, is the name? You, Lady Akeldama, are down as primary owner, with three other members of rank listed as the Honourable Primrose Tunstell, Professor Tunstell, and one Mr Lefoux. Is that correct?"

"Indeed it is."

"If you wouldn't mind filling in your staff and crew roster for restocking purposes here?"

He handed Rue the stylus, which Rue immediately passed to Prim who kept better track of such things and had vastly superior penmanship. The two customs officers watched this, hawk-like. They seemed to be paying inordinately close attention to the proceedings. Oddly, they were as focused on Lieutenant Broadwattle as they were on Prim and Rue. Was Lieutenant Broadwattle under suspicion of misconduct? Rue cocked her head at the young man. He seemed twitchy, but nothing out of the ordinary for a gentlemen faced with Primrose in a pretty dress and good temper.

He did seem perturbed that Rue had passed off the paperwork, perhaps because it now occupied the whole of that young lady's attention. He rallied enough to ask, "Do you know the nature of your stores and local contacts, Lady Akeldama?"

Rue shook her head. "No, I have people for that."

"Of course you do."

"Will there be anything else, lieutenant?"

"I have the length of your stay down for one week starting tomorrow. Is that sufficient for your needs?"

"As long as I can complete my social calls during that time. May I extend if necessary?"

"Indeed, my lady. However..." He trailed off, distracted by Prim.

Rue sighed. She was used to it. "I take it most activity commences after dark, when it is cooler."

Primrose was puzzling over a list of numbers in the margins of the paperwork.

The two customs officials tensed.

Then she moved blithely on with an obvious mental shrug.

"Sir?" Rue drew Lieutenant Broadwattle's attention back to herself.

"Yes, after dark. Speaking of which, some of the local diplomats, their wives, and a few officers are meeting for a garden party at sunset this evening. Would you care to join us? The ambassador's wife has authorised me to extend the invitation. I must say, we would welcome fresh faces and new society, not to mention unmarried ladies."

"Lieutenant Broadwattle!" reprimanded Primrose, pinking in pleasure. "You go too far." Thus proving she had not been entirely focused on the paperwork.

The young man lowered his head in mock shame.

Rue, on the other hand, did nothing to disguise her delight. She loved a garden party, and to have one materialise that very evening in an exotic land. Topping! "We should love to attend."

"Will you bring the two gentlemen as escorts?" he asked, clearly hoping the answer would be no.

Rue hated to disappoint. "Possibly one, probably not the other, but they are difficult to predict."

Prim finished listing relevant names and details and handed the parchment back over. "Any other customs business?"

The young man remembered his duty. "Do you have anything to declare for the record? Imports, business engagements, other taxable items? We were told that this is purely a pleasure jaunt."

Rue and Prim shook their heads solemnly.

"I do not recommend visiting the city proper without a guide, which I would be happy to arrange. Would tomorrow early morning suit? Sun-up? It is best to get as much done as possible before the heat."

After exchanging looks with Prim, Rue said, "That would be ideal. Will he come to the ship?"

"Absolutely."

"Thank you very much for saving us the bother. Now, Lieutenant Broadwattle, gentlemen, if that concludes our business? I think we will take the unspoken suggestion of the entire city and return to *The Spotted Custard* for a nap. This heat is most oppressive."

"Very good, ladies. I should say one gets accustomed to it, but I've been stationed here for nearly three years and I have yet to acclimatise."

Primrose was impressed. "Three years? I should never have guessed."

"You flatter me."

Rue grabbed her friend by the elbow and popped up her parasol with purpose. Things were about to get sappy – she saw all the signs.

Reluctantly, Prim did the same. "Will we see you at the garden party, Lieutenant Broadwattle?"

"I anticipate our renewed acquaintance with pleasure," replied the young man smoothly.

Prim continued, because she was a flirt, "As do I."

The officer blushed and stood hastily when they did. "Welcome to India, Lady Akeldama, Miss Tunstell." He bowed them off.

Rue and Prim twirled about, conscious that they looked as well in their expensive dresses retreating as they had done arriving, and returned across the mudflats to their gently bobbing airship.

"Must you make every man we meet fall in love with you?" Rue wanted to know, without rancour.

Prim gave this serious thought. "Yes. It's a point of pride, you see?"

"Ah, well, carry on then."

"Oh, but didn't he have fine eyes? The finest, I think, I ever saw."

The problem with Primrose was she also fell in love back. Rue could do nothing more than pat her friend's arm sympathetically.

Everything was still and quiet on board the *Custard*. The decklings, cocooned in their hammocks, snored softly, and everyone else was down below in quarters. Only Spoo and Virgil sat watch, crouched under the parasol at the helm, playing a lazy game of pumpernickel and bickering softly.

They stood to attention as Rue and Prim moved slowly up the gangplank.

"All right, you two?" Rue inquired.

"Tip-top, Lady Captain," said Spoo.

"Surviving well enough," added Virgil, which earned him an ear-boxing from Spoo.

"Delightful company you're keeping, Virgil." Rue grinned.

"Delightful," answered the valet, deadpan.

Spoo boxed his ears again, harder.

"Ow, now look here!" He turned on her.

Spoo put both hands behind her back and whistled a little tune.

Rue hustled Prim belowdecks before they were called to arbitrate.

Rue settled in for tranquil repose, difficult as that might be in the dark, oppressive stuffiness of her cabin. Graceful and well-appointed as it may be, it was not made for Indian weather. Nevertheless, she attempted to ignore both the heat and increasingly strident tones of the two directly over her head.

Then the tenor of the argument shifted. There came a yell that was by no means normal squabbling, and a loud thud.

Rue leapt out of bed, wearing nothing but her thin shift, grabbed her mother's parasol, and climbed up the captain's ladder to the quarterdeck. She emerged blinking into the late afternoon light to find Spoo sitting triumphantly on the head of someone while Virgil resided on the legs. Both of them were rising up and down, as if riding a wave, as the individual in question convulsed in an effort to de-seat them.

"What on earth?" Rue asked.

Virgil's eyes widened at her scanty attire. "Why, Lady Captain! What are you doing above boards dressed like that?"

Spoo was not perturbed.

Rue was beginning to suspect that nothing perturbed the girl. "Spoo, report!"

"Intruder, captain! We caught the blighter trying to sneak straight up the gangplank."

At the mention of the word "captain", the blighter in question stilled. He was clothed in plain unbleached material shaped into a very baggy shirt and some even baggier trousers. More of the same was wrapped about his head, face, and neck. Or what Rue could see of his head from under Spoo's bottom.

"Spoo, get off him, do."

"You're sure that's wise, captain?" Spoo's expression suggested that she sincerely doubted Rue's ability to defend herself with only a parasol.

"Yes, I'm sure."

Spoo got off.

The man turned to look at Rue. He had beautiful large almond-shaped eyes and copper skin. Too beautiful. And awfully familiar.

"You? How did you follow us so quickly? Percy will be so sad. He thought we were making especially good time."

The lady in question drew off her head wrap and spat out some bit of Spoo that had lodged in her teeth.

Spoo and Virgil gasped. Possibly because they now knew they sat on a woman, more likely because she was so beautiful. It spoke volumes for Virgil's presence of mind that he did not move from her legs – stunning female or no, she was still an intruder.

Miss Sekhmet said in that cultured British accent with only a hint of lilting foreign tones, "Really, children, was that strictly necessary?"

Rue popped open her parasol and used it as a shield to hide her indecent apparel. "We haven't been here very long," she said mildly. "We were not expecting visitors."

The woman sat up and attempted to shed Virgil from her legs.

Virgil did not budge and, after hopping about indecisively from foot to foot, Spoo joined him there, doubling the burden.

Rue contemplated telling them to get off, but Virgil looked quite militant in protection of his Lady Captain and Spoo seemed to be having far too much fun. So Rue let them stay, wondering how her unexpected caller might cope with rascals intent on military occupation of her lower extremities. It was almost pleasing to see such a very elegant female so very put upon.

Miss Sekhmet stopped trying to remove the parasitical small persons after finding them quite tenacious. She wrapped herself in dignity and sat there, talking to Rue as though there were nothing amiss and she commonly found herself on the deck of a ladybug-shaped airship with younglings tenanting her person.

"I warned you, metanatural, about India."

"So far, Miss Sekhmet, this moment has been the most unpleasant thing to occur here. And you, I hasten to add, are the one at the disadvantage, not I."

The woman wrinkled her aristocratic nose. "Oh, do tell them to get off. I'm not going to harm you. If I were, I've already had ample opportunity."

Rue arched an eyebrow. "Are you going to be any more forthcoming, or do you intend to persist in mysterious warnings?"

Miss Sekhmet huffed in annoyance. "It is a matter of some" – she glared at Virgil and Spoo – "delicacy."

"You have a message for me?" Rue hazarded a guess.

"I have been appointed speaker, more's the pity." Miss Sekhmet seemed annoyed by responsibility.

"And you couldn't have given it to me...before?"

"No one realised you were unaware of the situation. Why else would I warn you off?"

Ah, thought Rue, *there it is. She does represent the other players after the tea.*

Miss Sekhmet continued. "I wanted to meet you. One of the greatest wonders of our age. I did not intend to be involved further." She sounded like a finicky child being forced to eat her vegetables. "Once I realised that you were sent on purpose and already involved, I found I had no choice. I have my responsibilities, just as you do. Surely you understand?"

It was funny to see such a refined lady look like a petulant child. Despite herself, Rue warmed to the enigmatic Sekhmet. She couldn't help it. She had a soft spot for the disgruntled. That's why she kept Percy around. "You may give me the message and have done with it. I assure you these two are capable of keeping secrets." Her look said Virgil and Spoo had better be.

Spoo and Virgil nodded with gleeful yet solemn expressions.

The woman hesitated, muttering to herself in her own language. Finally she said, "I am instructed to ask that you attend tonight's garden party. Someone there will be prepared to discuss terms." She looked sceptically at Rue's hideous parasol, loose hair, and bare feet.

Without admitting that she was already intending to go, Rue nodded. "And how will I know this person?"

"Oh, you will know."

"Not you?"

"That would be awkward for other reasons. Besides, I am exhausted."

Rue frowned, trying to see beyond the intense beauty. There it was: the poor thing did look wan, even sickly. Her almond eyes were bloodshot, her skin drawn.

Miss Sekhmet took a small steadying breath, then asked, "Is the muhjah aware of the activities here?"

Rue nodded. Her mother had, after all, sampled the tea. Still it was an odd thing to bring up.

Miss Sekhmet stayed on the subject. "She approves?"

Rue nodded seriously. Tea was a serious business.

Miss Sekhmet shook her head. "But it is such an imbalance."

She must be alluding to the smokiness of the blend. "The muhjah is very advanced in her tastes. There will be mixing."

The woman's thick eyebrows arched in shock. No wonder that, for Lapsang-style teas were thought beyond the British palate. Only recently had they become accepted in the best drawing rooms, and even then it had been confined to Chinese imports. This woman, even if she were the proprietor of a very respectable tea export business interested in cutting out Dama's interests, would not yet be privy to such information.

"Very well. As a gesture of good faith, we are prepared to negotiate with you in parental absentia. And even that concession took all of my persuasive power. Tread carefully, skin-stalker."

Rue nodded. "Anything else?"

"If you could wear a recognisable colour?"

Rue considered both her and Prim's wardrobes. "Purple, I think."

"Very well. That is all."

Rue nodded to Spoo and Virgil. "Let her go."

"But, Lady Captain!" protested Spoo.

"Can't we keep her?" Virgil wanted to know. "She's so pretty."
As if she were a stray cat.

"Virgil, don't be rude," remonstrated Rue.

Reluctantly, the two relinquished the woman's legs. Miss
Sekhmet stood gingerly, then stretched slightly as if working out
Spoo-induced kinks. She made a polite little bow to all three and
then hurried at an indecently eager pace off *The Spotted Custard.*

Rue considered. "I think, my dear Spoo, you might activate the
gangplank drawback mechanism. No more unexpected visitors
today. Do you concur?"

Spoo snapped to attention. "Yes, Lady Captain." And went to
round up the necessary decklings to assist her in this task.

"Virgil?"

"Yes, Lady Captain?"

"Keep an eye to the accessories, please. There may be a lioness
around with a taste for parasols."

"Is that some kind of code, Lady Captain?"

"My dear young man, I only wish it were." With which Rue
returned to her nap and dreamed of cold tea.

EIGHT

In Which Percy Encounters a Pepper

To the surprise of everyone, including himself, Percy agreed
to attend the garden party that evening. Rue forbade him
to bring any books. Quesnel looked as if he could not decide
whether to be amused or distressed. Primrose disappeared with
her brother in order to monitor his apparel choices. Virgil was
in a near panic. He'd never dressed his master for an actual *event*
before, even something as casual as a garden party. Prim provided a most necessary service, for Percy emerged looking almost
respectable.

Of course, while his sister finished her own toilette, the professor mucked about in the library and managed to get covered
in dust, skew his cravat, and wrinkle his waistcoat. A very long-
suffering Virgil marched him abovedecks.

"Hopeless," pronounced his sister in exasperation before turning her ire on Rue.

Without Dama to impose upon her, Rue leaned in favour of
ease rather than style. She had selected a gown of pale lilac muslin that was startlingly plain and nearly four seasons old. It had
no train and only a single band of dark purple velvet at the hem

and collar. There was a demure pattern of cream appliqué on the bodice and over the forearms, and dark purple puff sleeves. That was all. It had a matching velvet hat with silk sweet peas in the same lilac colour and a ribbon like an undertaker's down the back. Without a lady's maid, Rue had resorted to twisting her mass of hair up quite simply. Dama would have disowned her on the spot.

Prim was moved to tisking disapproval. "And here I thought Percy was the only one who required assistance."

Rue smiled at her. "This is a working event for me, my dear."

"What if you get run over? People would read about what you were wearing when you died in the papers."

"Don't tempt fate, Prim. Besides, I need something practical."

"There is absolutely no call for you to use *that* horrible word. And what do you mean, *working*? You've never worked a day in your life, I'm happy to say."

Rue detailed, with some suppressed excitement, her naptime encounter with Miss Sekhmet.

Prim was, as ever, an excellent sounding board. "But why did this female feel it necessary to approach you on the ship and not wait until you were out in the city?"

Rue had no answer, only adding, "And why such urgency? Dama implied it was a secret economic concern. Admittedly, if he's right and this new variant of the plant takes, others will be interested, but to go to such lengths for tea?"

"Be fair; tea is important," Primrose remonstrated.

"And why mention my mother?" Rue continued. "To be sure, her job revolves around securing the safety of the empire, but that could hardly be a matter integral to a rove vampire's tea concerns." Percy and Prim, because of their mother's intimate friendship and vampire state, knew of Rue's mother's position on the Shadow Council. So Rue felt she was not betraying any confidences by involving them. Percy wasn't paying attention anyway.

Primrose looked serious. "You're certain about that?"

Rue considered the ramifications of her mission. "Perhaps these new plants are more significant than even Dama thought? Or perhaps he misled me as to their nature."

"Oh, now, Rue dear, I hardly think your Dama would let you walk blindly into a labyrinth of intrigue."

Rue didn't entirely agree. Already one agent had contacted her using the name Puggle, a name only Dama used. "I'm his beloved daughter, true, but he is still a vampire and he doesn't perceive danger in quite the same way as we mere mortals."

Quesnel appeared, looking stupefyingly gorgeous in a grey suit, purple cravat, and crisp white shirt. The ladies fell silent.

He fingered his cravat. "You see, I went with the theme." He'd obviously heard Rue ask Prim to wear purple.

Rue wasn't certain why she felt it necessary to run a scheme – perhaps it was simply in her nature to enjoy chaos. Plus any chance to perform was not to be missed.

Prim's dress was far more Lady Akeldama-ish, so she would probably get the lion's share of any attention in that regard. Those who had only heard of them were always easy victims. Prim's gown was stylish and modern with a slit-front bodice over a fine Chantilly lace shirtwaist and a lavender and gold brocade jacket matched to the skirt. Everything was cut simply to showcase the beautiful pattern of the fabric – and Prim's excellent figure. A wide sash emphasised Prim's narrow waist, several inches smaller than Rue's own. Yes, they looked alike in basics but, side by side, Rue was darker of complexion and substantially curvier. Prim lamented this frequently for it meant she could not borrow Rue's dresses, thereby doubling the size of her own wardrobe.

In keeping with her mother's wishes, Prim also wore a cream lace hat, perfectly matched to her dress, decorated with lavender ribbon and a bouquet of silk violets. Of course, the event was to take place after dark, and the sun was beginning to set in orange profusion over the Arabian Sea – thus hats were not strictly necessary. But custom dictated that a garden party meant hats, so hats they would wear. No doubt Aunt Ivy would learn of the breach if they didn't, even thousands of leagues away.

Rue's party elected to walk. The ladies utilised closed parasols as walking sticks. Fortunately, as they had absolutely no idea where they were going, Lieutenant Broadwattle was waiting for them on the shore.

Primrose took the lieutenant's proffered arm with alacrity. Rue thought she saw the young officer cast her a wistful look. She dismissed it as highly unlikely – for no young man of sense preferred Rue over Prim – and accepted Quesnel's all-too-casual offer. Percy slouched after them without any effort to participate in the social niceties of ambulation. Why had he bothered to come?

It turned out to be only a short way along the outside of the barracks to the impressive, almost church-like structure of the officers' mess. As they walked, of all out-of-place things, the sound of bagpipes permeated the air. Rue had never visited the Scottish Highlands, but she suspected nothing could be more different than Bombay. Without explaining the noise, the lieutenant led them through the mess and out the other side into a beautiful walled garden boasting overarching trees, a square pond, copious graceful – if flimsy – chairs and tables, and the milling throng of Bombay's resident elite.

Rue bounced in happily. Everything was so pretty and colourful. She and Prim were dressed to confuse. Tea espionage was afoot. This was going to be fun.

No one announced them but it was clear that the unvarying

nature of society abroad made four newcomers a welcome curiosity. There was no doubt that they had been the talk of the party
prior to their arrival. Rue felt rather like the pudding course of
a fancy meal, viewed with desire by some, suspicion by others,
and discomfort by those who had already partaken too freely.
She adored it of course, delighting in engendering discomfort. It
was, after all, her forte.

Lieutenant Broadwattle abandoned them at the stairs, presumably to alert the hostess.

Rue turned to her three companions and said with an air of
celebration, "Let's keep them as confused as possible, shall we?"

Quesnel looked game to play along.

Primrose nodded, an almost evil gleam to her dark eyes, before
assuming an expression of pleasant enthusiasm. Percy rolled his
eyes.

A large battleaxe of a woman bustled up to them, Lieutenant
Broadwattle in her wake. "Ladies. Gentlemen. You are most welcome to our modest gathering. Most welcome, indeed. Such an
honour. Now who is...?"

Lieutenant Broadwattle, doing his duty, said politely, "Lady
Akeldama, Miss Tunstell, if I might introduce our lovely host-
ess, the ambassador's wife, Mrs Godwit? Mrs Godwit, this is Lady
Prudence Akeldama and the Honourable Primrose Tunstell."

"Forgive me my dears, but which is which?"

Primrose stepped smoothly in before Lieutenant Broadwattle
could elucidate. "Oh, Mrs Godwit, you'll get accustomed to our
little idiosyncrasies quite quickly. Allow me to introduce Professor Tunstell and Mr Lefoux."

Percy's bow was almost too perfunctory to be polite.

Quesnel stepped forward, knowing his duty. The Frenchman
twinkled at their hostess in a most agreeable manner, entirely dis-
tracting that good lady from the question of confusingly similar
brunettes in purple dresses. "How do you do, Mrs Godwit?"

"A pleasure, a pleasure. Mr Lefoux, was it?"

"Indeed, dear lady."

Prim said, all gossip and good cheer, "I must say, the weather since we arrived! Is it always so hot this time of year here in India?"

"Oh, my dear young lady, I assure you this is mild, demulcent even, compared to the true summer suffering of this heathen land. You are lucky – or should I say, propitious? You have timed your visit very well indeed – the monsoon season has only recently ended. Such rains as we have been having already this month, a pabulum, a tempering of our customary languish—"

Rue stopped listening. The ambassador's wife was clearly a woman who enjoyed the sound of her own voice. She dropped flowery vocabulary about her like an incontinent hen might deposit eggs. This would not have been so horrible except that the voice in question was unpleasantly nasal. The banality of the subject matter only added insult to injury. Mrs Godwit was clearly a bore. But a powerful bore. Which meant Rue happily consigned her to Prim's tender mercies.

Quesnel, one mock desperate look in Rue's direction, was dragged along by Primrose.

Percy, unable to tolerate blathering, drifted towards a table of comestibles. It was laid with tea and coffee, ginger wine, and hard-iced milk with soda to quench the thirst. Percy was helping himself to a small plate of buttered scones and prunes soaked in rum when he was swarmed by a gaggle of giggling young ladies. Presumably these represented the eligible among the officers' and ambassadors' daughters. Percy, as usual, had drawn them to him like jam to toast.

Rue was left alone with Lieutenant Broadwattle. She noted a few other officers were present, wives in tow, but none seemed particularly scruffy or wolfish. "I'm assuming the werewolves will be joining us later, when it is fully dark?"

The lieutenant nodded, his attention on Prim's graceful form. He offered Rue his arm and they drifted after the others. Mrs Godwit was still detailing the weather.

Prim guided the conversation towards more lucrative territory. "My dear Mrs Godwit, I have heard much of Brigadier Featherstonehaugh. Will he and his wife be attending this evening's festivities?"

Mrs Godwit played along obligingly. "Oh, dear child, you haven't heard?" Her expression held all the joy of a hedgehog faced with a bowl of bread and milk. Rue suspected this meant that the topic could only be tragic.

"Oh, my dear Mrs Godwit, he is not ill, is he?"

"Far worse! Oh, my dear, do brace yourself. This is an untamed country, wild even. And so very dangerous. It is not the brigadier but his wife. Mrs Featherstonehaugh – *young* Mrs Featherstonehaugh – has been kidnapped! By native dissidents. Possibly those wretched Marathas. You know some of their women...Oh, it's too much, too much for young ears."

Primrose pressed her to continue.

"Some Maratha women do not wear skirts."

Even Rue was shocked by that statement.

"You mean...?" gasped Prim, eyes wide.

"Oh no, dear. Not that. But sort of trousers instead. They ride along with their men into battle. It hardly bears thinking about, so ungenteel. Anyway, where was I? Oh, yes. Young Mrs Featherstonehaugh, only a few days ago now – kidnapped! Along with some recently collected taxes. Although, of course, one cannot even contemplate the loss of the money when compared to what that poor girl must be suffering."

Rue wanted to ask if they would force Mrs Featherstonehaugh to go skirtless, but didn't want to interfere with the flow Primrose was coaxing forth.

Prim patted Mrs Godwit's arm. "So sad."

Mrs Godwit needed no more encouragement. "Of course, the dear brigadier is most distraught. Overwrought and despairing. All his attention of late has been occupied with investigating his wife's disappearance. Poor lamb. So of course, he is unable to attend. The werewolves, I understand, will be looking in to tender their respects to you, our honoured visitors, before heading out to continue tracking. But the chances of recovering the unfortunate girl seem slim."

Prim gasped.

Quesnel murmured appropriately aghast niceties.

Rue turned to Lieutenant Broadwattle. "Is this true?"

The lieutenant replied, "To the best of my knowledge. But I am only a lowly lieutenant and not on friendly terms with the brigadier."

Rue was concerned for the Featherstonehaughs' plight, of course, but having not met any of the players, she failed to be emotionally involved. Her attention drifted and she scanned the party, looking to identify Miss Sekhmet's contact.

Lieutenant Broadwattle said, "Oh dear, I do believe most people believe Miss Tunstell is you. I suspect it is her continued conversation with Mrs Godwit, not to mention the elegance of her dress." The gentleman caught himself at that. "Not that your gown isn't pretty . . ." He trailed off, uncomfortable. "Should I make an announcement to the contrary? I mean, about you being you."

"Please don't trouble yourself on my behalf." Rue was waiting to see if anyone, taken in by the scam, was desperately trying to get Primrose alone to pass on a message. But the cycles of social interaction seemed perfectly ordinary for a garden party, even one in Bombay. "Have there been any ransom demands?"

The lieutenant looked confused.

Rue elaborated: "For the brigadier's missing wife?"

"Not that we've been told."

"Odd."

"Not very – this is India, Lady Akeldama. They do things differently here."

"Yes, but *that* differentially? Why else would they want her?"

The young man looked grossly embarrassed.

Rue hastened to elaborate. "You think she was an accidental bonus and the taxes were the intended target?"

"Why else would natives want an Englishwoman? I'm not privy to the details but I believe the werewolves were blamed. It was supposed to be a cushy job, transporting the taxes and bringing the brigadier's wife back from the hills. Yet the pack botched it. They are rather in disgrace. I'm surprised Mrs Godwit invited them."

Rue said only, "Ah, I see." She was thinking, however, that Kingair had a reputation for botching up their assignments. Troublesome, her father had called his former pack whenever Rue asked about her Scottish relations. He'd thought it best that Rue not meet them.

"Lady Akeldama, could I beg your indulgence for a moment of private conversation?"

Rue only then registered that, as they talked, Lieutenant Broadwattle was steering her away from the party towards the far end of the pond and the privacy of several bushes there.

"Lieutenant Broadwattle, we have only just met!" To arrive at a garden party and immediately disappear in the company of an eligible man – she was as near to causing a serious scandal as she had ever got in her whole life. And it was Prim's good name at stake – since everyone thought Prim was Rue, it must follow that they also thought Rue was Prim. She could just imagine Aunt Ivy's face should reports of her daughter's behaviour reach London.

She drew back, intending to return to the party.

"But, Lady Akeldama, I have some very important information to impart. From Lord Akeldama."

Rue gasped. Lieutenant Broadwattle was Dama's contact?

She lowered her voice. "About *tea?*"

"I have been trying to get you alone since you arrived, but first those blasted customs officials – local spies for the Rakshasas of course – and now this party. No one here can be trusted," Lieutenant Broadwattle whispered darkly. "Especially not with tea."

Rue looked around. Everyone seemed to be respectably upper crust: the hats were in order, the hair was curled, the uniforms were crisp, even in the heat. "If you say so, lieutenant."

He bent over as though murmuring romantic nothings. "I do apologise, but we must give them reason to believe that my interest is genuine. I cannot be suspected – things have already gone pear-shaped."

Rue reluctantly agreed. "Quickly, then."

"I have been instructed to tell you that I have a message but you will need the honeysuckle."

"What? Oh. Yes, I see." He most likely had a cypher for Aunt Ivy's book and a message of encouragement from Dama.

Lieutenant Broadwattle angled himself so as to shield Rue with his body from the curious eyes of party attendees. He handed her a slip of paper. Rue glance at it briefly – it was notations on a grid, which she recognised as a received aetherographic transmission. Unfortunately, there were no letters but instead it featured only a series of numbers and spaces.

Rue knew a code when she saw one. This was some kind of message. "No cypher?"

The young man looked genuinely shocked. "My dear lady, I am only the redundancy agent. Newly minted, I am not privy..."

"Yes, yes, you are not privy to any secrets." Rue tucked the slip of paper down the bodice of her dress, much to the young man's embarrassment. "Now that Miss Tunstell's reputation is in tatters, shall we rejoin the party? I believe we have given them enough gossip for one evening."

"Indeed. Possibly even more than the kidnapping. At least that was respectable. This is good for *my* reputation, however." The young officer smiled at her and Rue wondered if he really was one of Dama's boys, as it were, and needed to establish notoriety as a lady's man. Or if he were simply referring to barracks bragging rights.

A thought occurred to her as they strode back, arms linked. "What happened to his previous agent?"

"Lord Akeldama didn't give you the name of your contact?" Lieutenant Broadwattle was surprised.

"He did not." Rue was beginning to regret her decision to sneak off in the wee hours of daylight without saying goodbye to Dama. Clearly, she had missed more than fond farewells. "I departed precipitously, for fashion reasons."

"His first agent was Mrs Featherstonehaugh."

"Oh dear," said Rue dropping his arm.

As soon as they joined the throng about the refreshment table, Quesnel and Prim abandoned Mrs Godwit and attached themselves, one on each side of Rue.

"Rue," hissed Primrose. "What are you about? My reputation!"

Quesnel added, "Yes, her reputation. Not to mention you're flirting shamelessly with that sorry excuse for an officer."

"Oh, stop it, both of you. He's Dama's not-so-specialist tea contact."

"What?" said both accusers as one.

"Keep your voices down. We'll discuss it later."

Quesnel would not let the matter drop. "You seemed to be enjoying yourself."

This inexplicably annoyed Rue. "Mr Lefoux, I always enjoy

myself at a garden party. And now, I believe the regimental were-wolves have arrived."

The werewolves made a grand entrance. They could hardly do otherwise. The pack was a standard size, looking to be eight or so members, but above-standard on an individual level. Each man was built on the brick wall end of the spectrum of human shape. They were also scruffy, boisterous, and wearing exotic formal wear. This involved a plaid skirt-like object instead of trousers. Luckily, Rue had been warned of this garment on more than one occasion.

All arguments and accusations forgotten, Prim edged closer to Rue and snapped open her fan, the better to whisper behind it. "Oh my goodness, are those *kilts*? I've never seen them outside the history books. They *are* an appealing fashion statement, aren't they?"

Rue could not help but agree – after all, how often did one get to admire a gentleman's knees in polite society? "Practical," she said. "I suppose they allow for a certain breeziness in this heat."

Primrose was clearly on the road to becoming a great admirer of the apparel. "Don't they *just*? Do you think they wear, uh, bloomers underneath?"

"I should think, as werewolves, they'd have my problem with bloomers."

"Tails?"

"Tails."

Prim's fan fluttered excitably at the unspoken conclusion – *nothing at all under kilts.* "My, but they do grow them large and handsome in the north now, don't they?" Prim's interest in Lieutenant Broadwattle was entirely forgotten in the face of this new invasion.

Rue had thought never to encounter a man as big as her father, but now she realised he was merely representative of the breed. She felt almost dainty. The rest of the assembled garden party seemed to be doing their best to ignore the newcomers, quite a feat given their size. Mrs Godwit had said something about the pack being in disgrace, the loss of Mrs Featherstonehaugh and the taxes placed in their paws.

The kilted masculinity rippled at a disturbance from the back, and an unlikely individual pushed her way roughly through the sea of plaid. There stood, feet braced, an ill-dressed older woman to whom the pack instantly deferred. She was also quite tall and tough as old boots, her expression uncompromising and her stance one of controlled power. Her long greying hair was plaited like a schoolgirl's, showing off strong features and a face that no one would ever call pretty.

Without waiting for an introduction, the lady marched across the lawn straight at Prim and Rue – who were still hiding behind Prim's fan.

Primrose hastily closed the fan and tried not to stare at this odd female.

Rue, on the other hand, regarded her with open interest. She knew of Lady Kingair. Who didn't? The only female werewolf to have been made in generations. Bitten into immortality by Rue's own father. But to meet the legend in person? To encounter the stuff of nightmares – it was thrilling.

Lady Kingair was dressed in a way that suggested all sense of style had been sacrificed on the altar of practicality. Her gown was made of sensible muslin in deference to the heat, with copious pockets and a wide leather belt from which dangled various useful objects including a magnification lens, a medical kit, and a bar of soap.

Lady Kingair stopped in front of the two girls. She was not confused by their similar appearance. She focused on Rue, narrowing a pair of awfully familiar eyes. Those eyes were the same as the ones Rue saw in the looking glass each morning before breakfast. Eyes that were such a pale brown as to be almost yellow. Rue's father's eyes. Rue's eyes.

"Good evening, auntie. We meet at last," said Sidheag Maccon, Lady Kingair.

Rue played along. "Niece!" she said, tempted to throw her arms around the woman. She held back because hugs were not acceptable conduct at garden parties, even among family members. Maybe in the Americas, but not here, not even at the fringe of the empire.

Rue continued, eyes twinkling. "What a pleasure to meet you at last, *niece.*"

Lady Kingair seemed taken aback by Rue's enthusiasm. "My, but you are different from your parents."

"What a lovely thing to say!" crowed Rue, even more delighted to meet this long-lost relation. Because it seemed to unsettle her relation, Rue acted even more bubbly. She bounced a bit on the balls of her feet and coloured her gestures with awkward, barely supressed energy – like Spoo.

Lady Kingair shook herself slightly. "And how is old Gramps?"

"Paw was fine when we left London – topping form, really."

"Oh indeed? Isn't he getting a little...old?"

Rue blinked at her. *What is she implying?* All werewolves were old, except the newly made ones, of course. "You'd never guess it to look at him."

"Of course not. But I didn't intend to ask after his appearance, more the state of his soul."

Rue didn't understand the question and so misdirected it. "He was in good spirits when I left London."

Lady Kingair tilted her head, as much as to say she respected Rue for avoiding all direct questions.

Rue accepted the unspoken accolade and said, "But I am remiss. Please allow me to introduce my travelling companions. This is the Honourable Primrose Tunstell and Mr Lefoux, and that is Professor Tunstell."

"Indeed? Fine company you keep, auntie."

"Primrose, Quesnel, this is my great-great-great-great-niece, Sidheag Maccon, Lady Kingair. I *think* that's the right number of greats."

Prim and Quesnel made polite murmurs. They did not find the relationship confusing, having grown up among vampires. Very strange things happened to family trees once immortals got involved. The Tunstell twins experienced similarly baffling relationships regularly. Their mother had been bitten to immortality when she was only a few years older than they were now. Primrose and Aunt Ivy looked, in effect, like sisters. Eventually, as Prim got older, her mother would look younger than she, like a daughter, and then a granddaughter. Vampires and werewolves had all sorts of rules in place to stop such things, but Ivy Tunstell had been made vampire by accident. And Rue's entire existence was a massive mistake. Lady Kingair had been made werewolf under even more unusual circumstances.

We are all of us, thought Rue, *not exactly meant to exist.* It made her feel a kinship beyond blood with this acerbic Scotswoman.

"Let us be candid, auntie. Are you here to order us back to London?" demanded Sidheag.

That was when Rue realised that there was something more behind her parents' refusal to host the Kingair Pack or visit Scotland. Something had gone wrong between them, something sinister, before Rue's birth.

However, it didn't stop her from ribbing her relation. "Order you to town, Lady Alpha? Why on earth would I do that? Everyone seems so eager to keep you *out* of London." Rue could imagine the carnage should this pack and her father's pack try to occupy the same city while at odds. London was big, but it wasn't *that* big.

"But you *are* here at your father's behest?"

"Which father?" Rue could play this game happily until the sun came up.

The Alpha werewolf lost a little of her aggressive posture. "I have always wondered which one would have the most influence. Well, if you aren't here for us, why are you in Bombay, Prudence Maccon?"

"It's Prudence Akeldama. And this is just a pleasure jaunt, esteemed niece. Dama gifted me with this lovely little airship and I thought I might see a bit of the world. I heard India was pleasant this time of year."

Lady Kingair rolled her eyes. "Double-talk, nothing but double-talk. It's like being back in finishing school."

"If I may be of service, Alpha?" said a smooth voice. And out of the pack of large, kilted Scotsmen slid a slight Englishman as calm, quiet, and nondescript as any civil servant wandering the House of Commons. His urbane nature made him as incongruous and as appealing as cheese in a pickle shop.

Lady Kingair relaxed and glanced at the man almost affectionately. "Yes, you're far better at arranging these kinds of things, aren't you, Beta?"

Prim dismissed the man instantly as uninteresting and stepped forward to engage one of the largest and best-looking of the kilts in conversation, clearly having decided that Rue had this encounter well in hand. Quesnel stayed fixed at Rue's elbow, although blessedly disinclined to open his mouth.

The unassuming Englishman gave Rue a little bow. He had sandy hair and pleasing if unmemorable features arranged under a small set of spectacles. His evening attire was perfectly appropriate to the place and venue but nothing more, with no hint of modishness. Everything about him was simple, unadulterated, and proper. Rue was not surprised that she hadn't noticed him when the pack first entered the room. He hadn't wanted her to.

"How do you do, Lady Akeldama?" said the man. "Professor Randolph Lyall, at your service."

Rue had heard somewhat of Professor Lyall. She knew he had been her father's Beta but left when she was too young to remember. He'd gone off to take up the mantle of Kingair Pack Beta, and Uncle Rabiffano, newly made werewolf at the time, had taken his place at Rue's father's side. Professor Lyall wasn't spoken of often by the London Pack, but when they did it was with a respectful wistfulness. Even Uncle Channing, who didn't really like anyone but himself, hadn't a bad word to say about Professor Lyall.

Rue smiled at him. As with Lady Kingair she resisted the urge to give him a hug. For entirely different reasons. A hug would have unsettled her niece; Professor Lyall simply looked like he needed one. "Uncle Lyall, how nice to meet you at last. Please call me Rue."

Professor Lyall blinked at this instant acceptance, mildly bemused.

Lady Kingair, on the other hand, seemed to take it amiss. "She *is* here for us. It must be time, Lyall."

The Beta shook head. "Don't be hasty, Alpha. I would have been warned."

"Oh, are you still so well connected to London you can sense their mood from India?"

Professor Lyall gave his Alpha a level stare. "I know how to write letters and so do they."

He turned his back on his Alpha, something only a very strong Beta could do and stay alive.

Lady Kingair, surprisingly, took the snub and shifted away, giving them a modicum of privacy.

Professor Lyall offered Rue his arm. "Would you care for a stroll about the garden, Miss Rue?"

"Oh dear, I'm afraid Prim's reputation couldn't stand any more garden strolling tonight."

"Pardon?"

"Could I take Primrose along as escort? Miss Tunstell, I mean."

"You trust her?"

"Of course."

"She is not so silly as her mother?"

"Not at all."

The sandy-haired werewolf nodded his approbation. "Remarkable."

"Mr Lefoux, would you fetch Prim for me? She seems to have been kilted."

Quesnel gave Rue a disgruntled look but made his way into the group of Scottish werewolves, who were getting a little rowdy, honing in on Primrose with consummate skill. He extracted her deftly and returned.

Rue said, "Professor Lyall would like the pleasure of my company for a stroll about the gardens. Would you kindly act as chaperone?"

"Oh, *now* you think about my reputation."

Quesnel trailed along as well, although Rue would have preferred he didn't.

Rue made quick introductions. "Primrose, this is Professor Lyall. Uncle, this is the Honourable Primrose Tunstell."

Primrose said, "How do you do, professor? My mother speaks highly of you."

The Beta's eyebrows rose. "Does she, indeed? How kind. The respect of a vampire queen is no small thing."

They meandered further into the garden, leaving pond and society behind. The grounds were full of exotic plants of strange shapes. There was steam-powered mechanical statuary as well, built to resemble animals or many-limbed gods, but capable only of dancing a pattern over and over, like the ballerina in a musical box. Here and there monkeys chattered abuse and hurled projectiles at them.

"They don't think much of werewolves," explained Professor Lyall.

Prim and Rue raised their parasols in defence. Nuts and small hard fruit made harmonious drumming noises as they bounced harmlessly off the taut cloth.

Rue said, "Well, Uncle?"

"I only wanted to say, Miss Rue, that the pack and I are at your disposal. Sidheag can be grumpy but she knows her duty to queen and country or we wouldn't be stationed here. If you are acting under the auspices of any of your parents in their formal governmental roles, we will aid you by any means necessary."

Rue was startled by such an offer. "Why, thank you very much."

Professor Lyall bowed. "And I am, most particularly, your servant."

"You trust me more than she does – why is that?"

"I've received several letters over the years extolling your virtues."

There was a mild despondency to his tone. Again, Rue sensed deeper troubles with his connection to the London Pack.

"Why does my niece think I am here to force Kingair back to London?"

"A bargain was struck, debts need to be paid. She has been waiting for the summons for years now. It has been longer than any of us expected."

"Oh, indeed?"

"Your mother's presence, I think. Amazing woman, your mother. She changes everything she touches, doesn't she?"

"Oh, yes? What kind of *everything* do you mean exactly?"

"Fate, one might say. And you, little one, are you the same? I have so many questions. Have you mastered your metanatural state? I have greatly missed the opportunity to learn the scientific details as you grow. How does the shift feel for you? What is it like to be a vampire one moment and werewolf the next? If you touch both simultaneously can you be both at once?" Academic curiosity must be how he had earned the moniker *professor*. He was also obviously trying to divert her attention.

"Please, professor, why is Lady Kingair needed in London?"

"Ah, no. It's me they need."

Rue rocked back slightly. "What?"

The reserved man shook his head in refusal and apology. "If your parents did not tell you, it's not my place."

A horrible thought occurred to Rue. "Are you, by chance, the negotiator? Is that why you need to speak to me alone? Are you representing Miss Sekhmet and her interests?" She hoped it wasn't the case, for that would mean the werewolves were acting against her father the vampire. Two supernatural interests at odds was never a good thing. Whole empires had crumbled because of it.

Professor Lyall arched an eyebrow. "Sekhmet? The Egyptian goddess?"

Rue was relieved by his confusion. *Right then, so far, purple dresses notwithstanding, they had yet to meet Miss Sekhmet's contact for the other side of the tea situation.* "Never mind," said Rue.

Professor Lyall was calm in the face of mystery. He said only, "Little one, the purpose of this conversation is merely to say that I am here if you need to call upon a werewolf." He gestured, without rancour, to his bare forearm. "In any capacity you require, metanatural. Any capacity at all. You understand?"

Rue inhaled in shock. It was the first time a werewolf had ever offered to share his form without question or restriction. Usually, she had to steal supernatural shape from a reluctant donor and apologise for it later. She found his offer touching.

"Thank you very much, Uncle Lyall. I am honoured, but I hope that won't be necessary."

The Beta smiled. "As do I, Miss Rue, as do I." With another small bow he glided off, leaving Rue, Primrose, and Quesnel slightly dumbfounded.

They watched his slight form disappear through the trees, dodging monkey projectiles with supernatural swiftness.

"Did he just offer what I think he offered?" asked Primrose.

Rue nodded, eyes wide.

"What an odd little man," said Prim. "Nice, but odd."

"He seems very capable," replied Rue. "I like him."

Quesnel, being French, picked up on emotions. "He seemed rather sad." It was an oddly serious thing for him to say and he shrugged it off with, "Beautifully tied cravat for a werewolf."

They followed said werewolf's retreating form, conscious that they had been neglecting their collective social duties and had left Percy, of all people, to take on the lion's share of the obligation.

They found the redhead holding his own in a spectacular manner. Surrounded by eligible young ladies, and a few who were not at all eligible, Percy was waxing loquacious on the breeding habits of chilli peppers. He was explaining, with the comestibles on offer as his sample specimens, why ingesting spicy food caused overheating of the body, heart palpitations, and occasional irregularities in the magnetic energies of the human brain – particularly in impressionable young ladies.

Said impressionable young ladies were duly impressed by this lecture.

The hostess was looking acutely embarrassed at the very idea that she had included truly spicy native cuisine in her offerings.

Percy caught sight of them coming up. "Here, let me demonstrate – try this." He held out a small bit of flatbread, dipped into a reddish curry.

Rue, who was always game for a new experience, took it and ate it with alacrity.

All the impressionable young ladies, who had no doubt eaten the same on more than one occasion before Percy had come into their midst and begun soliloquising upon its dangers, gasped. They watched her with round eyes, anticipating tragic gastronomic reactions.

Rue liked the flavour well enough but, in truth, it was spicy. "Goodness," she said, politely, to Mrs Godwit, "that's quite lovely. It is a bit hot. Might I have a spot of that milk and soda water to wash it down, please?"

Mrs Godwit, grateful for Rue's complacent response, gestured at one of the staff to pour.

Primrose followed Rue's lead, trying a bit of the curry herself. She coughed a little, but carried it off beautifully, "Delicious."

Neither young lady fainted, came over with some exotic rash, or appeared to experience any magnetic misalignment.

Percy harrumphed. "It must not be all *that* spicy." He broke a bit off the bread and, pinky up in the air, dipped the tip tentatively into the curry sauce. Then he tried a tiny nibble.

Pure chaos ensued.

"Argh – water – I'm dying!" yelled Percy.

The impressionable young ladies closed in, offering him drinks, cooling cloths, and scented handkerchiefs.

Percy screwed his eyes shut and grabbed his throat, wheezing and coughing.

"Give the man some air," suggested Quesnel, barely disguising a guffaw. "Can't you see he's suffering?"

Percy cracked one watering eye to glare at him. "It burns!"

Rue, sensing the mood, shouldered into the solicitous group and grabbed Percy, just as a caring older sister might. "Come along, Percy dear, I think it's time we got you home."

The impressionable young ladies all twittered objections and sighed in distress. As indeed did Primrose, who, even with the Kingair Pack departed, would have been happy to redirect her flirting back at the hapless Lieutenant Broadwattle for the rest of the evening.

Rue, on the other hand, wanted to read her coded message. Or at least try to. And there seemed no indication that Miss Sekhmet's contact was going to approach either her or Primrose. So she assisted the sputtering Percy in making their farewells.

They walked back to the ship, Percy hacking dramatically the entire way.

"Prim, did anyone try to negotiate anything with you? As if you were me? Anything to do with tea perhaps?" Rue asked.

Prim said, "One of the officers tried to invite me to tea tomorrow without a chaperone. I turned him down, of course. I have more of a care for your reputation than you do mine."

"I am sorry about that. But it was necessary."

"Mmm, that's always your excuse."

"I talked with Dama's contact, finally, but I wonder what happened to Miss Sekhmet's tea negotiator. He seems never to have shown up, which means we wore purple for nothing."

"He probably went where all good tea negotiators go. Bottom of a cup."

"Prim, that is not helpful."

At that juncture, Percy's coughing reached such a crescendo that they could no longer carry on a civil conversation. Many of those acquainted with the Tunstell twins believed only Prim had inherited their parents' flare for drama. But Rue knew full well that Percy could produce more than his fair share of theatricality when called upon.

Chilli pepper consumption appeared to call for it.

Quesnel, for his part, was taking every opportunity to whack Percy on the back, as hard as possible without causing permanent damage.

"Your brother is a ridiculous man," said Rue to Prim. "It wasn't *that* spicy."

Primrose said, "In his defence, it did burn all the way down. Not unlike cognac."

Rue was arrested. "How do *you* know what cognac tastes like?"

Prim replied, as though it were nothing of significance, "Queen Mums likes a snifter of an evening."

"Baroness Ivy Tunstell, vampire queen, drinks *cognac*?"

Prim grinned. "Apparently Madame Lefoux introduced it to her back when they were girls."

Quesnel did not look surprised at the sudden appearance of his mother in this particular conversation. Rue wondered if that meant that Madame Lefoux made a habit of corrupting young ladies with cognac.

Rue blinked in amazement. "Your mother shared this habit with you?"

"Not exactly. Percy and I used to sneak a sip upon occasion, because we weren't supposed to."

"Percy drinks cognac?"

"Ladies," rasped Percy, "I'm walking right here."

Rue and Prim ignored him.

Prim said smugly, "Well, yes, old Percy's very cultured in the matter of spirits."

"Madness." *I guess one can still learn something new about friends of twenty years.* "Clearly I'm going to have to instruct our cook to stock cognac."

Primrose looked at her brother thoughtfully. He glared back, eyes still watering slightly. "Perhaps not the best idea. Percy has been known to overindulge."

"Still *right* here," he said.

Rue and Prim continued to ignore him.

"Percy gets looped?" Rue hooted.

"Yes, rather like now."

Percy drew himself up and said with considerably dignity, "I am not at all looped. It's simply that I don't like chilli peppers."

"I should like to see Percy looped," commented Rue, meaning it.

Quesnel took a strange sort of pity on Percy. "Are they always like this around you, old man?"

Percy was morose. "My whole life."

Quesnel said, "No wonder you're so deranged."

Percy sniffed. "Thank you very much."

"It's a wonder you don't drink *more* cognac." Quesnel didn't bother to hide his grin.

Percy sighed. "Yes, well, if you've all had enough fun teasing poor old Percy for one evening?"

"It never gets old," answered his sister.

The tide had progressed inward, causing *The Spotted Custard* to tie in closer to the promenade, making their walk back shorter than their walk out. The hot evening had become almost temperate, quite bearable. Rue was enjoying herself – she'd met Dama's contact, received a code, uncovered possible scandal from her parents' past, and encountered long-lost relations. Not to mention the fact that there had been a kidnapping recently. India, she thought, was turning out to be a delightful place.

Unfortunately, when they arrived back at the ship things took a turn for the worse. They could not board, for the gangplank was hauled in. Arranged up on the main deck was a row of fierce-looking sooties, decklings, and Greaser Phinkerlington, all armed with slings and other projectiles. Down below, standing on the shore, trying to look like he didn't care, was a man.

"'Ware, Lady Captain," shouted Spoo, the moment they were within earshot. "We got us an uninvited vampire."

CHAPTER NINE

Rakshasas

The vampire turned to face them. Rue expected him to look like any other vampire, only Indian in appearance. Mostly, he did. Mostly. But it was in the vein of how a broad bean looks like a runner bean – different, but both still beans. He had thick dark hair, a straight nose, high cheekbones, and a dark complexion combined with the clear smooth skin indicative of immortality. His facial topiary was questionable, being one of those large thick moustaches that curved down and around below the cheeks before connecting to the hair above the ears. An unflattering statement at best, but not one he could really be blamed for selecting. It was probably the height of fashion when he was metamorphosed. Poor vampires – so obsessed with style yet often cursed to look decades behind the times.

The crew of *The Spotted Custard* had, at least in part, been assembled by a vampire. One might expect them to be amenable to a visit from the supernatural. However, it was clear why they stood arrayed against this vampire, for he was too different a bean.

This was quite possibly the most unpleasant-looking creature Rue had ever had the misfortune to meet. His fangs were larger than those of British vampires and closer to the front of his mouth so that they protruded, and could not be tucked respectfully away under the lips. And those lips, while well-shaped, were red and moist and curled at the edges. His eyes appeared sunken into his skull with circles so dark that the skin looked black. His fingernails were long and wickedly sharp and shone with some oily substance in the moonlight. He smelled of carrion.

All vampires smell of rotten meat to werewolves. Rue was not in wolf form, yet her inferior human nose wrinkled in disgust at the powerful odour. Vampires at home were not as obvious about what they were and how they ate. Dama, for example, always smelled of lemon pomade. He also had no moustache to speak of. This creature showed outwardly that he was a bloodsucker, with no pretence at anything civilised. The lack of artifice was off-putting, not to say embarrassing, and explained the crew's reaction.

The vampire had an unctuous way of moving. His eyes were so full of malevolence that Rue actually thought he might charge and bite without even the courtesy of a greeting, let alone an introduction.

Rue stepped to the front of her group and pulled off her gloves. She was repulsed by the very idea of touching this creature. She would not want to turn into such a being, even as a lark, but she had better be ready in case it became necessary.

Quesnel took position on her left, pushing back his coat and shirt sleeve to expose the dart emitter strapped to his wrist. She knew without having to check that Percy had extracted the long sharp wooden cravat pin he always wore and that Prim had pulled out the tiny little crossbow she carried in her reticule and armed it with a wooden dart. All four of them had parents who saw no harm in training children to protect themselves. And all of those parents – whether supernatural or not – knew what form that protection should take when faced with a vampire.

The creature drew back his lips further and actually hissed at them like a rat.

"Pardon you," said Rue. If one already looked as ugly as he did, there was absolutely no call for hissing.

He darted at her. Rue raised her bare hands. Her best threat to any supernatural was her metanatural state. Few immortals could face the idea of being mortal, even for a short space of time. It was what made Rue's preternatural mother so universally despised. The idea that not only would he lose his form, but someone else would have access to it, was adding insult to injury. Where a soulless was merely the enemy, a soul-stealer was dishonourable, a defiler of the supernatural state. Rue was not just despised, she was vilified.

It was pure instinct which caused Rue to raise her hands in defence. And it was that very instinct which gave her away.

The vampire turned all his attention on her and spoke in broken English. "Soul-stealer. Go home. The Rakshasas do not welcome you here."

It was so reminiscent of Sekhmet's first approach that Rue wondered if this was the contact she was supposed to have met at the garden party. "Quite the unoriginal sentiment, I'm afraid," she said.

"You are not invited to India."

Rue sucked her teeth in exasperation. "I do not *have* to be invited. I am not a vampire."

"Go home to your tiny island. Or we will consider this a breach of our agreement with your queen."

Percy said, "There's no mention of metanaturals in that treaty."

Of course. Rue was pleased. *Percy read it before we arrived.*

"No, but she is like soulless. Like muhjah. And muhjah is forbidden."

"I must say, like most daughters, I resent being accused of

emulating my mother." Rue jerked forward, pleased when the vampire lurched away. "Come a little closer, bloodsucker, and you'll see how *un*like her I am."

The vampire only repeated, "Go home, soul-stealer."

Percy said, taking a risk, "Actually, you yourself are currently in breach of the agreement. Local vampires are empowered by the crown as tax collectors, are you not? And we recently learnt those taxes have gone missing."

The vampire hissed again. "Soon. We will find the thief and return your taxes."

"Very well," said Rue primly. "After you have done that, I will go home. That seems a fair bargain."

The vampire growled something in his own language and slid off, moving as if he were skating on the promenade. He wore garments very like those of Sekhmet earlier that day, but dark in colour. As he slithered away, supernaturally fast, he seemed to fade into the night.

"What a pestilential gentleman," said Prim, putting her little crossbow back into her reticule. "Not at all like Queen Mum's vampires, I must say."

"Although equally responsive to threats of paperwork and legal action, thank you, Percy." Rue was grateful for Percy's keen interest in local bureaucracy.

"The Rakshasas," said Percy pedantically, "are a different breed altogether from our vampires. Much in the way that poodles and dachshunds are different breeds of dog. Rakshasas are reviled in India. Their position as tax collectors is an attempt by the crown to integrate them in a more progressive and mundane manner."

Rue said, "Oh, how logical. Because we all know ordaining someone as a tax collector is the surest way to get them accepted by society."

Prim said philosophically, "That's the government for you."

Quesnel seemed drawn out of his dislike of Percy into the science of the business. "Like Mr Darwin suggests? Vampires, like other creatures, evolved differently in different parts of the world?"

Percy was only too happy to elaborate. "That's one theory. They are, after all, the terminal predator. Perhaps in this part of the world, to feed on humans vampires needed more fang and darkening around the eyes. Who's to know for certain?"

"Very attractive," said Prim.

"Some reports claim the Rakshasas eat living flesh as opposed to merely sucking the blood," Percy continued.

"Like a moon-mad werewolf?" suggested Rue.

Noticing his sister's repulsed expression, Percy added, "There are also stories of Rakshasas desecrating the dead and feasting on rotten corpses, but these may be more like our own early legends of vampires as monsters, before we got progressive and learnt the truth."

Rue considered the way the Rakshasa had smelled. "Or maybe not."

"Regardless, darling," said Prim to Rue, "you are clearly most unwelcome."

"Evidently. Shall we stay a while?" The two exchanged mischievous grins.

Quesnel rolled his eyes. "Lord save us all from beautiful young ladies too accustomed to the supernatural for good sense. You are pigeons in front of a hawk."

"Poppycock," said Rue. "I'm not beautiful."

"Don't be ridiculous," said Prim at the same time. "Pigeons have no natural predator except Rue."

Rue added, "And hopefully Footnote. And, frankly, I resent being compared to a pigeon. Nasty, dirty, chubby creatures. Are you saying I'm nasty, dirty, and chubby?"

Quesnel smiled. "Nope, I'm saying you are delicious and fluffy and squawk all the time. Perhaps I should call you ma petite pigeonneau."

Rue refused to dignify that with an answer. Instead, she called up to her crew, who had been watching the entire interchange with interest and were still fully armed. "Permission to come aboard?"

Aggie Phinkerlington, much as if the ship where her personal property, said, "Permission granted." The redheaded greaser shouldered her crossbow. Hers was larger and more deadly-looking than Prim's and it was interesting to note that she owned one. Rue would wager on Greaser Phinkerlington being an excellent shot. Rue had no concrete reason. Aggie simply seemed the type of female mean enough to be good with a crossbow. Aggie disappeared belowdecks, presumably before anyone could engage her in civilised conversation or attempt to be nice to her or anything revolting like that. The sooties followed. Rue had intended to commend them for managing the Rakshasa situation. Too late now.

"Lower the gangplank, please," requested Rue politely of the decklings.

Spoo's voice called out, "Aye aye, Lady Captain."

The gangplank cranked down in a massive puff of steam, the decklings chattering and groaning with collective effort.

Rue's party climbed on board. Rue ensured the gangplank was pulled in and locked closed, and that the ship was belayed to float as high out as possible, beyond the leaping distance of even the most powerful werewolf. Primrose settled the rattled nerves of the youngsters with soothing talk and profiteroles. Percy slouched uncomfortably, and Quesnel took a moment to ensure everything was in working order.

Rue felt utterly exhausted. It seemed to have been an overly long evening. The others looked much the same, but when they would have dispersed to their beds, Rue insisted that Quesnel, Primrose, and Percy join her in the stateroom for a consultation.

"Prim dear, would you make a note, please? I think we should stock additional crossbows, and darts both silver-tipped and wooden. Perhaps we should put some thought into a defensive training program for decklings and deckhands?"

Primrose nodded.

"Oh, wonderful," said Quesnel. "You anticipate more such encounters?"

Rue said, "I come from a long line of people who attract trouble. It's best to be prepared, don't you feel?"

"When you put it like that, perhaps we should hire militia when we return to London?"

Quesnel was joking but Rue felt the suggestion was worth considering. "Prim, make a note of that too, please? I could ask Paw. He might know some candidates. Now, so we can get off to bed, the reason I asked you for a quick conference." Rue fished about in her cleavage.

Quesnel looked away.

Percy said, deadpan and brotherly, "Rue, please spare us. We have already had sufficient appreciation of your assets for one evening."

Rue gave him a quelling look and produced the slip of paper Lieutenant Broadwattle had given her. "As it turns out, the good lieutenant was Dama's contact in the matter of the tea. You remember the reason we are in Bombay? This is what he gave me."

The three passed the slip of paper between them. It ended up in front of Percy.

"It's a code of some kind."

"Yes, it is. Brilliant deduction, Percy. Now, you're the don of this operation – what does it say?"

Percy stood to retrieve a roll of parchment and a stylus from a nearby sideboard. He began making notes and doing sums, while Prudence explained about Lieutenant Broadwattle being Dama's redundancy agent and the fact that her real contact was the recently kidnapped brigadier's wife, Mrs Featherstonehaugh. She also explained that she felt there was another interested party, also after the tea, represented by Miss Sekhmet and possibly the Rakshasas. While she had expected to be approached at the party, that element had never appeared.

Eventually, Percy looked up from the bit of paper. "Nothing basic. Nor is it algorithmic. It may be something I'm not quite able... That is... the numbers don't translate to letters of the alphabet nor is it any variation or foreign language with which I am familiar. My guess is that it is based on a book of some kind. See here? The first is always a number between one and about two hundred, the second between one and thirty, then the third between one and ten. It follows that the first is a page number, the second a line number, and the last the word in. So each set of three numbers represents a word in a text, thus constructing a complete correspondence. Without knowing the book, it's meaningless."

Rue and Prim looked at one another.

Rue said, "I think we know the book. Prim, if you would be so kind?"

Prim scurried off to Percy's library, returning a short while later clutching *Sand and Shadows on a Sapphire Sea: My Adventures Abroad* by Honeysuckle Isinglass.

Quesnel picked it up and read a few lines. He sputtered laughter.

Percy looked utterly mortified. "Why on earth would you think anyone would choose *that* as a cypher? And what are you doing with it, Tiddles? I thought we swore an oath never to grace it with—"

Prim said, "It's not my copy. It's Rue's."

"Rue, how could you?" Percy looked genuinely betrayed.

Rue held up a hand. "Before you accuse me of trading in family secrets, it was given to me by an agent of Dama's at the Maltese Tower. I had no idea why or what for, and I didn't know it had any bearing on your family. Now I suspect it is the means by which Dama transmits messages."

"Isn't it just like that vampire to use something so domestically embarrassing?" grumbled Percy.

Rue gestured encouragingly. "Go on. Test it and see if it works."

Percy did so, paging through swiftly and jotting down words until he had a full message written out on his parchment.

While he worked, Quesnel asked, confused, "Why domestically embarrassing?"

"Oh, it's nothing much, simply that Aunt Ivy wrote that book," answered Rue.

Quesnel chuckled. "The Wimbledon Hive Queen? Fantastic. Wait until I tell Maman."

"Don't you dare," instructed Rue. "It's a family secret. You are now sworn to safeguard it to the grave as a potentially damaging moral hazard. Not to mention our communication cypher."

Quesnel arched an eyebrow. "Am I, mon petit chou? I don't remember any swearing."

Rue narrowed her eyes at him.

Percy put down his stylus. "Well, there it is. The message makes perfect sense, so this book must be the code-breaker. Unfortunate indeed, but such is life."

"Ever full of our mother's embarrassments?" suggested Prim.

"What does it say?" Rue was dying of curiosity. She may have squirmed a bit in her seat. This was all so deliciously espionage-ish.

Percy passed it over so she could read it, at the same time offering up his own interpretation. "Essentially, he's changing our mission. He found out about his agent being kidnapped while we were in transit."

Rue examined it and then continued with her interpretation of the message. "It appears he wants me to go after Mrs Feather-stonehaugh. He thinks she may have betrayed him in the matter of the tea and that's why she was taken. The tea is in danger."

Percy crossed his arms and glared at Rue. "Tell them the rest of it."

Rue stuck her tongue out at him. She didn't want the others to know the remainder of their new instructions. Quesnel would make a joke of it and Primrose would worry.

Percy said, because it looked like she wouldn't, "Rue has been given sundowner dispensation."

"Oh, just *lovely*." Instead of teasing her, Quesnel lost all merriment and looked annoyed.

"That's me, licensed to kill supernaturals," said Rue blithely, feeling the strain at the back of her eyes, but making light of the matter for the sake of Prim, who looked like she might cry. "Ain't it topping?"

"I think Lord Akeldama is worried about the Rakshasas. Doesn't trust them. Thinks they may have stolen the taxes themselves," Percy added.

Rue shook her head. "I think it's most likely Paw overreacting. I bet he heard about the kidnapping, fears the worst, and pressured the Shadow Council into granting me permission to exterminate supernaturals. Or Mother thinks I'm going to accidentally kill an immortal and wants to reduce her paperwork."

"How did we go from tea to death so quickly?" wondered Quesnel.

"Sometimes," said Prim darkly, "there is a very fine line between the two."

"There's no *we*!" insisted Rue. "This is my responsibility. I've been given the role. Dama obviously doesn't trust any other agents here in India."

"Don't be an idiot," said Prim firmly. "Of course there's a *we*. Now, shall we do some collective cogitation? What did everyone learn at the party about this kidnapping?"

It was a great deal later on in the evening before they retired.

Rue was surprised to find, when she went to open the door to her captain's quarters, that Quesnel had followed her from the stateroom. She hoped the other two hadn't seen.

"You aren't going to take this sundowner burden to heart, are you, chérie?"

Rue looked into his violet eyes, her own yellow ones twinkling. "It is a sacred duty."

"Are you this flippant about everything?"

"That's rich coming from you." Rue only then realised he was being serious, or trying to be. Quesnel didn't wear serious very well. It looked ill-fitting on him – his mercurial face was pinched and his eyes sombre.

He said, "Dealing out death changes a person. I should not wish to see you so very altered and . . ." He trailed off.

Rue wondered what he might have said. "How would you know what death does?" she asked, not unkindly.

"I've been around it all my life. You know I was partly raised by my great-aunt when I was younger?"

"Yes?" Rue encouraged. She knew very little about Quesnel's childhood. When they'd first met, he was already at university.

"A ghost."

"Oh. So you watched her fade to poltergeist?"

"I did."

"But you have not killed anyone yourself?"

A quick flash of his old charming grin. "Not as far as I know. Perhaps in matters of the heart."

Rue made the only promise she could. "I will do my best not to use this power, but if we are going after this kidnapped woman and the Rakshasas do have her..."

"You would do it?"

Rue tried to be serious. She wasn't all that good at it either. It probably looked worse on her than it did on Quesnel. "I believe I could kill one of *them*, if I had to. He was *very* rude."

"Yet they are vampires, and you were raised by a vampire. You would have more trouble than most, I think." Still so serious.

Rue wanted to tell him to stop. This conversation was making her uncomfortable. "Perhaps that's why the Shadow Council decided to grant me sundowner status. They knew I would struggle with death dealing – morally as well as physically."

"I cannot believe your mother would allow such a burden."

Rue stiffened. She may not always get along with her mother but she would not have her maligned. "My mother knows her responsibility to queen and country. She would not have permitted the conference of sundowner status if she didn't think I could handle the repercussions." Perhaps that was part of Rue's own ready acceptance: *Mother is actually treating me like an adult.*

"Indeed? And has she ever been a sundowner?"

"No, only a licensed exorcist. But Paw's held the title since he became head of BUR."

"And how has your father handled the repercussions?" Quesnel wondered.

Rue considered this question. Really considered it for the first time in her life. She had always known that her adored Paw was one of the few men in Britain authorised to hunt and kill vampires and werewolves as needed. But she'd never thought much about how he felt about that, nor indeed how the rest of the supernatural community might regard him as a result. It must be lonely. That Rue could understand. Her three parents had tried hard to bring her up without spoiling her overmuch, but Rue knew she was unique in the world. There weren't even historical records of metanaturals, only rumour and hearsay. It was an odd kind of loneliness, like being the last of a dying race. Would she be further ostracised if she killed as well?

"Paw is Paw – things mostly roll off him. How else could he survive marriage to my mother?" she answered at last.

Quesnel cradled her face in his hands. "Don't accept sundowner status, chérie. You can say no."

Rue shook her head against his touch. "All three of my parents serve the crown with grace and integrity. If the Shadow Council trusts me with this, I will accept the responsibility. It is an odd birthright, but it's mine. Besides, why do you care?"

Quesnel lowered his hands. "You are amazingly frustrating. Has anyone ever told you that?"

"Frequently. It's part of my charm."

Quesnel turned all French on her in an instant. His eyes back to twinkling. "Very well, mon petit chou, I think I should kiss you now, before you are corrupted by circumstances beyond our control."

"Very melodramatic of you. And yet here I find it is you who is bent on my corruption." Rue tilted her head, as if considering an offer of new gloves. Inside she was properly thrilled. They shouldn't, of course, but Rue had never had a real kiss from someone she actually liked. And she suspected Quesnel might be pretty good at it.

She closed her eyes. "Very well then, do your damnedest."

Quesnel, as it transpired, was a good kisser. All those fancy ladies, Rue supposed. Not that she had much fodder with which to build comparisons. But she certainly enjoyed it. His lips were warm and firm, but not too firm. Halfway through she could feel him smile in the creasing of his cheek against hers.

Only Quesnel, she thought, *would have the temerity to smile during an embrace.*

His arms were gentle around her, strong enough to know she was supported, but not so tight as to feel confining. His hands curled about her waist, warm and strong. He took his time, exploring her lips with his, and eventually her body with those hands. *He's rather wicked*, thought Rue happily.

Rue was a believer in experts. She felt it was always best to identify the expert and trust their abilities in the matters of shoe leather or embroidery work or opera singing. Quesnel had the reputation as an expert in the matter of seduction, so Rue committed herself utterly to his expertise. She supposed that made him a rake, but a good one.

She tried tentatively to imitate some of his actions. She was worried about being thought inferior in the matter of intimate relations. Or worse, prudish. Rue took seriously a statement Primrose once made in admiration when they were ten that Rue was "always game for a lark".

Rue found she was battling Quesnel's lips for dominance and was not sure about that. But she did enjoy running her own hands over his warm back, exploring the indented line of his spine and even – greatly daring – trailing her fingertips down to his posterior.

At which juncture Quesnel stopped kissing her.

Rue was disappointed.

"That's more than enough of that," he said. His voice was a little raspy and his accent stronger than normal.

"Oh, is it? Just when I thought I might be grasping the way of things. Did I bungle it? I haven't had much practice."

"Oh, chérie, I assure you you did very well indeed."

"I did?"

"Hidden talents." His violet eyes positively sparkled.

Rue was chuffed. "Marvellous. I always wanted to be good at something."

"Well, don't go practising with just anyone now, please?" Quesnel looked faintly serious again but only in a flirty way, which was reassuring. They were back on familiar ground. Or as familiar as just having kissed could get.

Rue paused, pretending to consider the suggestion. As if there were anyone else around suitable to further experimentation. "Oh, very well, if you insist."

Quesnel grinned, showing dimples. "I do."

Very daringly, Rue said, "I could take you on in a trial position, as a kind of tutor? You are, after all, years older than me and very experienced."

Quesnel looked a little shocked.

Look at me go, thought Rue. *More daring than the rake himself!*

"Can I think about it?" he quavered.

Rue stuck her nose in the air, hurt that he hadn't leapt at the chance. "Well, if you feel you can't be discreet with my reputation..."

Quesnel's eyebrows arched. "I think it is more that you had better be clear with me on the perimeters of the position on offer."

Rue frowned. "Well, you know, courting and romance and stuff. I'd like to learn, personally, in a low-risk, scientifically experimental situation."

Quesnel made a funny *eep* noise. "*Low risk?* Should I be insulted?"

Rue laughed at him. "Don't be silly. You and I both know you have a reputation to maintain."

"Oh, do I?"

Rue continued blithely on. "The reputation of not playing for real stakes and keeping your wagers small and, mostly, circumspect."

"Ouch, mon petit chou. You wound me."

"The truth, she hurts sometimes. So I think we could play this as a private game, don't you?" Rue thought she should pucker up her lips seductively to get him to kiss her again. Then she thought she'd look fish-like. Or would she? This was why she needed his help!

Coincidentally, Quesnel looked not unlike one who had swallowed said fish. Apparently, his suave manners in the arena of romance paled before Rue's bluntness. "I think it would be best if I headed to bed at this juncture. Alone. Good night, chérie."

"Good night, Quesnel." Rue was amazed to think she had actually scared him off.

She noticed that he walked a little funnily as he wended his way down the hallway to his own room.

Of course, later on, Rue could not help running back over the experience in her head, staring into the darkness despite her exhaustion and the lateness of the hour. Perhaps she shouldn't go around attempting to arrange a liaison with her chief engineer. Then again, how else was she supposed to learn anything useful about romance? Quesnel had always flirted but never for one moment had she supposed him serious in his interest. He couldn't fear for his bachelorhood, could he? She shuddered at the very idea she would set out to trap anyone in to matrimony. However, the only other explanation for his reluctance was worse. Surely he couldn't be so very *not* serious that he wasn't attracted to her at all? Had he been faking everything? Perhaps she was too respectable? Rue was tolerably certain she did not want to be accused of being another one in a long succession of Quesnel's fancy ladies. On the other hand, she also didn't want to be Mrs Lefoux anytime soon. She'd thought that she'd come up with a good solution. Why had he reacted so badly? Had she not made her feelings clear?

For the first time in her life, Prudence Alessandra Maccon Akeldama actually wished for the advice of her mother. Unfortunately, said mother was thousands of leagues away, and probably wouldn't be much help. She'd simply suggest hitting Quesnel over the head with a parasol. Her on-board confidants would be equally useless. Primrose was too respectable and Percy too disinterested.

I'm on my own with this one.

Early next morning Spoo roused them with the information that Lieutenant Broadwattle's promised guide was waiting onshore. The guide turned out to be female. She looked terribly familiar, an inordinately tall and beautiful woman swathed in white robes.

Rue was beginning to understand the difference between masculine and feminine garb, and these were the drapes worn by men. Did Miss Sekhmet wish to be mistaken for a man? She supposed the woman was tall and thin enough to carry it off, with her face covered. While her movements were smooth and sensual, they were not precisely feminine.

Rue could see that such apparel might be cooler than her own red-check walking dress with the cream pleated shirtwaist, high neck, and puffed sleeves. She wondered what might be said if she wore a loose tunic and trousers. Since she'd started down the path towards doom by canoodling with a mechanically minded Frenchman only last night, the possibilities seemed endless. *Why stop there? Dress reform!*

All unaware of Rue's revolutionary thoughts, Quesnel and Primrose joined her, and they all made their way down the gangplank.

Quesnel seemed actually tongue-tied in the face of Miss Sekhmet's beauty. A state no doubt entirely unfamiliar to him.

She seemed to have little or no interest in the engineer.

She showed, however, good grace when meeting Primrose.

"You're our guide?" Prim whispered, her vaunted composure shaken.

Rue, who liked stirring the pot, said, "Miss Sekhmet here represents the counter-interests I was telling you about. Speaking of which, what happened to your negotiator last night? I wore purple and everything."

Sekhmet's lip curled. "Hence the reason I am here now and not your scheduled guide." She looked awfully tired. "Rakshasas got him. Glad you weathered the encounter last night."

"Not very nice, are they?"

"I did warn you. You knew we were not the only players in India."

"Of course, but I didn't think the others would be so very supernatural."

Sekhmet gave her a funny look at that statement.

"How come you yourself are unable to conduct negotiations?" Rue asked.

Sekhmet gave her another funny look. "Do I seem like the type? Among other things, I'm a woman. I can't speak for *them*."

"Local custom? If you say so. You seem capable enough to me."

"And now it's daytime. So we must wait again."

"What's your interest then?" Rue wanted to know.

"Me? Balance, I suppose." Miss Sekhmet got all philosophical. "And keeping you safe. You are our miracle."

Rue was instantly suspicious. "Did Paw send you?"

"I know not of the Paw. But, Lady Akeldama, you are the *only* one of your kind."

"You say that as if she were some rare exotic species and you a collector," Primrose interjected softly. Prim was prone to getting protective of Rue when people saw only her friend's metanatural state, and forgot she was also a person.

Miss Sekhmet made that funny little bow. "I apologise. No insult was intended. I understand your wish for freedom, I more than anyone." It sounded like a vow. "But I also value your uniqueness. In this instance, however, my function is only to act as a liaison and, at the moment, a guide. Come, allow me to show you this amazing city."

Rue didn't know why but she trusted the austere beauty.

Primrose was more cautious. Under cover of getting Rue to help secure her sun hat, she said very quietly, "She's too beautiful for words, but she's more than that."

Rue giggled. "Very astute observation." Her friend seemed to have been thrown for a loop by their new acquaintance, which never happened to Primrose.

"Oh, stop it!" said Prim, blushing. "Give me time to assess her character further. I'll be more articulate then."

Rue stopped grinning with an effort. "Come on – looks like we must rescue Quesnel. He's trying to flirt and she is having none of it."

Rue warmed to Sekhmet even more. Not only had she discombobulated Prim, but Quesnel was red-faced and stuttering. None of his charm had any effect on the goddess-like female. Miss Sekhmet was merely glaring at him as if he were some unpleasant bug, and rewrapping her head with the white cloth to hide her face.

"It's best if I'm not recognised and easiest if the locals think me a man," she explained when Primrose gave her an inquisitive look.

"Oh," ventured Prim, surprised by her tone. "Then you aren't a local yourself?"

"Somewhat further west," was their guide's reply. Odd thing to say, since west of Bombay was nothing but water.

Prim would have pressed but Miss Sekhmet began striding off

at quite a masculine speed, expecting them to follow. Quesnel offered the ladies his arms and they scuttled after. They caught up about halfway down the promenade, only to be hailed by one additional member to their party.

Percy came panting up behind them.

Introductions completed, Primrose regarded her twin, twirling her yellow parasol suspiciously. "You realise, brother dear, we are walking into a city full of people, not books?"

Percy stuck his nose in the air. "Yet there must be some reading material available to purchase or it wouldn't be a proper city. And how am I to learn the breeding habits of chilli peppers if I remain behind?"

"Very broadminded of you," commended Rue. "We certainly cannot be trusted to obtain the correct book without you." With which she raised her parasol and trotted after their guide, who seemed eager to get to the busy hubbub that was Bombay.

"Exactly," said Percy, running to catch up. Then, in a disquieting display of gentlemanly etiquette, he offered Rue his arm.

Rue took it. Prim took Quesnel's. Rue pretended not to feel a very slight twinge of envy that she would not get the benefit of Quesnel's teasing. Although the Frenchman seemed more sombre than usual. *Is he regretting our kiss?* Rue was saddened by the idea. *Or is it awe in the face of Miss Sekhmet?* Rue couldn't blame him for that.

The woman in question led them purposefully towards an open-topped steam carriage, arranged, she explained, because it was some distance to the nearest market. They climbed in and Prim lamented that she had chosen a walking dress instead of a carriage dress. The driver cranked up the engine, the stoker fed it anthracite, and they were off.

They drove north, away from the governmental structures and military areas, into the city proper. Immediately it became a

great deal more what Rue had expected of India. Miss Sekhmet
proved an excellent guide. She seemed genuinely to like the area
and pointed out landmarks, from the Black Bay Baths to the
Aetherographic Office of the Controller to the Scottish Cemetery.
They loosely followed the path of the railway lines to their right
and the elephant trolley skylines above.

Eventually, they rounded a corner onto Princess Street and their
steam carriage was forced to stop by the sheer number of people
assembled there. Miss Sekhmet explained that the famous Cloth
Market was to their right. She instructed the driver to wait and
they climbed down. Rue knew her eyes must be as big as saucers.
Prim's perfect rosebud mouth was slightly open in amazement.
Percy looked to be taking copious mental notes. Even Quesnel
was awed. Fortunately, it seemed local custom was not opposed to
staring. Even among such a crowd, Rue's group was a novelty and
much as they stared others stared back.

The Cloth Market was a hubbub of colourful fabrics and chattering humanity. Mostly people walked but some pushed massive baskets on wheels, others guided donkeys or camels loaded
with goods. The occasional horse and carriage bobbed through
the throng as well as bicycles, mono-wheels, human-drawn carts,
and other more peculiar means of transport. The sky rail above
their heads rumbled back and forth in seemingly endless rounds
of transportation from dock to industry and from military to
government, loaded down with massive swaying vats of cloth, or
lumber, or pottery, or furniture, or whatever else was important
at the time. Unlike London's transports, this sky rail seemed less
of an ugly imposition on the landscape with its cheerful elephant
visage. The wreaths of lanterns and flowers draped about its colossal head tilted at a jaunty angle.

Prim, enchanted, asked Miss Sekhmet about the elephant's
appearance.

"As far as I know, he has always been that shape. But the flowers and the others, that is for the celebration of Ganesha. Worshippers extol the elephant god this time of year. There is a particularly beautiful festival soon."

"How interesting." Prim sparkled at Miss Sekhmet, almost as if she were flirting, both her hands clutching the handle of her parasol in excitement. "And is the elephant a very revered god in local mythology?"

"Indeed he is. Most benign and helpful. One prays to him when one has a burden or an obstacle."

"And this festival?"

It was hard to tell when only her eyes were visible, but Rue thought Miss Sekhmet was smiling. "Among other things, they carry the god to the beach where he is put into the sea."

"Likes to bathe, does Ganesha?" wondered Percy.

Miss Sekhmet gave him a dirty look. "All elephants like water, Fire-hair."

They began to try moving through the street, clumped together because the crowds were so thick. Off to one side, a group of stunning dark-eyed dancers twirled, arms waving noodle-like in the air, gyrating to music so odd Rue actually wondered if it ought to be called music at all. It had a whining, haunting, angular quality.

It appeared that all daily business was conducted in the middle of the road. Men moved around in gossiping turbaned groups. The higher ranking women, in colourful shrouds, were followed by groups of servants and showed a marked preference for large brightly coloured fringed parasols which Primrose called "most respectable." Fruit and meats were exchanged, pottery and fabric haggled over. Rue even spotted a live snake.

"Everything is so bright and cheerful." She spun in delight. "And everyone smiles so much!"

Sekhmet asked Prim, "Is she always this excitable?"

Primrose, looking extremely dignified, answered, "I'm afraid so."

"How exhausting," replied their guide.

"You're telling us," grumbled Percy.

"It's one of her charms," defended Quesnel.

But it *was* so bright and cheerful.

Rue was particularly fascinated by the consumption of a specific hot beverage, the earthenware mugs of which were then cast aside into the street to crumble to dust under the many feet walking by. Everyone seemed to be drinking it. Where was the vendor?

A Cederholm Condenser muscled its way through, obstructing Rue's view and blasting hot steam from its carapace. The people around scampered away to avoid being burned. The smoke from its small antennae stacks was somehow dyed bright pink, which coloured the unwary with speckles of pigment, to no one's surprise or avoidance. Prim shrieked, parasol up in defence of her yellow walking gown, although the smoke was nowhere near her.

Rue was seized with a mad desire to dance through it – it looked like fun.

Eventually, they made their way to the Cloth Market proper, which was, as advertised, mainly cloth with a few other vendors. Tethered at corners of the square were hot-air balloons, the primitive floating technology of yore still alive and well in parts of the empire. Rue's mother had once told her a story of the Balloon Nomads of the Sahara, how they floated their patchwork giants above the desert. *Anitra*, remembered Rue suddenly. Hadn't she said something about floating? Perhaps that was the connection. Here the balloons were also patchwork, and Rue wondered if these were distantly related tribes, or if it were merely the nature of ballooning that lent itself to patchwork.

Despite being early morning, it was not a sleepy gathering. The locals were enamoured of singing and yelling and laughter. Grey and black monkeys scampered through the crowd, hands in everyone's baskets and business. Miss Sekhmet picked up a stick which she applied adeptly to any monkey, curious child, or beggar that approached Rue's party with overly familiar intent. The monkeys, she explained, were considered reincarnated politicians, which made Rue laugh and the stick entirely understandable.

Quesnel had to restrain Primrose forcefully since she was intent on diving towards a display of colourful fabric. "Oh, but Queen Mums would so love that colour," she kept saying. And then, "I'm delighted I wore my brightest dress today. Yellow seems in keeping with the spirit of the festivities, wouldn't you say? Only *look* at that shawl."

"Later, Prim," Rue would reply, and then, "Yes, excellent choice. My peach feels quite drab. No, not the shawl! We are attempting to get the lie of the land, not shop."

Inevitably, they found themselves in an area where the amalgam of goods saw Rue's party spontaneously split apart despite her best efforts. Primrose spotted a sari shop full of such stunning embroidered cloth as to be utterly impossible to resist. Quesnel saw that the massive steam Ganesha had come to a stop overhead and went to look for a way to climb aboard and examine the machine up close. Finally, Percy noticed a combined chilli vendor and books stall and all was lost.

"So much for the group tour." Rue found herself alone with Miss Sekhmet in the centre of a busy marketplace.

The guide seemed pleased with this. "A chance to speak privately."

Rue gave a pointed head waggle at the craziness around them — anything but private.

Miss Sekhmet continued. "I must confess to an ulterior motive,

Lady Akeldama. As you may have guessed they will not meet you
here, not when one of their own has already been eliminated. We
are at an impasse and I would like to prevent conflict. Have you
had an opportunity to contact the muhjah? Has she changed her
mind concerning involvement?"

Rue nibbled her lip. "Last night, at the garden party, I did receive
some unexpected instructions. It was a busy evening. I must look
into another matter now. Your interests will have to wait."

The guide looked disappointed. "They will not be pleased.
They expected at least an amendment to the agreement."

Rue raised a hand. "Wait a moment – what agreement? Look,
are we discussing the missing tea or the missing taxes? I know I
should be all secretive and talk in code and all that rot, but there
are a lot of threads loose right now. My concern is the tea."

"You disguise your negotiating with bluntness? Very shrewd,
Lady Akeldama. Very shrewd indeed." Even only seeing her eyes,
Miss Sekhmet looked frustrated and exhausted. She signalled
and a man came over, a carafe of steaming beverage strapped to
his back, dispenser tubes down one arm with thumb-activated
nozzle, and mugs dangling from his waist. *So that's how they did it.*
Miss Sekhmet purchased two cups of the hot drink and led Rue
over to one side of the marketplace where they could sit atop a
low wall in relative privacy.

The beverage proved to be a tea unlike any Rue had sampled
before. Someone had actually thought it necessary to spice the
sacred drink with ginger, cardamom, cinnamon and a few other
things that had absolutely no place in tea. It was sweetened as
well. Rue grimaced but sipped it for the sake of politeness. She
found if she imagined it were a liquid pudding instead of tea it
went down easier.

Rue took a deep breath. She liked this odd woman. She wanted
to be liked in return. "Your pardon but I believe we may be at
cross-purposes. I mean no artifice at all, I swear it. You see, I had

understood our earlier conversation to be on the subject of some very valuable tea."

"Tea?"

"Yes, tea."

The guide's eyes crinkled in confusion. "But it was not."

Rue nodded. "I am realising that now. So what *have* we been discussing? I'm afraid you must think me very thick, but I cannot seem to get a straight word out of anyone since I was jumped by a lioness in a tower teahouse."

Miss Sekhmet seemed to sink into depression at that. She muttered, "Then the muhjah is not aware of the nature of our activities?"

Rue sighed, frustrated. "I am not privy to the workings of my dear mother's brain, thank goodness. She knows more than most, but she told me nothing significant about my travels here to India before I left. Did you send her a message hoping for a response from me? Or perhaps you represent a local political body?"

Miss Sekhmet seemed only more inclined to obtuseness by Rue's revelation of ignorance. "Why are the British always so against locals?"

"I don't follow. Have I offended in some way?"

The woman merely sipped her funny tea, deep in some moral quandary. "I thought you might be supportive. Or at least scientifically interested. But if they are once again denied? What point is there in my urging them to try? Everything is in confusion."

"You're telling me," said Rue with feeling.

"It's too sunny and I have a headache," Sekhmet complained.

"You do look knackered. Should you even be out playing our guide?" Rue resisted pressing Miss Sekhmet's hand in sympathy. "If you could articulate what is happening? The nature of the trade? The specifics of your demands? I might be able to help, even without my mother. I do have my own particular set of talents." She tried to be modest.

It was all lost on Miss Sekhmet, who was working herself up into an exhausted frenzy. "You know that your relationship is with the wrong ones, don't you?"

Rue was exhausted by the continued mystery and was starting to get a headache too. Finally she took a stab. "Do you represent the dissidents? The ones who stole the taxes and the brigadier's wife?"

"Is that what they are claiming has occurred?"

"Isn't it?"

Miss Sekhmet's beautiful eyes narrowed. "I assure you, Mrs Featherstonehaugh came of her own free will."

Aha, at last we are getting somewhere. "Oh, did she *indeed?*" *Dama's agent is a traitor! So what about the tea? Did she take it with her?*

Instead Rue said, "And the taxes, did they come of their own free will as well?"

Miss Sekhmet gave her an exasperated look. "Money attracts attention."

"You have my attention. What are your demands?"

She shook her head. "Oh, no. Not for me to say. I must tell them that you have not been contacted, challenged, or autho-rised. We will see what happens next. This is a grave setback."

Rue smiled. "I have been authorised, just not as you might assume."

"Yes?" she perked up at that.

"Oh no, if you can be cagy, so can I." *If they don't have the tea, no point in telling them about it. Whoever they* are.

They finished their repast, at an impasse. Betraying no little annoyance, Miss Sekhmet tossed her rough earthen cup to the packed dirt of the square where it shattered. Greatly daring, Rue followed her example. It was quite satisfying.

The marketplace was only getting more crowded and hot and

stifling. Rue would not have thought this possible a mere ten minutes ago.

"Perhaps," she suggested, "we should round up my companions and you can guide us back to our craft? Then you can contact your friends for the next move in this little game?"

"Very well." Miss Sekhmet looked unhappy about it, but there was no other course of action.

So it might have happened, except that a roving flower stall, heavily laden and pulled by a steam locomotive of antiquated design, rolled to a stop in front of them, neatly trapping them in their small corner of the square.

"Ho there!" said Rue, banging on the top of the engine with her parasol.

Miss Sekhmet leaned over to talk to the driver, a discussion that escalated rapidly into a virulent argument in the local dialect, punctuated by copious hand gestures.

Then the flower stall exploded.

Rue acted on instinct. Growing up with parents like hers, she'd become accustomed to spontaneous explosions – of beauty products, parasols, or tempers, depending on the parent. She threw herself back and over the low stone wall she'd so recently been sitting atop. She rolled and landed, surprisingly gracefully, on the other side, crouched down, parasol raised up over her head to shield herself from the rain of flowers, leaves, and stalks.

She peeked over the wall in time to see Miss Sekhmet, insensate, being loaded into the now empty flower stall. A team of suspicious-looking black-clad men scuttled about as nefariously as anything. They were arguing with one another. Rue stared, and then flinched when they pointed in her direction.

One moved towards her.

Rue stood, parasol at the ready. She would not crouch behind a stone wall like a coward.

The man was clearly reluctant to follow his orders, as frightened of Rue as she was of him. If he knew that she had metanatural abilities he clearly did not understand that they functioned only at night. Why else be wary of an Englishwoman alone and abroad?

Rue braced herself. He was but one man. She had a parasol.

He lurched in her direction as if he intended to leap over the wall. Rue prodded at him with the parasol tip as if she were a lion tamer. "Back, you ruffian! Back!"

Surprisingly, he backed away bewildered.

One of his fellows joined him. This appeared a source of courage, for they moved in, less frightened as a group.

There came a shout of anger and then a whizzing hiss sound. One of the men looked profoundly surprised for a split-second and then pitched forward, a dart sticking out of his neck. Rue did not risk a turn to see whose dart. She could very well guess. The second one shouted to his fellows before grabbing his fallen comrade and backing away from Rue.

Rue hopped over the wall — or, more precisely, *clambered* — and brandished her parasol at him threateningly.

The men loaded their fellow in on top of Miss Sekhmet, slammed the flower cart shut and, in a blast of pink steam, chugged off into the busy marketplace.

The steam cleared enough for Rue to see Quesnel standing, arm out, wrist following the departure of the stall, a look of such anger on his face as to strike fear into even Rue's questionable soul.

He said something quite rude in French.

"We must follow them!" insisted Rue. "I was almost getting answers." She pulled up her skirts, prepared, if necessary, to run the engine down on her own two feet.

Quesnel gave her a look that said he thought her unhinged. He was, perhaps, not wrong. For the flower cart had disappeared into the milling throng of a foreign city, with too many other steam engines and too much activity already hiding it.

Rue sighed. "Oh, very well." She crouched down and looked about the area where the explosion had occurred. She did not quite crawl among the fallen flowers, but that was only because she had not entirely forgotten her upbringing. She used her parasol to poke among the heads of decapitated blossoms and fallen leaves. She wasn't certain what exactly she was looking for but any clue was better than the nothing that currently befuddled her.

Quesnel came over and bent down. "What are we looking for?"

"Clues. Miss Sekhmet knew about the kidnapping and the dissidents. Someone didn't want her to tell us what she knew. I should not have engaged in such a public conversation with her. She kept trying to involve my mother. I think there is something seriously political going on. And we do not have nearly enough information. Curse Dama, he could have said *something*."

"Perhaps he didn't know?" suggested Quesnel.

"That would be highly unlike him but possible, I suppose. Too focused on tea."

Quesnel looked a little worried. "Are you in any further danger?"

"I don't think so. Hard to tell. You know, she said Mrs Featherstonehaugh went with the dissidents voluntarily. Then she said it had something to do with an *agreement*."

"The agreement that makes the Rakshasas the tax collectors?"

"That would be my guess. After all, the taxes were stolen too. Do you think we've stumbled into local economic hostility? How droll."

"Perhaps those black-clad men were Rakshasa drones putting a stop to any information that might be relayed against them."

"Or possibly these dissidents are setting the Rakshasas up to take the fall in an effort to keep the money themselves? From what Percy said, the locals are terrified by the very idea of vampires.

Do they have the courage to undertake direct opposition? Who is Miss Sekhmet working with?"

The flowers yielded up nothing concrete. Rue did find a small necklace – a bit of stone strung on a length of cord. The stone was carved to look like a monkey. Rue popped it into her reticule, uncertain of its significance – if any – and whether it might be connected to Miss Sekhmet, her kidnappers, or merely dropped by one of the hundreds milling about the square.

Rue said, "We'd better find Percy and Primrose. We must get back to the *Custard* and we've no guide any more."

They extracted Prim, laden down with bolts of cloth and packages full of embroidered shawls and scarves. "What happened? Where's our lovely guide? A flower cart exploded? Oh, Rue, really."

Quesnel said, deadpan, "Miss Tunstell, might I suggest in future that any time you hear an explosion, you check to see if our Prudence is involved?"

Rue objected. "It wasn't my fault. Never you mind it now, Prim. I will explain once we collect Percy. No sense in telling the story twice."

Percy was immersed in books and chillies. He was neither surprised nor worried to learn of the explosion, nor their lost guide. "I have a map of Bombay," he said, as if that alone could safely get them through an alien city.

Rue said on a sudden realisation, "Percy, we need books that illuminate the nature of the Rakshasas, and anything to do with the Indian agreement to the Supernatural Acceptance Decree. Anything at all. That is the parliamentary act under which the agreement that made local vampires tax collections would fall, yes?"

Percy was easily distracted. "Nature of the Rakshasas? Analytical or mythological books?"

"Both."

He dived back into the stacks all around him, emerging with

various volumes and bound journals, a few rolled parchments, some looking quite old, and a string of dried red chillies draped about his neck. "It won't be inexpensive."

Rue said, "I shall put them on the ship's account. You're going to have a great deal of researching to do when we get back. None of the rest of us reads Hindustani."

Percy gave her a look as much as to say *tell me something I don't know* and *could you please come up with something more challenging next time?* He said none of this, however, only grunted.

They purchased the books and the chilli necklace because it was better to stay on Percy's good side at the moment. Laden down with these, as well as Prim's fabric, they had to move quite slowly through the crowded streets.

Quesnel refused to carry anything and insisted that Rue keep her parasol hand free in case of further attack. So the twins bore the brunt of the burden, with no little complaining. But their enemy, whomever they might be, seemed content having extracted Miss Sekhmet.

No small thing, as it turned out. Without her guidance, it took them over an hour to find their way back to the steam carriage. Even with Percy's command of the language, it was another two hours to direct the driver back to the ship. All this despite, or perhaps because of, Percy's map. They had to stop several times for more of the spiced tea, which Rue was growing to enjoy and find most restorative, even in the heat. Starvation necessitated a pause for luncheon at a street-side stand where chunks of some mysterious meat of a remarkably vibrant red colour were roasted on sticks over large clay pots. Rue, Quesnel, and Prim nibbled happily, finding the flavour delicious. Percy refused, for fear of chilli, and only ate some fruit.

To try to raise their spirits, Quesnel told them all about the working of the elephant head. Unfortunately, no one was quite as excited as he about engineering. Still, it was nice of him to try.

Tired, dusty, sore, and overly hot, they finally returned to *The Spotted Custard.*

Percy immediately made for his room to begin reading. "Percy," instructed Rue, "do concentrate on the Rakshasas and how they relate to the agreement. This issue may become life-threatening by the time the sun sets. Please, don't get distracted."

Percy took offence. "Me? I never get distracted."

No one dignified that with an answer.

Prim retreated to her chambers to soak her sore feet in rose water, repair her hair, and admire her newly acquired fabrics.

Quesnel paused before going to his rooms.

Rue was too sunburned and grumpy to hope for another kiss.

Apparently, he felt the same, for he only gave her a long look. Or possibly he still hadn't decided if he wanted to be her tutor in matters of romance.

"You are unharmed from the incident with the flowers, chérie?"

"Only my pride. Thank you."

"If you're a true sundowner, where is your royal gun?" Quesnel asked, offended on her behalf.

Rue arched an eyebrow. "Good question. I shall bring it up with my family as soon as I get home."

"In the meantime, would you consider some form of projectile weapon? For my peace of mind, mon petit chou?"

Rue said, "The difficulty is in how to keep it with me if I change shape."

"Rue." He almost growled her name.

"Fine," said Rue. "I'll consider it."

"That's all I ask." With which he made to leave.

Rue forestalled him, "And have you been considering *my* offer? It's nothing important, you do realise? It was only a thought."

He actually winced at that, which hurt in a way she hadn't anticipated. Rue had thought she had presented him with an opportunity, but perhaps he saw it as a burden. Perhaps he had always seen her as nothing more than a meaningless flirtation and now she had placed him in an awkward position, as her chief engineer.

But his charm returned in an instant. "It is a gift, mon petit chou, and it *is* important."

Rue stumbled on, "But if it's too much a bother, I could seek elsewhere."

Quesnel's face shuttered over. "You must do as you see fit, chérie." Which, of course, was no answer at all. He gave her a small bow and retreated to his own quarters without even trying to touch her.

Rue thought she saw a flicker of movement in the doorway of Percy's room but wasn't certain. Percy would already be occupied with his research. Perhaps Virgil was being nosy? Hard to keep one's business private on an airship. She and Quesnel would have to be more careful about assignations in future.

Rue caught herself out with that. *Future assignations indeed! He hasn't even considered my terms.* He had taken Prim's arm as they walked that morning. And he'd been very taken by Miss Sekhmet. Clearly, she had overblown his flirting, and her own appeal.

He must be regretting last night's embrace. In which case, Rue was back to square one as far as romance was concerned. It was a lot more painful than she had anticipated, rejection.

Rue retired to her room to stare up at the ceiling and, in order to not dwell on a certain flirtatious French engineer, tried to think about who might have a grudge against Indian vampires. Which was the problem with vampires – almost everyone had a grudge against them.

CHAPTER

TEN

Vanara

R ue was wearing an old-fashioned skirt of lilac satin, mismatched to a bodice of burgundy velvet with elaborate beadwork about the neck. It was heavy for the weather and hugely inappropriate to Rue's rank.

"Goodness, chérie, you look like a lady of the night," was Quesnel's assessment. But his eyes were delighted and not at all critical as he took in her very well-emphasised figure.

Rue tilted her black velvet hat at him. Three seasons old when there had been a blessedly brief fad for sewing small gears to hatbands. "Do I really? Excellent!"

"Prudence Maccon Akeldama!" was Prim's opinion, rendered in a very high voice. "Is that rouge? On your lips? And your cheeks! And what on earth do you think you are wearing?" She looked as if she might faint.

Quesnel said, "I think it's delightfully flattering."

"It's certainly rather tight." Rue was trying not to breathe too deeply for fear of the seams bursting.

Percy said, "Suspiciously accurate, as these things go, if you ask me."

Prim responded to her brother. "No one did ask. And I'm shocked you would know."

Rue was further delighted. She twirled. She'd even left her hair down. It felt very wicked. "Is it possible I have a bad case of the spotted crumpet?"

Quesnel laughed. "The worst."

"I think we are ready to depart then." Rue and Quesnel turned to leave.

"This is a terrible idea," said Prim. Not for the first time.

"I agreed that Quesnel could come along only if you stopped questioning my judgement," responded Rue. Also not for the first time.

Before Prim could say anything more, Rue left the ship.

Quesnel followed, chuckling.

It was dark as they marched towards the werewolf barracks. It was the barracks that accounted for Rue's attire. Only one type of woman visited a soldier's den after hours. Rue tried to sashay in a manner she though such women might walk. This was not a role she felt comfortable in; she wasn't familiar with the nuances. She tried for movements and expressions that would appear worldly, but from Quesnel's ill-disguised grin she wasn't doing very well.

Quesnel was dressed in the part of her curator. Showing less skin, sadly, although his trousers were fantastically tight. His favourite top hat was turned to the seedy side through the addition of some very loud plaid ribbon. He'd even donned a small waxed moustache.

The fortress was quiet – presumably most of the military were off looking for the missing Mrs Featherstonehaugh, or fighting dissidents, or wheeling cheese, or whatever. The werewolves, unable to work during the day, would no doubt be conducting the night-time search. Rue hoped to catch them before they left. Or more precisely, she hoped to catch her Uncle Lyall.

There was a sleepy guard posted at the side entrance. He jumped to his feet at Quesnel's throat clearing, but didn't seem to know quite what to do when faced with a flesh dealer and his wares.

"Good evening," said Quesnel. "Mr Pinpod and a lady to call upon the Kingair Pack. Please inform them that we are here."

The man stuttered, "I wasn't told. That is – your names are not on the list. Sir and, uh, *lady*."

"They most certainly are," insisted Quesnel.

The young man looked terrified. He couldn't leave his post to check with his superiors, and he didn't want to cause a scandal.

"Oh dear. If you could wait a moment, miss, my lady? They should be surfacing soon."

No doubt he meant it literally. Werewolf attachments were often housed underground, for everyone's safety.

"At ease, private," came a calm soft voice, and Uncle Lyall materialised out of the shadows behind the relieved guard. "The lady is not unexpected."

Rue batted her lashes. "La, sir!" she simpered.

The guard eagerly ceded all responsibility to Lyall's authority. He resumed his post while the werewolf guided them inside and out of sight around the corner of a munitions building. "Herself is in a temper. I wouldn't bother her if I were you. Can I help?" He didn't even flinch at Rue's attire.

Rue smiled hopefully. "Actually it was you I wanted to see. It's Mrs Featherstonehaugh – I think she may be more important than anyone realised. I'd like to know more about her. Anything you can tell me would be useful."

Uncle Lyall shrugged. "We didn't socialise, I'm afraid. The brigadier is happy to have a werewolf attachment but unhappy to have a Scottish one. The pack was never invited to his private functions. Mrs Featherstonehaugh seemed nice enough, rather young. Bookish."

Rue perked up. "What did she like to read?"

"I never had the opportunity to ask. Do you think it important?"

"I've been charged with investigating," Rue replied cautiously. Was this estranged former member of Paw's pack trustworthy?

Uncle Lyall didn't seem to take this amiss. "Have you indeed? Well, my offer stands."

"What do you mean?"

"I mean the brigadier's quarters are there, second storey window. You could borrow my form and take a look for yourself if you like. He's out of town. Guards on the first floor."

Rue considered. "If I'm seen, Kingair would be blamed."

Uncle Lyall shrugged. "We're already in the soup for losing the chit in the first place."

Quesnel looked suspicious. "That's right. It was pack acting escort. You're certain you didn't socialise with Mrs Featherstonehaugh at that time? It's a long journey back from the hills."

Uncle Lyall didn't resent his honesty being questioned. "I wasn't with them. Left behind to act as pack anchor." His tone spoke volumes. Clearly he felt that if he had been with them, they wouldn't have lost the girl, and he blamed himself for not having kept a closer eye on things.

Rue thought for a moment. "Then I accept your offer. Have I ever stolen your form before, uncle?" She had been a holy terror in her childhood on this matter.

Uncle Lyall chose not to answer.

Quesnel said, "Mon petit chou, shouldn't you consider your nice dress?"

Rue snorted at him.

Quesnel managed to look both guilty and determined. "Well, I suppose we could get you another one."

Rue wasn't sure why but something in his tone both embarrassed and thrilled in a way that no romantic comment would have. *He likes it when I look a little less buttoned up, does he? I'll have to remember that.*

Uncle Lyall looked sharply at the young man but was too much a gentleman to say anything. Rue had the distinct impression he was taking mental notes on the flirtation.

Rue took her gloves off and touched the back of Uncle Lyall's bare hand to distract him.

It was painful. It was always painful. More painful even than the day before she got her monthly courses. She remembered, before she had matured as a woman, that the shift had not hurt when she was a child. But when she stopped growing and her bones firmed into their adult shape, the fracturing of those bones into wolf was no longer mere discomfort – it was agony. But she had withstood it before and she would again.

Her revealing tight velvet bodice tore beyond repair. The skirt, tight over hips and posterior, also ripped. Rue wanted to console the crestfallen Quesnel that she could certainly lay her hands on more tight dresses. Goodness, if that was what it took to get him looking at her like that, she'd start a new trend as soon as they returned to London.

The hat stayed on her head. It was small enough to perch between her ears. Rue let it be. At least she could save one article of clothing.

Uncle Lyall, being the type, made quick work helping her to extract herself from the remains of her costume.

Rue yipped her gratitude and bounded towards the officers' residence.

"How on earth is she going to look through books without fingers?" Quesnel wanted to know.

"I take it once she touches one of us she is in wolf form and can't turn back to human voluntarily?"

"Not that I've ever heard." Quesnel was careful not to give anything away.

"*Very* intriguing," said Uncle Lyall.

Rue bounded back, supernatural ears having caught the entire conversation. She crouched in front of Quesnel expectantly.

"Oh no," said the young man, blushing tomato red. "Chérie, I couldn't possibly. Not *ride a lady.*"

The corners of Uncle Lyall's mouth twitched. He smelled like the pomade Dama and Uncle Rabiffano favoured. *Guess it is more popular than I thought. He must import it at great expense.* She sniffed deeper. There was also a hint of sandalwood and fresh linens, and perhaps smoked fish on his breath.

Rue growled at Quesnel. He smelled of boiler smoke and hot coals and a little lime.

Uncle Lyall said, "She's right. Time is getting on. Best if I don't go. If you're caught, someone has to get you out."

"But you've lost your wolf form."

"Did I say I would need to fight? Dear boy, no, that's not my style at all."

Rue growled at Quesnel again.

With a sigh he slung a leg over and squatted on top of her gingerly.

Rue rose up precipitously.

Quesnel made a pathetic noise of discomfort.

Professor Lyall gave him brief instructions on wolf riding — how to lean forwards and tuck his feet up and back. Quesnel leaned, stiff and uncomfortable. It was a good thing he was relatively slight or Rue's supernatural strength would have struggled to make up for the awkwardness of disproportionate mass.

"You have your father's markings, little one," said Uncle Lyall. "But, like me, you're not so very big. Speedy, I suspect?"

Rue lolled her tongue in agreement.

"He's as settled as he's going to be. In future, you might consider training your crew in wolf riding." Professor Lyall stepped away, not a hair out of place. Well, to be fair, it was very good pomade. He did not seem at all perturbed to be mortal. In fact, he seemed to be enjoying himself. Hard to tell – he was a master of the impassive. Rue envied him that.

Quesnel was as affixed as he was likely to get, so Rue took off. She got up a good speed, showing off for her Uncle Lyall, and leapt. The brigadier's window was large and wide open. Being inside a military fortress and up a storey, the man clearly felt little need to take precautions. Well, there was a werewolf regiment nearby, and his wife was *already* missing.

Rue sailed through, landing softly in the sitting room.

Quesnel tumbled off, shaken. "Not quite like riding a horse, is it?"

Rue growled at him. *Never liken a lady to a horse.*

"Pardon, how crass of me. I do apologise. Now, what are we looking for?"

Rue nosed towards the bookshelves.

Quesnel perused the titles. "Mostly military history, how exhausting. This must be the husband's collection."

Rue left him to it and trotted off to look for other clues. She sniffed her way to the bedroom, following the scent of shaving soap and sweaty sheets. It was clear whose side of the bed was whose. One smelled like horse and leather; the other like violets and shaved metal. Also, one side had a monocle and a tin of snuff – *In bed? Disgusting* – and the other a pot of cold cream and a lace bedcap. There was a book under the cap, all about the mythology of India.

Rue barked softly and Quesnel came running.

Her nose was pressed on the book.

Quesnel looked at it doubtfully. "You sure?"

Rue growled.

Quesnel pocketed the small volume.

Rue heard clattering outside in the hallway. She charged back towards the sitting room.

Quesnel followed. "What? What is it?"

She crouched.

"Already? There are a few books over there and I've barely recovered from the—" Then he heard the clattering. Military never could move quietly.

He jumped onto Rue's back and seated himself, although not quite as well without Uncle Lyall's guidance. Rue wanted to tell him to hold on tight but she hadn't the vocal cords so she simply growled again.

The door behind them burst open. "Who's there?" barked a voice.

Several soldiers came crashing into the room.

Rue leapt out of the window, landed, and took off, Quesnel jostling atop her.

"Was that a werewolf and a ruffian?" she heard one soldier ask another.

"Sure looks like. Curses, I knew Kingair couldn't be trusted."

The soldiers attained the window. Rue knew this without looking because they started firing rifles at them.

She charged towards the side entrance, hoping Uncle Lyall would keep the pack from getting involved. Soldiers couldn't catch her, but if the pack gave chase she hadn't a chance.

Shots fired again. Rue dodged and twisted mid-leap.

Quesnel made a keening warble of distress.

For one horrible moment she thought he had been hit.

But then the wolds resolved themselves into: "My hat. My favourite hat!"

The rifles fired again. Quesnel flattened himself against her, modesty and hat forgotten. He wrapped strong arms around her neck. Rue was glad for her supernatural form or she might have been strangled. She dampened down worry by telling herself that surely his hold would slacken and she would smell blood if he were hit. Still, her best option was to get him out of range quickly. She put on a burst of speed – rifles continued to fire. She wasn't going to make it to the doorway.

She veered right, and with a tremendous heave, went up and over the outer wall, just clearing the ramparts with her back paws. She landed, stumbling only slightly and zipped away, impressed with herself, only to skid badly on the looser dirt of the promenade. She scrabbled and managed to stay on four feet, wondering how much longer she would have them. It was very dry in India so her tether to Uncle Lyall was most likely longer than the equivalent in London. But she was about to test those limits.

It turned out to stretch pretty far. She almost made the ship before the tether snapped.

Then poor Quesnel found himself sitting on top of a very naked, very human Rue in the middle of mudflats.

Rue said, the instant she recovered her voice, "You aren't shot?"

Quesnel seemed to be less concerned by bullets than by decency. He proved himself uninjured by leaping off her as if she had stung him. He took a few steps, resolutely facing away. Then remembered manners and returned to help her stand. Then clapped one hand over his eyes.

Rue started to laugh. He looked as near to nervous hysteria as she had ever seen. "Stop. You'll do yourself an injury."

He faced away and began backing towards her, breathing deeply. "Mon petit chou, it is not that I am not impressed, but I seem to lack the resources to cope with this particular situation."

Rue's laughter turned to snorts. "Give me your coat, silly man."

Rue had hoped it would be under more romantic circumstances that Quesnel would rip off his jacket with enthusiasm and speed. Truthfully, she had hoped to be naked with him in a more intimate setting. And not covered with foul-smelling mud. Sadly not the case.

Heads poked over the rails of her ship.

She could tell, even in the dim of evening, that Primrose was frowning. Percy too, probably.

She pulled on Quesnel's frock coat and stood with as much dignity as possible under the circumstances. Her legs were showing like a French dancer's but – and Rue could be proud of this – she had rather nice legs, even covered in mud. She felt a certain satisfaction in the way Quesnel's breath hitched and the small side glances he kept sneaking despite himself. Then again she was practically naked – perhaps any rake would do the same in a similar position. Rue chose to be flattered.

Spoo ran down the gangplank and over to them.

"Lady Primrose sent this." The deckling shoved one of Rue's voluminous robes into her hands. "Lady Captain, that was aces! I didn't know you could be all over wolf and such."

"Thank you, Spoo." Rue pulled on the robe over Quesnel's coat.

Spoo said, "Can you teach me?"

"Afraid not. You have to be born this way."

"Well, can I ride sometime, then?" Peppery as all get-up, was Spoo. "I'm sure likely to be better at it than him. Jiggling all over the place and falling off like that."

Quesnel recovered some of his faculties. "Now wait just a moment there, you scrubber!"

Rue thought about Uncle Lyall's recent advice. Teach her crew to ride, should she? "Sometime, Spoo, sometime soon." With which she led Quesnel, still pale with shock, and Spoo, ginning hugely, back aboard the ship.

The riflemen, having run down the stairs, through the yard and out of the barracks the regular way without supernatural speed, arrived at the promenade in time to see a very odd-looking family boarding their even odder-looking ship. The mother wore a robe, the man had only a shirt and waistcoat, and the child was dressed like a sailor. Assuming they were circus performers, the soldiers turned away to look for the werewolf intruder with the ruffian rider.

Rue instructed Quesnel to give the book to Percy to investigate and ignored the twins' disgusted expressions.

"I may have to send 'round to the werewolf pack for the remains of my dress," she said to Prim.

Prim sniffed. "Why bother?"

Quesnel looked crestfallen. "Not your dress *and* my hat? I hope that book was worth it."

Rue patted at her head. Miraculously, her own hat had made it all the way through. Small blessing. Feeling buoyed by its survival, Rue scooped up her trailing robe and glided queen-like towards her quarters, leaving muddy footprints on the nice clean deck.

"I'm exhausted," said Rue. "I believe I shall retire for a nap. Rouse me if anything interesting happens."

"Rue," said Primrose. "Do take a bath first, won't you?"

Rue hadn't been completely lying. It felt as if she hadn't slept a wink since they landed in Bombay. She was dozing off when a knock came at her cabin door.

Groggy, she went to open it and found Percy, head down, absorbed in the book they'd so recently liberated.

"Yes, Percy?"

"Oh, good afternoon, Rue."

"Night, I think it still is?" corrected Rue.

"Yes, well, what did you want?" Percy was staring at the book.

"You knocked on *my* door."

"I did? Oh yes. I know who might have kidnapped that bridge's wife, Mrs Flibbertyblue."

"Brigadier's wife, Mrs Featherstonehaugh. She wasn't kidnapped – at least, we don't think so any more. And, Percy, I don't think it proper for you and I to be alone together in my boudoir."

Percy looked at her, genuinely bewildered. "Worried you might be overcome and take advantage of me?"

"No, Percy, not exactly. Strangely enough, I seem to be one of the few women in existence able to resist your copious charms."

"I know," said Percy morosely. "Terrible tragedy."

"Oh, Percy, do stop it. I get enough of that from Quesnel."

"Another tragedy."

Rue sighed. "Fine, be like that. What was it you had to tell me? Do be quick before someone catches you here." She turned and marched back to her bed, flopping on top of the counterpane. Percy followed, sitting gingerly next to her on the very edge.

"What have you learnt?" Rue asked, and regretted it the moment she said it. Too open-ended a question for Percy.

Percy took a deep breath and prattled. "Under Her Majesty's Supernatural Acceptance Decree – referred to by the unfortunate colloquial moniker of SAD – all agreements between the East India Company and undead of conflicting nationalities are standardised. Bombay Presidency doesn't deviate. It is based on the traditional legal language maintained unbroken over thousands of years. Very correct and vampiric, as one might expect. Hives have these things well in hand, and most local vampires are eager to treat with the British Empire because England has such a progressive stance on open acknowledgment and incorporation of the supernatural."

Rue blinked at him. What had this to do with anything? Oh yes, she had asked him to look into the Rakshasas before they stole the book on mythology. "Percy, did you find something out particular to the Rakshasas?"

"No, not that."

"Percy!" Rue was not in a temper to play flighty word games

with her resident academic. Nor was she a particular fan of the Socratic method. It impinged upon efficiency. "Just tell me."

Percy sniffed. "Very well. I believe we may be dealing with Vanaras, not local dissidents. Or, more precisely, the Vanaras may be local dissidents."

Rue had never heard the word before but she wasn't going to dignify him with continued questions. She crossed her arms and glared.

Percy, in classic Percy fashion, remained oblivious to her frustration. He said nothing further, apparently feeling that this one statement was sufficient to explain everything that had happened to them since they landed in Bombay.

Rue finally crumbled. "Percy, what do you mean by Vanaras? Is it a different tribe? A thing? A population category? Please, O brilliant one, illuminate me."

Percy relaxed, enjoying his superior knowledge. "Actually, this book held the key. She had the pages marked. It was almost too easy."

"Please, Percy, enlighten me with your genius."

"Since you ask so nicely. Vanaras – to wit, mythological creatures featured in Hindu legends, most specifically the Epic of Ramayana which your Mrs Festtenhoop was reading." He tapped a passage in the book Rue had so recently retrieved. "They are extolled as brave and inquisitive, amusing and mildly irritating, honourable and kind, and so forth. They are reputed to have, at various points in the distant past, assisted local kings and generals in resisting Rakshasa domination."

"You think these legendary creatures might have intersections with reality?"

"Well, the first British explorers determined them mere legend, flights of local fancy. Since then, British forces in India have never encountered evidence of Vanara existence. But what if they were real? After all, the Rakshasas are real, although perhaps not exactly as depicted in the myths. What if Vanaras simply didn't *want* to be found? India is a very big country."

Rue nodded. "Go on. What other evidence do you propose to support their tangibility? After all, there are myths about Ganesha but I don't hold that we will see a giant elephant-headed man with multiple arms marching over the horizon any time soon."

"I am afraid I must appeal to Mr Darwin on this. We have now seen evidence with our own eyes that Indian Rakshasas differ from European vampires. Vanaras are reputed to be shape-shifters."

"Are you saying these Vanaras are what amounts to India's version of werewolves?" Rue couldn't help but be deeply enthralled by the idea.

"Why ever not? Different kind of vampires, ergo different kind of werewolves. If we have supernatural men who change into beasts, what is to stop other countries from having their own version thereof? It would be terribly conceited of us to believe Europe unique in this matter. Only . . ."

"Only what?"

"I don't think they are wolves exactly."

"Oh, no?"

"If my translation is correct, of which I am certain, of course, for I am never wrong in the matter of foreign tongues, then the best wording would be, well . . ."

He trailed off, acutely embarrassed. Wherever else this new theory was taking him, it was into questionable territory. It must be very questionable indeed to unnerve the man who once publicly hypothesised that bacon could be blamed for the explosion of Mount Vesuvius.

"Go on, Percy. Out with it," urged Rue.

"I suppose the best way of putting it would be . . . weremonkeys."

Rue couldn't help it – she snorted a surprised laugh. It seemed so very undignified. "Men who change into monkeys?"

Percy nodded. "Very, very large monkeys."

"Goodness, it hardly seems worth the effort. There is not so much difference, is there?"

Percy shrugged. "I suppose monkeys are stronger, faster, and can climb with greater dexterity."

Rue cocked her head. "Climbing could be useful. So where in India might we find these Vanaras, should they exist?"

"All the various epics describe them as forest-dwelling. So, unless all my suppositions are entirely misguided—"

"Never that."

"Exactly, highly unlikely. Your Mrs Fetherpottoot—"

"Featherstonehaugh."

"Will be in a forest. I suspect there's one nearby."

"You don't know?"

"I can't do everything for you," protested Percy, forgetting who'd procured him the book in the first place.

It was as good a theory as any and at least it indicated a course of action. This was a great relief to a girl of Rue's particular character. She could now start planning. "Percy?"

"Yes, Rue?"

"Please go and find out the location of the nearest forest."

"But, Rue, I haven't even finished this book."

That's Percy for you. "Well, if you can't help, I suppose I could ask Quesnel to check his areal..."

"You think I can't figure it out? I have maps."

"Of course you do, Percy."

Rue suddenly thought of something and went to rummage about in her peach dress from that morning's tour of Bombay.

Absentmindedly she said, "Thank you, Percy dear, you've been extraordinarily useful."

Percy puffed up with pride. "Yes, well."

Rue emerged, triumphant. From the interior of her small bag

she discovered the stone monkey on the cord she'd found after the flowers exploded.

"Percy, what if Miss Sekhmet was speaking for them?"

"For whom?" Now it was Percy's turn to be confused.

Rue showed him the little statue. "The Vanaras."

"She was a very odd sort of woman."

"Terribly careless of us to let her get captured like that. But why didn't she just say something? Was that why she kept harping on about my mother? Did she think the Shadow Council knew about the weremonkeys?"

Percy looked shocked at the idea. "I highly doubt it. If they do exist – and it's just a working hypothesis, mind you, Rue – they have taken a great deal of care not to be known by the British government."

"Which would be why Miss Sekhmet kept being so mysterious. Then what was her negotiation about?"

Percy shrugged. "You can't depend on me for everything, Rue, especially if it isn't written down."

"Of course not, Percy. I do apologise. Still" – Rue tapped Mrs Featherstonehaugh's copy of the Epic of Ramayana – "exceptional work."

Percy actually blushed. "It's all in the books."

Rue smiled. "Now if you will excuse me, I must find someone to take a message to Uncle Lyall. Spoo, I think. I like Spoo, very plucky."

"Who?"

"Spoo."

"Oh, the little lad who is always tormenting my valet?"

"Sort of."

Percy nodded. "Yes, by all means send him off on an errand. Maybe Virgil will get some real work done for a change."

"Now, Percy, don't be mean. Virgil's very diligent in your care.

Why, I haven't seen you once without a well-tied cravat or neat waistcoat this entire trip."

"Oh, not *that* sort of work. There are manuscripts to dust and catalogue."

"Percy, he is your valet. You hired him to tend to your appearance, not your books' appearance."

"I did?"

"Yes, you did. If you want an archivist, go and get yourself a clerk."

Percy seemed much taken by this idea. "Do such useful persons exist for hire?"

"Of course they do. Now scoot."

Percy scooted and Rue went to find herself a tea-gown so she was presentable enough to climb up top. Fortunately, Dama's drones, accustomed to her predisposition for getting naked and stealing wolf shape, had supplied her with a full range of tea-gowns. They were technically the provenance of older married ladies, but allowances had to be made when balancing Rue's relaxed attitude against her reputation. Tea-gowns were easy to get into and out of, and elegant despite their simplicity. Rue selected her favourite, one of light blue gauze that wrapped crosswise over her chest, held fast by a wide belt. Over the gauze went an open overdress of dark blue velvet with white embroidery. It looked very modern and was comfortable, although perhaps not as cool as an evening in Bombay demanded. Nevertheless, she did not wish to offend the decklings' sensibilities any more than she already had that night. She climbed up on deck.

"Spoo, walk with me?"

Spoo swung out of her hammock and joined Rue in drifting to the other end of the ship, away from the curious ears of other decklings.

"Do you need my advice about something, Lady Captain?" asked Spoo with all the serious maturity of a ten-year-old.

"Of a kind, Spoo."

"That Mr Lefoux ain't good husband material," offered Spoo immediately, sounding a great deal like some disapproving aged aunt.

"Not *that* sort of advice, Spoo. Although as it happens, I wholeheartedly agree with you."

"What then?"

"I have a very grave and possibly dangerous mission for you."

Spoo straightened her spine, thrilled by the prospect. "I'm your man, Lady Captain."

Rue raised her eyebrows. "Well, if you put it like that. There is a werewolf in residence at the local barracks. He's with the regiment. Beta by pack standing, goes by the name of Lyall. Have you heard of him?"

Spoo shook her head, eyes wide. "Werewolf like you was earlier, Lady Captain?"

"Very like. Now, I need you to get a message to him and they may not be very welcoming to strangers right now. See that long brick building beyond the steeple of that church? You'll need to argue your way in and find the underground residencies. Say to anyone you encounter that you have a very important message for Kingair from Lady Akeldama about a recent upset. This is werewolf *not* military business. The werewolves might have left by now, but don't give the message to anyone but Professor Lyall, not even Lady Kingair."

Spoo nodded, small face very serious. "I understand, Lady Captain. What's the message?"

Rue gave Spoo the stone monkey on the cord. She trusted her instincts, and hoped that Professor Lyall would know enough about local custom to connect this to the Vanaras. Was he scientist enough to figure it out or would he be trapped in the belief that there was only one kind of shape – wolf? Rue didn't entirely believe Percy's theory herself. Hidden weremonkeys? The very idea! But then again, it might just be outrageous enough to be true.

Spoo looked at the funny little necklace doubtfully. "That's all?"

"And ask if I can have my dress and shoes back, would you? And Mr Lefoux's hat, perhaps?"

Spoo looked scandalised. "I don't think I want to know."

"Good, because I'm not going to explain further."

Spoo popped the monkey charm about her own neck. "Aye aye, Lady Captain."

Rue was about to rouse the others to extend the gangplank, when Spoo waved an airy hand. "Gangplanks are for you proper types." Without further ado she ran, grabbed a dangling rope on the landward side of the ship, and leapt over the railing.

Rue's hands went to her mouth, stifling a scream. Then she realised this must be a common deckling activity, for the rope was rigged to respond to Spoo's slight weight. It belayed down rapidly but not too rapidly. Spoo continued swinging back and forth until it had lowered her almost to the ground, at which juncture she let go and dropped the remaining distance. The rope rebounded, winding back up to the ship, leaving Spoo alone on the mudflats. She stuffed her hands into her jodhpurs, lowered her cap, and scurried towards the military fortress in a purposeful manner.

"I wonder if I can get her to teach me that trick," said Rue.

"Absolutely not," said Primrose, coming up behind her. "Now come and have some tea. You look like death warmed over without exorcism."

CHAPTER

ELEVEN

The Shape of Things to Come

Everyone awoke from their naps refreshed. It was late night and the air had finally cooled. Primrose organised and served a delicious repast.

Unusually, it was Rue whose spirits flagged, for Spoo had not returned.

Rue tried to drown her worries in tea and conversation. Prim and Percy were both inexcusably cheerful. Percy was basking in the glow of his weremonkey discovery. Prim was luxuriating in the thrill of her recent acquisitions and enjoying chastising Rue for ungenteel behaviour. To top it all off, Quesnel had rediscovered his flirtatious good humour. The three eventually ended up engaged in a lively discussion on the subject of weremonkeys.

Quesnel was as scientifically charmed by the idea as Percy. "Imagine the possibilities. I mean to say, if India has weremonkeys, what about other countries? How ignorant are we concerning the evolution of the supernatural? Are there other forms of vampires? The Rakshasas seem a minor physical variation. What if there are other adaptive variations? It is thrilling to speculate." His eyes turned to Rue encouragingly.

But even speculation could not draw Rue into the conversation. She kept glancing over the rail of the ship towards the land; trying to see in the darkness a small form scuttling back across the now diminished flats. The tide was coming in, *The Spotted Custard* floated nearer the promenade, and yet Spoo was nowhere to be seen.

Did I give her too much responsibility?

Quesnel's expression said much of his surprise at her lack of interest in such entertaining ideas as the probable existence of werefoxes somewhere in the Islands of Niphon and whether some variant of vampires might actually suck brains instead of blood.

Rue only shook her head at him and rose. Carrying her tea-cup and saucer with her, she made her way to the decklings, huddled together in one corner of the quarter deck.

One of them said, "Lady Captain, we wouldn't want to betray one of our own, but we're a mite worried. We checked the entire ship and Spoo is definitely missing."

"I know. I sent her away."

The decklings instantly relaxed. "Oh, that's all right then."

"However, I think we should make it easy for her to return. Take us as close as possible into shore and lower that useful little rope of yours so she can climb back up. Or, if that's not how it works, drop over a rope ladder."

"Very good, Lady Captain." They scampered off to do her bidding.

Rue returned to the others.

"Conservation of mass," Percy was saying, "would seem to dictate only certain animal forms are available for use. Are monkeys too small? We must ask ourselves this. After all, even the supernatural cannot defy physics. Rodentia and the like, we must assume, are right out. As are the more massive elements, like ungulates."

Quesnel nodded. "Agreed. And I think we must acknowledge

that mammalian bone and skin are also the only real option, the synchronicity of forms suggests nothing reptilian or invertebrate. Although that would be amusing, a werejellyfish."

Percy's hands were steepled in thought. On the subject of undiscovered shape-shifting creatures, Percy and Quesnel seemed entirely in accordance. "Or aquatic. Gills, you know."

Quesnel nibbled a muffin. "Although there are legends concerning shape-changing seal creatures in the far north of Scotland and parts of Ireland. I never gave them much credence but—"

Percy nodded sagely. "Indeed, the Silly."

Quesnel frowned as though he might contradict. "Is that what they're called?"

Primrose, less interested in speculation as to the nature of supernatural creatures not immediately likely to attend her evening gathering, stood and went to join Rue, looking over the rails at the shore. "Is everything in order, Rue?"

"I don't know," replied Rue honestly.

The distant city was lit up with torches, lanterns, and the occasional gas lamp. The decklings gathered near the rope ladder they'd deployed. They were unsettled in the absence of their leader. Spoo had come so recently among them yet made quite a lasting mark. Virgil joined them in their vigil, his small face set. Rue wished she could stand with them, but she didn't want to betray to the others that anything was seriously amiss. Extended fraternisation with decklings would be too suspicious.

There was a jolt and a scuffle and a few startled cries from the assembled group of young persons. The decklings scattered as a great furry creature landed where they had been standing. A monster of myth, which apparently needed no rope ladder to board an airship. Nor did she require an invitation. The creature had leapt from the ground below to land gracefully on deck in one massive display of supernatural strength.

While Prim, Percy, and Quesnel gaped, Rue smoothed her

skirts nervously. Then with – she hoped – captain-like dignity, she made her way to the lioness.

"Welcome back, Spoo. And Miss Sekhmet, I assume?" Of course Rue should have known, but it was like the Vanaras – she never considered that there would be other shape-shifters. British scientists only spoke of werewolves. A quintessentially imperial attitude, of course, to ignore native mythology. But if there were weremonkeys, why not werelionesses?

Nevertheless, in case she was wrong, Rue approached Spoo and the lioness with caution. "Glad you were able to escape your captors. Welcome aboard *The Spotted Custard*. Spoo, you had us worried."

Spoo, sitting with immense pride astride the cat, slid off and moved away only to be instantly surrounded by decklings, the returning hero. They hustled her off in a nattering group, like a gaggle of excited geese.

The lioness looked up at Rue as if waiting for something.

Rue said, "I'd be delighted to offer you use of my quarters and a dressing robe. It is Miss Sekhmet, is it not?"

The cat tilted her head, whiskers twitching.

"The robe will be short on you, I am afraid. I am assuming, as our first meeting took place in the Maltese Tower, that you are not afflicted, like werewolves, with an inability to float? But I get ahead of myself. We have much to discuss that I am afraid requires you to be in human form."

The werecat nodded her sleek head. Rue wondered if in this she was the same as werewolves. It was a mark of age and skill to possess all of one's facilities while in animal shape. Oh, she had so many questions!

Quesnel and Percy, having stood at the arrival of their visitor, abandoned their tea to approach.

"Rue," said Percy. "Are you talking to a lioness? Is that wise? Aren't they hazardous to the health?"

Without batting an eye Quesnel said, "Of course – Miss Sekhmet, is it? That's why you shrouded yourself in fabric under the direct sunlight this morning."

"No wonder she looked so exhausted," added Rue, trying to carry everything off with aplomb when inside she was now trembling with excitement: *A werecat. I found a werecat! Well, she found me, but still!*

"And too weak to fight off her kidnappers," added Quesnel. "Or should I say, catnappers?"

The lioness looked displeased at that statement. She flattened her ears at Quesnel.

"Spoo, would you show our guest to my chambers?"

"My pleasure, Lady Captain. Right this way, miss." Spoo trotted off, the lioness trailing behind.

They disappeared.

Percy said, "Is she staying? Footnote is not going to be happy." And then, after a moment, "Where has my sister gone?"

Primrose, as it turned out, had fainted.

The decklings collected around her in a chattering worried mass.

Rue applied smelling salts and Prim revived relatively quickly. Her big dark eyes were smudged with concern. She sat up.

"I'm feeling better. I do apologise. Terribly silly of me."

"It's the heat," said Rue, giving Prim an out and offering her a hand up.

"Just so I am clear, do we now have a werelioness on board?" Primrose rose slowly.

"Yes," said Quesnel, helping her solicitously to sit back in a deck-chair.

"And did she take us shopping this morning?"

"Yes, she did," confirmed Rue.

Percy, following at long last, said, "Werelioness? Of course. It fits perfectly. Do you think that's what the Vanaras are? Hardly makes sense. That's not how they are described in the text. Not cat-like at all. Do you think she'll let me write a report for the Royal Society?"

Quesnel gave him a disgusted look. "Can't you think about anything but your academic standing? This is a revelation of epic proportions! We now have proof that there are other shape-shifting creatures besides werewolves."

"Exactly! The scientific community should know. I'm being altruistic. Selfish would be to keep this information secret."

The two men stood – forgetting Primrose's delicate state – the better to argue.

Quesnel said, "Our caller has obviously gone to great lengths to keep her condition out of the public arena. You should respect her wishes!"

"Oh, should I indeed? And your concern wouldn't have any-thing to do with the fact that she is an incredibly lovely female specimen? Would it?"

Rue decided to ignore them in favour of her friend. "Do you think you could manage a little restorative tea, Prim?"

Primrose said, "I think so. Thank you. I haven't forgiven you though, Rue. You knew she was coming and did not warn me? And here I am not in a receiving gown."

"Is that why you fainted?"

Prim ignored this dig to continue her lament. "What will she think of me?"

Rue rolled her eyes. "For your information, I didn't know she was coming. And even if I had made the connection, I thought she was kidnapped. I'm trying to act debonair. I'm surprised to have fooled you. I didn't put it all together until she leapt on board." She let the wide grin she'd been suppressing sweep across her face. "Isn't this the cat's whiskers? Werelioness. Did you ever imagine? Do you think she'll let me steal her soul for a bit? I would so love to be a cat."

Prim raised a hand. "Rue, stop; too much excitement. It's worse than you being all suave. Calm down. How did she get here, then?"

Rue shrugged. "I sent for the werewolves but I suppose they've gone hunting. She must have found Spoo, or Spoo her. And stop worrying. She will think very well of you – everyone does. You look lovely. You always do."

Rue helped Prim to butter a muffin. Prim's hands were still shaking, and Rue knew exactly how she liked her muffin buttered. She then foisted another cup of tea on Primrose. Though a touch cold, Prim drank it gratefully as she nibbled her well-buttered muffin.

Once revived, Prim gave Rue a suspicious look. "You're being awfully nice. What are you plotting?"

"Nothing as yet."

Prim was not convinced. "You're wearing a tea-gown and no gloves." She stated the obvious. "And you sent for werewolves. Haven't you had enough soul-stealing for one evening?"

Spoo returned, Miss Sekhmet following. The werelioness wore a robe of quilted velvet, opulent and flattering, if a little small. With her hair loose and flowing, free of all accessories, she was more beautiful than ever.

Rue decided, magnanimously, to forgive her for it. However, it did appear to rather drive all her companions, even Primrose, into a tongue-tied state.

"Please excuse the casual dress, ladies, gentlemen. I was going to follow the werewolves on their hunt and then I ran into your messenger and she had this." Miss Sekhmet tossed Rue the monkey charm. "They have made contact with you directly in my absence?"

Rue took the necklace and, because she thought it might be the safest thing to do, put it on, grateful that she had rejected the massive hat that fashion dictated be pinned atop her head at all times. She gestured for the werecat to sit. Which she did, quite gracefully.

While Primrose poured more tea, Rue avoided the question by asking one of her own. "Is it really true that Mrs Featherstonehaugh went with them willingly?"

Miss Sekhmet nodded. "She is acting as surety for British cooperation. She has a childish faith in their being good and noble."

Rue frowned. "And you are working for them as what?"

"Nothing any more. I said I would speak for them and I did. We expected your mother, not you. Her, I wanted to meet. An original, and I'm fond of originals. Not that you are not unique, skin-stalker."

Quesnel pressed the question. "Then who do you work for?"

Miss Sekhmet looked insulted by his impertinence. If she'd had her whiskers, she would have twitched them.

"Milk?" asked Prim, raising the jug questioningly over the tea-cup.

"The more the better, lovely child. The more the better," responded the werecat with a look of avarice.

Prim blushed and poured. She handed over the cup.

They half expected Miss Sekhmet to begin lapping. But she was perfectly respectable about it, sipping with pleasure at the over-milked cold tea.

"They asked me to speak their case. So I spoke it. You did nothing. Now they wonder who is on whose side. They question my motives. They question yours. You have handled this badly, skin-stalker."

Rue took offence at that. "I thought it was all about the tea."

Miss Sekhmet smiled a very cat-with-cream smile. "They hold, how you British might say, all the cards."

Rue was annoyed. "But what do they *want*? I must say, you haven't done well in making their position clear."

Miss Sekhmet paused so long the silence became awkward.

"Something fresher?" offered Prim nervously, signalling to one of the stewards with the intention of sending him to the meat locker.

The werecat shook her head. "No. Thank you for the thought. This will do well enough. Wait. Are those kippers? Marvellous. It's been years since I had a kipper."

Prim served their guest a generous helping of kippers in brown butter sauce and fried egg. All quite cold by now, but the werecat didn't seem to mind congealed food.

"How did you know they were sending anyone?" Rue asked.

"Your father wrote a letter to the pack here. Asking them to keep an eye on his biggest treasure. Of course, I thought he meant his wife. We all did. She's travelled without him before. Didn't realise you were all grown up and floating about without them."

Rue said, "Time moves differently for immortals."

"Just so." Miss Sekhmet nodded. "Nor did we think England would let you out of the country."

"I am not a prisoner because I am metanatural!"

"No, but you are, as your father put it, a national treasure."

Rue frowned darkly. *Overprotective, interfering Paw!*

The werecat laughed. "Child, you don't have to explain to *me* a love of independence."

Rue moved them on. "Let us be frank, Miss Sekhmet. These people you keep alluding to – the ones who have Mrs Feather-stonehaugh and the taxes – are they indeed some form of were-monkey, or are we merely dealing with nationalist dissidents?"

Rue was reminded of that old saying: trying to get a straight answer out of a cat is like trying to find the soap in the bathtub.

Miss Sekhmet swallowed her mouthful of kipper and looked smug.

Percy said, "The agreement, SAD. Of course! Things could get messy, politically, if Vanaras do exist. The Rakshasas would have to share power."

Miss Sekhmet tried hard to hide her surprise. "Your government would acknowledge them legally?"

Percy sat a little more upright. "My good woman! The British have always dealt fairly with the supernatural. It is *tradition*."

Miss Sekhmet's lip curled. "But not with the natives."

Percy looked surprised. "We bring civilisation and enlightenment to all the empire."

"Is that what you call it?" The werecat finished her kipper and leaned back in her chair, sipping tea. "Mrs Featherstonehaugh believes similarly. The Vanaras are not so sure. And then when you refused to talk..."

"I didn't refuse!" said Rue. "I didn't know."

"And now we are at an impasse. For I am no longer speaking for them and you have yet to ask me the right question." Miss Sekhmet put down her cup.

Rue frowned. "Werelioness, are you aware that I have been made sundowner?" That little bit of information managed to shock the werecat. *So she doesn't know everything.*

"Chérie!" Quesnel's voice was gruff with warning.

The werecat inclined her head. "A threat, little bird? I comprehend. Then they do not treasure you as much as they think you are useful. Very interesting."

Rue laughed. "That would appear to be the case."

"So?"

"So can you take me to the Vanaras?" *They want me to negotiate in my mother's name and Dama wants me to find the tea. Only Mrs Featherstonehaugh knows where it is. I suppose I am going into the jungle whether I like it or not.*

"Very good, skin-stalker. That is the right question. And yes, yes I can."

At which Prim, Percy, and Quesnel all started talking at once.

Prim and Quesnel thought this a terrible idea. Percy thought he ought to accompany Rue for research purposes. At which statement Quesnel said no, he should come along, for he could help defensively as well as scientifically. Prim said if Rue had to go, they should take *The Spotted Custard* and crew into the forest en masse.

Rue held up a hand. "Do you think the government would not have tried to find Mrs Featherstonehaugh by air before now? I suspect this forest to be overly lush. No, the hunt must be conducted on foot. Or more precisely, on paw."

Quesnel and Prim protested this vociferously. "It's too dangerous!"

Rue considered. "In lioness form, I can carry two easily." Only Prim had any idea how thrilled she was to say that. *Oh please, oh please, oh please.*

Miss Sekhmet looked thoughtful, rather than objecting outright.

Rue was delighted. She felt compelled to explain. "Not by weight. I could take more. I'm as strong as any normal werecreature. At least I think I would be. I've never done cat before, but by size—" She gestured expressively at her short curvaceous figure. "As you might have noticed, I did not benefit from my parents' proportions. Two is the most that will fit on my back."

Quesnel said, "I do not like where you are going with this."

Rue said, "It has to be me in shape. If I'm riding, the risk is too great of a skin slip-up. I will be safe as a lioness. It is Miss Sekhmet here who will have to take the risk."

The werecat, following her plan, nodded. "I am old enough not to fear a second death. And you are my first skin-stalker. It should make for an interesting experience. I am also old enough to rarely encounter interesting experiences any more."

"Curious as a cat, Miss Sekhmet?" suggested Primrose rather daringly.

Said cat gave her a little smile of approval.

Primrose blushed.

Quesnel stood up from his deck-chair and began to pace. "You expect the rest of us to stay behind?"

Rue ignored him and asked Miss Sekhmet: "Have you studied the British policy on supernatural agreements in any depth?"

The werecat shook her head.

"Very well, Percy will make up the third of our party."

Percy looked part delighted, part terrified to be included.

Primrose blanched. "Rue, Percy's not accustomed to adventure. Or forests. Or the outside world, really."

Rue said, "I know, but he did some wolf-riding when we were little. At least I know he can stay astride. And he's pretty deadly with his cravat pin."

Quesnel said with a cheeky smile, despite obvious tension, "Mon petit chou, any time you want me to ride you again, I would be happy to learn how to do it properly."

Primrose gave a shocked little squeak at that statement.

Rue was privately thrilled. *Perhaps he's decided he'd like to tutor me in romantic encounters after all.*

Then he added, spoiling matters, "Just stay behind where it's safer."

Rue was moved to reprimand. "I know you are upset, Mr Lefoux, but do try to control yourself."

Quesnel persisted, "You don't know what danger you face, how long it will take, or how you will get back out. You are intending to run into monkey-ridden doom with no more support than a werecat made mortal who we don't know if we can trust and a ruthlessly incompetent academic."

"Ho there, old boy!" objected Percy.

Miss Sekhmet said, "Ah, family arguments. Makes me miss my old pride."

Rue and Quesnel said to her at the same time, "We are *not* related!"

Miss Sekhmet shrugged. "Neither were many in my pride."

Quesnel was not to be thus distracted. "Chérie, please, don't go."

Rue could feel her face getting hot in frustration. *Why is he countermanding my decisions in front of the others?* She was mortified. Miss Sekhmet would think her a mere child. "This is the best option we have."

"It is an *imbecilic* option!" Quesnel's jaw muscles worked as he clenched his teeth in an effort to keep himself from yelling.

Rue wanted his interest — of course she wanted his interest — but not this overprotective nonsense. She wanted flirtation and desire, not yet another parent. Sekhmet was right — he was acting like family. "What care you? You, yours, and the ship will remain safe."

Quesnel stood up and came to lean over her. "Now *you* are being an imbecile."

Rue didn't know how to relate to a Quesnel who was over-emotional. She thought for one terrifying moment that he intended to kiss her again, right there on the poop deck in front of all the decklings and a visiting werecat. There seemed an equally good possibility that he might strike her.

He did neither, only saying, "I am concerned about your safety. This is like you tearing after the lioness all over again."

Rue was stung. "It isn't that at all. I'm telling you what I'm doing ahead of time. And I'll be tearing off *as* the lioness!"

Quesnel slapped his forehead with his hand and began striding about, copious arm gestures displaying his French ancestry. "And it will be your first time in that form. You don't even know if you're any good at it. You grew up being a wolf! And that is not even the point, the point is—"

Rue interrupted him, standing up herself. She puffed out her considerable chest and drew herself upright, not as tall as Quesnel but doing her best. "*Enough.* I am still the captain. You should not contradict me in front of the children." She gestured to where, a little way away, the decklings had stopped chattering to Spoo and were watching Quesnel's spectacular display of temper with wide, frightened eyes.

Quesnel stopped pacing, vibrating with anger, and then pulled himself together. "Yes, Lady Captain," he said coldly, and stormed away belowdecks.

Rue did not stop him.

There was a long silence while Prim and Percy pretended not to have heard anything, and Miss Sekhmet tried not to look curious.

Rue took a deep calming breath. "Primrose, you have command while I am away. Technically, I suppose it ought to be Mr Lefoux but since he is proving a tad unstable, I think you had better see to the necessities. I'll leave you to tell him so later." Which would also save Rue from having to call down to the boiler room with the transfer of command and get another earful from Aggie Phinkerlington.

Prim said tentatively, "Might I suggest a gunpowder display sparkle? If you took one with you and trouble arises, you could set it off and summon help? Any local militia would surely respond."

Rue was not above sensible suggestions. "Excellent notion."

Prim crinkled her forehead. "I'll find you one of the smaller ones and tie it about your neck in a reticule. Also, I think you should take one of those long scarves I bought this morning in case you have to change shape in the middle of a forest. Or in case something happens to Miss Sekhmet."

The werecat looked a little nonplussed. "I don't know exactly where they are in the forest. We have always discussed things through an intermediary. Territory is territory, after all."

"Then we have to follow Mrs Featherstonehaugh's trail."

The lioness asked, "Do your skin-stalker abilities extend beyond the mere stealing of form? Do you possess enhanced tracking skills as well?"

"Naturally," lied Rue. This may be her only chance to be a lioness. There was no way she was going to suit up in thick clothing and ride Sekhmet into the forest. It had to be the other way around.

The werecat said, "Very well, then, no time like the present. We are only losing darkness."

Prim scuttled off to the stores and reappeared with a flint and tinder, one of the sparklers, a reticule that looked like a water lily, and a large orange scarf.

Percy made a sputtering noise about not being ready for a trip, until Virgil appeared at his elbow with a warm jacket, a belt from which dangled various tools in pouches, and a satchel full of books and scrolls. Percy said, "Is the ancient Hindustani language derivation text there?" Virgil nodded. "And the Epic of Ramayana?" Another nod. "And my maps?" More nodding. "Well," said Percy, in surprise, "perhaps you *are* good for something."

Virgil said, "Don't stay out too late – Footnote will worry."

Rue gestured for Miss Sekhmet to accompany her belowdecks to her private quarters, Prim alongside, for the sake of appearances. The aforementioned Footnote encountered them in the hallway, got one whiff of the werelioness and puffed his tail hugely, sidestepped on his toes, and took off back to the library. Miss Sekhmet gave a funny hiss-like laugh.

In her room, Rue slipped behind the changing screen and switched her gown for a loose robe and nothing else. She emerged and turned to the werecat.

Miss Sekhmet looked impassive, but Rue suspected the werecat was nervous.

"Very well, then." Rue looked at Prim. "Ready?"

Prim nodded.

"Miss Sekhmet?"

The werecat nodded. And before she could think to change her mind, Rue stepped in and touched her bare hand.

It was as painful as ever. In that matter, werelioness was no different from werewolf. Rue felt herself morphing, falling, and shifting all at once.

Her bones re-formed into those of a fleet four-footed creature. Her hair became fur all over her body. Her spine stretched out into a long tail. Her fingernails became claws. Her nose expanded and moistened. Her teeth elongated. Her sense of the world shifted. Colours faded and became less important.

All that was similar to a werewolf, but other things were different. Sounds were clearer and more minute. The balance of her muscles was altered. This form was made to climb and to leap. Her long tail could balance back, her claws could flex and extend.

Rue sniffed. The sense of smell was good – perhaps not quite so good as wolf but still infinitely superior to human. There was Prim, all flowery powders and soaps, and a faint sheen of sweat she would be mortified that Rue knew about. Miss Sekhmet, still standing close, smelled of exotic spices and dry grasslands. There was the hint of kipper still on her breath, mixed with remnants of milky tea.

Miss Sekhmet said, "Amazing. Truly amazing. You lift cat away from me so easily. And I have carried her with me for so very long."

Prim said sympathetically, "Do you feel abandoned?"

"By my own immortality? No more than when a preternatural touches me. And before you ask – yes, I have met a soulless. But it is remarkable not to have to remain touching. How long is the tether?"

Prim was always circumspect with other people's secrets, especially when they were right there listening. She said only, "That is a conversation for you and Rue to have when she can speak again."

"Indeed, indeed. Forgive my curiosity – a curse I was born to. Believe it or not."

Prim said, "I fully understand. Now, I assume you have ridden a lioness before?"

Miss Sekhmet nodded. Her face, more expressive in mortal form, looked sad. "A long time ago. But, yes."

Well done, Primrose, now we know there are more of them. Or once were.

Miss Sekhmet settled herself astride Rue. "Can she communicate?"

Prim nodded.

"Fully?"

"She can understand you. She has possession of all her capacities, unlike a newly changed werewolf. But she no more possesses the ability to articulate with the tongue than you would as a lioness."

Rue gave a little mew of inquiry and felt Miss Sekhmet twine her hands into the thick fur of her neck, a sign that she was ready. Rue tried to purr her approval, but nothing but a stuttering sputter emerged. Rue gave up and ran through her quarters out into the hall and leapt up the staircase out onto the quarterdeck.

She almost overshot it. Lioness shape was powerful in distinct ways from werewolf.

Percy was waiting for them, looking impatient. Virgil was fussing about his master, ensuring Percy was all buttoned up for the evening ride, that his boots were dusted, and his hat in place.

Rue stopped next to him, tail thrashing.

Percy looked her over doubtfully. It had been a while since he had ridden her as a wolf, and this form was vastly different. Plus, while he had grown bigger, Rue had mostly not.

Rue yowled at him, dictatorially.

Percy legged over and sat, tucking his knees up, presumably wrapping his arms about Miss Sekhmet's waist.

"I do beg your pardon, miss, having only just met you and all."

"Oh, for goodness' sake, you British and your manners. Just grab on to me, man!"

"Yes, miss," said Percy meekly.

Rue merped a question at them both.

"All set," said Percy, his voice a little strangled.

"Ready," added Miss Sekhmet.

With which Rue dashed over to the shoreside railing of the ship and, in one great leap, cast herself and her passengers over the edge.

It was a spectacular manoeuvre. The decklings behind gave a gratifying communal gasp. It was further down than Rue had thought. Fortunately, it was not too far for her supernatural body to absorb the impact. She landed and stumbled only slightly, righting herself so quickly even Percy didn't fall off. She suppressed a small surge of disappointment that Quesnel had not bothered even to look out of the engineering port hole to see her away. Shaking off thoughts of the difficult Frenchman, Rue set off through the city.

CHAPTER
TWELVE

Hijacking an Elephant Head

Percy said, "My research suggests the Tungareshwar Forest as the likely location for Vanaras."

"You are good, professor," said Miss Sekhmet.

"Rue here doesn't keep me on board for my good looks, I assure you."

"Are you certain?"

Percy ignored whatever supposition the werecat was making about his – or possibly Rue's – character and went pedantically on. "It's the largest vegetation close to Bombay. And there appears to be a sacred temple at its heart."

Rue could feel Miss Sekhmet nodding.

Percy was like a small child, always eager to share knowledge recently acquired, as if it were some artistic creation of his own devising. "Vanaras are supposedly allied with local religions and superstitions. In the epics they are friendly with gods, if not gods themselves."

Rue did not wait for him to continue. Percy, she knew, could keep parroting on for ever. She headed north, up the peninsula, fast enough for his words to be lost in the wind as she ran. Or, more precisely, fast enough for her to pretend that this was the case.

Bombay at night was quite different from Bombay during the day. There was little activity – odd, since it was so much cooler. *Perhaps it has to do with fear of the Rakshasas?* It made Rue nervous like nothing else had in India. It was very foreign, the stillness. London came alive at night with vampires, werewolves, ghosts, drones, clavigers, and associated sycophants roaming the streets. Military pubs and bars served werewolves and their fellow soldiers all night long. Theatres featured operas, dances, and comedy plays open to all. For the vampires and their companions there were private clubs, symphonies, arts houses, and late-night museums. Whole streets of shops stayed open all night long, catering to the shadow society and their fashionable inclinations. BUR agents swept the streets with warm conscientiousness and the unsavoury elements saw to other needs.

Bombay had none of this. After dark it was as quiet as it had been during the high heat of day. A few stray dogs and rats milled about. Packs of mangy monkeys roamed the marketplaces scavenging the remnants of the day's gatherings. The city was theirs.

To Rue's cat nose Bombay was all exotic stale smells. Odours ranged from rotting vegetation, mouldy meats, and excrement to the more pleasing scent of cut rushes, roast lamb, fragrant spices, and perfume oils. Burning kerosene and gas permeated everything, as did the undercurrent of machinery and steam technology – coal dust and motor fluids.

Rue moved quickly through the empty streets. Faster than a horse at full gallop, not as fast as a train, or a dirigible in aetherosphere, but good enough to get her through Bombay and out to the far reaches in a quarter of an hour. The weight atop her back was no inconvenience except when it impinged upon her agility.

She ran on through the northern reaches of Bombay, where

slums gave way to the factories of industry. There she stopped, her whiskers twitching, which they seemed to do without her input. Here the air was harsh with the smell of fishing, tanning, and illness. She was glad not to be werewolf or the odour would have been near overwhelming. Here were the sanitoriums, orphanages, burial grounds, and associated livelihoods that all cities pushed to the outskirts. Even humans could smell the foulness of misery. Rue paused, tail lashing. She could see the shimmering of white above a nearby cemetery: local ghosts hoping for conversation, or poltergeists in the throes of second death. She had no time to stop and investigate which.

"The locals call ghosts Bhoot," said Percy, as if hearing her thoughts.

"Just ahead there," said Miss Sekhmet.

Rue's cat eyes were near solid black as she stared into the darkness. The salt smell of the sea was sharp and biting. Rue could make out a narrowing of the peninsula, a crossing only wide enough for a road and train tracks. The sky car cable stretched above, empty for the moment. This narrows was one of the Great Works, a land bridge built by the East India Company. When they selected Bombay as their port, they turned seven islands into one peninsula.

Rue ran through the narrows, big paws silent, leaving behind Bombay and heading into the untamed countryside. The roads were rough and dirty, smelling of iron-rich clay, rust, and old blood. The vegetation to either side was untamed, the likes of which she had never scented in England. There were no neat hedgerows of holly, no oak or apple trees, no fields of heather. Monkeys and other alien creatures scampered away, leaving scent trails of fur and meat.

At each fork in the road, Miss Sekhmet instructed her, guiding them further north, angled slightly inland. Rue could tell this from the fading ocean smells. She began to scent what must be jungle. The odour of thick green mosses, layers of leaves, and damp roots hit her well before she crested a small hill and saw a massive forest. Under the silvered moonlight, the world ahead of them seemed nothing more than a rolling nest of shadow trees.

Percy said softly, so as not to disturb the moment, "This isn't Tungareshwar. Believe it or not, this is a smaller forest, only a few leagues wide, unnamed on my map. Tungareshwar is on the other side."

Rue followed the pathway forwards and into the dark of overhanging branches. She knew that a jungle was no ordinary wooded glen of the respectable English countryside. It boasted not only huge trees, ferns, and copious undergrowth but vines that grew up and through and over everything. It lacked discipline, too much wildness, like a woman full grown who did not turn up her hair. It was unsettling, even to Rue. And Rue was one of those young ladies most disparaged by society for being wild. She put on a burst of speed, stretching her supernatural strength to the maximum, rushing through the undergrowth so fast anything that might jump out at her would only manage a mouthful of tail tip.

She felt Miss Sekhmet and Percy tighten their legs about her waist and hunker down. Miss Sekhmet lay forward across her neck, as Prim was wont to do, her hot breath near one of Rue's ears. It twitched in reaction.

"Gently, kitten," she murmured, loud enough for Rue to hear but not Percy. "There is nothing in these woods that can harm you as you now are."

Rue could not explain that her fear was for those who sat astride her. Her responsibility was to their mortal forms, which now seemed very fragile. *Why did I bring Percy? Prim will kill me if anything happens to him. He's not made for this.* She thought of turning around and taking him back to the *Custard*, but it was too late, and he'd probably make a fuss if she did.

A half-hour of running and Rue burst through and out of the unnamed forest.

Only to find that she was at the edge of a steep cliff. Far below, a river cut along the gorge. The water was so far down, her nose hadn't warned her of its presence before her ears did. She skidded to a halt, turning up road dust and scrabbling for purchase with her paws.

She lost her passengers.

Percy, fortunately, weighed down by his book satchel, fell to one side, landing safely in the bushes with a cry of distress.

But Miss Sekhmet, already leaning forward, tumbled over Rue's head and fell down into the gorge.

Rue's instinctive reaction was to give the werecat back her immortality. If she could snap their tether before Miss Sekhmet hit the water far below, or worse, the rocks, she might survive. So Rue whirled and dashed back the way she had just come, leaving Percy alone at the top of the cliff.

Though tired, Rue could move a great deal faster without the burden of riders. Her only concern was to put distance between herself and the woman whose form she had stolen. Rue hoped against all hope she was not also in danger of stealing Miss Sekhmet's life.

She ran with such speed even a vampire could not have caught her.

Abruptly, between one stride and the next, Rue found herself sprawled on the dirt road. She was naked, aching from the painful suddenness of the shift, shivering in the cool of the night. The vegetation around her sharpened into focus, greens she had not seen as a cat became vibrant even under moonlight. Individual smells were lost, replaced by a mild scent of dust and jungle.

Did it work? was her first worry. She had no way of knowing if her tether to the werelioness had been severed because Miss Sekhmet died, or because Rue had reached tether limits and lioness form rebounded, saving Miss Sekhmet from that brutal fall.

She had no way of finding out either, for now Rue was some distance away from that fateful cliff.

She stood, taking the scarf from about her neck and wrapping it around her body in a crude attempt to preserve modesty. She left the sparkler hanging in its lily reticule and turned, resigned to trudging back the way she had just come. She cursed herself for going so fast initially. For not checking with Miss Sekhmet as to the nature of the forest edge. For not making better use of her unfamiliar supernatural senses.

It was a much longer walk bare-footed and without supernatural speed. Stones in the path cut her feet where the pads of her lioness paws had felt nothing. She was more afraid that the scent of her blood would attract predators than she was upset by the pain. One lucky result of shifting to wolf form on a regular basis – if one could call it *lucky* – was that Rue could withstand pain better than most normal genteelly bred Englishwomen. She ignored her feet and walked, occasionally calling out in the hope that Percy would hear her. One never knew with Percy. He could have decided to move towards her, or he could be attempting to assist Miss Sekhmet, or he could be walking into Tungareshwar Forest alone, or he could be sitting in the roadway reading a book about swimming hedgehogs.

Three-quarters of an hour later, tired, dusty, bleeding, and tetchy with worry, Rue arrived back at the fateful cliff.

Percy was nowhere to be seen.

Rue hobbled to the edge and looked down into the gorge.

Miss Sekhmet's beautiful form did not lie crumpled far below.

Nor was she walking along the riverbank as a lioness, looking for some convenient way to leap up.

The werecat had vanished.

Rue straightened and took a long look all around her, feeling very alone. Behind her lay the vast reaches of the unnamed forest she had already traversed. It would take all night for her to walk back through it. Before her lay the gorge. Across that loomed another jungle, even larger, darker, and lusher than the previous one.

Rue set her shoulders. She still had the sparkler. She could signal for aid, as unlikely as it was that anyone would respond this far from civilisation. If Miss Sekhmet were somehow behind her and alive, she could follow Rue's trail from the bleeding of her feet. Percy was a worry. But having come so far, Rue saw nothing for it but to continue on alone.

There were two bridges around the corner from where Rue had dumped her riders. On the left side was a railway bridge, which crossed and then veered away from Tungareshwar towards the coast. Above that stretched one of the sky cables. It headed straight into the forest, although admittedly high above it. Slumbering there, right before the crossing, was yet another of the great elephant sky trains. It hung partly suspended above the gorge, as though it had stopped for a nap mid-run. Its interior was dark, its necklace of lanterns unlit. Rue supposed it was under orders, like the rest of the country, not to work after dark. It swung gently, rocking its slumbering cargo and crew. Rue wondered if she could shout them awake and ask for aid. But what could she say? *I'm an underdressed Englishwoman looking for weremonkeys? Oh, and I seem to have misplaced a professor and a werelioness.* And how would she make that statement clear using pantomime, since she didn't speak the language?

To the right of the elephant was a foot-traffic bridge made of slats of wood and rope, of the suspension type. It was designed for people, not animals or wheeled transport. Only pilgrims were permitted entrance into Tungareshwar.

Rue put a hesitant foot on the first board. The bridge swayed under her weight.

She was not afraid of heights. One could hardly captain a dirigible and be scared to look down. But Rue felt more in control of *The Spotted Custard* than this bridge, and without supernatural form it did seem a long way down and a shaky means of crossing a river.

Rue paused, considering her situation. She had nothing more to her name than a reticule shaped like a lotus, a flint and tinder, a sparkler, and an indecently small shawl. Her feet ached something awful. Best, she thought, to devise some means of locomotion and not walk if she didn't have to. She looked at the elephant in the sky. She was no fit company for a crew of young steam jockeys.

Nevertheless, she damned modesty to the winds and left the bridge, heading for the nearest support tower. It was basically a tall pole sunk into the ground at the edge of the gorge. It had metal rungs all the way up. Rue took a fortifying breath and began to climb.

The smooth metal was cold, but kinder to her feet than the rough road. It seemed not too long before she was at the top.

Making certain the scarf was secure about her body and the reticule about her neck, Rue swung herself up, legs wrapped about the cable, and began to shimmy along towards the train. It was challenging work. *I should consider taking on labour as a deckling to improve my climbing skills, not to mention arm strength.* Being not so very fit, Rue had to take it gradually, otherwise her muscles might give out. Even so, halfway along, her arms began to shake. But she made it – a fact that she noticed only when her head bashed into the trunk of the metal elephant.

The trunk disguised multiple guidance gears that fitted into tracks on the cable. It presented a bit of difficulty to Rue, who could no longer crawl dangling from the cable towards the head of the beast. And that was her objective since Quesnel had said it housed the navigation chamber.

She twisted this way and that, finally managing to flip herself over and on top of the trunk so that she could scoot up it, legs and arms desperately wrapped around the scales of metal, moving on her belly. Her poor tummy was entirely unused to the sensation of cold rough metal, or indeed any exposure. *Imagine what Mother would say*, thought Rue, *of me brandishing my midriff to an elephant*. She didn't have to imagine. Mother would have called her all kinds of heathen and ordered her to get dressed immediately. Rue had the whole conversation in her head as she squirmed along.

"My daughter is a barbarian dressed in an orange peel!"

"But, Mother, I am stranded in the middle of a tropical forest."

"Pish tosh," said imaginary Mother. "Trivial detail. Your reputation is a stake. What will they think of you?"

"Who? The local grubs?"

"How do you know grubs don't have delicate sensibilities? Cover yourself this instant, infant," was her mother's illogical opinion.

"Oh, really!" imaginary Rue said in exasperation.

Funny that even in my fantasies I lose arguments with my mother.

Eventually, the trunk dipped below the cable and widened enough for Rue to crawl on all fours, leaving the cable above her. She found herself face to face with one elephantine eye – an eye that was really a window through which the conductor might see.

Rue looked inside, shading out the moonlight with hands on either side of her face. The navigation chamber appeared to be empty. She supposed there was little fear of someone attempting to hijack an elephant train in the middle of an unpopulated jungle.

Rue wasn't certain at what point her subconscious had decided to hijack the air train – probably while the rest of her argued with her mother. With language and nudity against her, her chances of convincing the crew of her point of view were slim. Plus she was too embarrassed to turn up in front of them making demands, like a barbarian in an orange peel.

So as she continued crawling, she began to plan a theft. She kept in mind Dama's lessons in this regard, even though such lessons had mainly centred on objects a great deal smaller.

There must be crew somewhere, and the moment Rue started the engines that crew would come and stop her. She needed to uncouple the freight cars that made up the elephant's body from the locomotive of the elephant's head. The elephant was made to look as if it were basically dangling from the cable by its trunk but she knew that, in function, sky trains were much like a normal trains, hooked in at multiple points.

Rue crawled up and over the top part of the noggin, wiggling around the point where the head attached to the cable. From there, she manoeuvred down between the massive leather ears.

She lost purchase, swallowed a scream and slid down the back of the head, landing with a jarring thud at the coupling point.

The locomotive was chained and locked with a massive hitch to the freight cars. Rue wished once again for stronger arms or supernatural strength. Barring both, she managed eventually to brace herself between the two sections, and use her legs to lever the hitch up and off its hook. She then uncoiled the massive redundancy chains.

Rue could only hope she managed to get the elephant head moving quickly enough to break away before any crew awoke and reconnected the hitch, or jumped from the car to the locomotive.

Turning to face the head, Rue inched around the side, balanc-

ing on a little lip at the creature's chin, no doubt a remnant from
the original construction. It was precarious and remarkably lacking in handholds, but eventually she made it to the engine room.

No doubt the door was easy to open when one was at a station,
or even on one of the pole-top platforms. It was not as easy mid-
air. The door was directly below one of Ganesha's ears. Rue leaned
in and rattled the handle as quietly as she could while still clinging desperately with her free hand to the elephant's side. The door
swung open so abruptly that she lost her balance and grabbed the
ear. Fortunately, the leather was riveted on and held. She dangled
there like a Rue-shaped earring, breath caught in her throat. By
sheer will, for it could not be ability, she managed to rock and
grab the top of the door-jamb and swing inside, closing the door
firmly behind her. It was unbelievably reassuring to be safe in the
cabin. It took a very long time for her heart rate to subside.

The man who had been sleeping beneath the guidance console
woke up and stared at her in astonishment.

Rue could only imagine what she looked like, wearing nothing but a dislodged orange scarf, a reticule that looked like a lily
flower, and a monkey charm necklace. Her hair was wild and
loose. Her feet were bare and bleeding. Her skin was particularly
pale in the moonlight and covered in scratches.

The man did not yell – he merely gaped in surprise and then
began to prostrate himself as if she were visiting royalty. Or possibly some religious icon brought to life.

He kept repeating the word "Gauri," and bowing, then occasionally he would add, "Lakshmi." In between these, he spewed
forth a long string of sentences and cries and possibly small songs
or lines of poetry in his own language. His attitude was one of
profound reverence. He kept looking from the ground to his own
clasped hands to Rue's face to the reticule about her neck.

*I guess I'm a goddess. How is a Hindu goddess in a sky train supposed
to act?*

Rue smiled beatifically and made a gesture with both hands, a little like swimming, in a crude imitation of the dancers she'd seen at the Cloth Market. *Arms like graceful noodles*, she instructed herself.

The man gasped at her movement and fell silent.

Rue tried to convince him to rise, fanning her arms up and down in a ridiculous manner, but he seemed disinclined to do anything but kneel and bow.

Unsure what else to do, Rue lifted up her reticule, an object of much fascination. She removed it from about her neck and took out the sparkler.

The man moaned in fear and anticipation, eyes as wide as saucers.

Rue carefully put the flint, tinder, and sparkler aside on the steering column. Those she might need. And then she cast about the cabin for something meaningful.

To one side was the boiler, accompanied by the ubiquitous pile of coal. Rue picked up a small piece of the black and placed it carefully into the reticule, drawing it closed. Making several more of the dancer gestures over the bag with one hand while she held it in the other, feeling like a particularly poor conjuror, she hummed a little ditty. Her mind was so befuddled it latched upon a bawdy favourite of Paw's pack, "Eat Bertha's Muscles". Fortunately, the man kneeling before her was unfamiliar with the tune. Rue twirled three times in place for good measure and then handed the bag of coal to the man, who was kneeling with his hands cupped up in front of him like a beggar.

The man bowed his head, repeating those two words "Gauri" and "Lakshmi" over and over and attempting to hum his own version of "Eat Bertha's Muscles".

Rue wished she knew how to say the words "leave me" in Hindustani but, lacking any grasp of the language, she stood completely still with what she hoped was a stern, impassive, goddess-like expression and pointed to the door.

She didn't know what she expected. Perhaps for the man to leave by climbing around the elephant cheek the way she had.

Instead, he ran to the door, pushed it open and leapt out.

Rue suppressed an un-goddess-like shriek. She didn't want to kill the poor man!

She rushed after him, only to see that he had deployed some kind of parachute, which he must have grabbed from near the door. It looked a lot like a large conical parasol. He floated down to land a good distance away, on the other side of the gorge, in the unnamed forest. Rue heard him shout in elation and then the glad tones of "Eat Bertha's Muscles" wafted up to her. Presumably he was happy with life and the blessings of his holy visitor.

Well, thought Rue, *at least I made somebody's evening.*

The sky train Ganesha might look like a creature of Hindu mythology come to awesome mechanical life, but inside the guidance cabin was all classic British engineering. It was actually a rather simple, old-fashioned steam engine out of the Poedunkle-Boof Manufacturing Company in Bacon End. Rue's eyebrows arched as she read the plaque – it was a decade or more out of date! *It's been a while since the far reaches of the empire received upgrades. This is nothing compared to Quesnel's domain back on* The Spotted Custard. She stopped that thought before it started. Rue did not want to think about Quesnel. Given the catastrophe that her evening had become, he had not been as far from the truth when he had tried to stop her from starting all this.

The firebox was cold and dead which was odd as, even overnight, most steamers simply banked their coal. Also, the boiler was half full, hardly enough water for much of a journey. Perhaps there was a watering station on the other side of Tungareshwar?

Rue was undaunted. All she had to do was get everything up to temperature and the steam going, make certain all her dials, levers, and settings were configured correctly, keep the firebox stoked, and the elephant head would move. *Actually, that's rather a lot.* Fortunately, she had flint and tinder with her.

It took some time to stoke the boiler. The moon had moved a great deal since she started her escapade – the night was near half done. Eventually, she did manage the happy bubbling and steam emission of an operational engine. It was not easy to guide the Ganesha and stoke at the same time. Luckily, the elephant was inclined to stick to the cable although it did rattle a great deal. All steam engines by their nature need at least two people to run efficiently. With only one at the helm *and* stoking the boiler, the locomotive moved in fits and starts along the cable, an embarrassing stuttering that to any observer would seem as though the elephant god was overcome with occasional malaise. Not to mention that it was merely the head of the creature, with no body following behind.

If her thievery of the front of the sky train had been noted by the crew sleeping in the freight cars, Rue couldn't hear them shouting over the clanging of the engine. And if they had tried to jump the coupling, they were unsuccessful, for no one came after her. Some distance along, Rue took a moment to open the door and crane her head back to see, and there was no one following.

She stoked the boiler and jerked onward. She had no concrete plan except to take the Ganesha on into Tungareshwar's heart. Hopefully, there she might see or receive some sign.

Rue developed a pattern of stoking, checking her dials, pumping the guidance lever, and glancing out of the two windows.

Occasionally, she cracked the door and looked down into the for-est, hoping for an inkling of Percy or Miss Sekhmet, not certain what form that inkling might take. After all, she was the only one with the fire sparkler. And if there was a path beneath her, it was overarched by trees.

After an hour or so of stoking, Rue was beginning to think her arms might never recover from the night's experience. *And I still have to climb back down.* She considered stopping next to one of the poles, but her stubborn streak kicked in and she soldiered on.

Idiotic stubborn streak as it turned out. Because on her next check of the cable ahead Rue realised several things at once.

First, there was no more cable.

Second, the upcoming pole was her last and she was moving too quickly towards it.

Third, the boiler had been cold and the water reserves low because this engine wasn't meant to go anywhere at all. It was meant to test the stability of the line at each stage of installation.

Fourth, that was why it was so antiquated. As it was only there to check the cable, they had used cheap old technology.

Fifth, the man in the cabin to whom she had appeared as a goddess was not an engineer but a guard.

Sixth, no crew would be chasing her because there was no crew.

Rue realised all of this even as she grabbed for the brake lever, hauling back on it as hard as she could with a strength mere moments before she would have believed impossible. If only she had a second person to cool the boiler, to rake back the coals. Alone, her best option was a mechanical one. She hoped the lever wasn't too old. Her arms screamed in pain almost as loudly as the brake screamed in reality.

The Ganesha head slowed. The brake locked down, no longer requiring Rue's measly strength. The engine shuddered against it. Freed suddenly, Rue dived for the firebox. Grabbing the rake, heedless of her own safety, she pulled the coals out into the slop grate, although part of her knew it would not be sufficient to cool the boiler. A few embers fell to the floor of the cabin, scorching Rue's bare legs. She hardly noticed.

The firebox was empty and the brake had managed to slow the elephant head, but not enough. With relentless precision Ganesha crawled towards the last pole, after which the cable dangled down like a limp snake.

Rue slammed open the door and looked for a second parasol parachute — nothing. At a complete loss of what else to do, she grabbed her sparkler and dipped the fuse into the slop grate, aiming for a still smouldering coal. It lit. She leaned out of the door and threw it as hard as she could up into the air.

She heard its loud bang and the forest below lit up with a flood of yellow light. Everything was in sharp and sudden relief, the vibrant green of the trees extending endlessly in every direction, every leaf painfully clear. Rue could see the end pole with its builders' scaffolding, obviously in the middle of construction, coming relentlessly closer.

And then Rue saw something she wasn't expecting. The face of an extremely unfriendly-looking monkey pressed upside down to the window of her cabin.

Rue screamed and backed away from the door, slamming it shut.

The monkey creature swung over the top of the elephant head with consummate skill, performing a flip that put him on the other side of the door. A door he proceeded to rip off of its hinges and discard casually into the jungle below.

Well, I call that unnecessary. The door has a perfectly good handle.

The creature swung through the opening to land gracefully on the floor facing Rue.

He was much bigger than a monkey should be and stood fully upright like a human, but with more muscles than any human

Rue had ever seen – except maybe one strongman at a carnival. He had very long arms and an extremely articulate tail. He was wearing a loincloth of expensive blue silk, a breastplate of beaten gold, and a great deal of jewellery.

Rue stared at him, open-mouthed. Impressed despite herself. *Well, golly. I guess Vanaras do exist.*

Without an attempted introduction or making any noise whatsoever – *could he speak in that form?* – the creature advanced towards her. His eyes were riveted on the monkey charm necklace.

He made as if to pick her up.

Rue held out her hands, warding him off, not because she didn't want the help – if he wanted to rescue her, she had no objection to being rescued – but because she would likely steal his form just as she could steal that of a werewolf or werelioness.

With a noise of disgust, the Vanara ignored her non-verbal protest as a hysterical female reaction and scooped her up with his tail. Wrapping it tight about Rue's *naked* midriff.

Only to suddenly have no tail at all.

The man who now stood before Rue was comely with dark almond eyes, ridiculously thick eyelashes, and velvety tea-coloured skin. He was slighter as a human than he was in his monkey form, muscles having been redistributed into lankiness rather than bulk. As a monkey he was golden with black feet, hands and face, but as a man he was a true child of India, princely in his bearing and appearance. If not in his utter shock at being suddenly mortal.

Rue tried to look apologetic.

Only to find that it was very hard to do apologetic wearing a monkey face.

CHAPTER

THIRTEEN

Monkey Hijinks

The transformation was sudden and a great deal less painful than when turning werecat. Rue supposed not as many bones needed to break and shift about when going from human to monkey. Instead, it seemed mostly muscle being redistributed. Her hair turned short and extended to most of her body. It was a mottled dark brown colour, much like her fur in wolf form, only fuzzier. Her arms, previously so sore and tired, recovered and gained additional strength and length. Most peculiar of all was her tail. As a werewolf, Rue's tail rather took matters into its own hands, as it were, reflecting her moods and waving about indiscriminately. As a werecat, it had seemed only mildly under her command. But as a weremonkey, she had total control over this appendage, like an extra arm with only one finger. It was rather fun.

Rue had no time to dwell. The Ganesha head was still creeping relentlessly towards the end of the cable, and the embers she had brushed out of the firebox were beginning to find fallen bits of fibre and other combustibles, flaming to life on the floor of the cabin.

Acting on instinct, Rue did as the Vanara had attempted mere moments before. She grabbed her metanatural victim with her amazing tail and ran to the doorway, carrying him behind her.

The man cried out in fear.

Rue stumbled slightly. Her legs did not work quite the same way as in human form. Her large dextrous hands found purchase on the doorframe. She was incredibly strong as a Vanara. It was delightful – like a particularly well-brewed tea.

The pole top was now in front of her. The Ganesha was definitely going to overshoot it. No time to think, Rue leapt onto it, using her extra-long arms to grab down and stabilise her landing. The man clutched in her tail acted as a counterweight. It was unexpected, that weight, and Rue rocked back and forth, nearly falling. She modified her stance a split-second before they both tumbled over the edge, then held herself down and relaxed into the sensation of a man in her tail. The Vanara stilled in her grasp, sensing the danger in this newly made weremonkey's shaky understanding of her own agility.

With a climbing speed unequalled by any other form she'd stolen, Rue made her way down the scaffolding to the ground. There she placed the man carefully on his own two feet and stood before him, feeling guilty. She *had* tried to warn him. She wondered if she could formulate words with her monkey face and explain herself. *Nothing to do but try.*

Her voice came out, slurred and much lower than before, but functioning.

"Ruehh," she said, gesturing to herself.

The man babbled at her in Hindustani.

Rue shook her head. "Englisssh," she said slowly, trying to enunciate.

The man had gone from fear to anger now that he was safe on land. He began yelling and pacing, and pointing at her and then him as if trying to instruct her to give him his shape back.

Rue shook her head. *It doesn't work like that. I can't control it.*

And now I intend to keep it. It's much warmer and my arms don't hurt any more. I'm very sorry. I didn't mean to steal from you. She said, "I thhried to warn you not to toucsssh me."

The man continued yelling. Then in one furious move, he reached forward and yanked the monkey charm from around Rue's neck.

Above them, the head of Ganesha reached the end of the line. At the same time, the fire inside made its way to the oil reserves that lubricated the engine's gears. It roared into an inferno. A massive elephant head fireball slipped off the cable and fell down into the forest with a tremendous crash.

The man in front of Rue jumped and whirled. Realising what must have happened, he turned back, yelled at her some more – apparently this was also her fault.

Rue shrugged at him.

He finally realised that there was nothing she could do about having stolen his shape. Or he determined she wasn't giving it back. At least she had not run away. He made a rude gesture and turned, striding into the thick foliage, holding his loincloth up with one hand when it threatened to slide off his now lean hips.

Rue checked to ensure that her modesty scarf was secured. Her monkey chest was a good deal wider than her lady chest, but her endowments were smaller, so that section had stayed in place. During the course of her climbing adventures the bottom part had loosened, but that meant it fit her now wider, muscled hips. Her legs and arms were covered in the brown fur. Rue wasn't certain how she felt about *that* but she supposed it might count as a modesty covering. The society madams would have had something snide to say but Rue strongly suspected that, should she encounter one roaming the Indian jungle, arm hair would not be high up on the list of complaints.

She shuffled after the indignant man, realising that her legs were bowed like a sailor's when not climbing. Rue hoped that he would lead her to someone who could interpret English or this was going to be a very long night indeed. She considered ways she might pantomime the meaning of *metanatural* as a monkey. It seemed nigh on impossible.

Tungareshwar from within was a great deal different than Tungareshwar from above. The undergrowth was mostly made up of thick plants with large wide leaves and a few bushes which looked like sage. Trees of all sizes stretched upwards – Rue recognised palm and banana – and vines grew over everything. It was delightfully tropical. She was no horticulturalist but she spotted a few orchids – her night vision seemed quite decent in weremonkey form. Occasionally they crossed a small stream, its embankment covered in a thick carpet of maidenhair fern. Rue would have enjoyed a stroll through Tungareshwar during the daylight. It must be stunning, everything verdant and lush, green broken only by the black of tree trunks and bright splashes of exotic flowers.

Then her ears started roaring. She thought it might be a weremonkey thing and tried surreptitiously shaking her head.

Eventually, she realised they were heading up the side of one stream into a valley and the sound was coming from a large waterfall. They rounded a bend in the river and there it was ahead of them, extraordinarily picturesque. The moon hung in three-quarter glory directly over the white falls, trees dipping in all around. To each side of the falls built out of – but also part of – the cliff was a massive sandstone temple. Rue assumed the stones ranged in colour, although at night she could only see shifting shades. It was clearly very old – the dominating motif was one of steep arches rather than spires or onion shapes. It was naturalistic, modelled on leaf shapes, its doorways like open flowers and its columns like tree trunks.

Rue gasped appreciatively. "It'ssh beautiful!"

Her unwitting guide did not turn when she spoke, merely continued marching up the right side of the waterfall. This side of the temple was lit by a large bonfire in the enclosed front courtyard. Around this was a group of shadowy figures. Some crouched, others perched, a few sat in proper formal fashion on top of strangely modern large spheres. The figures jerked and twitched in a frenzied manner, unable to keep still. They all wore a quantity of gold plate which gleamed in the firelight. They were all quite furry.

The newly made mortal man marched through the wide entranceway towards the group, trailing Rue behind him.

The assembly was engaged in some manner of civilised discourse, sipping earthenware cups of spiced tea. It comprised a dozen or so Vanaras, Miss Sekhmet, and Professor Percival Tunstell.

Behind the group and up a level was a beautifully ornate silver birdcage – many times larger than a normal birdcage – in which Miss Sekhmet's lioness form sat, looking disgruntled but unhurt. Rue wondered if the silver cage kept her from turning back to human shape or if there were some other reason she remained a cat. Piled next to her and around her was more gold. The Vanaras were obviously fond of the stuff.

Percy sat in the centre with silver manacles around his wrists chained to a matching set around his ankles and from there to a ring in the stone floor.

Rue and her escort took up position near Percy in front of the weremonkeys, who all stopped talking and stared at them.

The spheres they sat upon proved to be transport containers,

brass-made and slitted open on the sides in wedges like a sporadi-
cally eaten orange. Each one held a quantity of dirt and a selection of healthy-looking seedlings, suspended above which was a
series of tubes and bulbous bladders that could only be an automated watering system.

Dama's missing tea!

Upon registering that one of their number was apparently
involuntarily human, the Vanaras all stood up and began talking
at once, in Hindustani of course. Rue's mortal victim threw the
monkey charm at the feet of his fellows in evident disgust.

At the same time Percy, who could not stand, leaned forward,
squinting in the firelight and said, "Rue, is that you?"

"Of coursh ish me. Pershy, what ish going on?"

Percy blinked at her myopically, having lost his spectacles at
some point. "Aside from the fact that we just watched the head of
Ganesha emit a fire sparkler, catch fire, explode, and fall into the
forest?"

"Ah, yesh," said Rue. "That would be me assh well."

Percy's expression said he found this utterly unsurprising. "Our
hosts thought it a sign from the gods."

Rue nodded. "I sheem to be reshponshible for a number of
those thish evening."

Percy evaluated her newly fuzzy form. "Interesting outfit you're
wearing for an evening call."

"Yesh, well, Primrosh did insisht I bring the scarf. It would be
churlish of me not to wear it."

"That wasn't what I meant to imply. Are you covered in hair?"

"Pershy, you're as blind as a billiard ball. I'm a weremonkey."
She cocked her hip out and flicked her tail. "The tail ish remarkably useful. Even better than the cat one. You know, I should like
a tail as a rule. Difficult in skirts, I sushpose."

"Oh?"

Rue decided they'd engaged in sufficient banter for the moment. "Enough of thish, Pershy. What's been happing? How did you get here? Why ish she still a lionessssh? And mosh importantly, what are they saying?"

Percy made as if to push his non-existent specs up his nose. Finding them gone, he lowered his hand awkwardly. "That's a number of questions to answer all at once. Where should I start?"

"Begin at the beginning. Ish very becoming, not to mention organised."

Thus, while the Vanaras argued with one another, apparently questioning the veracity of everything their mortal compatriot was telling them about Rue, Percy explained.

Rue had, indeed, managed to race away fast enough so that when Miss Sekhmet hit the bottom of the gorge, she was a supernatural and unhurt. She'd climbed out and found Percy waiting at the top. She'd changed into lioness form so that Percy could ride. They had been about to go looking for Rue when they were assaulted from above. The Vanaras had dropped down out of the trees in a coordinated attack, and thrown a silver net over Percy and Miss Sekhmet.

"But I thought she was allied with them?"

"Not close enough to be forgiven for bringing me along, I guess. And there was something about a missing necklace. She could hardly explain. She's been stuck as a cat ever since. They trussed us up as if we were a loin of pork. Then wrapped us in a thick blanket over the net, presumably to protect themselves from the silver. One of them carried both of us through the forest, Miss Sekhmet struggling the whole while. They must be very strong. Once here, they put Miss Sekhmet into that cage and manacled me. Silver" – he pointed to his feet – "or silver-plated, so I think they may believe I'm a werewolf or something. I tried to explain I wasn't, otherwise why would I ride when I could run? But they ignored me."

Occasionally, one of the Vanaras would walk over and circle Rue, staying well out of tail reach, but clearly curious.

"How do you do?" Rue would say politely, examining each in return before returning her attention to Percy.

There were no females among those assembled so they must have the same issue as other supernaturals with metamorphosing women. Or perhaps female Vanaras assembled separately, like after supper in England? Still, given the Vanara interest, either Rue herself as a female was an oddity, or the story that the mortal Vanara was telling about Rue was sparking intrigue.

Rue endured it while directing Percy to continue.

"Whash been happening sinsh you were captured?"

"They realised I could speak their language – although theirs is an exotic dialect, I'm thinking perhaps quite ancient, very exciting—"

"Pershy, pleash don't get dishacted with minutia."

"They had me sit, gave me this odd tea to drink. They are very fond of tea. Value it above all things. Collect it as tribute, I understand. Where was I? Oh yes, they won't let me talk unless it's to answer one of their questions. So I haven't been able to discern much. Besides which, I don't quite know what I'm permitted to reveal to them. Officially, or, erm, militarily, as it were. There have been a number of awkward silences. Reminds me of an opera."

"Oh, really, Pershy."

"Well, what can I do?"

Rue tapped her foot. Then was forced to engage in a rapid exchange of small bows with one of the Vanaras. "Have you learnt anything of ushe?"

Percy frowned. "Culturally? Vanaras are accustomed to being

considered beneficial sacred beings – even gods. They expect reverence, gold, and tea. They openly and understandably resent the very idea that we British purport to bring enlightenment to the locals. They think of this as their role. They blame us for the fact that they must hide here in the forest. They like Tungareshwar well enough, but this is their offering temple and retreat, not their home. Before the British arrived, they spent the majority of their time closer to cities. They have been hiding here for nearly forty years."

Rue was frustrated. "Why? We are a progreshive empire. We have alwaysh made contact with the local supernaturals and recruited them to our cause. We have alwaysh tried to passh on the ideal of incorporating supernaturals *into* society." In her frustration, Rue was learning to control the shape of her new jaw. Her speech became clearer. "If they already were an accepted part of Indian society, why didn't they meet us openly at the start? We might have treated the entire country differently, if we had known of their existence. The fact that they were already progressed would have been taken by Queen Victoria as a sign of enlightened thought. Wars might have have avoided."

Percy cocked his head and, strangely, defended his captors. "My dearest Rue, have you forgotten who first made contact here in India?"

"Oh dear, of course. Bloody John." The East India Company was a vampire concern. Rue's monkey face crinkled up. Her tail switched back and forth in irritation, like a cat. Her forms were getting confused. "Are you telling me that we inadvertently allied with one side of an ongoing supernatural civil war?"

"That might indeed be the case."

Turning to Percy, one of the Vanaras gesticulated at his own furry throat. Then he said something in his native tongue.

Percy replied in stuttering Hindustani before explaining to Rue. "They want me to interpret."

"Please do."

This particular Vanara was the most important – if one were to judge by the quantity of gold draped upon him.

Rue was taken aback by the sheer number of gold bangles he wore. Among London's fashionable set such an amount of jewellery was the height of vulgarity. However, barring any other indication of authority, she curtseyed to the speaker deferentially. It was awkward to curtsey in bowed monkey legs with no skirt. She thought it quite the achievement – not falling over.

Percy spoke for the Vanara. "Foreign Devil Woman, why have you stolen our companion's monkey self?"

"*Foreign Devil Woman?* Really?" said Rue.

Percy replied, "It's the best direct translation I can think of, unless you prefer Alien Daughter of Evil?"

Rue ignored this and said to the Vanara, "Apologies. I tried to warn your friend not to touch me. This is not something I can control."

"Lies, White Devil Female."

"Percy, must you repeat that particular part?" hissed Rue, and then: "I do not lie." She decided to risk her own safety for the sake of negotiation. "Your fellow can get his monkey shape back by moving away from me."

Percy paused before translating. "Rue, you risk yourself unnecessarily."

"If all else fails, I'll dive in and touch another one."

"You're sure?"

"Repeat what I said, pleash, Pershy." Rue once more found her jaw disobeying her. She wondered if English was ill-suited to monkeys.

Percy did as she asked.

The Vanara responded with a gesture at Rue's victim. Without comment, the handsome man turned and trudged away.

"He'll need to go further than that."

He kept up his steady pacing until he was lost around a bend of the stream, back into the depths of the forest.

Eventually, Rue felt a tell-tale initial tremor and then her bones and muscles were re-forming. The pain made her wince but she managed to keep from moaning. Her tail vanished and she mourned its absence. The fur retreated back up her body, becoming her own tangled brown hair once more – that, at least, was gratifying. Rue was vain about her hair. She fluffed it forwards to cover as much of her torso as possible. She felt unmistakable physical loss as her monkey strength dissipated. This was so annoying that she was forced to consider seriously doing more physical exertion in the future. *If I am to continue this new life as an adventuress I may have to train for it.* The very idea! Her orange modesty scarf loosened about her waist and she quickly grabbed it and re-tied the side.

The Vanaras all about her gasped in awe. A few spoke out of turn, but the bejewelled monkey in front of Rue made a silencing gesture with his wrinkled, hairy hand. They fell quiet, if not still. Vanaras, Rue was beginning to realise, were never still.

Her victim reappeared, walking back down the stream, once more in Vanara form, and pleased about it. Or as pleased as a man with a monkey face could look, which was more a stretching of the lips into a grimace.

The highly decorated Vanara, who Rue decided must be Alpha, began talking once more. Percy resumed translating.

"Remarkable, Foreign Devil—" Percy forcibly stopped himself. "But what kind of creature are you, who is no Vanara in truth but a thief of our shape?"

Rue was glad to have her own voice back – it was much less troublesome. "I know not the word in your language. We would say *metanatural*, the child of a soulless. *Flayer*, say the werewolves. *Soul-stealer*, say the vampires. Miss Sekhmet there calls me a *skin-stalker.*"

Percy did his best to translate, using Hindustani where he could, English words where he couldn't.

The Vanara Alpha did not respond for a long time. He turned and went to speak quietly with one of the other weremonkeys, a smaller, delicate-looking creature with almost-white fur. Eventually he returned his attention to Rue.

"We have legends of Vanaras in the past who could take many forms in service to the gods. Are you one of these? A lost kinswoman?"

Rue said, "I'll take it. Kinswoman is better than Foreign Devil Woman any evening. If it helps, I too am fond of tea. Perhaps it runs in the family?" But despite her enthusiasm, the Vanara did not relax in his aggressive stance, even though it was he who had extended the offer of kinship.

He continued, "This seems a reasonable explanation. Tea love is always good, but sadly we cannot hold you as family in truth. Our foreign brothers whose form is one with Bhairava's mount have lost their way and fight for the Rakshasas and their pact with your queen."

Percy interjected at this point: "'Bhairava's mount' is their term for werewolves. Although, according to legend, I believe the mount was a dog of some variety."

"Yes, thank you, Percy."

Behind the twitching Vanaras, in her silver birdcage, Miss Sekhmet suddenly spat and hissed in agony or frustration.

The Vanara Alpha ignored her and continued talking to Rue. "So you too, kinswoman, might be an agent of evil. Turned by the Rakshasas against us in the service of conquerors."

It was an insulting way to put it but Rue had to admit, from his perspective, it was a fair assessment. How on earth was she to explain British politics, the position of the East India Company, or the very idea of social progression, to a bunch of monkeys?

She gave it her best shot. "The Rakshasas are unpleasant. On this matter we entirely agree. But our vampires at home are not the same. And you must understand, Her Majesty did not know of your existence."

"This is irrelevant to the fact that you allied with them. You gave daemons money, trade, technology, *tea*."

Rue struggled with a way to defend what seemed to be a grievous political error the British Empire hadn't even known it was committing. "We are a civilised nation. It is our policy to ally with the supernatural wherever we are in the world. Our politicians draw little distinction between werewolf and vampire, between Rakshasa and Vanara. Forgive me if this seems an insult. In the queen's eyes all are special. All are worthy."

Around her, as Percy repeated her words, the Vanaras chittered in annoyance. Rue wasn't certain if they were angry with her, with what had happened with first contact, or with the implication of her words.

When a little of the noise died out, Rue took a chance at asking her own question. "Is this why you have stolen the taxes, an Englishwoman, and my father's tea? Is it an opening to negotiations? Do you wish to change the terms of India's supernatural treaty with England? You needn't have kidnapped a lady to make a point. I am sure Queen Victoria would have opened negotiations the moment we confirmed your existence. You need not have hidden."

Once more the Vanara around her erupted into yelled conversation. Percy did his best to repeat some of what he heard. "With the Rakshasas on your side? All attempts would be corrupted. They foul everything they touch. The British gave them control over money and technology and communication and thought those daemons would not use it to drive us away? To see us extinct? Is she mad? How could anyone ally with the Rakshasas and not know their true nature? They're evil, always been so."

Oh dear, thought Rue. *I might not be doing any good whatsoever.*

She said loudly. "Where is Mrs Featherstonehaugh? May I see her? Is she unharmed?"

Percy actually tried to shout her words, looking mortified at having to raise his voice.

The Alpha Vanara heard him. "Now is the time to stop talking, kinswoman. You have given us much to think on and discuss. Dawn is soon to come."

But someone else had heard Rue's query and, high above, out from behind a series of arches, stepped a lady. She was perhaps a year or so younger than Rue, dressed sensibly in a travelling suit – four seasons old – of grey canvas with a black velvet-trimmed collar. Under the jacket was a ruffled shirtwaist and a gentleman's-style waistcoat. Perched atop flaxen hair scraped into a bun was a straw boater with black velvet ribbon. She held a wooden cane with an ivory handle in one hand. She had a face too long to be pretty but her attitude was becomingly frank. Her stance was firm and Rue noticed that *she* had not been manacled. Perhaps the Vanaras did not like to restrain women. After all, Rue herself had not been shackled. Yet.

Rue looked her over as she approached. "Mrs Featherstonehaugh, I presume?"

FOURTEEN

Ladybugs to the Rescue

Mrs Featherstonehaugh walked around and down, the limp that required the cane one of inconvenience rather than pain. Either that or she'd learnt not to show her discomfort. The Vanara treated her courteously, if not with any particular reverence. Nor were they overly familiar. She was a guest and free to move around, but not considered particularly important.

Rue said, with a small curtsey, "Prudence Akeldama at your service. How do you do?"

The woman's face showed no sign of recognition. Either she was very good at being impassive or her status as Dama's agent did not confer with it knowledge of his family connections. Or she didn't know who her master really was.

"How do you do, Miss Akeldama?" Mrs Featherstonehaugh stopped a few feet from her. Omission of title? Was Mrs Featherstonehaugh trying to insult her? Lady Akeldama's name was so prevalent in the society column that it was odd the spy didn't recognise it.

"My dear Mrs Featherstonehaugh, we thought you were in grave danger."

The lady dismissed any concern with a twitch of her cane. Nor was she the type to be taken in by Rue's sympathetic tone. "Very kind I'm sure, but who is *we?*"

Forthright indeed! Rue felt it only right to respond in kind. "Oh, you know, your standard concerned party of miscreants."

The woman looked her up and down. Had she a monocle, she would have peered through it suspiciously. "I see. In which case, you will understand that I cannot trust you."

Rue thought hard, frowning. Trying to remember the name spoken by that young woman, Anitra, in the Maltese Tower. *Oh yes.* "Goldenrod sent me."

Mrs Featherstonehaugh paused. "You are not his normal type."

Rue might have agreed, had she not met Anitra. "Neither are you."

Mrs Featherstonehaugh acknowledged the hit with a slight dip of her chin.

Having no other proof to offer than that she knew Dama's code name, Rue tried an attack. "My dear Mrs Featherstonehaugh, are you trying to start a war?"

"They do not find my presence nearly as unsettling as they do yours. You are the threat."

"Ah, but I am not a brigadier's wife."

"Is he looking for me?"

"With his army. And he blames the werewolves for losing you."

"Does he now?" Mrs Featherstonehaugh's face was hard to read. Did this fact upset or relieve her?

Percy said, "If I ask nicely, would you explain what is going on? This place, these creatures...remarkable." He sounded impossibly academic.

Mrs Featherstonehaugh noticed him for the first time. She reacted – as did most ladies, married or no – with a small verbal flutter. "Oh, how do you do, Mr——?"

Percy tried to rise, but his restraints kept him from standing. All he could do was make a sitting bow from the large square stone upon which he was chained. "Professor Percival Tunstell, at your service."

Mrs Featherstonehaugh curtseyed. "Professor, pleased to make the acquaintance of a man of learning."

"And as such I am eager to *learn* of your success in discovering these noteworthy beasts." He was also, no doubt, eager to learn if she intended to publish her findings or if he could have first crack.

Percy's flattery had the desired effect. Mrs Featherstonehaugh was delighted to enlighten him. "As you can see, Vanaras really do exist. Painstaking inquiry among the natives yielded only rumour. I needed to apply to the local religious observers and delve into the tea trade to uncover the truth. That's why I needed Goldenrod's plants. Even then, I travelled into this jungle on mere speculation."

"Remarkably intellectually modern of you, madam," encouraged Percy.

Mrs Featherstonehaugh blushed. "Why, thank you kindly. You'll never guess what else?"

"My dear lady, you have the entirety of my attention." He attempted a winning smile.

A blush resulted.

Rue had thought until that moment that Percy's charm was largely unintentional – now she was beginning to wonder.

Mrs Featherstonehaugh glowed under his regard. "I have learnt that we British offended them with our actions. It was our fault for appearing to have chosen sides. Or, better, the East India Company's fault for establishing a treaty with the Rakshasas."

Percy said, compelled to add detail to any situation, "Under the standards of the Supernatural Acceptance Decree?"

"Exactly so, professor."

Rue defended her countrymen. "That is policy. To favour and

recruit the disenfranchised supernatural element to our cause. It is how we win wars."

The blonde girl flushed. "I know policy! I am loyal to the crown."

Rue said, "Current circumstances would seem to indicate otherwise."

Mrs Featherstonehaugh ignored Rue in favour of Percy, appealing to his intellect, for Rue clearly had none. "It was a mistake not to research more before bargaining for Rakshasa alliance. Policy is to involve *all* of the native supernatural elements. By ignoring the Vanaras, we offended not only them but the local humans as well."

Rue said, "That is not fair. No one knew there were shapeshifters in India. Who would have thought to look for weremonkeys? Goodness, it's going to be a chore convincing home of the very idea, let alone the fact that they are many, organised, and easily offended by imperial decrees. Besides which, open hostility between supernatural races is so rare."

Mrs Featherstonehaugh said, "As I am sure the professor here knows, ancient history would beg to differ."

Percy nodded his support.

Rue felt a twinge of betrayal.

Rue had more faith in coexistence than anyone, having been raised by both vampires and werewolves. "The wasp does not battle the wolf – they ignore one another."

Mrs Featherstonehaugh looked frustrated. "This is not wasp and wolf. This is daemon and demigod."

"My dear lady, there are no such things as daemons." Rue would not budge on this.

Percy was compelled to interject at this point. "Well, actually, Rue, the technicality of the term is no different. Rakshasa means daemon – it's the same word. It was we who classified them as a type of vampire on the basis of sanguinary subsistence. They would not have known to identify themselves as such. And the wasp and the wolf comparison is a metaphor, not an actuality. Werewolves are no more like real wolves than vampires are like wasps. It's only a naturalistic model."

"Yes, thank you, Percy, for your valuable input," said Rue. *Less betrayal than pedantry, which might be considered worse.* "Regardless, why did the Vanaras not make themselves known to us sooner?"

Mrs Featherstonehaugh was annoyed. "Unlike everyone else, I bothered to learn the local language and I read considerably into the Hindu epics. If the legends are to be believed, for thousands of years Rakshasas and Vanaras have been enemies. There is even some suggestion that the Vanaras were created by Brahma specifically to battle the Rakshasas. They kill one another on sight. The moment Bloody John parlayed with the local vampires, England made an enemy of the Vanaras. These courageous, kind, and noble beings took to the forests." She spoke with trained eloquence, her free hand moving broadly.

Rue had to admit that someone had blundered with the Supernatural Acceptance Decree in India. *But what's done is done. The question is how to repair the damage? This woman is overly enthusiastic in her support.* A horrible thought occurred to Rue. "Mrs Featherstonehaugh, have you . . . gone native?"

Mrs Featherstonehaugh clutched her hand to her breast. She took a restorative gasp and lashed out. "Miss Akeldama! I am *not* the one dressed only in a scarf!"

Rue had forgotten that fact, warmed by the bonfire, not to mention the vigorousness of their debate. "I've had a difficult evening."

They paused, at an impasse. All the Vanara around them stood watching in twitchy interest – even without knowing the language, the exchange fascinated them. They reminded Rue of her father's pack witnessing similarly heated exchanges between Rue and her mother. It was as if the Vanara knew that if they uttered the merest peep, the womenfolk might turn on them.

Rue said, "And the tax money?"

Mrs Featherstonehaugh was offhand. "The Vanaras have certain expectations and I wished to parlay. Besides, those nasty Rakshasas don't deserve the funds!"

"And Dama's tea? You were given a sacred charge." It was, after all, the reason Rue had come to India in the first place.

Mrs Featherstonehaugh looked frustrated. "The Vanaras like nothing better than tea – it's the perfect bribe. He should understand."

Rue considered her Dama's feelings on the matter. "I doubt it." After all, this was some very important tea.

At this juncture, the Vanara Alpha stepped up to Mrs Featherstonehaugh and prattled out a query. The lady answered him, her flow and mastery of the language far superior to Percy's. Percy looked appropriately impressed.

Rue, who had initially admired Mrs Featherstonehaugh's boldness, was now finding it abrasive. Mrs Featherstonehaugh reminded Rue of a small blonde version of her mother. Which was only a good thing when they were on the same side. Currently, and through no fault of her own, Rue had been forced into justifying a policy made ten years before she had been born. A policy that she had only recently learnt of and that, until a week ago, had had no bearing on her life whatsoever. If they hadn't been arguing so aggressively, Rue might actually come around to agreeing with this horrible woman.

Rue tried to think about it without the spur of conflict, from the Vanara perspective. What if this was the war against Napoleon and she had come in and allied herself with the French because she had a policy that said she favoured all French emperors under a certain height? Absurd. Britain's current supernatural policy might seem equally absurd to the Vanaras. If Vanaras and Rakshasas never thought of themselves as kin – despite being both immortal, both supernatural, both undead – then they would, perforce, think of themselves as different species. *Scientific truth or not, some definitions are a matter of cultural tradition. It all comes down to categorisation in the end.*

Rue said, "Percy, do you remember anything about the SAD treaty with India, the original document as written between Bloody John and the Rakshasas?"

Percy said, "Of course I do. I remember most of it."

"You didn't happen to bring a copy in that satchel of yours, did you?"

"The Vanaras took it away from me." He was petulant, a schoolboy deprived of his sweeties.

"Well, cast your mind back, would you? Are the Rakshasas named as allies by title, or does it use the word vampires, or does it simply say local supernatural representatives?"

Percy thought about this for a long time.

Rue said, knowing she was up against his pride as an academic, "This is important, professor. Please don't say it either way if you can't remember exactly. You know how solicitors get."

Percy's face was glum in the flickering bonfire. "I can't recall the precise wording, Rue. But I think I follow your reasoning. They would have used the standard SAD paperwork which hasn't changed since Good Queen Bess. That one employs the vague descriptive 'native supernatural element' specifically so that vampires can't be named before werewolves, or vice versa. In which case . . ." He intentionally trailed off.

Rue turned back to Mrs Featherstonehaugh. She had stopped her conversation with the Vanara Alpha and was watching Percy intently. "Mrs Featherstonehaugh, did you study the original agreement with India under the Supernatural Acceptance Decree? The one that has been causing all this fuss?"

"No."

"Has your friend there?"

Mrs Featherstonehaugh asked the Vanara Alpha. "No."

"Then there is a possibility that the solution has existed all along. The standard treaty calls for an alliance with local supernaturals. Whether the Vanaras considered themselves of a similar type to the Rakshasas or not, Her Majesty did and does. They have been allied with us all along. Of course, we would have to make the case that whoever signed it for the Rakshasas also signed for the Vanaras."

Mrs Featherstonehaugh said, "How do you know they want to be our allies?"

Rue almost stamped her foot. "But it is a solution! They could come out of hiding, join forces with a progressive nation, collect back taxes, trade for all the technology they want. The queen would treat them fairly, I know she would."

Mrs Featherstonehaugh cocked her head, translating and then listening to the Vanara Alpha's thoughts on the matter. "He says they did very well before the British arrived. They do not want our help, our technology, or our entanglement. He says India is theirs."

"Oh dear," said Rue. "They really are dissidents."

Percy shook his head. "It's too late now. Industry is in place – sky trains and rails criss-cross this land. If he knows history firsthand, he knows that there is no progress backwards. There is only the engine of empire, advancing. We are civilisation and order. They would do well to ally with us now if at all possible." It seemed a ridiculous statement coming from an effete academic strapped to a rock.

Mrs Featherstonehaugh was upset by such broad imperialist sentiments. As the wife of a brigadier, she really shouldn't be surprised – it was her husband's business to enforce expansion. Still she said, "But, professor, they are so lovely and unsullied here in their forest. Can we not leave them in peace? Allow them to continue their battle with the Rakshasas. Pretend we never met them at all."

Rue said, "You were the one who wanted contact. You were the one who insisted they had been wronged. That the treaty should be righted."

Mrs Featherstonehaugh's face fell. "I did not consider the repercussions."

Rue said, "Progressive is not only what England is. It is what we do unto others."

"But is that *right?*" the lady wondered as if for the first time. Her arrogance was somewhat lost in moral quandry.

Rue considered her own existence. At any other time or place than England in the reign of Queen Victoria, she would not be alive. Even now, in this enlightened age, most of Europe hunted and killed supernatural creatures whenever possible, with increasing efficiency. Scientists were always making more and better anti-supernatural weapons. England had managed a balance which included acceptance of once-feared monsters. Perhaps the Great British Empire forced that acceptance upon others, but it was a policy that at its heart Rue could not help but endorse. It made up her world and, more importantly, her family.

So she took a stand on behalf of her government. "I exist because of Her Majesty's progressive politics. That Vanaras fight Rakshasas is their choice. We are sorry to have stumbled unwittingly into their war. But there is only one solution – the Vanaras must be included in the treaty. Our policy has always been to befriend both vampire and werewolf. It matters not to the queen if those vampires are daemons or those werewolves are weremonkeys."

Mrs Featherstonehaugh turned to relay this to the Vanara Alpha. He crossed his arms, angry, and spat something back to her.

She turned back to Rue. "They will not ally with those who are allied with the Rakshasas. No exceptions."

Percy said, clearly frustrated, "Don't be a fool. It is only a trade treaty. If they sign as well, they are on an equal footing. We could bring them back into the world. I know scientists would pay good money simply to talk to any one of them." Then he made as if he would say this exact thing to the Vanara.

Rue had great faith in diplomacy but she didn't know what to try next. *Should I lean on Vanara pride, insist that they can't allow the Rakshasas to have all the perks of an alliance? Or would an offer of special technology work better? And do I even have the authority to make bargains?* She was frustrated with her parents for putting her in such a position. *Officially, I can kill any of them with impunity, but I do not know what is right. That, in and of itself, is a mark against the empire's foreign policy.*

Then, from the top of a nearby tree, came a chittering of alarm. The weremonkeys all began to behave in a very odd manner. They started scrambling, reaching for their weapons: curved wooden blades, sharp and deadly, particularly to vampires. They looked up into the sky, monkey faces grave.

Rue inched closer to Percy. "What's going on? What are they saying?"

"They are under attack."

Mrs Featherstonehaugh joined them. "What have you done, idiot girl?"

Rue glared at her. "I say! No call for insults."

"Oh, I think there is. I had a good negotiation underway. They were beginning to talk to me, if not trust me. Then you come stumbling in here after a werecat and a professor and mess everything up."

"Speaking of Miss Sekhmet, why is she trapped in a birdcage in lioness form? I thought they liked her."

"I told them to put her there. I don't trust her. Her agenda is unclear. She is new to this territory and not of their kind. She said she would negotiate with the crown's representative but we have heard nothing from her in days. Then she shows up with a professor who clearly doesn't represent the crown."

"No," said Rue. "That would be me, I suppose."

Mrs Featherstonehaugh looked at her indecent attire doubtfully. "You don't know for certain?"

"You were expecting someone else?"

"I thought once I notified Goldenrod as to my suspicions surrounding the Vanaras that he would send one of his agents."

Rue sighed. "That message must have been intercepted. All we knew was that you had been kidnapped by dissidents. I was supposed to be following the tea. Nothing more. Then after you went missing I was supposed to find you and determine what you did with the tea."

"Bugger the tea!" Mrs Featherstonehaugh showed her soldier roots. She cast her eyes up to the heavens for support. Not uncommon in those debating with Prudence. "Oh my goodness me! What is that?" She had finally, along with almost everyone else, looked up at the sky.

Rue followed her gaze. "Well, blast it!"

The Spotted Custard was headed in their direction, making speed — well, speed for a dirigible out of aether, which wasn't very speedy at all, more a sedate breeze-born meander. She bobbed under the silver moon — a large spotted ladybug, running a search pattern over the forest, following the line of the sky rail, tacking back and forth in a zigzag pattern.

"I guess they got your signal," said Percy to Rue drolly.

"Did I leave instructions for them to be the ones to rescue me? Did I instruct them to follow? They must have been tracking us all along or they couldn't have got here so quickly. Quesnel. I'll murder that Frenchman, I will."

"Um," said Percy. "You might not get the chance."

The Vanaras, deducing that this new threat somehow had something to do with Rue and Percy, had turned their attention and their weapons upon them.

"Oh, this is wonderful," said Mrs Featherstonehaugh. "Just wonderful." She began desperately to explain the situation in Hindustani.

The Vanaras were having none of it.

"They think we encouraged the ship to follow to flush out their location," explained an eavesdropping Percy unhelpfully.

"Yes, Percy, so would I under similar circumstances."

Rue tilted her head back. Knowing the ship was well out of earshot, she nevertheless yelled up to it. "You muttonheads! Go away." She turned to Percy as if this was all his fault. "What in the aether do they think they are doing? We don't have any militia on board. Who do they intend to have rescue us? And what weaponry will they use?"

"Those biscuits Cook served yesterday were almost hard enough for ammunition," said Percy in all sincerity and truthfulness.

"Don't be flippant. No one on board knows how to shoot!"

Percy gave her a look that said he rejected all responsibility and that there was no way this could be other than entirely her fault.

The Spotted Custard spotted them, probably by the light of the bonfire. The ship headed determinedly in their direction, sinking down until she almost brushed the treetops.

Rue could see the faces of a few decklings looking over the railing, the ones who weren't scampering about manning sails, venting gas, and hauling up ballast. They were grinning and waving madly. Everything was a lark to a deckling, even a major political incident.

Rue made frantic backup motions at them.

They were pushed aside to be replaced by Quesnel. The chief

engineer was looking harried but smiled in relief the moment he saw her. He did not wave and he ignored her gesticulations.

Soon enough the *Custard* was close enough for them to yell back and forth. Which was also close enough for the Vanara to start hurling projectiles. The weremonkeys were armed with longbows, lances, and darts. Most of these bounced off the hull – the balloon section was shielded by the gondola – though a few gouged the pretty wood.

"My beautiful ship!" yelled Rue at the Vanara. "Stop it!"

Quesnel said, "Chérie, you're all right!"

"Of course I'm all right," replied Rue crossly.

"Where are your clothes?"

"That's the first question you can think to ask? Quesnel, please don't take this the wrong way, but *go away*. You're messing everything up. I almost had things sorted."

This was clearly not the reception the young man had anticipated. "We came to rescue you."

Prim's head appeared next to Quesnel's, her poof of hair topped with a flowered straw hat decorated with an entire rose garden. She waved her handkerchief. "Toodle-pip, Rue."

Another smaller head popped up. "What ho, Lady Captain?"

"Good evening, Prim. Spoo."

"We came to rescue you!" crowed Spoo.

"Yes, so Mr Lefoux said." Rue knew better than to lose her manners with a subordinate over good intentions. "Thank you kindly for the thought, but I don't actually require rescuing just this moment."

Prim said to Quesnel, "I did tell you that would be the case."

Spoo said, "Jolly good," and disappeared again.

Prim was interested in other, more pressing matters. "Is that bubbles of tea I see everywhere? Spheres of the plants in growth? Amazing. I've never thought to see so much in one place." She

ducked and a half-heartedly hurled wooden spear got one of the
silk roses sticking up from the top of her hat.

"I say there." Prim was not pleased.

Rue said, "Prim, you are witnessing the discovery of long-lost
shape-changing immortals, monkeys of legend, and you're excited
by tea bushes?"

"Do you realise how many cups of tea all that would make?"
said Prim. "Besides, the tea doesn't seem to cherish a vendetta
against my hat." She ducked again. "And Miss Sekhmet is more
impressive as alternate animals go, don't you feel? Where is she
by the way? Oh, there she is. Good evening, Miss Sekhmet. Why
the cage?"

Quesnel was not to be denied gratitude. "But we saw your
sparkler. You signalled for help."

Rue said, "Oh, that. Yes, you see someone *else* rescued me first.
Well, to be perfectly fair, he tried to rescue me but then I ended
up stealing his form and rescuing both of us. It's all been a bit of
a trial since then. But I was getting things all straightened out
with the Vanaras – oh, really, monkeys, do stop throwing things
at my ship! – when you came floating in and botched it. Now
they'll never trust me."

"Uh-oh," said Prim.

"What do you mean, 'uh-oh'?" Rue did not like the guilty
tone in her best friend's voice.

"Well, I'm afraid we aren't the only ones coming to rescue you."

Rue was instantly on her guard. "Prim, what did you do?"

"Nothing. It's only that I believe you were watched when you
left with Miss Sekhmet and Percy. Oh, hello, Percy? How are
you? Still revolting? Good. Anyway, where was I? Oh, yes, I
think you were watched when you left, possibly followed – as
much as one is able to follow a werecat."

"By whom?"

"Werewolves, I am given to understand. Your Uncle Lyall isn't wholly to be trusted. And I *know* that we were watched and followed as we floated over Bombay. For a little while at least."

"Oh, indeed, and who was that by?"

Prim and Quesnel exchanged glances.

"The Rakshasas," said Quesnel finally.

Rue said, "That's just wonderful. Wonderful."

"Well," said Prim, "we determined it wasn't too great a problem. After all, vampires are restricted in territory and they can't leave the city. If it was only their drones who could follow us, what harm could they possibly do?"

"They'd have a devil of a time tracking us from the ground once we hit the forest, anyway," asserted Quesnel.

Rue was not so relaxed about this new bit of information. Knowing what she did about the ongoing enmity between the two supernatural creatures, she could predict what the Rakshasas would do. Moreover, she *knew* exactly what any hive vampire in England would do. Rue would bet good money it was Rakshasas who intercepted Mrs Featherstonehaugh's message about the Vanaras to Dama, and Rakshasa drones who kidnapped Miss Sekhmet. They had a vested interest in keeping the Vanaras secret and estranged from England. She realised she must try to warn the Vanaras – somehow convince them that danger was coming, and not from her beloved ship.

Before she could do so, she was interrupted.

Behind them all, in her lonely cage, Miss Sekhmet yowled. The sound cut through the flurry of weremonkeys gibbering and shrieking.

A werewolf howl is unlike any other. It touches primal instincts embedded in skin and spine, causing hairs to raise up and uncomfortable tingling sensations. It is the sound of something large and furry that is about to come charging out of the night, intent on indiscriminately tearing out throats. It is not a nice noise.

The yowl the werelioness made was worse.

The Vanaras stopped throwing things at *The Spotted Custard*. This was good as they'd started dipping oil-tipped arrows into the bonfire, preparing to set the *Custard* ablaze. The werecat's wail caused them to pause in their torture of the floating lady-bug. The whites of their eyes showed as they glanced frantically around, the fur on their arms and about their faces fluffed out.

Rue was upset by the very idea of flaming arrows. After all, apart from yelling at her, *The Spotted Custard* had not made any attempt to return fire. In fact, her crew had behaved admirably under adverse conditions.

"Drat it!" she said to Mrs Featherstonehaugh. "There's no call for flames. The ship only came to rescue me. They don't intend the Vanaras any harm. They won't counterattack without my order. Can't you tell them that?"

Percy said, "I already tried."

Mrs Featherstonehaugh bustled over to the Alpha. He rudely pushed her aside, all discussion ended.

Rue said, "Don't they understand that the danger isn't from us? It's from—"

Miss Sekhmet yowled again – long and loud, enhancing the general nervousness. Everyone turned to stare at her. Whatever she was trying to articulate went well over their heads. Only Rue felt like she had a pretty good guess.

"Percy, Mrs Featherstonehaugh, we must get to the ship," she said. Then turning once more to look up, "Quesnel, Prim, it's going to get messy soon. Prepare for defensive action."

Prim said, "And monkeys with projectiles aren't messy?" She had a right to be perturbed – one of the Vanara arrows appeared to have bisected her hat.

"Why?" Mrs Featherstonehaugh left off trying to convince the Alpha weremonkey and came over. "What's going on?"

"The Rakshasas know we are here, which means they know that we've made contact with the Vanaras. If they're smart, they'll realise that British policy is to try to integrate newly found were-animals. Your husband still thinks you've been kidnapped. I know what I'd do if I were a Rakshasa queen and I hated Vanaras."

Mrs Featherstonehaugh paled. "No!"

"The army has been told where we are."

The frontline attack of any British night campaign is always werewolves. They form the perfect vanguard – supernaturally strong, amazingly quick, fierce, tireless, and immortal. Werewolf packs had won England her territories, and vampire hives had determined how to keep them. It gave Queen Victoria an empire upon which the sun never rose. As the famous saying went, "It is always night somewhere, so somewhere werewolves are fighting." Tonight that somewhere was Tungareshwar Forest.

The Kingair Pack charged into the fire-lit grounds of the Vanaras' sacred temple. There were not many but they made a good show – bristling and fierce, battle-hardened, and fighting-fit. The Vanaras turned their weapons away from *The Spotted Custard* and onto this new threat, but they did not strike the first blow. Instead the weremonkeys stood, furry arms drawn back, spears and arrows at the ready, awaiting their Alpha's command.

So too did the werewolves. Kingair was an old pack, once not very stable, but in Lady Kingair they had a strong Alpha. She could hold them in check by sheer force of personality, even with all their instincts urging them to attack.

With the attention of both parties diverted, Rue looked up

and caught Prim's eye. She gave a sharp nod. Prim gestured with her handkerchief.

Spoo dropped a rope ladder which unfolded swiftly, thunking softly to the top of one of the temple walls.

Rue signalled to Mrs Featherstonehaugh. "Best to get out at this point. Everyone's finished conversing."

"I can't accept that. Can't we convince them that this is a set-up? Somehow?"

"Look at them. This is no longer our battle."

Mrs Featherstonehaugh did not budge.

Rue couldn't give her any more time. *My first priority must be to save Percy. He is my responsibility and if the fighting gets deadly or moves towards the fire, he's trapped at the heart of it.* Rue couldn't decide how to break his chains. She wished for good old-fashioned vampire abilities. Or possibly some training in how to pick a lock.

She inched close enough to touch Percy.

The Vanaras and the werewolves remained at a stalemate. Clearly, the Kingair Pack was under orders to keep the enemy in place and not engage. The Vanaras were under no such orders, but their weapons were designed to fight vampires. Nothing was tipped in silver. They could hurt with wood, but cause no serious injury.

Rue examined Percy's shackles as surreptitiously as possible. They looked to be silver-coated iron. She needed a tool.

Everyone had gone rumbly. The werewolves, hackles up, emitted low growls and the occasional snarl as one drew back his lips to expose sharp canine teeth. The Vanaras were equally vocal, their rumbles higher pitched and gibbering, their weapons as sharp as those teeth.

Rue could think of no other approach so she sidled away, slowly, softly. A few heads turned to track her but no one chased. She stopped under her ship.

"Toss us down an axe or something similar, would you, Spoo? There must be firemen tools on board."

Spoo's head appeared, proving that she had been eavesdropping on the proceedings. Then vanished at the order.

Prim and Quesnel turned to glare after the former sootie.

Mrs Featherstonehaugh watched with interest.

Quesnel said, "Rue, what are you about?" A marker of his annoyance that he used her actual name.

Spoo reappeared with the requested axe.

Rue stepped out of the way hastily. Spoo dropped the tool overboard. It clattered on the sandstone and Rue gathered it up.

At this, one of the Vanaras veered away from his standoff with the werewolves and leapt over, spear at the ready. Rue brandished the axe and whirled to face him.

Quesnel shouted from above and took aim with his dart emitter. Before either of them could do anything, one of the werewolves leapt in a spectacular display of muscle over the bonfire and interposed himself between Rue and the attacking Vanara.

Herself.

This must be Lady Kingair, because none of the other wolves broke position. Also, this wolf had Rue's eyes. The wolf's fur was tinged grey like Lady Kingair's hair.

The Alpha of the Kingair Pack growled low and herded the Vanara warrior away from Rue and back into his group.

The weremonkeys chittered at each other. Something was keeping them from casting the first blow. Though the one facing Lady Kingair looked like he desperately wanted to hurl his spear into her side, he kept looking to his Alpha for a signal. The Vanara leader did not give him one.

Neither Vanara nor werewolf wanted to be responsible for starting an *incident*. Rue wondered if this was based on a sense of kinship between the two shape-shifting immortals, or the result of old age. Rash battle, as a rule, was the provenance of the young and ignorant.

Unimpeded, Rue made her way to Percy.

She crashed the axe down hard on his chain.

Nothing happened. Except everyone jumped at the noise.

"Sorry," said Rue into the quiet that followed.

Percy looked embarrassed to be causing a fuss.

None of the Vanaras tried to stop her. They merely looked amused at her puny mortal efforts.

How am I supposed to get Percy to safety if I can't even break him free? Clearly I have no other choice – I have to steal Vanara form.

Rue left the axe with Percy, so as not to appear threatening, and advanced towards the nearest Vanara. She strolled casually, hands behind her back, swaying slightly – all innocence. If she hadn't felt it too theatrical, she might even have whistled. Never taking his gaze off the werewolf pack, he slid out of reach.

Lady Kingair returned to her previous position, back to the forest, flanked by her pack, facing the bonfire. The Vanaras were arrayed on the other side, backs to the temple, and there were a good deal more of them. Either they hadn't the same procreation problems as werewolves or they formed bigger groups. Rue supposed monkeys naturally preferred large collectives so perhaps the Vanara followed primate tradition.

Rue arrowed in on the next nearest Vanara.

He too shifted away.

Rue snorted and tried for a third victim.

It was turning into a slow-moving quadrille – Rue with multiple weremonkey dance partners. Without appearing to watch her, each one deftly moved away the moment she was within arm's reach.

Rue grumbled under her breath, "We could do this the easy way – you could simply unlock him."

One of the werewolves at the back of the pack, a smaller, almost fox-like creature, looked as if he were trying not to laugh at that. Not that he could laugh in wolf form, but Rue knew wolf amusement when she saw it.

Rue was nowhere near as fast as any supernatural creature, so she couldn't dart in and grab a Vanara. But she might be a tad more cunning. If nothing else, the Vanaras had shown themselves to be curious by nature.

So Rue pretended a sudden scarf malfunction. Humiliating in the extreme, but she could think of no other ruse. She gave a squeak of alarm and bent over to adjust the knot at her waist, casually letting the fabric slide, exposing the top bit of her fundament for all the world to see. She went red at the thought of Quesnel, who might, very possibly, faint at the sight.

She heard Prim, behind her and above, give a squall of horror.

Percy said, "Oh, my word."

Out of the corner of her eye, Rue saw one of the Vanaras bend in to see what all the fuss was about. Just a little bit closer and . . . there.

Rue threw herself forwards, trusting in her metanatural abilities to steal monkey form before she actually hit the ground, saving her from any major injury.

Gravity was unpleasantly quick.

Supernaturally fast, the weremonkey dodged but not far enough. Rue's fingertip touched his wrist. He lost his advantage. And Rue shuddered in pain as her muscles shifted, her bones lengthened, and her hair turned to fur all over her body.

Prudence Alessandra Maccon Akeldama was once more a weremonkey.

She didn't know what she expected. Perhaps for the Alpha Vanara to set his other warriors to attack her. Instead, he gave her latest victim a disgusted look and made an aggressively dismissive gesture, his monkey face disappointed.

The now fully human Vanara, ashamed, made a subservient half-bow and turned to run into the temple, presumably to get away from Rue as far and as fast as he could in order to snap her tether.

Which meant Rue didn't have much time in her stolen form.

She leapt over to Percy, grabbed up the fallen axe and, before anyone could stop her, began hacking through his shackles.

The chain broke.

Rue scooped Percy up with her tail, despite his protestations, and carried him bodily back to her ship. She climbed the temple and most of the way up the rope ladder with amazingly graceful ease, before using her tail to toss Percy up and over the railing onto the main deck of *The Spotted Custard*.

Percy landed with a thud but was already yelling, "My satchel! Rue, you fiend! They still have my books! I can't leave without them!"

Rue said, surprising everyone on board the *Custard* with the fact that she could talk in wereform, not to mention the low slurring of the voice coming out of her massive monkey chest, "I'll try. You find a copy of the Act. Now, Pershy."

She looked to his twin. "Primrosh, given a chansh, steal back the tea bubbles."

Prim blinked. "What?"

"You hearsh mesh." Rue hadn't the time to explain further.

She didn't wait to see if either followed her instructions, nor did she join her crew on deck as they expected. Instead, she leaned out on her long monkey arms, swung the rope ladder twice, and with an elegant flip dropped back down to balance on the wall.

"No," cried Quesnel. "Don't!"

Rue ignored him. There was still Miss Sekhmet to rescue. Her loyalties were unknown, but Rue was tolerably certain the werecat wanted to prevent conflict. In this they were allies. And frankly, Rue liked her.

She leapt over to the cage and gave the bars a test tug. Yes, the silver burned Vanara flesh just like werewolf. The palms of her hands, free of fur, were tender and exposed. Before she could further pit her supernatural strength against the silver and the pain, a new agony suffused her body. Her monkey muscles were shrinking. The world shifted, her senses altering. She was a mortal human once more. Her Vanara victim had reached the edge of the metanatural tether.

Rue shook off the disorientation and crouched down, meeting Miss Sekhmet's brown eyes through the bars. She wrapped a hand about one bar, the metal no longer burning her skin. She could see upclose that the Vanaras had wrapped a silver net around the lioness. It fastened at her neck and draped over her body in loops and coils. That would make it impossible for her to change shape. Even if she were strong enough to shift despite the weakening effect of silver mesh, she would then be left pressing sensitive naked flesh against it instead. That explained why she was still a cat – she needed the protection of fur.

Rue grinned. *That* she could help with. The cage had large threaded knobs holding on a door that dropped down. Rue grabbed at these, loosening them as much as possible. Then she reached in and buried her hands in Miss Sekhmet's smooth sandy-coloured fur.

CHAPTER

FIFTEEN

Weremonkeys in Dressing-Gowns

O uch. After two stints as a weremonkey, Rue had almost forgotten how much more painful full animal shift was. Her bones broke and re-formed. Her senses altered entirely – her nose became primary, her ears secondary, her sight limited by the reds fading away. Given that everything was taking place under a silvered moon and in flickering firelight, colour was not so great a loss. It was a bit like suddenly forgetting how good cheese tasted: convenient in that it kept one from craving cheese; inconvenient in that one no longer got to eat cheese.

Rue's whiskers twitched. The Vanara odour was all warm fur, dried moss, and some exotic fruit. They had neither the predator meat odour of werewolves, nor the carrion rot of vampires. A slight breeze wafted through the temple, bringing with it the overwhelming scent of tea plants. It caused her to sneeze sharply, once, before she named it in her head and forced it into the background.

Rue didn't wait to see if Miss Sekhmet would determine how to get out of her birdcage. If she was smart, she'd stay there – safer until after hostilities. If hostilities happened. She was now fully mortal, after all. And hostilities could be damaging to mortals.

So far, however, the standoff hadn't changed and didn't look to. And now, Rue couldn't argue with anyone, although she dearly wished to. Back to the cheese situation. Her tail lashed in annoyance.

Then out of the forest materialised the cavalry component of the British Army. Rue craned her head back – several large airborne dots were also heading in their direction. The brigadier had mobilised the float reserves. Most of the regiment was in pursuit of his beloved wife. Or the taxes. Or both. Rue could maybe support such action over tea, but taxes and wives? It seemed excessive.

The brigadier, distinguished by a particularly large and dictatorial hat, raised a large hand. Behind him the cavalry stilled, flanking the werewolves. Now the British outnumbered the Vanaras, and surely the infantry would follow soon.

Rue slunk through the line of tense Vanaras and the group of werewolves to leap into a tree near the brigadier. She attempted to hold her tail up in as non-threatening and perky a manner as possible. The tip was a bit difficult to control – it dangled and twitched like a small, furry, excited flag. Nevertheless, there was a gratifying gasp of fear and the sound of several rifles cocking, which suggested the cavalry thought her a real and dangerous lioness. She wondered how they reconciled the artfully draped orange scarf.

Brigadier Featherstonehaugh didn't seem to notice her even when dangling above him on a tree branch. He was a large man on a large horse. He smelled of said horse mixed with expensive cigars, curry dinner, and coconut pastry. Clearly the loss of one's beloved wife was not allowed to interfere with one's enjoyment of supper. Beneath his impressive hat there was very little hair. He had pronounced eyebrows and a substantial moustache paired with an oddly diminutive beard.

He was accompanied by a young native gentleman in turban

and British uniform, who was obviously his translator. This man
was struggling to harmonise his position as herald in the face of a
group of his own gods. He was bowing over and over to the Vanaras from his saddle.

The brigadier glared at him and said, "Stand to, soldier!" Then
he turned to face the Vanaras.

"Monkey people," he said. "Give me back my wife and the
queen's money, and we will be lenient with you."

Mrs Featherstonehaugh limped forward into the light of the
fire. She raised her cane in salute. "Jammykins!"

"Snugglebutter!" said the brigadier. He was easily twice the
age and size of his wife, but there was evidently at least some
affection between them if the tenor of their endearments was to
be believed.

"They have been very kind to me. The Vanaras are good-
natured civilised creatures, much like werewolves. And the
empire has accidentally mistreated them."

"Now now, Snugglebutter, you know the empire is never
wrong. I've read of this phenomenon. It happens sometimes
with impressionable young ladies, taken in by the enemy – they
become sympathetic to local causes."

Mrs Featherstonehaugh stamped her foot. "Jammykins, I have
not gone native."

"No, dear heart, no, worse. Now you hush up and let your Jammykins handle this. It's the queen's business. Don't you trouble
your little head about it."

Mrs Featherstonehaugh gave Rue's tree a desperate look. Rue
was actually enjoying the spectacle. Prim and Quesnel had out
The Spotted Custard's grappling hooks and were stealthily drifting
about, throwing down and pulling up as many spheres of tea as
possible. Since this was going on behind the Vanaras' backs and
they were concentrated on the army before them, none of *them*
had noticed. A few of the cavalry were giving the *Custard* odd

looks, but they were soldiers and knew better than to interrupt a brigadier with questions about custards. The werewolves couldn't say anything even if they wanted to.

Mrs Featherstonehaugh could not argue further without sounding like a hysterical female unless she revealed herself as an agent of Goldenrod. She needed someone with official authority to stand up to her husband. Rue, even had she been able, was pretty certain she couldn't reveal her position openly either. Besides, as a young, unmarried, and mostly naked lady, she would have been summarily dismissed.

Brigadier Featherstonehaugh said to the Vanaras, "Who among you will speak in your defence?"

His assistant translated his words.

None of the Vanaras moved. They all remained quiet, weapons at the ready, watching their Alpha out of the corners of their eyes.

"Very well, you leave me no choice. I will take back my wife and Her Majesty's money by force!" The brigadier raised up his sabre. "Company. Prepare to charge."

The weremonkeys stiffened.

The werewolves all looked to their Alpha.

Rue tensed her muscles, ready to leap. Although she wasn't certain who or what she was going to leap at.

Then, into the silence, a voice said, "Wait!"

Miss Sekhmet walked into the firelight. She'd found a length of Vanara cloth from somewhere, which she'd wrapped regally about her body. Her brown shoulders were bare but for her long thick hair and the silver net, draped like a mantel. In mortal form she was only a little more tan-coloured than as an immortal, and still so painfully beautiful it was almost unreal. Somehow the wrapped cloth, the hair, and the silver net combined to make her look like a goddess of legend, more so than the Vanaras. Rue leapt down and ran to her, coming to stand at her left side. Lady Kingair was a heartbeat behind. The werewolf stood on her right.

The Vanaras, the werewolves, and the cavalry all stared in awe at the vision before them.

Behind the brigadier, in the jungle, Rue's werecat hearing picked up the crashing of booted feet. The infantry was approaching. Above the forest, the float enforcements moved relentlessly forward. Soon the full might of the British military would be upon them. Miss Sekhmet didn't have much time.

Miss Sekhmet said, "Brigadier, this is all a terrible misunderstanding. These are the Vanaras of the epics, weremonkeys, kinsmen to your very own werewolves. They have the right to petition for sanction under the Rules of Progression and the Supernatural Acceptance Decree."

"Confound it, they kidnapped my wife!"

Miss Sekhmet pulled her slim shoulders back and said, "Not precisely correct. She took the initiative to come here and talk to them voluntarily. I think she is to be commended."

"You? And who are you to involve yourself with my *wife*? And what about our taxes?"

Miss Sekhmet said obliquely, "I represent those interested in facilitating the safety and integration of supernaturals. Your wife made for a lovely ambassadress. Under her gentle touch, the Vanaras might have been amenable to an introduction. Now, however, we must work to salvage this situation."

Rue thought that Miss Sekhmet must have had experience with negotiation – excellent use of the word "we".

Mrs Featherstonehaugh said, "I rather overstayed my visit, Jammykins. It was no one's fault. I have been treated with all honour as a guest here."

Brigadier Featherstonehaugh continued to glare at Miss Sekhmet. "Oh yes? And who exactly do you represent?"

"I am not at liberty to say. Friendly interests, to be sure, sir," replied the werecat primly.

The brigadier crooked a finger at his wife. "Now, Snugglebutter, you just come over to me. Slowly."

Mrs Featherstonehaugh looked with desperation back and forth between her husband and the Vanaras. The Vanaras made no overt effort to keep her with them, but everyone knew the moment her husband considered her safe he would attack. He'd now have his eye not only on the missing taxes, but all the gold mounded up in the temple.

"Silly chit," said the brigadier when she did not move. He gestured to one of his flanking riders. "Major Dwillrumple, fetch me my wife."

Major Dwillrumple did not look pleased with this order. Said wife was standing behind a bristling line of Vanara spears and arrows.

"Sir?" Major Dwillrumple was an older, pudgy gentleman whose rank looked to be in his skill at strategy rather than with the sabre.

"Now, major."

The major did as he was ordered, trotting his horse forwards slowly, both of them glistening with sweat in the firelight.

The Vanaras firmed their line, closing ranks as if they too were military trained.

Behind them, Rue watched Prim, Quesnel, and the decklings haul in another sphere of tea.

Mrs Featherstonehaugh, in a desperate attempt to forestall bloodshed, limped through the Vanara group and around the bonfire.

The major trotted up to her and bent to offer her a hand, swinging her sidesaddle in front of him. Mrs Featherstonehaugh clutched her cane awkwardly in her lap and looked terribly afraid. The major spurred his horse back to rejoin the ranks.

Mrs Featherstonehaugh stared at Rue the entire time, as if she were trying to tell her something mind to mind.

Everyone prepared for battle.

Rue looked to her ship.

Prim and her crew had managed to capture most of the tea containers. The bubbles rolled about the deck like many round brass eggs in a gondola-shaped basket. Rue worried they might fall overboard should the ship list in any particular direction. She wanted to yell up orders to keep the *Custard* steady, prevent tea-crushing accidents. But she still had no voice. In lieu of an actual speech, she turned to Miss Sekhmet and, lips curled away from the burn, bit at the silver mesh, trying to pull it off her.

Miss Sekhmet understood and with a grace that seemed to suggest some long-gone acrobatic ability – *had she once been a dancer of some kind?* – she shrugged off the net.

Rue jerked her head at her and Lady Kingair.

Miss Sekhmet looked to the Alpha. "May I?"

The pack leader nodded, wary. Miss Sekhmet mounted up. Lady Kingair turned and ran into the forest. A wolf carrying a goddess atop her back, thought Rue poetically.

Everyone but Rue was confused by this.

"What in the aether is that crazy female up to?" demanded the brigadier as he watched his werewolf Alpha break for the trees. Almost as one, the rest of the Kingair Pack whirled and followed. They may ostensibly fight for the British army but werewolves fought for their Alpha first. If that Alpha wanted to dash off into the jungle with a mysterious goddess on her back on a whimsical evening run in the middle of a prospective battle, they would go with her.

Rue was pretty certain Miss Sekhmet would rather keep her

identity as a werelioness secret. It was all very well to reveal wer-emonkeys to the British government but werecats was taking things too far. Rue agreed. It wouldn't do to broaden their tiny political minds too quickly. One werethingy at a time. She made for the trees, in the opposite direction.

"What on earth?" the brigadier demanded of the vacant air. "Deserters! I'll have your guts for garters." He did not have long to dwell on prospective courts-martial, for without the werewolves between him and the Vanaras, his attention shifted to more urgent matters. The Vanaras were advancing steadily towards him and his cavalry.

The weremonkeys respected their wolf brethren more than anyone realised. Now that the pack was gone, they were intent on taking this battle into the forest, home turf, where they could use their climbing abilities to greatest advantage. Everyone there knew this.

Horses could only hold ground in a clearing. So, before the cavalry could be pressed under the canopy, the brigadier signalled the charge.

"No!" yelled his wife desperately. "Miss Akeldama, do something!"

Rue was among the vines and out of sight up another tree.

Brigadier Featherstonehaugh would brook no contrary women around him in battle. "Major, get my wife away from here."

"Sir!" The major wheeled and, while Mrs Featherstonehaugh struggled against him, he held her fast and urged his horse into a gallop away from temple, seeking safety.

Afterwards, even though she occupied a good vantage point on a nice sturdy branch, Rue could not remember who struck the first blow. All she knew was the twang of bow strings, and the air filled with arrows flying in one direction and bullets in the other. Soon after came the sound of clashing steel and wood, of sword and spear, as the cavalry closed in on the Vanaras. She smelled the sour salt of fear sweat, and the copper richness of fresh blood.

It was not a fair fight.

Without the werewolves and their supernatural strength, the abilities of the Vanara warriors would inevitably carry any conflict against mortals. Not knowing, or not believing, that they might be up against shape-shifting immortals, the brigadier and his men were not armed with silver, only steel sabres and leaded bullets. These the Vanaras could shrug off, hardly slowed by injuries that closed and healed even as they collected new ones. There were no licensed sundowners in this regiment, no specialised ammunition to take down supernatural creatures. The British army ordinarily made it a particular point *not* to fight the supernatural, certainly not on native soil. How could England be thought a civilising force if they disobeyed their own policies abroad?

So when the weremonkeys attacked, throwing their spears and shooting their arrows with deadly accuracy, they were attacking an army trained to work with them, not against them. Oh, the cavalry was efficient, although they could never hope to be so strong or so fast. The riders shot bullets and hurled knives in perfect formation, and for a short moment it looked as if they were driving the supernatural creatures back. But the Vanaras were stronger, more agile, and better trained. In a coordinated charge, half the weremonkeys leapt to the horses, swinging nimbly about from tree branch to saddle, lifting and throwing riders off bodily with long strong arms and prehensile tails until only a very few — the brigadier among them — were left seated. The horses, even the best-trained, were driven off into the jungle riderless and afraid.

The Vanaras closed in on what little cavalry remained.

That would have been the end of it except that the initial stalemate had lasted too long. It had given the infantry enough time
to catch up. At a quick march they pushed through the forest and
emerged to form ranks exactly when it looked as if all might be
lost for the British.

Now the Vanaras, immortal though they may be, faced a solid
line of a hundred harsh-faced soldiers ready to do battle. Even
against monsters of legend.

The Vanaras may be more numerous than a werewolf pack but
even at a dozen strong and fierce, they were not made to take on
a whole regiment of fighters. They retreated to the bonfire and
regrouped. The Alpha yelled out commands and instructions in
ancient Hindustani combined with monkey clicks.

There was another brief pause. Fallen cavalry, those who could,
pulled themselves upright to stand with the infantry.

The brigadier joined his reinforcements, a fierce look of tri-
umph in his eyes.

At that point, Rue realised that the Vanaras had carefully tried
not to actually kill anyone. A few of the cavalry stayed down but
their bodies were not wounded, and it appeared that they had
merely been knocked unconscious.

Something odd was going on in those fuzzy monkey heads.
Something that kept them from wanting all-out war with the
British Empire. Rue wished fervently she could yell at the brigadier to notice this restraint. To realise that his enemy was holding
itself back. For him to stop and consider. For him to comprehend
that they may not be an enemy at all.

Then Rue felt her bones breaking, felt a scream of unexpected
pain pass her lips. Well, *that* was embarrassing. She was left panting, clinging precariously to a tree branch in human form. The
branch was a lot higher up to human Rue than it had been to
lioness Rue. Nevertheless, she swung around to hang from her
arms and let go before she could really think about it. She landed

badly, ankle twisting. With no time to worry she limped towards the fray.

So it was that as the infantry came to their cavalry's defence, they were just in time to see a pale British lady of aristocratic bearing and generous proportions wearing *nothing at all* limp into the firelight. Rue's orange scarf, after much torture and two bouts on a weremonkey, had given up the ghost as a rum deal and stayed hanging in the tree. She ought to have realised that. But she didn't until it was too late.

The Great British army had seen many things as it conquered the empire. Yet, they had never seen anything like Rue. Not an actual British female, entirely unclothed. The very idea.

Not a lot could stop an infantry in full march, but Rue supposed she was now one of the few to claim that dubious honour. If only some of the now conquered lands had known – *naked aristocrats is all it takes*. Rue stood up and dressed herself in nothing but sublime dignity. She tried to think about it as one of life's new and exciting experiences.

The brigadier said again, even more surprised, "God's bones, who are you?"

Rue ignored him and, with as much hauteur as possible, bent and retrieved Mis Sekhmet's discarded silver mesh. It would provide no real covering but she had a feeling she might need it later.

The Vanaras, having already seen most of her, were not as easily distracted by the apparition of Nude Englishwoman. They took the infantry's sudden stillness as an opportunity to retrieve fallen spears, preparing to defend themselves against the near-overwhelming odds of an entire regiment.

Rue, with great stateliness under the circumstances, made her way over to her ship. *The Spotted Custard*, in its dedicated pursuit of tea, was hovering off to the right side of the temple now, away from the stream. The crew watched the battle and tried not to get involved.

A rope ladder dangled.

Deciding that a naked Englishwoman in the middle of a jungle in India, no matter how unexpected, wasn't worth any more of his valuable time, the brigadier returned to the attack. Bolstered by foot reinforcements, he barked out a new set of instructions. Tearing their eyes away from Rue's rounded – and retreating – buttocks, the infantry obeyed the brigadier's orders. They regrouped into that concentrated efficiency for which England was famous and marched forwards, pushing the Vanaras further into temple grounds, away from the advantage afforded by trees.

As Rue climbed the rope ladder, she noticed that the air support was almost upon them.

Those dozen weremonkeys were destined for annihilation. Should the infantry not possess enough leaded bullets to keep them down against all supernatural healing abilities, the dirigible floatillah was armed with ammunition strong enough to blast the group from above. It might not kill them completely, but it would certainly incapacitate them long enough to facilitate capture. There also was an ominous pinking in the eastern sky which meant that the sun was soon to rise. If Vanaras were anything like werewolves, such an all-out attack could *certainly* kill all but the very oldest and strongest with the help of sunlight.

Rue landed on deck to find herself instantly surrounded by chattering crew. Prim threw a dressing-gown about her. Quesnel looked her determinedly in the eyes, telling her off for risking her safety in no uncertain terms, at the same time giving her a full report on the state of the engines. Percy was waving a piece of parchment at her and using a number of long legal words. Spoo was trying to explain something about tea pods and grappling hooks.

Rue could not have felt more at home. The moment her bare feet hit deck she relaxed.

She held up a hand for quiet. "No time to visit. Prim, do we have all the tea?"

"Yes, captain."

"Spoo, could you switch the grappling hooks for a large fishing net – you know the one we use for hauling up cargo? Also, please put this silver one on the drop lines."

"Yes, Lady Captain."

"Percy, is the treaty as we guessed? Does the agreement specify Rakshasas?"

"Yes, captain – I mean to say, no, captain. I mean to say, Rue, the Vanaras are legally included under the pertinent clauses because the agreement only utilises the term *supernatural*. They simply need to sign it."

Quesnel stopped yelling and reporting at Rue and said seriously, "You have a plan, don't you, chérie?"

"Yes, I most certainly do. And don't call me chérie in public."

"So I may do so in private?" Quesnel brightened.

Rue snorted to cover a smile. "Crew, listen, please."

Those assembled all straightened expectantly.

"Let's steal this war away from them, shall we? Spoo, I want you and the decklings to use that silver net and target one particular Vanara – the one who is wearing more jewellery than the others. He is their Alpha. Try to catch him. Once you've caught him, keep him dangling – don't reel him in; too dangerous. Let me know the moment you've got him secure."

Rue pointed to two of the deckhands – larger bulkier men who did a great deal of the heavy labour that the smaller nimbler decklings couldn't. "You two, man the rope net and try for the brigadier. Unless I'm wrong about personalities, those two will try to fight one another directly, so they should be close together. Understand?"

"If you say so, Lady Captain."

Rue glared. "We are trying to stop a major international ker-
fuffle here. This isn't for larks. I want the two leaders netted
before the floating reinforcements get here. Which reminds me –
Quesnel, Percy, we need to make aether and outstrip that floatillah if possible. Both of you, prep your stations. Percy, I want due
notice. You keep an eye to the incoming puffs and let me know
with a countdown before we lose our window to outrun them."

Percy and Quesnel didn't bother to answer. They both ran off
to do as ordered – Quesnel for belowdecks and Percy for the navigator's station on the poop deck.

Prim and Rue took up position on the main deck, ship's centre,
one on either side, looking down over the railing to watch the
action below from two different angles.

"Percy, take us in and down," yelled Rue.

"A little to starboard," added Prim.

"And a little more," said Rue. "Spoo, how's it coming?"

"Nearly there, Lady Captain."

Below, Rue saw the Kingair Pack materialise from the trees.
Lady Kingair was at the front, Professor Lyall, the sandy fox-like
one, close to his Alpha. The rest of the pack followed in formation.

The sound of the battle below was almost deafening but, nevertheless, Rue leaned over the edge and yelled down to her kinsfolk. "Yoo-hoo, niece of mine?"

Lady Kingair looked up, yellow eyes flashed once.

"I'm trying to steal this war. Give me some time?"

Lady Kingair nodded and, with great elegance, she sat, right
there at the edge of the jungle. As one, all the pack sat with her –
refusing to participate in the fight.

Fortunately, the brigadier had not yet seen them. So far the
werewolves could only be accused of desertion, but if he saw them
and ordered them to participate, they could be accused of wilful
disobedience or even mutiny. Pack attachments could act with a
certain amount of autonomy, but not *that* much.

Just then a shout came from one of Rue's deckhands. They'd managed to net the brigadier right off the back of his surprised horse.

Rue saw him dangling, struggling in his net, trying to cut his way free with a hopelessly tangled sabre. His hat had fallen off and he looked much less imposing without it. She changed her orders. "Pull him in and bring him on board. He might get out otherwise."

"Yes, Lady Captain."

"Spoo, how are you doing with your Vanara trap?"

"He's a fast one, Lady Captain. A little help wouldn't go amiss."

Rue went over to see if she could assist, but just as she came up, Spoo gave a cry of victory.

"We netted ourselves a weremonkey!" she crowed.

Rue blessed the element of surprise. Whatever else they had been expecting, the Vanaras were not prepared for an attack from above. Not that she wanted to think of herself as attacking. She leaned over the railing and there he was – all monkey anger, gleaming gold and rich silks, struggling in a silver net. It burned his exposed skin, palms and feet not protected by fur. He tried to rip his way out but the silver not only burned, it sapped supernatural strength. His own net defeated him.

At that moment, the deckhands reeled in the brigadier and dumped him unceremoniously on the deck, as if he were a load of fish. He flopped about trying to unwind himself – no one bothered to assist him. Rue didn't have any militia on board to keep him controlled. Now that he was her prisoner, there was nothing else for it but to rise high and fast so he couldn't jump overboard safely, even if he wanted to.

Of course, she had no idea what would happen to a Vanara in the aetherosphere. To the best of everyone's knowledge, supernatural creatures and aether did not mix. Werewolves got violently ill. Vampires went mad or worse. No one wanted to talk about that one test, back at the beginning of aether travel, when a rove had fallen from the skies like Icarus. But Rue had read the reports. Then again, Miss Sekhmet had been perfectly fine in the Maltese Tower.

There was only one way to find out. "Percy, take us up."

"Yes, captain."

Even as she gave the order, Rue had a sinking suspicion that Vanaras were like werewolves, linked to pack. She didn't want to damage their inadvertent guest permanently. She only wanted to give everyone time to calm down. Perhaps serve tea. Tea was very soothing.

So, even as Percy began to puff up the *Custard*, Rue said, "Hold position for one moment."

Behind her on the forecastle, the brigadier shuffled off the net and cast around, looking for someone to blame. He spotted Rue and made for her, murder in his eyes.

Spoo was shouting something about not being able to hold on to the Vanara Alpha much longer.

Rue leaned over the railing and yelled to the wolves, still sitting patiently on the sidelines.

"You ever consider hunting monkey, auntie?" Lady Kingair put her muzzle up in the air and barked. "I don't mean you to hurt them – simply bring them along, track us on the ground."

Lady Kingair cocked her head as if considering the situation.

Percy said, "This is your warning, Rue – incoming floaters are nearly on us."

Rue had inherited many things from her parents, but she hadn't any of their pride. She was not above begging. "Please, niece. Please, I need your help."

Lady Kingair barked again.

At which the werewolves waded into the fray.

Rue didn't wait to see which side they were on. "Percy, take us up, fast as you can. But don't go into the aether; we need to

be seen from the ground. And take us out, away from the floatillah. Hopefully, they're too confused down there to realise we netted us a brigadier. With any luck, the floatillah will go down to
liaise with the troops before they realise they should be chasing
us instead."

"Aye aye, captain." The *Custard*'s propeller ramped up to speed
with its customary flatulent sound. Rue was grateful for the noise
of battle which hid it. She stayed glued to the railing, watching
the fight.

The Kingair Pack moved in with remarkable stealth. Werewolves trained in many manoeuvres and, while covert tactics
were unusual, Kingair specialised in being secretive. They slithered through the battling infantry, who had the leaderless Vanaras surrounded. The monkey warriors, somewhat lost without
their Alpha, still stood strong, defending themselves against the
mass of attacking mortals with lightning-fast twists of spear and
sword. They still seemed to be trying not to kill.

The wolves broke through the ranks. The Vanaras paid them
little mind. They did not expect their lupine kinsfolk to attack
them.

Lady Kingair went first. Instead of charging and going for
monkey throats, she oiled in and dived under one of the Vanaras.
The hapless weremonkey suddenly found himself riding a wolf.
At a loss for anything else to do, the Vanara wound his legs and
tail about the Alpha's furry waist and his hands into the ruff at
her neck.

The others of the pack imitated Lady Kingair until each wolf
had a monkey riding him.

The Vanaras, after the initial shock, decided to cast themselves in with their wolf compatriots. They knew they could not
win against overwhelming odds, particularly not when holding
themselves back from dealing mortal blows. They could also
sense that the sun was soon to rise. Without an Alpha to order

them otherwise, the remaining Vanaras threw themselves pillion behind their fellows so that each wolf carried two weremonkeys. As a group, the supernatural creatures turned and dashed through the infantry ranks, heading at speed into the trees.

The army was left behind with nothing to fight and no means of following.

Dirigibles can never be said to *race* anywhere. They were designed originally as pleasure crafts and all the technology of the modern age had yet to make them fast. Even with the propeller cranked up high, and having found a brisk favourable wind, *The Spotted Custard* could only be said to *drift with purpose*. Within the aetherosphere was a different thing entirely, but right now, Rue needed distance without height. They had to stay high enough so that one of their guests didn't take it into his head to jump, and low enough so the other didn't suffer from tether snap separated from his pack. It was a delicate balance that took a great deal of Rue's attention, even as Brigadier Featherstonehaugh came stomping over and started yelling at her. He looked like he might punch her, and had she been anything but British and female he would certainly have done so.

"Woman! Do you know what you have done? You have betrayed your country. You have countermanded a military action. I will see you court-martialed, you fatuous bint."

Rue looked down her nose at him, which was hard as he was twice her size in most directions. "Now now, brigadier, language. This is my ship you're on. I wouldn't be so hasty if I were you. Besides I'm not in the army, so you can't try me in a military court."

"Oh no?"

Rue ignored him at that juncture, squinting down into the

jungle, hoping the werewolves and Vanaras were managing to keep pace. It was too thick to tell.

"I'll be with you in a moment, brigadier. Spoo, how's our other guest?"

"Still secure, but I'm not sure for how long. That silver net isn't quite meant for lifting, I don't think, Lady Captain."

Rue nibbled her lip. "Percy, please make for a clearing. There must be somewhere big enough to set to ground, perhaps with enough overhang so we could tuck out of view. That possible?"

"I'll do my best." Percy said this without looking over at her.

The brigadier said, "Young lady, take this ship down immediately! Or turn us around to rendezvous with my floatillah."

"Absolutely not. Now hush up; I'm thinking."

The brigadier gaped at her as if he were a fish.

"Prim," called out Rue. "A little help?"

Prim came bustling over. "My dear brigadier, sir. Welcome aboard. Would you care for some light refreshment?"

The brigadier blinked in utter amazement at the audacity of such a request, but social niceties were never to be ignored, even under the most trying circumstances. Brigadier Featherstonehaugh was a good British officer to the last. "How do you do, Miss—?"

"Miss Tunstell, the Honourable Primrose Tunstell. How do you do?"

"Not little Ivy's daughter?"

Everyone was startled at that. Prim replied quickly, eager for any way to distract the military man from arguing with Rue, "Why, yes indeed, sir. You know my dear mother?"

"Why, yes, yes, I most certainly do." A soft expression suffused the big man's fierce face like a walrus having discovered a much beloved oyster. "We were engaged once, a long time ago. Such a sweet young lady. Ruined by association with that harridan."

"Engaged?" Prim pressed her gloved hand delicately to her lips. It was always distressing to discover one's parent had an amorous past. Recovering her poise, Prim linked her arm gracefully with the brigadier's and gently led him to the poop deck, the tea trolley, and folding chairs which had miraculously survived all chases and battles. "How romantic. Do come and tell me all about it."

The brigadier thus distracted, Rue could return her full attention to Spoo's netted Vanara. They were high enough up so that, as a mortal, he would die if he jumped, but as a supernatural he would survive if he wrestled himself free. Which meant Rue had no other option than to make him mortal.

She dashed over. Spoo and her crowd of decklings who stood, muscling the three ropes that held the Vanara Alpha suspended below the gondola.

Rue rolled back the sleeves of her quilted dressing-gown. "Pull him up to this railing, slowly. Nice and steady."

The decklings began to haul.

By careful degrees the Vanara came closer. When he was within arm's reach Rue folded herself over the railing and flailed down, fingers stretching. She caught the whites of his terrified eyes – *this man does not want to be mortal* – precisely before her hand brushed his cheek. He craned his neck to bite her finger but it was too late. He was now suspended there – a mortal Indian prince netted out of legend, all dark eyes and liquid beauty. Rue was now a weremonkey once more, wearing a very proper English dressing-gown of ice-blue silk with pastel embroidered flowers up the front. Her tail made the back of the robe tilt up in a ridiculous manner. But at least she was covered. She thought that a nice tassel wrapped about her tail tip to match the tassels down the front of the gown would complete the look to the height of absurdity. Or possibly a fez. However, she had no time to attend to tassels.

She now understood why werewolves hated to fly. Her stomach turned into a hive of wasps that had been recently poked with a sick. All her muscles, many of them new and extra big, ached as if fevered. This had nothing to do with shifting shape. She felt queasy and dizzy. She contemplated succumbing to the vital humours in a faint, or having a bout of hysteria. On top of all that discomfort, it was as if she could sense the aetherosphere high above her. This was difficult to articulate, even in her own head, but she felt it in her blood like a thorny stinging blanket draped inside her, between skin and flesh. She had a certain instinctual knowledge that flying up any further and entering that grey nothingness would drive her mad with pain and loss.

She swallowed down all of it – her monkey face must look quite green – and put a supporting hand on the railing to steady herself.

"Right, decklingsss, pull him all the way in," said Rue in her low slurring voice, surprised it wasn't shaking with strain.

The decklings, with admirable lack of upset at their captain suddenly having a monkey's face, obeyed her order.

Despite feeling ill, Rue stayed to act as muscle. She had supernatural strength and speed, so she was needed to keep their newest guest under control should he decide to fight. Primrose would not be as effective with this warrior, potent weapon of etiquette though she may be.

The mortal Vanara Alpha was docile under the ministrations of the decklings as they stripped him of his silver mesh. He stood tall and calm until he was entirely free. Once liberated, he made no move to try to fight or escape.

Rue nodded at him and made a gesture towards the poop deck, indicating he should follow her. Percy couldn't leave his post to translate so the Vanara must be taken to Percy. His bearing proud, the Alpha followed Rue with an air of one who was granting a favour.

They arrived at the tea trolley, where the brigadier and Prim were nibbling cucumber sandwiches. Percy was guiding the ship almost casually, biscuit in one hand, helm in the other.

Rue said, voice tired, "Pershy, how low can we shafely go?"

Percy looked at her. "Rue, you feeling quite the thing?"

"No, this floating as a supernatural is no lark. I feel like curdled milk. Can you safely take us down and still evade the floatillah?" Rue covered her mouth on an ugly burp.

Percy gave her a worried look and said, "If we go down much more, we'll lose this favourable breeze. But if we have to, I will."

Rue thought about it. They were not yet far enough out to risk loosing the advantage simply for her personal comfort. The floatillah, once it realised what had happened, could still chase them down before dawn. "No. We need speed. I'll hold on a bit longer. Any sign of a likely clearing?"

"Yes, ten minutes to the north. See – there?"

Rue saw. "Very good. I can make it."

Percy took her word for it and returned to his duties.

Rue sagged into one of the deck-chairs.

Gingerly, the Vanara did the same.

The brigadier stared at them.

After a pause, Prim poured them both tea.

"Milk?" she asked the Vanara.

He ignored her.

"Sugar? One lump or two?"

"Give him two," Rue suggested. From her experience with the spicy native version, the locals took their tea sweet.

While Rue battled nausea and weakness to stay at least seated upright, Prim engaged the brigadier in conversation. The Vanara Alpha calmly sipped his tea with an expression of mild shock. No doubt he was as confused by this situation as everyone else. Or perhaps he was merely as surprised by the taste of British tea as Rue had been by the local spiced variety.

Nine and a half minutes later, Percy brought them in and down to hover below treetop height over a bare patch of land. They remained high enough so that neither visitor could jump to the ground without injury. Nor were the Vanaras and werewolves – who soon collected in the clearing to wait expectantly – able to leap up.

Fortunately they were low enough so that Rue's stomach settled and the oppressive blanket feeling of the aetherosphere no longer troubled her with its spiky presence. In fact, she felt perfectly normal, or as perfectly normal as a girl can when in monkey shape. Percy left navigation to Virgil and Spoo, and joined them at tea to act as translator.

Rue found herself delighted with the civilised nature of it all. She guessed that she had about fifteen minutes before the floatillah arrived and opened fire. Could one broker an end to hostilities, rectify a missed opportunity for peace, and facilitate the introduction of a new species in fifteen minutes?

CHAPTER
SIXTEEN

In Which Tea Solves Everything

Negotiations, Rue soon came to understand, required a great deal longer than fifteen minutes and were better suited to a personality not hers. Not to mention someone who had mastery of monkey voice and face – she would keep slurring her words. The Vanara Alpha and the brigadier refused to see reason. They didn't seem likely to come to an agreement before dawn, let alone before her beloved ship was attacked by her own country.

Percy had them almost to the ground and tucked away, partly hidden by overhanging trees. But as soon as the floatillah was close enough they would be easy to spot. The great red, dotted balloon of the *Custard* poked up too high, slightly out of the trees in such a way as to look like a massive embarrassed mushroom.

Around them in the clearing below, the monkeys and wolves cavorted together.

Lady Kingair had changed shape after Spoo helpfully tossed down one of Rue's spare dressing-gowns. Occasionally, that good lady would shout something autocratic up at them. She wanted to know exactly what in *all atmospheres* was going on! Prim would lean over the railing and yell down as much of an explanation as she could.

Rue kept up with negotiations. Uncle Lyall sat in the background, amused by the entire situation.

The pack and the Vanaras settled into a game, something along the lines of *chase my tail, chase your tail, flip over, and wrestle.* Between these two species, at least, accord had been found. They remained determinedly oblivious to the fact that the floatillah was coming and that the werewolves may be cashiered and the Vanaras imprisoned. Rue supposed for the werewolves it was a little like finding a lost pack, knowing they were not alone in the world, that there were other types of shape-shifters. The Vanaras seemed happy to be out in the open at last, to reveal themselves to their wolf cousins.

Where is Miss Sekhmet? Rue wondered. The werelioness would be most useful in these negotiations.

Rue said to the Vanara for what she felt was the millionth time, "Jussssh sign the Supernatural Acceptance Decree and I'm certain our queen will see reason. The brigadier here would be bound by the termsss, yesh?"

Brigadier Featherstonehaugh huffed into his tiny excuse of a beard. "Well, I don't see that it's obvious these creatures are the same as werewolves, in which case..."

"Except that I can pershonally assure you they are immortal supernatural shape-shifters." Rue waved her monkey tail at him in annoyance. "Ish no difference."

Percy translated for the Vanara prince, who said, "We are not interested in your queen and her agreements."

Rue tried to frown. It was challenging with a monkey face. "What if I offered you a treaty with a separate branch of the British government?"

The brigadier looked as if he would like to object but as Percy translated what Rue had said, the Vanara Alpha perked up.

"Nothing to do with Rakshasas or their alliance?"

Rue thought fast, calculating what she knew of the Shadow

Council. How would her mother react? Dama, she suspected, would want peace. As potentate he tended to favour the most civilised non-violent road if possible. But he'd want his tea back. The werewolves and the Vanaras were getting along well enough that the Kingair Pack would return a favourable report to the dewan. So she could probably count on his vote. Her mother? Well, her mother could be persuaded eventually. So Rue felt safe in offering an alliance with the Shadow Council, as if it were an independent entity. The Vanaras need not be told of their intimacy with Queen Victoria. She wondered if the brigadier even knew of the existence of the Shadow Council. She would have to speak with circumspection around him. Nevertheless, it seemed the most promising course of action.

"My father," she said, "has some business interests here in your land." She purposefully did not mention which father. Better if the brigadier thought she spoke of Lord Maccon, otherwise he might let slip the fact that her adopted father was a vampire. The Vanaras wouldn't like *that* at all.

Everyone looked perfectly blank at this seemingly unrelated statement.

"He, like you" – Rue acknowledged the Vanara Alpha with a nod – "ish a great fan of tea. Thish new breed" – she gestured at the spheres all around them – "will grow well in this climate, in the fields next to Tungareshwar Forest. If we were to offer the Vanaras a trade agreement, perhaps governorship and control of these new tea plantations? As part of an alliance?" *Dama is not going to like this.*

The brigadier looked upset. Rue turned to him and said under her breath, "Bloody John has its alliance with the Rakshasas. It's time to balance the books."

It was not an outright admission that she was going against the East India Company, but it was implied. If the brigadier was anything like most military men, he opposed the Company's military influence. Rue listened to Paw's pack gossip and more often than not they objected to the might of Bloody John. It was politically challenging because of vampire involvement in the Company, but Rue had guessed right, for the brigadier's militant expression relaxed.

He huffed, more thoughtful than combative. "Are you saying this agreement would circumvent the East India Company?"

"Yes, exactly. And the Rakshasas." She nodded at the Vanara prince.

Both men looked interested. Rue was pretty certain she'd get an earful from Dama about bargaining away his private tea investment for an alliance with local weremonkeys, but he was a reasonable man and if all else failed, she could use her daughterly wiles.

Percy said for the Alpha Vanara, "Tell me more?"

Then Percy said for Percy, "Oh, I say!"

The floatillah was upon them.

Cannons deployed out of the base of the airships, trained on *The Spotted Custard*.

Rue's entire crew held its breath and stared at the brigadier. No doubt all of his subordinates in the floatillah had binoculars trained on him. The only reason they had not been instantly attacked was the fact that the brigadier was sitting unharmed in the company of a British lady, taking tea. It wasn't exactly a hostile situation – Vanaras or not.

Beads of sweat appeared on the brigadier's brow. If he signalled his ships to fire, indicating that he was a hostage, then he risked his own demise, as well as the end of any possible treaty.

Primrose reached one trembling white hand forward. "Please, good sir, call off the floatillah. For my sake?"

He looked to the pretty young aristocrat and said nothing.

"For all our sakes?" Prim pressed her luck, batting eyelashes.

Rue wondered if Prim would risk mentioning Aunt Ivy given that there seemed to be history between them. That proved unnecessary, for mere moments later, a lioness leapt aboard the ship, carrying Mrs Featherstonehaugh atop her back.

Mrs Featherstonehaugh was less excited to ride a leaping lioness than Spoo had been. She dismounted looking as fragile as fine china. She'd lost her cane and had to limp to her husband and the tea table, one of which – the husband – rose at her arrival.

"My dear!" He rushed to her. "The major let you go? I'll cashier the blighter."

Mrs Featherstonehaugh looked at the werecat. "The major had no choice, Jammykins. The lioness was most insistent."

The cat in question disappeared belowdecks, no doubt to borrow another robe. If Miss Sekhmet would keep shifting form on board, Rue supposed they should stock a selection of those colourful drapes she preferred and assign her a wardrobe.

The brigadier looked at Rue. "Is that your cat?"

Rue considered, then used the escape she had given Sekhmet at the beginning of their acquaintance. "You know cats. They don't really belong to anyone."

Primrose said, still sitting demurely at the table, "Mrs Featherstonehaugh? Do join us for tea."

Such a smart girl, Prim, for in that simple request, she had ensured everyone's wellbeing. Mrs Featherstonehaugh couldn't refuse tea and still be thought anything like a respectable lady. And the brigadier wasn't going to let his floatillah attack a ship with his wife on board. He may risk his own life, but he wasn't going to risk hers. Not again.

He waved away the looming ships, all casual, but there was a complex hand signal involved. They moved a little way off. The three ladies – Rue still a monkey – entertained the three gentleman with politics. And the three ladies, as is often the case when women of sense serve tea to men of passion, prevailed.

For the Vanara Alpha, Rue spun a yarn about this new breed of tea and how it might provide economic independence. She bragged of her personal political connections, implying that she could draw up an agreement based on the tenets of SAD that would name the Vanaras as allied not with the queen but with others, one of them a werewolf. Percy faithfully translated it all and did not laugh once.

"In fact, I'm sure Percy here could write you up a nice mock treaty while you rest for the day. Would that be acceptable? Of course, I would have to take it back to England for the official seal of approval but I think I can guarantee it will be passed through committee. In the interim, if you, brigadier, would abstain from any further action?"

"Yes, dear," pressed his wife. "Do abstain, do. It's very manly to think seriously about a course of action and not go rashly dashing into war."

"Is it indeed, Snugglebutter?" huffed the husband.

"Why yes, don't you find, ladies?"

Grave nods all around.

Rue suggested, in a mild tone, "This new treaty, we might consider naming it the Featherstonehaugh Accord."

The brigadier and his wife looked positivity delighted. The brigadier said, "Well, I *am* needed in Waziristan. If we could finish up here relatively quickly, I might just forget to file a report on this matter until I return from campaign."

Sensing a favourable shift, Prim called for celebratory muffins and jam.

Muffins and jam seemed to sooth everyone's temper, particularly the Alpha Vanara's whose delight in the jam was that of a child discovering blancmange for the first time. Rue could sympathise. She often felt that way about really good jam, not to mention blancmange. And this was, after all, gooseberry.

The sun was soon to rise, at which point the werewolves would lose their wolf forms and the Vanaras – including Rue – their monkey shape. All but the very strongest supernatural creatures would be driven into shade and sleep, and any chance at further discourse would have to wait until the following night. Rue was prepared to land her ship and invite all on board, offering up sleeping quarters if she had to.

Muffins consumed, jam admired, and bellies full, Primrose said in her most motherly tone, "Well, dears, bedtime?"

Rue rose. "Perhaps, gentlemen, if we all slept on it? Percy, I believe it is time to take us to ground. Then, Spoo, I think it is safe to lower the gangplank. We have guests to accommodate."

The brigadier and the Vanara Alpha were looking almost relaxed. The brigadier could even be called jolly.

Rue thought of Lady Kingair and her Scottish pack. "Do we have any shortbread?" she hissed under her breath.

"Good notion," said Primrose, crooking her finger at a harried-looking steward. "All the shortbread stores, please."

The Spotted Custard went down as low as possible to hover above the moss of the clearing. The floatillah sailed off about other business. The brigadier's signal must have included a set of instructions. The decklings lowered the gangplank and Professor Lyall and Lady Kingair trotted up it. Then, when Rue issued a formal invitation, all the werewolves and all the Vanaras followed. Virgil ran off to find robes. Prim hustled the wolves belowdecks to change shape in seclusion. The Vanaras were enthralled by the ship, and Rue wondered if they had ever been on board a dirigible before. It moved her to a certain affection regardless. After all, a lady likes to have her ship admired.

She had thought that Miss Sekhmet would reappear at that

juncture. But perhaps she didn't want to remind either party of her presence and felt that Rue was well able to settle the treaty situation. Rue was honoured by such trust. Always assuming, of course, that peace had been the werecat's objective all along. Hard to tell objectives and reasons with a cat.

A short time later found the ship's stores of shortbread greatly strained, and the cook in near hysterics at having to feed not only a pack of werewolves but also a troop of weremonkeys. A generally gregarious quarter of an hour ensued – except for the cook – while everyone sorted themselves out, slurped tea, and nibbled.

The werewolves, now back to human shape, borrowed whatever dressing-gowns were available, including a few of Prim's more frilly styles. They carried these off with the aplomb of very large Scotsmen, who, on a regular basis wore skirts anyway. It must be said, however, that large hairy men ill-suited pink ruffles. It was like seeing a mastiff in an ostrich feather boa.

Nothing was left of the muffins but crumbs, and the gooseberry jam jar had actually been licked clean by a Vanara warrior, for which Primrose rapped his knuckles in rebuke. However, it did look as if hostilities had abated.

Rue offered their best spare room to the brigadier and his wife, who accepted with alacrity and made for it with indecent haste.

"We have, after all, been separated for several days," whispered Mrs Featherstonehaugh so only Rue could hear.

If she had eyebrows, Rue would have raised them high. Given the age and aesthetic differences between the two, not to mention Mrs Featherstonehaugh's clandestine activities, Rue had thought there was little real affection between the couple – apparently not.

Mrs Featherstonehaugh giggled – actually giggled – as her big bear of a husband helped her down the staircase, following Prim to guest quarters.

After some further jocular exchanges, oddly pantomimed between

Vanaras and werewolves – Percy dragged to and fro to interpret –
it was agreed that the following night the wolves would be taken
on a tour of Tungareshwar by the monkeys. The Vanaras thought
that wolf-riding might indeed be their new favourite thing *ever.*
The werewolves requested they remove some of their gold armour
for the event, as it tended to dig. Both parties agreed that dozing on board the *Custard*, with an infantry still unsure of their
orders tramping about the forest, was probably the safest option.
All twenty or so strapping immortals, which felt like a great deal
more, wandered belowdecks to sleep wherever they might find
a spot.

Rue requested that they try to stay out from underfoot as she
did still need to run her ship. The storeroom, she suggested, was
an excellent option. Although she feared greatly for the supplies.

Prim returned and they found themselves in possession of the
upper decks, with the exception of all the spheres of tea. Rue,
Percy, Prim, and the decklings watched the sun rise over the
trees, listening to a great cacophony of birds singing it up and
wondering what had happened to the army.

"I suppose the floatillah might be off to track them down and
let them know," said Rue.

"Let them know what exactly?" said Quesnel, coming up to
join them. "What did I miss, mon petit chou?"

"We brokered a peace deal, I think." Rue tried not to be so
very pleased to see him. Not to mention pleased with herself.

"You – *peace*?"

"I know, incomprehensible, isn't it?" She grinned.

Quesnel's huge violet eyes were huger than normal, the wide-
eyed look of having been up for twenty-four hours. One cheek
was terribly smudged with coal dust. Rue repressed the urge to
clean it with her thumb. She also suppressed the urge to push the
floppy bit of blond hair back from his forehead.

"Don't be mean," defended Primrose staunchly. "I think you did very well, Rue dear."

"I had to lie by omission, but I believe the Shadow Council will agree to my terms once I have explained the cultural and historical reasons for an aberration."

Quesnel frowned, still not understanding, "You negotiated a peace treaty between the *Shadow Council* and the Vanaras? Without asking?"

"I didn't name them, of course, but I think it'll work. Aside from the dewan – who's likely to be the most on my side anyway – I do have the ability to persuade the other two members."

"One being your mother; the other your adopted father?"

"Exactly."

"And what about Queen Victoria?" said the Frenchman, looking more shocked than proud.

Rue, who had expected praise, was put out. "What about her?"

"You aren't related to her, are you? How will she take being ousted from the agreement? Circumventing the power of the crown to negotiate a deal between supernatural creatures and their foreign counterparts? What kind of precedent does that set?" Quesnel's tone was almost harsh. So far Rue had seen him angry and now coldly calculating. She wanted her old irreverent, flirtatious Quesnel back. These other versions of him weren't nearly as nice.

However, it made sense that beneath all his frivolity Quesnel would think like that. He'd been raised in a hive but his mother had other allegiances. He would be taught always to question the supernatural agenda.

Rue felt a sudden sagging in her stomach. She hadn't thought about the perspective of daylight folk. She'd only thought about keeping the Vanaras safe. She'd neglected the human component entirely and with Queen Victoria that was likely to get a girl in real trouble. "Well, rats. I guess I won't get to keep my sun-downer status."

"Probably not." Quesnel brightened.

"And I never even got to use it, not really."

"Buck up, chérie, you may still have a chance. I tripped over two werewolves sleeping in the hallway. We could take them up to the aether."

"Why, Mr Lefoux," said Prim. "I had no idea you were so bloodthirsty."

The Frenchman smiled winningly at both ladies, and went to fish hopelessly about in the muffin crumbs.

As the sun fully crested the horizon, Rue lost her monkey shape. She was relieved to be human. Changing shape so many times in one night gave a girl a bit of a crisis of identity. It couldn't possibly be good for her character.

Primrose unpinned her straw hat, only then noticing it was speared though with a Vanara arrow.

"Ruined, I'm afraid," said Quesnel, placing a gentle hand on Prim's shoulder.

Rue's lip curled at the fact that he could be so sympathetic to Prim's plight but not her own political blundering.

"I rather like it that way," said Percy.

Rue agreed. "You should sport it proudly when we get back to London and start a new trend."

Percy said, as if he had been actually thinking about Quesnel's point, "You know who else is not going to be happy about this treaty? The Rakshasas."

"There you are, chérie, now aren't you glad you're still a sun-downer?" Quesnel used it to try and get back in Rue's good graces.

Rue turned her full attention on Percy. "You're right. They aren't. We might want to ask the brigadier to lend us the Kingair Pack for the remainder of our stay in Bombay. They'd be the best deterrent if the Rakshasas want to take revenge."

"Rue, are you actually considering asking someone else for help?"

Rue gave Quesnel a superior look. "I can be taught, thank you very much."

A polite cough interrupted any further bickering. Miss Sekhmet walked out onto the deck, under direct sunlight. Admittedly, she wore Prim's largest and most highly decorated hat in addition to Prim's favourite full coverage purple robe – with fringe and a train. She looked not unlike a very fancy lamp-shade.

Rue had assumed the werecat was holed up somewhere, sleeping off the night's activities. Instead, she'd been pillaging Prim's wardrobe. Primrose looked more embarrassed at her dressing-gown being worn on deck with a walking hat, than inclined to object.

"Miss Sekhmet. Thank you very much for retrieving Mrs Featherstonehaugh."

"I thought, given her attitude, she might be useful."

"Useful for what exactly?"

"Brokering peace, of course."

"Was that always your mission?"

The werecat inclined her hat-covered head. Hard to tell if that was agreement or approval.

Rue's own head teemed with questions. *Are all werecats able to be out in daylight? Are they all able to withstand great heights close to the aether? Were did Miss Sekhmet come from? What is her real name? Who does she work for? Why did she not reveal herself as a werecreature from the start?*

"A remarkable young lady, Mrs Featherstonehaugh. Perhaps a little hard-headed," said the werelioness when Rue remained quiet.

"Next time, hopefully, she won't go tearing off on her own pretending to be kidnapped. I suspect Dama will be none too pleased," said Rue.

"As the potentate, he got a nice little treaty out of it," protested Primrose.

Which proved how little she knew of Rue's vampire father's objectives. Unless Rue was very much mistaken, Dama would be upset over the shift in power. He liked balance above all things. Plus, "He lost his precious tea in the end."

"Why, chérie, are you in trouble there too?" Quesnel was trying to sound sympathetic but Rue sensed he was secretly pleased.

Why did I ever want him? Rue wondered.

Miss Sekhmet interrupted. "Mrs Featherstonehaugh is deeply excited about a public revelation of Vanara existence. She is planning on writing a slim travel volume on the Tungareshwar Forest."

"Inspired by Honeysuckle Isinglass, is she?" Rue raised her eyebrows.

"The hell she is!" sputtered Percy, going red in the face. "Not if I get there first. Rue, we must return to England this instant! The integrity of the scientific community is dependent on it."

Everyone ignored this outburst. Rue remembered that she hadn't managed to get Percy's satchel for him. They'd have to float back to the temple to retrieve it. He would insist and he'd earned it.

She said, "Are you all right out in the sunlight, Miss Sekhmet? We could retire to the stateroom."

The werecat looked at her strangely, guessing the prying interest behind the solicitous care. "I'm fine for a short while. It's not as bad as it once was." A tiny bit of information, doled out gently. She was good.

Rue gestured to a vacant deck-chair. They were all sitting at this juncture, in an exhausted circle about the vanquished tea trolley. Even Rue, who generally had more energy than any other human on the planet, looked wan.

Miss Sekhmet sat gratefully. "Interesting night."

"My dear lady," said Prim, about to pour the last of the tea. "You have a gift for understatement." She checked herself and instead poured the remains of the milk jug into a tea-cup and handed that over.

"You are a thoughtful thing, aren't you, little one?" The were-cat took the milk and sipped it gravely.

Rue thought it odd that Prim blushed so much at the compliment.

"Miss Sekhmet, who do you work for exactly? I thought you were with the Vanaras but they put you in a birdcage. But you can't be with the Rakshasas – they put you in a flower cart. You aren't one of Dama's, so who?" Rue decided on the direct approach. She tried to emulate Primrose's welcoming charm, but was too tired for acting.

The beautiful woman gave a self-satisfied smile. "My dear girl, I am cat. I don't *work* for anyone."

"Then why did you involve yourself?"

"For exactly the same reasons."

Quesnel snorted. "Cats."

Miss Sekhmet waved a hand. "Exactly."

Rue thought back to their first meeting. "You were curious; you wanted to meet the world's only metanatural. Perhaps have your form stolen and be mortal again?"

"My, now who values herself highly?" said the werelioness.

But Rue was beginning to finally get the werecat's measure. If one thought of Miss Sekhmet and her behaviour as entirely cat-like, even when human, it actually made odd sense. "You're exactly like Footnote."

Percy, who was still mulling over the dangers of preemptive publication, rejoined the conversation at that. "I say, what?"

Rue laughed. Miss Sekhmet's tactics were becoming clear to

her. There was the gentle way with which the werelioness coaxed and complimented Primrose. The verbal equivalent of winding in and out of her legs, with a purr. Primrose, of course, was necessary to befriend for she controlled the ship's larder. Sekhmet also teased Percy with exactly too little information. She had witty exchanges with Quesnel, not to mention ignoring him when he flirted. And then there was her, Rue. How was the cat wooing her? Blasé attitude, slight reverence for Rue's metanatural abilities – the thing of which Rue was most proud. And of course she kept herself a mystery, knowing that all of them – Quesnel, Percy, Primrose, and Rue – were taken in by a mystery.

Rue leaned forward. "Percy has a cat, named Footnote. Or as Virgil put it, Footnote has a human, named Percy. I have this sinking suspicion that we – all of us here on *The Spotted Custard* – are about to have a cat too. I have a suspicion because, right now, I feel as though we are being had by a cat."

"Prudence Alessandra Maccon Akeldama. *Manners!*" reprimanded Primrose.

Miss Sekhmet only laughed. "So where are my quarters? You'll need something you can secure. Full-moon night is full-moon night, even for a werecat."

Rue grinned back. *Excellent. Now I can winkle out all her secrets.* "That's assuming a bit much, isn't it, Miss Sekhmet?"

"Call me Tasherit," said the werelioness. "It'll be nice to have a pride again."

Because she obviously wanted to be asked if that was her real name, Rue didn't ask. This was going to be so much fun.

Oddly enough, it was Primrose who raised the only objection. Percy and Quesnel seemed delighted by a new addition to their crew: Quesnel liked beautiful women and Percy liked cats. Plus, if the werelioness was with them, she was proof of Percy's new discovery of non-werewolf shape-shifters.

"Rue." Prim's voice trembled. "Are you sure about this?" It was a mark of her agitation that she said it there at the table, in front of Tasherit.

"Don't worry, Prim. She'll settle in fine. Besides, you already know how she takes her tea – that's half the battle when integrating a new acquaintance. And now, we too should sleep."

The decks were mostly deserted. Everyone was exhausted. Except Spoo and Virgil who, with the unflagging energy of youth, were engrossed in a game of tiddlywinks on the poop deck, crouched between two of the massive tea spheres. Unfortunately, someone adult had to stay above deck and raise the alarm if the infantry came calling. Or the floatillah decided to return. Or the Rakshasas sent drones to attack.

"Anyone awake enough to sit watch?" Rue asked hopefully.

None of them said anything.

Rue nodded. She supposed the joy of being captain brought with it all kinds of unpleasant responsibilities. "Very well, I'll take first watch. Prim, you and Percy can have second. Quesnel, you raise Greaser Phinkerlington and the two of you will take third. Tasherit, I'm assuming you can't sit a whole watch in full daylight, unless you tell me otherwise."

The werelioness said nothing.

It was a marker of how fatigued they all were that the others stood without objection, even Quesnel.

The Tunstell twins made their way below with sleepy alacrity. They leaned against one another in a manner that almost indicated sibling affection.

Quesnel, despite Tasherit's gaze, stood to lean over Rue, trapping her in her deck-chair with his body.

"I'm glad you're unharmed, mon petit chou."

Rue blinked at him. "Oh, well, thank you."

He did not kiss her, not with the werecat sitting there watching with interest. He certainly looked as though he wanted to though.

"That other position you offered?"

"Yes?" Rue squeaked. Her heart went all the way up into her throat and started beating there, clogging and unclogging her breath.

"I accept."

Rue was suddenly both elated and terrified on top of being tired.

Quesnel straightened and said to the werecat. "Coming below? I'm sure I can find you a spot somewhere."

The stunning beauty said mildly, "I think I might stay awhile, keep little Prudence here company. Unless she objects?"

"Delighted," said Rue. But she wasn't really thinking about the werelioness any more. What had her big mouth got her into this time? Quesnel's pansy-coloured eyes, though tired, were very, very twinkly.

Quesnel said mildly, "Behave, both of you. We've had enough excitement for one evening." Then he made his way across the deck, lean and sure, blond hair a dandelion fluff about his head in the morning breeze.

"Fine young man there – good bones, nice posture, just enough brains," commented the werecat, as if contemplating a meal. "Would they mind, your parents?"

Rue was not too tired to play the game, and still in shock at this new prospect to furthering her education. "Quesnel is a bit of a rake." *And I've got him for a lover. Or something very like. I think.*

"Best ones usually are."

"Are you trying to be helpful, Tasherit?"

"Is it working, Prudence?"

"Rue, please. Call me Rue. And I assure you, I have plenty of relationship wisdom at my beck and call."

"Then I shall endeavour to offer you other wisdom."

It was on the tip of Rue's tongue to shock her by asking what Tasherit thought of Rue just going to bed with Quesnel. For the experience, of course. She suspected the cat would be in favour of anything that stemmed from curiosity. But it was too soon and too early for such confidences.

"How do you feel about pigeons, Tasherit?"

Without blinking the werecat replied, "Can't stand the nasty things."

"In that case, I should like to welcome you – officially – on board *The Spotted Custard*. Now, here's your first order. Go to bed."

Oddly, for a cat, she obeyed.

Rue was left alone with her ship and the sunrise and a sense of profound peace that lasted exactly as long as it took Spoo to get into an enormous argument with Virgil about tiddlywink protocols.

Acknowledgements

Grateful thanks to Calin and Pantea for their expertise in 1800s India. And to all those who followed my blog, sympathised with my plight, and were willing to wait for *Prudence* – I am so very grateful for your understanding.

extras

orbit

meet the author

Photo Credit: Vanessa Applegate

New York Times bestselling author GAIL CARRIGER writes to cope with being raised in obscurity by an expatriate Brit and an incurable curmudgeon. She escaped small-town life and inadvertently acquired several degrees in Higher Learning. Ms. Carriger then traveled the historic cities of Europe, subsisting entirely on biscuits secreted in her handbag. She resides in the Colonies, surrounded by fantastic shoes, where she insists on tea imported from London.

introducing

If you enjoyed
PRUDENCE,
check out the series where it all began, starting with

SOULLESS

The Parasol Protectorate: Book the First

by Gail Carriger

*Alexia Tarabotti is laboring under a great many social
tribulations. First, she has no soul. Second, she's a spinster
whose father is both Italian and dead. Third, she was rudely
attacked by a vampire, breaking all standards of social etiquette.*

*Where to go from there? From bad to worse apparently, for
Alexia accidentally kills the vampire—and then the appalling
Lord Maccon (loud, messy, gorgeous, and werewolf) is
sent by Queen Victoria to investigate.*

*With unexpected vampires appearing and expected vampires
disappearing, everyone seems to believe Alexia responsible.
Can she figure out what is actually happening to London's
high society? Will her soulless ability to negate supernatural
powers prove useful or just plain embarrassing? Finally,
who is the real enemy, and do they have treacle tart?*

CHAPTER ONE

In Which Parasols Prove Useful

Miss Alexia Tarabotti was not enjoying her evening. Private balls were never more than middling amusements for spinsters, and Miss Tarabotti was not the kind of spinster who could garner even that much pleasure from the event. To put the pudding in the puff: she had retreated to the library, her favorite sanctuary in any house, only to happen upon an unexpected vampire.

She glared at the vampire.

For his part, the vampire seemed to feel that their encounter had improved his ball experience immeasurably. For there she sat, without escort, in a low-necked ball gown.

In this particular case, what he did not know *could* hurt him. For Miss Alexia had been born without a soul, which, as any decent vampire of good blooding knew, made her a lady to avoid most assiduously.

Yet he moved toward her, darkly shimmering out of the library shadows with feeding fangs ready. However, the moment he touched Miss Tarabotti, he was suddenly no longer darkly doing anything at all. He was simply standing there, the faint sounds of a string quartet in the background as he foolishly fished about with his tongue for fangs unaccountably mislaid.

Miss Tarabotti was not in the least surprised; soullessness always neutralized supernatural abilities. She issued the vampire a very dour look. Certainly, most daylight folk wouldn't peg her as anything less than a standard English prig, but had this man not even bothered to *read* the vampire's official abnormality roster for London and its greater environs?

The vampire recovered his equanimity quickly enough. He reared away from Alexia, knocking over a nearby tea trolley. Physical contact broken, his fangs reappeared. Clearly not the sharpest of prongs, he then darted forward from the neck like a serpent, diving in for another chomp.

"I say!" said Alexia to the vampire. "We have not even been introduced!"

Miss Tarabotti had never actually had a vampire try to bite her. She knew one or two by reputation, of course, and was friendly with Lord Akeldama. *Who was* not *friendly with Lord Akeldama?* But no vampire had ever actually attempted to *feed* on her before!

So Alexia, who abhorred violence, was forced to grab the miscreant by his nostrils, a delicate and therefore painful area, and shove him away. He stumbled over the fallen tea trolley, lost his balance in a manner astonishingly graceless for a vampire, and fell to the floor. He landed right on top of a plate of treacle tart.

Miss Tarabotti was most distressed by this. She was particularly fond of treacle tart and had been looking forward to consuming that precise plateful. She picked up her parasol. It was terribly tasteless for her to be carrying a parasol at an evening ball, but Miss Tarabotti rarely went anywhere without it. It was of a style entirely of her own devising: a black frilly confection with purple satin pansies sewn about, brass hardware, and buckshot in its silver tip.

She whacked the vampire right on top of the head with it as he tried to extract himself from his newly intimate relations with the tea trolley. The buckshot gave the brass parasol just enough heft to make a deliciously satisfying *thunk*.

"Manners!" instructed Miss Tarabotti.

The vampire howled in pain and sat back down on the treacle tart.

Alexia followed up her advantage with a vicious prod between the vampire's legs. His howl went quite a bit higher in pitch, and he crumpled into a fetal position. While Miss Tarabotti was a proper English young lady, aside from not having a soul and being half Italian, she did spend quite a bit more time than most other young ladies riding and walking and was therefore unexpectedly strong.

Miss Tarabotti leaped forward—as much as one could leap in full triple-layered underskirts, draped bustle, and ruffled taffeta top-skirt—and bent over the vampire. He was clutching at his indelicate bits and writhing about. The pain would not last long given his supernatural healing ability, but it hurt most decidedly in the interim.

Alexia pulled a long wooden hair stick out of her elaborate coiffure. Blushing at her own temerity, she ripped open his shirtfront, which was cheap and overly starched, and poked at his chest, right over the heart. Miss Tarabotti sported a particularly large and sharp hair stick. With her free hand, she made certain to touch his chest, as only physical contact would nullify his supernatural abilities.

"Desist that horrible noise immediately," she instructed the creature.

The vampire quit his squealing and lay perfectly still. His beautiful blue eyes watered slightly as he stared fixedly at the wooden hair stick. Or, as Alexia liked to call it, hair *stake*.

"Explain yourself!" Miss Tarabotti demanded, increasing the pressure.

"A thousand apologies." The vampire looked confused. "Who are you?" Tentatively he reached for his fangs. Gone.

To make her position perfectly clear, Alexia stopped touching him (though she kept her sharp hair stick in place). His fangs grew back.

He gasped in amazement. "*What* are you? I thought you were a lady, alone. It would be my right to feed, if you were left this carelethly unattended. Pleathe, I did not mean to prethume," he lisped around his fangs, real panic in his eyes.

Alexia, finding it hard not to laugh at the lisp, said, "There is no cause for you to be so overly dramatic. Your hive queen will have told you of my kind." She returned her hand to his chest once more. The vampire's fangs retracted.

He looked at her as though she had suddenly sprouted whiskers and hissed at him.

Miss Tarabotti was surprised. Supernatural creatures, be they vampires, werewolves, or ghosts, owed their existence to an overabundance of soul, an excess that refused to die. Most knew that others like Miss Tarabotti existed, born without any soul at all. The estimable Bureau of Unnatural Registry (BUR), a division of Her Majesty's Civil Service, called her ilk *preternatural*. Alexia thought the term nicely dignified. What vampires called her was far less complimentary. After all, preternaturals had once hunted *them*, and vampires had long memories. Natural, daylight persons were kept in the dark, so to speak, but any vampire worth his blood should know a preternatural's touch. This one's ignorance was untenable. Alexia said, as though to a very small child, "I am a *preternatural*."

The vampire looked embarrassed. "Of course you are," he agreed, obviously still not quite comprehending. "Again, my apologies, lovely one. I am overwhelmed to meet you. You are my first"—he stumbled over the word—"preternatural." He frowned. "Not supernatural, not natural, of course! How foolish of me not to see the dichotomy." His eyes narrowed into craftiness. He was now studiously ignoring the hair stick and looking tenderly up into Alexia's face.

Miss Tarabotti knew full well her own feminine appeal. The kindest compliment her face could ever hope to garner was "exotic," never ' "lovely." Not that it had ever received either. Alexia figured that vampires, like all predators, were at their most charming when cornered.

The vampire's hands shot forward, going for her neck. Apparently, he had decided if he could not suck her blood, strangulation was an acceptable alternative. Alexia jerked back, at the same time pressing her hair stick into the creature's white flesh. It slid in about half an inch. The vampire reacted with a desperate wriggle that, even without superhuman strength, unbalanced Alexia in her heeled velvet dancing shoes. She fell back. He stood, roaring in pain, with her hair stick half in and half out of his chest.

Miss Tarabotti scrabbled for her parasol, rolling about inelegantly among the tea things, hoping her new dress would miss the fallen foodstuffs. She found the parasol and came upright, swinging it in a wide arc. Purely by chance, the heavy tip struck the end of her wooden hair stick, driving it straight into the vampire's heart.

The creature stood stock-still, a look of intense surprise on his handsome face. Then he fell backward onto the much-abused plate of treacle tart, flopping in a limp-overcooked-asparagus kind of way. His alabaster face turned a yellowish gray, as though he were afflicted with the jaundice, and he went still. Alexia's books called this end of the vampire life cycle *dissanimation*. Alexia, who thought the action astoundingly similar to a soufflé going flat, decided at that moment to call it the Grand Collapse.

She intended to waltz directly out of the library without anyone the wiser to her presence there. This would have resulted in the loss of her best hair stick and her well-deserved tea, as well as a good deal of drama. Unfortunately, a small group of young dandies came traipsing in at that precise moment. What young men of such dress were doing in a *library* was anyone's guess. Alexia felt the most likely explanation was that they had become lost while looking for the card room. Regardless, their presence forced her to pretend that she, too, had just discovered the dead vampire. With a resigned shrug, she screamed and collapsed into a faint.

She stayed resolutely fainted, despite the liberal application of smelling salts, which made her eyes water most tremendously, a cramp in the back of one knee, and the fact that her new ball gown was getting most awfully wrinkled. All its many layers of green trim, picked to the height of fashion in lightening shades to complement the cuirasse bodice, were being crushed into oblivion under her weight. The expected noises ensued: a good deal of yelling, much bustling about, and several loud clatters as one of the housemaids cleared away the fallen tea.

Then came the sound she had half anticipated, half dreaded. An authoritative voice cleared the library of both young dandies and all other interested parties who had flowed into the room upon discovery of the tableau. The voice instructed everyone to "get out!" while he "gained the particulars from the young lady" in tones that brooked no refusal.

Silence descended.

"Mark my words, I will use something much, much stronger than smelling salts," came a growl in Miss Tarabotti's left ear. The voice was low and tinged with a hint of Scotland. It would have caused Alexia to shiver and think primal monkey thoughts about moons and running far and fast, if she'd had a soul. Instead it caused her to sigh in exasperation and sit up.

"And a good evening to you, too, Lord Maccon. Lovely weather we are having for this time of year, is it not?" She patted at her hair, which was threatening to fall down without the hair stick in its proper place. Surreptitiously, she looked about for Lord Conall Maccon's second in command, Professor Lyall. Lord Maccon tended to maintain a much calmer temper when his Beta was present. But, then, as Alexia had come to comprehend, that appeared to be the main role of a Beta—especially one attached to Lord Maccon.

"Ah, Professor Lyall, how nice to see you again." She smiled in relief.

Professor Lyall, the Beta in question, was a slight, sandy-haired gentleman of indeterminate age and pleasant disposition, as agreeable, in fact, as his Alpha was sour. He grinned at her and doffed his hat, which was of first-class design and sensible material. His cravat was similarly subtle, for, while it was tied expertly, the knot was a humble one.

"Miss Tarabotti, how delicious to find ourselves in your company once more." His voice was soft and mild-mannered.

"Stop humoring her, Randolph," barked Lord Maccon. The fourth Earl of Woolsey was much larger than Professor Lyall and in possession of a near-permanent frown. Or at least he always seemed to be frowning when he was in the presence of Miss Alexia Tarabotti, ever since the hedgehog incident (which really, honestly, had not been her fault). He also had unreasonably pretty tawny eyes, mahogany-colored hair, and a particularly nice nose. The eyes were currently glaring at Alexia from a shockingly intimate distance.

extras

"Why is it, Miss Tarabotti, every time I have to clean up a mess in a library, you just happen to be in the middle of it?" the earl demanded of her.

Alexia gave him a withering look and brushed down the front of her green taffeta gown, checking for bloodstains.

Lord Maccon appreciatively watched her do it. Miss Tarabotti might examine her face in the mirror each morning with a large degree of censure, but there was nothing at all wrong with her figure. He would have to have had far less soul and a good fewer urges not to notice that appetizing fact. Of course, she always went and spoiled the appeal by opening her mouth. In his humble experience, the world had yet to produce a more vexingly verbose female.

"Lovely but unnecessary," he said, indicating her efforts to brush away nonexistent blood drops.

Alexia reminded herself that Lord Maccon and his kind were only *just* civilized. One simply could not expect too much from them, especially under delicate circumstances such as these. Of course, that failed to explain Professor Lyall, who was always utterly urbane. She glanced with appreciation in the professor's direction.

Lord Maccon's frown intensified.

Miss Tarabotti considered that the lack of civilized behavior might be the sole provenance of Lord Maccon. Rumor had it, he had only lived in London a comparatively short while—and he had relocated from Scotland of all barbaric places.

The professor coughed delicately to get his Alpha's attention. The earl's yellow gaze focused on him with such intensity it should have actually burned. "Aye?"

Professor Lyall was crouched over the vampire, examining the hair stick with interest. He was poking about the wound, a spotless white lawn handkerchief wrapped around his hand.

"Very little mess, actually. Almost complete lack of blood spatter." He leaned forward and sniffed. "Definitely Westminster," he stated.

The Earl of Woolsey seemed to understand. He turned his piercing gaze onto the dead vampire. "He must have been very hungry."

Professor Lyall turned the body over. "What happened here?" He took out a small set of wooden tweezers from the pocket of his waistcoat and picked at the back of the vampire's trousers. He paused, rummaged about in his coat pockets, and produced a diminutive leather case. He clicked it open and removed a most bizarre pair of gogglelike things. They were gold in color with multiple lenses on one side, between which there appeared to be some kind of liquid. The contraption was also riddled with small knobs and dials. Professor Lyall propped the ridiculous things onto his nose and bent back over the vampire, twiddling at the dials expertly.

"Goodness gracious me," exclaimed Alexia, "what *are* you wearing? It looks like the unfortunate progeny of an illicit union between a pair of binoculars and some opera glasses. What on earth are they called, binocticals, spectoculars?"

The earl snorted his amusement and then tried to pretend he hadn't. "How about glassicals?" he suggested, apparently unable to resist a contribution. There was a twinkle in his eye as he said it that Alexia found rather unsettling.

Professor Lyall looked up from his examination and glared at the both of them. His right eye was hideously magnified. It was quite gruesome and made Alexia start involuntarily.

"These are my monocular cross-magnification lenses with spectra-modifier attachment, and they are invaluable. I will thank you not to mock them so openly." He turned once more to the task at hand.

"Oh." Miss Tarabotti was suitably impressed. "How do they work?" she inquired.

Professor Lyall looked back up at her, suddenly animated. "Well, you see, it is really quite interesting. By turning this little knob here, you can change the distance between the two panes of glass here, allowing the liquid to—"

The earl's groan interrupted him. "Don't get him started, Miss Tarabotti, or we will be here all night."

Looking slightly crestfallen, Professor Lyall turned back to the dead vampire. "Now, what *is* this substance all over his clothing?"

His boss, preferring the direct approach, resumed his frown and looked accusingly at Alexia. "What on God's green earth is that muck?"

Miss Tarabotti said, "Ah. Sadly, treacle tart. A tragic loss, I daresay." Her stomach chose that moment to growl in agreement. She would have colored gracefully with embarrassment had she not possessed the complexion of one of those "heathen Italians," as her mother said, who never colored, gracefully or otherwise. (Convincing her mother that Christianity had, to all intents and purposes, originated with the Italians, thus making them the exact opposite of heathen, was a waste of time and breath.) Alexia refused to apologize for the boisterousness of her stomach and favored Lord Maccon with a defiant glare. Her stomach was the reason she had sneaked away in the first place. Her mama had assured her there would be food at the ball. Yet all that appeared on offer when they arrived was a bowl of punch and some sadly wilted watercress. Never one to let her stomach get the better of her, Alexia had ordered tea from the butler and retreated to the library. Since she normally spent any ball lurking on the outskirts of the dance floor trying to look as though she did not want to be asked to waltz, tea was a welcome alternative. It was rude to order refreshments from someone else's staff, but when one was promised sandwiches and there was nothing but watercress, well, one must simply take matters into one's own hands!

Professor Lyall, kindhearted soul that he was, prattled on to no one in particular, pretending not to notice the rumbling of her stomach. Though of course he heard it. He had excellent hearing. *They* all did. He looked up from his examinations, his face all catawampus from the glassicals. "Starvation would explain why the vampire was desperate enough to try for Miss Tarabotti at a ball, rather than taking to the slums like the smart ones do when they get this bad."

Alexia grimaced. "No associated hive either."

Lord Maccon arched one black eyebrow, professing not to be impressed. "How could *you* possibly know *that*?"

Professor Lyall explained for both of them. "No need to be so direct with the young lady. A hive queen would never have let one of her brood get into such a famished condition. We must have a rove on our hands, one completely without ties to the local hive."

Alexia stood up, revealing to Lord Maccon that she had arranged her faint to rest comfortably against a fallen settee pillow. He grinned and then quickly hid it behind a frown when she looked at him suspiciously.

"I have a different theory." She gestured to the vampire's clothing. "Badly tied cravat and a cheap shirt? No hive worth its salt would let a larva like that out without dressing him properly for public appearance. I am surprised he was not stopped at the front entrance. The duchess's footman really ought to have spotted a cravat like *that* prior to the reception line and forcibly ejected the wearer. I suppose good staff is hard to come by with all the best ones becoming drones these days, but such a shirt!"

The Earl of Woolsey glared at her. "Cheap clothing is no excuse for killing a man."

"Mmm, that's what you say." Alexia evaluated Lord Maccon's perfectly tailored shirtfront and exquisitely tied cravat. His dark hair was a bit too long and shaggy to be de mode, and his face was not entirely clean-shaven, but he possessed enough hauteur to carry this lower-class roughness off without seeming scruffy. She was certain that his silver and black paisley cravat must be tied under sufferance. He probably preferred to wander about bare-chested at home. The idea made her shiver oddly. It must take a lot of effort to keep a man like him tidy. Not to mention well tailored. He was bigger than most. She had to give credit to his valet, who must be a particularly tolerant claviger.

Lord Maccon was normally quite patient. Like most of his kind, he had learned to be such in polite society. But Miss Tarabotti seemed to bring out the worst of his animal urges. "Stop trying to change the subject," he snapped, squirming under her calculated scrutiny. "Tell me what happened." He put on his BUR face and pulled out a small metal tube, stylus, and pot of clear liquid. He unrolled the tube with a small cranking device, clicked the top off the liquid, and dipped the stylus into it. It sizzled ominously.

Alexia bristled at his autocratic tone. "Do not give me instructions in that tone of voice, you..." she searched for a particularly insulting word, "puppy! I am jolly well not one of your pack."

Lord Conall Maccon, Earl of Woolsey, was Alpha of the local werewolves, and as a result, he had access to a wide array of truly vicious methods of dealing with Miss Alexia Tarabotti. Instead of bridling at her insult (puppy, indeed!), he brought out his best offensive weapon, the result of decades of personal experience with more than one Alpha she-wolf. Scottish he may be by birth, but that only made him better equipped to deal with strong-willed females. "Stop playing verbal games with me, madam, or I shall go out into that ballroom, find your mother, and bring her here."

Alexia wrinkled her nose. "Well, I *like* that! That is hardly playing a fair game. How unnecessarily callous," she admonished. Her mother did not know that Alexia was preternatural. Mrs. Loontwill, as she was Loontwill since her remarriage, leaned a little too far toward the frivolous in any given equation. She was prone to wearing yellow and engaging in bouts of hysteria. Combining her mother with a dead vampire and her daughter's true identity was a recipe for disaster on all possible levels.

The fact that Alexia was preternatural had been explained to *her* at age six by a nice gentleman from the Civil Service with silver hair and a silver cane—a werewolf specialist. Along with the dark hair and prominent nose, preternatural was something Miss Tarabotti had to thank her dead Italian father for. What it really meant was that words like *I* and *me* were just excessively theoretical for Alexia. She certainly had an identity and a heart that felt emotions and all that; she simply had no soul. Miss Alexia, age six, had nodded politely at the nice silver-haired gentleman. Then she had made certain to read oodles of ancient Greek philosophy dealing with reason, logic, and ethics. If she had no soul, she also had no morals, so she reckoned she had best develop some kind of alternative. Her mama thought her a bluestocking, which was soulless enough as far as Mrs. Loontwill was concerned, and was terribly upset by her eldest daughter's propensity for libraries. It would be too bothersome to have to face her mama in one just now.

Lord Maccon moved purposefully toward the door with the clear intention of acquiring Mrs. Loontwill.

Alexia caved with ill grace. "Oh, very well!" She settled herself with a rustle of green skirts onto a peach brocade chesterfield near the window.

The earl was both amused and annoyed to see that she had managed to pick up her fainting pillow and place it back on the couch without his registering any swooping movement.

"I came into the library for tea. I was promised food at this ball. In case you had not noticed, no food appears to be in residence."

Lord Maccon, who required a considerable amount of fuel, mostly of the protein inclination, had noticed. "The Duke of Snodgrove is notoriously reticent about any additional expenditure at his wife's balls. Victuals were probably not on the list of acceptable offerings." He sighed. "The man owns half of Berkshire and cannot even provide a decent sandwich."

Miss Tarabotti made an empathetic movement with both hands. "My point precisely! So you will understand that I had to resort to ordering my own repast. Did you expect me to starve?"

The earl gave her generous curves a rude once-over, observed that Miss Tarabotti was nicely padded in exactly the right places, and refused to be suckered into becoming sympathetic. He maintained his frown. "I suspect that is precisely what the vampire was thinking when he found you *without a chaperone.* An unmarried female alone in a room in this enlightened day and age! Why, if the moon had been full, even I would have attacked you!"

Alexia gave him the once-over and reached for her brass parasol. "My dear sir, I should like to see you try."

introducing

If you enjoyed
PRUDENCE,
look out for

THE UNFORTUNATE DECISIONS
OF DAHLIA MOSS

by Max Wirestone

*Meet Dahlia Moss, the reigning queen of unfortunate
decision-making in the Staint Louis area. She is unemployed,
broke, and on her last bowl of ramen. But that's all about
to change.*

*Before Dahlia can make her life any messier on her own
she's offered a job. A job that she's woefully underqualified for.
A job that will lead her to a murder, an MMORPG, and
possibly a fella (or two?).*

CHAPTER ONE

The only time I ever met Jonah Long he was wearing a fake beard, a blue pin-striped captain's outfit, and a toy pipe that blew soap bubbles. He did not seem like someone who was about to change my life.

"I have a proposition for you," he told me. Admittedly, that does sound like the kind of thing a life-changing person might say. It's right up there with "It's dangerous to go alone—take this!" and "You are the chosen one." But a plastic bubble pipe really takes the edge off this sort of thing.

It was a nautical-themed party, which partly explained his ridiculous outfit. I thought he was hitting on me. "I'm in a non-dating phase," I told him. Not entirely true, but I repeat: bubble pipe.

"A financial proposition, Dahlia."

I had no idea who he was. I was irked that he knew my name, but it was clear from the way Charice was hovering over him that my roommate was involved. She was wearing an over-sized mermaid's outfit that made her look faintly seal-like—especially with her mugging at me as Jonah spoke. Eh? Eh? I felt like I should throw a fish at her.

But really, what could I do? I had seventeen dollars and twenty-three cents in my bank account at the time of this exchange, with less in savings. I could only use ATMs that dispensed tens. Despite my correct sense that Jonah was (1) ridiculous and (2) trouble, at the phrase "financial proposition," he had my undivided attention.

"Come into my office," I told him.

I didn't have an office, to be clear. Actually, this is a good time to come clean on all the things I didn't have, just to get them taken care of, right up front.

Things Dahlia Moss Did Not Have:

- a job
- an internship
- cheerful prospects of finding a job
- a reliable car
- a boyfriend
- supportive family members
- rent
- any skill or experience as a detective

Honestly, that's just hitting the highlights, but I feel they look less depressing as bullet points. Still with me? If you are, you can't say I didn't warn you.

Anyway, no office. What I did have was a room—or more technically, Charice's room, which she let me sleep in for free.

"Quite a place you've got here," said Jonah.

He was referring to the fact that there were no decorations of any kind, just cheap, misshapen furniture and blank beige walls. This is what happens when garage sales keep you financially afloat.

"What's your financial proposition?" I asked, gesturing for Jonah to sit in a sagging director's chair while taking the luxury of the folding bed for myself. At business meetings, I had read, it was best to take the position of power, although I doubt a folding bed is what *Forbes* had in mind.

I could tell that Jonah was getting serious, because he took off his beard.

"I want you to recover the Bejeweled Spear of Infinite Piercing."

This is the kind of statement that makes one pause, and it is especially the kind of statement that makes one pause when it immediately follows a debearding. First, the debearding: It was like one of those teen movies where the ugly girl takes off her glasses and is revealed to be a bombshell. Except that here we were moving from community theater sea captain to J.Crew model, which I would argue is a greater distance.

"The Bejeweled Spear of what?"

"Infinite Piercing," said Jonah solemnly.

"How can something be infinitely pierced?"

Jonah was not interested in this sad and overly literal question. "It's been stolen from me, and I want you to recover it."

"Maybe an earlobe shaped like a Klein bottle?"

But earlobe-based math puzzles were not why Jonah was here. "Don't get lost in the weeds," he said. "The important thing is that the spear was mine, and I want you to recover it from the thief who stole it away from me."

And here Jonah looked deeply satisfied and proceeded to blow bubbles from that damned plastic pipe. The noise was appealing, but it looked ridiculous.

It bears mentioning that this was not the first ridiculous boy that Charice had funneled through our apartment. Charice specialized in ridiculous, and so I got guests not unlike Jonah with relative frequency. They didn't usually have quests for me, but I've seen lots of strange birds pass through. Charice favors odd theme parties that just sort of happen, like flash mobs. Literally, I've gone to the bathroom for a span of time and come back to find three people dressed like vampires in our sitting room. My general strategy for dealing with Charice's parade of guests was to treat them as a sort of living theater. Occasionally, they were.

"All right, fine. Tell me more about the spear," I told him, only half holding back a sigh.

"It's an item from the Kingdoms of Zoth," said Jonah.

Ah. Now I saw where we were going. It still didn't make sense, but I could at least recognize the general destination. I waited for an explanation from Jonah, not because I didn't know what the Kingdoms of Zoth were, but because I had hoped that he would imagine I was the sort of person who didn't know what the Kingdoms of Zoth were. He didn't. Ah well.

Zoth is an MMORPG. That's Massively Multiplayer Online Role-Playing Game. One of those computer games with a million people playing at once. In this case, imaginary avatars dressing up in knights' armor and parapets and killing griffins—that sort of thing.

The truth is, I knew quite a bit more about it than that. *Zoth* was a niche game—there are other, bigger games you've probably heard about. *World of Warcraft*, or *EverQuest*, or *The Lord of the Rings Online*. Those were games that had commercials on Hulu. Inviting, easy-to-learn. *Zoth* was a game for the hardcore. There weren't commercials, because they didn't want everyone playing. This game was for the serious, for the connoisseur. For the type of detail-oriented guy who would put together an elaborate and expensive sea captain's costume, complete with bubble pipe.

"You want me to find a stolen item from an imaginary world?"

"Not imaginary, Dahlia. Digital. These are entirely separate things."

The conversation had gotten weird, even given my usually

high standards. To recap: A man dressed as a sea captain had sneaked away from one of Charice's nautical-themed parties and wanted to hire me for detective work in a video game. There were countless reasons to question this proposal. And even blinded by the prospects of an ATMable sum of money, I found a couple of them myself.

"Why hire me for this? Surely you can find someone more qualified."

Jonah clearly had been anticipating this question, because he answered in a smooth and curiously rehearsed way. "Oh, I think you'll do. I've heard that you've played *Zoth* yourself. And that you have some experience working for a detective agency."

That last bit was very carefully phrased. I wondered who had fed him the line and had to assume it was Charice. "Some experience working for a detective agency" is technically true if we understand that "some" means two days and "experience" means answering the phone as a temp. I explained this to Jonah, who did not seem to regard my confession as a revelation.

"It's immaterial," Jonah told me, "because I've already got everything all worked out. I already know who took the spear."

My grandmother used to say that there was nothing worse than trust-fund kids with plans, and I find myself thinking of her now as I type this account. Jonah had both in spades, although at the time I understood neither the depth of his wealth nor his designs on me. I just thought I was being presented with a suspiciously well-wrapped package. Emphasis on "suspiciously." But who were we kidding; I was a pauper, and I needed the package.

"What is it, exactly, that you would like for me to do?" I asked with a glimmering notion that this was the sort of question a drug mule might pose.

"I want you to meet up with the thief and shake him down."

extras

I was looking at Jonah, and he was clearly making the sort of face that Satan makes when he's on the cusp of adding a new soul to his collection. There I was, watching the mischievous gleam in his eye and thinking this was surely some kind of trap, but I couldn't escape the gravitational pull of money. Jonah could sense it too, because he volunteered details on payment without my even asking.

"One thousand dollars, right now. Another thousand after you've met with the thief. That's my offer; take it or leave it."

One thousand dollars buys a lot of ramen. Things had gotten so rough for me in the past few weeks that I had to walk to job interviews because I could not afford the bus. There was no choice here, not really.

"Well, Jonah. You just bought yourself a detective."

———————◆———————

Jonah handed me an envelope.

"Open it," he said with a twinkle in his eye. The kind of sparkle you'd find on Santa's face. Or a mental patient's.

I opened it. It was brimming with twenties. One thousand dollars in twenty-dollar bills. Hundreds would have been more sensible, but the weight of the twenties made me feel rich, and I suddenly couldn't stop smiling. I don't know if it was Jonah's intent, but nothing quells skepticism like money.

"There's a note as well," said Jonah.

And so there was. When I got over my euphoria, I discovered a small sheet of paper folded into thirds. I unfolded it and read the message.

To: KRISTO
From: REVENGE
What comes around goes around.

I recognized the font, a serif that screamed high fantasy while only whispering legibility, as being from *Zoth*, and so I asked:

"You're Kristo?"

"I am," said Jonah. "Level-sixty human thief at your service."

"Someone sent this to you after the spear was burgled from your account?"

"Exactly," said Jonah. "I can see that you are just the person for this sort of thing."

There was something patronizing in his tone of voice that I frankly should have wondered about, but I had made one thousand dollars in five minutes, and for that price I would take the patronage. Instead, I found myself wondering who would steal a spear and then leave a snarky note. It could only increase the risk of getting caught, and for what? A punch line?

"So you want me to figure out who Revenge is?"

"I know who Revenge is. His name is Kurt Campbell. I think you'll like him; he's very charming."

This was kind of a non sequitur, but I let it slide.

"How do you know that he stole your spear?"

This was a question Jonah had wanted me to ask, because his answer was another of his prepared speeches.

"Up until three weeks ago, he was my roommate and classmate, but through a series of *entanglements*"—and here Jonah put particular emphasis on the word—"Kurt lost his place in our graduate program. Following that, he lost his job, his income, and from there it was a short trip until I asked him to move out. He did not take it well."

I was more than a few months behind in rent, and I hoped Jonah did not know that I was living on Charice's largess.

"You aren't hurting for money," I said, gesturing to my envelope of twenties. "You don't need a roommate to contribute to rent. Why kick him out?"

"Oh," said Jonah, bored. "The principle of the thing."

"We're not talking drug addiction or something ugly here?"

"Ho, ho, ho," said Jonah, which was an incongruous laugh for someone in a sea captain's costume. Even beardless, one expected some sort of *yarr*. "No, Kurt's not that sort of guy."

"How did he lose his job and his spot in school in one fell swoop?"

"Entanglements," said Jonah.

I had somehow known that's what he was going to say.

When I was a second-grader, my older brother, Alden, was deeply into *Dungeons & Dragons*, and talking to Jonah suddenly reminded me of Alden's stories. He would design these elaborate adventures and was so desperate to have someone play with him that he would occasionally try to make me fit the bill. I loved playing—I always idolized Alden, plus the game had horses—but I never seemed to go where Alden wanted me to. He'd present me with a quest, and rather than killing the dragon, I would linger about the princess's castle. He'd always get all clammy on the details whenever I was somewhere he hadn't planned on me being. What's the throne room look like, Alden? *I don't know...gray?* Is there a banner? *I guess.* What does the banner look like? *It's also gray.* Are there pictures of flowers on it? *No.* But when you went to where Alden wanted you to be, you were drowning in description.

The roommate losing his job was a gray banner in a gray room. So I did what I had done with my brother. I tried to figure out where he wanted me to go.

"So," I said. "You ousted your roommate, and you think that he stole some bauble from you in *Zoth* as retaliation. Was anything else stolen?"

"No," said Jonah. "Just the spear."

"Did you play *Zoth* with Kurt?" Surely yes. I had played *Zoth* only a little, and the idea of breaking into someone's account and stealing something of value seemed daunting. How would you know what had value? Oh, the Bejeweled Spear of Infinite Piercing sounded impressive enough, but *Zoth* was one of those games in which everything sounded impressive. You'd load Truesilver Arrows of Unerring Path into your Wildwood Bow of Goblin Striking while sipping on Improved Plumberry Tea of Mana Replenishment. This was at level two.

"We played together, yes. He was part of my guild, the Event Horizons."

"A very techie name for *Zoth*, isn't it?"

"The guild migrated over from *Martian Chron*—"

"Who else is in your guild?"

And Jonah suddenly got rather sharp with me. At the time I assumed that it was because I had interrupted him. "The guild is not important," he said, his voice suddenly loud. And then he returned, just as suddenly, to his previous cherubic mood. "What I mean to say is that you do not need to trouble yourself with the rest of the Horizons. It's Kurt you should be interested in."

Given that Jonah had just given me one thousand dollars, it seemed wise to stay off topics that made him raise his voice.

"Kurt knew that the spear was important to you."

"Well, yes," said Jonah, pleased that we were back on track. "But everyone would have known that. *Zoth* has more than a half million players, and there is a single spear. Think about that."

I did think about it, and it did not impress me very much. But I was not a *Zoth* person.

"How did Kurt steal it from you?"

"He took it from my computer," said Jonah hastily. "The machine remembers my password, so if you have access to it, you have access to my account. But that's not important either."

And again, the effect was like being shuttled through one of

Alden's games. Look at that, not this. Nothing down that hall, silly girl. Investigate the dragon.

"How about you tell me what's important."

"The important thing is dinner."

Dinner was never the answer in Alden's games, that's for sure.

"As in, what comes after lunch?"

"Yes. The dinner that you're going to tomorrow. I've arranged for you to meet Kurt tomorrow at a nice restaurant. He thinks that he's meeting me. But he won't. He will meet you."

"And I will...?"

"You will tell him that I know that he took the spear. You will inform him that I have hired you as a private detective to ensure its recovery. And he will fold on the spot. Then I'll give you the second thousand dollars, and it will be the easiest money you ever made."

It all seemed impossibly dumb to me, but I was reminded of another of Grandma's sayings: A fool and his money are a golden opportunity. If Jonah was handing out cash for purposes as silly as this, I might as well benefit.

But he was wrong about it being the easiest two grand I ever made. For one, Jonah hadn't known about the Modern Woodmen of America scholarship, which was an easy two grand indeed, if a little hard to reproduce.

For another, he would never live long enough to give me the second thousand dollars.

———————◆———————

After Jonah left, I took a moment to count the twenties and inspect that it really was American currency and not some sort of gummy candy money. Something had to be off—money doesn't just fall out of the sky like that—but I couldn't put my finger on anything that was actually a problem. On the face of it, Jonah was some rich kid who'd been fed a line about my detective skills and was caught up in the romance of having his own private eye. But even as I failed to rub the ink off the money he'd given me, I couldn't shake the feeling that something greater was happening.

I took the bills and placed them inside my copy of *Northanger Abbey*. If I was going to be stolen from, I could at least take consolation from knowing that the thief liked Jane Austen. And then I crept back into the party.

I generally avoided Charice's parties, despite living among them. I was never one for parties, and I was especially against them since I had entered my long, dark era of unemployment. My parents, whom I would describe as sharklike real estate people, encouraged the idea, suggesting that Charice's gatherings were a good place to "network," but I could never stomach the "What do you do for a living?" questions, which are hard to take after thirteen months of failed job interviews.

I ventured out now. Guests in sailor suits danced while a woman pecked out the theme to *The Love Boat* on the marimba—which is to say that things were just getting started. Charice was making drinks for a boy who, from the looks of it, had dressed as flotsam. Even if my parents had been right about my needing to get my name out there, it's hard to know what you'll gain by networking with flotsam.

I passed by the driftwood and headed straight to Charice. I didn't turn any heads, which is good, because I felt underdressed. This is a Dahlia Moss superpower. With my "quiet girl at the library" look, I am genetically suited to not being noticed at parties. In my best moments, I think I look like Carmen Sandiego, with long wavy brown hair and sunglasses and a fedora. Setting aside the fact that I don't wear a lot of fedoras. In my worst moments, I think I look like Roz from *Monsters, Inc.*, but maybe everyone thinks that.

extras

"Did you put Jonah Long up to that?"

"No," said Charice. "Put him up to what?"

The question must have taken her by surprise, because it was not in Charice's nature to deny involvement with anything. Most of the time, this was simply because she *was* involved, but even in the rare case that she wasn't, it wasn't like her to just say no. More often you would get a raised eyebrow and Mona Lisa smile, suggesting that she was possibly involved, even if she didn't know precisely what you were talking about.

Charice was the head-turner at parties, by the way. I like to think of Charice as a *jolie laide*, which is my way saying that I don't really understand why men constantly throw themselves at her. She's not really—a *jolie laide* is supposed to have a "flaw" that somehow makes her more beautiful, like a big nose that's somehow entrancing and perfect. Or snaggle teeth. Or alopecia, although you see that one a lot less. But I couldn't tell you what Charice's flaw was. She looks like Peppermint Patty, but grown up and with 0 percent body fat.

I parried her question for now, but I knew that I would have to answer her eventually. "How well do you know him?"

Charice poured a sludgy red substance into a pink plastic cup and slid it over to me. "Drink this. It's my special mix."

Despite some long dark nights of the soul caused by Charice's special mixes, I gave the sludge a swig. It was just the sort of terrifying combination of fruitiness and liquor that I expected.

"How well do you know Jonah?" I asked again.

"Not well. He came to my Seed Time party a few months back. Great fun, but I never saw him again. A shame, because he's a good person to have around at parties. A gentleman of leisure."

I remembered that party. Charice had been inspired by *Harold and Maude* and sent people in teams to plant saplings all

over the city. I remembered two biologists getting into a fist-
fight over a cactus, but I couldn't recall Jonah at all.

"What you mean by 'gentleman of leisure'? He's rich? What
do his parents do?"

"His parents *don't* do. They *own*. A pharmaceutical, I think.
Anyway, he called me last week and asked me if I had any parties coming up. I told him about this one, and he showed up
in that fantastic outfit. I thought we were in for a grand time."

"But?"

"He only wanted to speak to you, Dahlia. He was barely
here before he went into your room, and when he came out he
bailed on me altogether. What did you do, punch him?"

"He gave me one thousand dollars."

Charice considered this. "I didn't realize you would turn out
to be such a high-class hooker."

I noticed that flotsam boy was taking quite an interest in
our conversation, and I brought my voice down to a whisper.
"Charice, he hired me to be a detective. You didn't feed him
lines about how I worked for an agency last year?"

"No," said Charice, her face practically splitting in half with
delight. "A detective? That's the best thing I've ever heard."